Also by Ana Huang

KINGS OF SIN SERIES

A SERIES OF INTERCONNECTED STANDALONES

King of Wrath

King of Pride

King of Greed

King of Sloth

TWISTED SERIES

A SERIES OF INTERCONNECTED STANDALONES

Twisted Love

Twisted Games

Twisted Hate

Twisted Lies

IF LOVE SERIES

If We Ever Meet Again (DUET BOOK 1)

If the Sun Never Sets (DUET BOOK 2)

If Love Had a Price (STANDALONE)

If We Were Perfect (STANDALONE)

if we were perfect

ANA HUANG

Bloom books

Sourcebooks, Bloom Books, and the colophon are registered trademarks of Sourcebooks.

Published by Bloom Books, an imprint of Sourcebooks
P.O. Box 4410, Naperville, Illinois 60567-4410
(630) 961-3900
sourcebooks.com

Originally self-published in 2020 by Ana Huang.

Cataloging-in-Publication data is on file with the Library of Congress

Printed and bound in the United States of America.
LSC 10 9 8 7 6 5 4 3 2 1

Playlist

"We Don't Talk Anymore" —Charlie Puth featuring
Selena Gomez
"Somebody That I Used to Know" —Gotye
"Apologize" —Timbaland featuring One Republic
"Can't Get You Out of My Head" —Peking Duck
"I Left My Heart in San Francisco" —Tony Bennett

CHAPTER 1

"HE TRIED TO GIVE ME A LAP DANCE, FARRAH. IN THE middle of a four-star restaurant." Olivia Tang paced the length of Ishikawa's black-marbled bathroom, her heels clicking against the tile floors in agitation. "I like this place. The sushi is great, and it scores at least an eight out of ten on everything else I require from my favorite dine-out places—service, ambiance, decor, location, clean bathrooms. I refuse to be banned for my momentary lapse in judgment in agreeing to dinner with a guy named Wesley."

Her best friend, Farrah Lin-Ryan, laughed, the silvery sound tinkling over their transcontinental call in a wash of familiarity. Olivia hadn't heard that laugh in person in months—not since she, Farrah, and their other friends, Courtney Taylor and Kris Carrera (soon-to-be Kris Reynolds), flew to Miami for a girls' trip in February. She missed having her best friend in the same city, but a phone call was better than nothing, especially when she was on yet *another* disaster of a date.

"Say you have an emergency and cut the date short," Farrah suggested. "I'll call you in a few and pretend I'm a close family member that got rushed to the hospital."

"I would, but I want to try the dessert." Olivia ran a hand through her sleek just-below-shoulder-length black hair and examined her reflection. She'd been optimistic about tonight and had run out of the office so she had enough time to get ready. Two hours later, her hair was perfect, her makeup accentuated her bright dark eyes and rosebud lips, and her elegantly provocative black dress clung to her slender frame. Comfy but sexy heels added an extra three inches to her five-foot-five frame.

What a waste.

All that time, energy, and makeup for nothing.

"They're famous for their dessert," Olivia added, oddly compelled to explain why she was staying. "Caramelized apple and kuromoji ice cream served with muesli."

There were few things she wouldn't do for good food. Maybe it was because she couldn't cook to save her life, so she relied on other people's cooking skills for culinary satisfaction. Whatever it was, Olivia's food obsession had taken her to sometimes sketchy, always delicious places since she was old enough to distinguish between a hand roll and a maki roll.

"Sounds yummy. Well, you're in the middle of the main course, right? You're almost there. Just make sure Wesley doesn't, um, pull another Magic Mike." Farrah sounded like she was trying not to laugh again.

"Yeah, yeah, make fun of me, you happily married newlywed," Olivia grumbled. "You're not the one slogging through the swamps of single life in modern America."

"Newlywed or not, I still love you."

"I know." Olivia sighed. "I better get back out there before Wesley thinks I fell in the toilet or something. I swear, this dessert better be worth it."

"I'm sure it will be. Call me later and let me know how it goes? Love ya."

"Love you too."

Olivia hung up.

The date had been a colossal waste of time, but it would be less of a waste if she stayed for dessert. She'd weighed the pros and cons already: sacrifice an extra half hour for dessert and leave with greater satisfaction, or escape early with no satisfaction at all (beyond the delicious sushi she'd already consumed). The past hour and a half were a sunk cost; she couldn't get it back.

She concluded that greater satisfaction outweighed thirty minutes of her time. Olivia had an obligation to herself to ensure her night wasn't a *total* waste, and she'd been dying to try Ishikawa's signature dessert since she read about it in *Mode de Vie*'s "Food Features" section.

She exited the bathroom and tried not to grimace when she saw Wesley polishing off another sake at their table. According to his dating app profile, he was a real estate agent who liked vintage wine and travel—just like Olivia—and he *was*. What it'd failed to mention—and what he'd announced ten minutes into their dinner—was that he also moonlighted as a stripper at the Cock Pit.

Yes, that was the name of Wesley's nighttime employer, and yes, according to her chatty date, all the non-stage-performer employees had to dress up as flight attendants.

Olivia had nothing against strippers. She loved *Magic Mike XXL*. A shirtless Channing Tatum, Joe Manganiello, and Matt Bomer all in the same movie? Yes, please. But there was a time and place for them, and tonight was neither the time nor place for Wesley to "show off his moves," as he'd announced he would do half an hour ago.

To be fair, he was also unabashedly drunk. For a six-foot-two, 190-pound specimen, he couldn't hold his alcohol *at all*. He had, however, managed to climb onto a speechless Olivia's lap before she shoved him off and excused herself to go to the restroom.

"You're back!" Wesley exclaimed, like she'd just returned from a trip to Italy and not the toilet. "How was the bathroom?"

"Fine." She pasted on a smile and flagged down a server. "Can we order dessert, please? Two caramelized apple and kuro-moji ice creams. Thank you."

She wasn't sharing, and if Wesley didn't like her dessert choice, too bad.

Olivia had put up with an unwilling near-lap-dance; he could put up with ice cream.

"Dessert already? You didn't finish your food yet." Wesley stared at the remaining sushi on Olivia's side of the table.

"I will by the time they bring it out."

He laughed. "No way—" He stopped when Olivia dug into her remaining food with the gusto of a starving thirteen-year-old boy who'd just come home from sports practice. Translation: she demolished the rest of her meal in two minutes flat. "Whoa. You eat faster than I do. That's hot."

Wesley got out of his chair.

Oh no.

This was what she got for meeting up with a rando from a dating app. It wasn't Olivia's first time meeting with an online match, but it was her first time agreeing to dinner with someone whom she hadn't properly screened. Usually, it took more than a day of messaging back and forth before she took things to the next level, but she'd needed to blow off steam after a grueling first year in her MBA program and an equally grueling summer dealing with her jerk-face colleagues.

Okay, fine, her last final had been five days ago, and she'd only worked with said jerk-faces for two days, but still. Olivia deserved hazard pay for dealing with their immature, sexist asses.

People thought Wall Street in New York was bad? They never met the San Francisco branch of Pine Hill Capital, the prestigious private equity (PE) firm Olivia had worked for since she jumped ship from investment banking five years ago.

"Wesley, sit," Olivia ordered, unconsciously using the same tone she used on dogs.

"I never finished showing you my moves earlier."

"I don't want to see your moves." Olivia flashed a tight smile of thanks at the server, who returned with their ice cream and shot a strange look in Wesley's direction but didn't say anything.

The top two buttons of Wesley's shirt were unbuttoned, revealing a sliver of muscled chest and spray-tanned skin. He wasn't bad-looking, but if he didn't sit down in the next two minutes, she couldn't be held accountable for where she might lodge her shoe.

Olivia scooted her chair closer to the table so he couldn't climb into her lap again. She spooned some ice cream into her mouth and—*Oh. My. God.*

All thoughts of sticking her heel where the sun didn't shine flew out of her head as she focused on the cold, creamy mound of heaven in her bowl. It was *amazing.* Definitely worth thirty minutes of her life, but once she finished dessert, she was hightailing it out of here—Wesley could take care of the bill—and she'd never have to see him again.

Olivia wondered if she could eat Wesley's portion of dessert too. The poor ice cream was melting, and he didn't seem like he would stop "showing off his moves" anytime soon. Saving that perfectly flavored scoop from dying a useless death was practically a moral imperative.

"Olivia, look," Wesley said, sounding suspiciously whiny for a twenty-nine-year-old. "You're not looking. This is my booty pop. Women love it."

Someone kill me now.

At least they were in the back corner of the restaurant, away from the kitchen and most other guests. The nearest diners—a handsome couple in their midforties—shot Olivia and Wesley the same strange look their server had earlier, but Wesley hadn't done anything *too* egregious yet, like take his shirt off. The couple soon got distracted by their food, while Wesley booty-popped to his heart's content.

"Sit. Down," Olivia repeated.

He didn't.

Fuck it. She finished her ice cream and swapped her empty bowl with Wesley's full one. He didn't deserve dessert.

"I can't believe you don't like my moves," Wesley slurred, sounding offended. He sidled closer, and she realized he'd unbuttoned several more buttons until half his chest was showing. If a restaurant staff member saw him, he'd be thrown out for public indecency. "I'm the star of the Cock Pit. Women *specifically* request me for their bachelorette parties. I make over a thousand dollars a night. I can squeeze a penny with my—"

Olivia never found out what he could squeeze a penny with—thank God—because she chose that moment to turn her head to the left. Just a few inches, really, until she could see over Wesley's shoulder. In the grand scheme of things, the small movement was nothing.

Or it *would've* been nothing had her gaze not collided with a pair of familiar onyx eyes that sucked her in like a black hole. Nothing escaped—not light, not sound, not the painful beats of her heart. Just like that, everything disappeared except for the man her younger, naive self had thought held her universe in the palms of his hands. Even Wesley ceased to exist, and he was practically on top of her.

Olivia's breath rushed out in a shaky gust of exhilaration, embarrassment, and loathing.

"Olivia?" Her name fell off Sammy Yu's perfect lips like a long-forgotten love song, evoking memories of golden days and beautiful nights.

Those dark eyes darted from her spoonful of ice cream—frozen halfway to her mouth—to Wesley's bared chest before finally resting on her face. She spotted glints of confusion and amusement, and it was the latter that fueled her with the strength to level a glare at Wesley so menacing, he immediately backed off.

"I'm going to the restroom," Wesley announced, indignation oozing from every pore. "It's clear my booty pops are not appreciated here."

He stalked off, his half-open shirt flapping in the breeze. He didn't spare Sammy a glance.

Sammy's mouth twitched. "I wasn't aware booty pops were on the menu."

"Funny. We—*I* was just leaving," Olivia said with as much dignity as she could muster. She set her spoon down. The ice cream had melted anyway, and she could bolt right now while Wesley was in the restroom.

Usually, Olivia would never do something so rude, but she was fed up with this day. It kept going from bad to worse—and running into your ex-boyfriend while on a terrible date definitely counted as "worse."

"You mean you don't want to go home with that fine, booty-popping specimen?" Sammy feigned shock. "Say it ain't so."

She glared at him. "Sarcasm doesn't suit you."

The Sammy she knew wasn't sarcastic unless it was in a fun, playful way, but the man standing before her *wasn't* the Sammy she knew.

He was still tall and handsome—so handsome the mere sight of him sent a pleasurable shiver through her body. Same eyes, same high cheekbones and strong jaw, same dark hair—though he wore it shorter now than in college. But his lean frame had filled out with more hard-hewn muscles, his eyes sparked with more cynicism, and he possessed a self-assurance one only gained with age.

With his camel coat, black dress shirt, and hard expression, Sammy couldn't have looked more different from the good-natured, math-pun-loving, lived-in-a-T-shirt college boy she once knew. He was all man now, and not one that had any love lost for her.

"What are you doing here?" Olivia demanded. He hadn't responded to her sarcasm dig, and the silence was bugging her. She almost wished Wesley were here so she'd have a buffer. What was taking him so long, anyway? Did he fall in the toilet?

Then again, Olivia had holed herself in the restroom for a good twenty minutes talking to Farrah, so she couldn't throw stones.

Sammy's eyebrows rose a fraction of an inch. "This is a restaurant. I'm here for dinner, same as the rest of the patrons. What are *you* doing here?"

"Uh, you answered your own question. Dinner." The *duh* was implied.

"You don't live in San Francisco."

"I do this summer. I'm working at the SF branch of my company instead of going back to New York." Olivia wasn't sure why she was telling him all this. They weren't friends anymore. Unfortunately, they had tons of mutual friends from their college study-abroad program, and they were constantly forced into the same space thanks to said friends. Farrah's wedding, Kris's upcoming nuptials, group trips, and reunions...things Olivia couldn't back out of because of either loyalty or a strong sense of FOMO (fear of missing out). Sammy's thoughts must've run along the same lines because he showed up at almost every event too.

As a result, they'd settled into an uneasy, somewhat civil truce that consisted of them ignoring each other and parking themselves on opposite sides of whatever room or table they found themselves in.

"Hmm." Sammy appeared displeased by the revelation that she would be in San Francisco for the summer. Thanks to Farrah, he knew she was working on her MBA at Stanford—Olivia had almost killed her for letting that piece of info slip, to which Farrah merely responded, "Why? Are you afraid he'll show up on campus and you'll have hot, sweaty makeup sex?"

Ha! As if. Eight years was a little too late for makeup sex.

As for Sammy's displeasure, too bad. He didn't own the city. She could *move* here if she wanted (she didn't, but she *could*).

"Olivia? Is that you?"

Olivia stiffened when a familiar blond sidled up next to Sammy. Golden hair that fell past her shoulders in shiny waves, red lipstick that matched her Ted Baker sheath dress perfectly, a face that would make a supermodel weep.

Jessica.

"It is you!" Sammy's girlfriend grinned. "Sam didn't tell me you were in San Francisco."

She called him Sam? *No one* called him Sam.

But Sammy didn't so much as blink an eye at the moniker.

"I'm here for the summer." Olivia forced a smile and repeated her explanation. "I just finished my first year of business school at Stanford, and I'm working at my company's SF branch until classes start again."

"I didn't know she was in the city until we ran into each other here." Sammy slid an arm around Jessica's waist, and Olivia fought the urge to upchuck. She'd only met Jessica twice before— once at Sammy's Fourth of July barbecue in New York three summers ago and once at Farrah and Blake's wedding. Funnily enough, she'd wanted to upchuck both those times too. "She was just leaving. She has to go before her date comes back." A tiny smirk tugged at the corners of his mouth.

Olivia glared at him; he stared back with one infuriatingly arched brow.

Jessica, to her credit, didn't press on why Olivia was leaving her date high and dry. Instead, her smile widened. "We should all have dinner sometime. There's a bunch of great restaurants in the city I'm sure you'll love."

Ugh. Why did she have to be so *nice?* It would be easier to hate her if she were a total witch. Not that Olivia had a reason to hate her ex's current girlfriend or anything. She didn't even like Sammy anymore.

"I'm sure Olivia's busy." Sammy's voice contained a note of warning.

"Too busy for dinner?" Jessica shot her boyfriend a look Olivia couldn't decipher.

"Thanks for the invite. And yeah, let's grab dinner sometime." Olivia would rather roll around in a puddle of sewer water than eat dinner with Jessica and Sammy, but this was the twenty-first century. People made vague plans with no follow-up all the time. "Listen, I have to go. There's an emergency at my apartment."

She needed to get out of here. Wesley was going to be back any minute, Sammy was sucking all the oxygen out of the room, and Jessica...well, Jessica was making her stomach churn.

Not because the blond was mean or had said anything wrong, but because she was there. With him. Olivia hated seeing them together, and she hated herself for hating it.

Jessica's brows dipped. "Everything okay?"

"Yes. I just have to go check on...stuff."

"You have Sam's number, right? If you need help, give him a call and we'll be there."

"Thanks." It was weird that a woman she barely knew was acting like they were best friends and even weirder that said woman seemed intent on throwing her boyfriend back with his ex, but that wasn't Olivia's problem.

Sammy remained silent, his expression unreadable.

Olivia mumbled a goodbye, paid for her dinner against her earlier plans—she didn't trust Wesley to cover their tab or tip appropriately—and hailed a cab home.

While the taxi wound its way through San Francisco's hilly streets, she tipped her head back and closed her eyes, exhaustion sinking into her bones.

God, what a night. First her ridiculous date, then running into Sammy and Jessica.

She hadn't reached out to Sammy when she'd moved to California last year, even though he'd been the only person she knew in the area. Stanford was a forty-five-minute drive from San Francisco, and she'd been swamped with schoolwork. Plus, while they were no longer on hostile terms, they weren't exactly friendly either.

"Get it together, Olivia," she muttered under breath.

Dwelling on the past was a waste of time, and if there was one thing Olivia hated, it was wasting time. The average life expectancy for a female in the U.S. born in Olivia's birth year was seventy-nine years. That was 28,835 days, 41,522,400 minutes. She had an ever-present clock in her mind, ticking down those days and minutes until they reached her inevitable, if unknown, death date. Some might find that morbid, but she found it reassuring. Olivia thrived on structure, and life had a beginning, middle, and end, as all things should.

The mental clock had the added benefit of reminding her how precious her time was. If she wasn't productive, happy, or relaxed, it was time wasted.

Tonight? A colossal waste, and she wouldn't drag it out by wondering, for the millionth time, if there could've been a different ending for her and Sammy. If she'd stood up to her mother, if she hadn't lied, if Sammy hadn't said the things he'd said...

Olivia shook her head, shoving thoughts of the past back in her mental Do-Not-Open drawer where they belonged. To distract herself, she pulled out her phone and tapped out notes for Monday's meeting until the taxi rolled to a stop in front of her apartment building.

San Francisco rent was even more ridiculous than New York—and that was a high bar—but she'd gotten lucky with the studio apartment she'd sublet from a friend's friend. She was still paying a ridiculous amount of money each month for something the size of a shoebox, but it could've been worse.

Olivia unlocked the door, eager for a hot shower and sleep. She couldn't wait—*what the hell?*

A thick, musty smell slammed into her nose before her brain registered the scene in front of her: the floors of her apartment glistened beneath two inches of water.

"You've got to be kidding me."

Her high, shocked voice echoed off the walls and absorbed into the puddles destroying her belongings. Her mattress, which she'd placed on the floor since her bed frame hadn't arrived yet? Donezo. Her beautiful wool area rug? Unrecognizable. The cardboard boxes she'd yet to unpack because she'd been so busy at work? Half-disintegrated.

There's an emergency at the apartment.

Olivia's earlier excuse came back to her, and she wanted to throw up. She wasn't the superstitious sort, but a tiny part of her wondered whether she'd manifested this nightmare. She'd only been gone for a few hours. How the *hell* had this happened?

She pressed her palm to her temple and tried to deepen her shallow breaths.

It was nine at night, she was exhausted, half her belongings were ruined, she had no clue where to *start* cleaning this mess up, and she had no friends in the city. No one to help her.

A wild sound emerged from her throat, and it took her a few seconds before she realized she was laughing. Hysterically.

For once in her well-planned life, Olivia Tang had no clue what to do.

CHAPTER 2

THE ICE CUBES CLINKED AS SAMMY PICKED UP HIS drink with one hand and flipped through the menu with the other.

"I might skip the sushi and go for the udon," he said. "I'm in the mood for noodles."

Silence.

He looked up to find Jessica staring at him with a half-knowing, half-judging expression.

"What?"

"You know what." The judging edged out the knowing by a smidge.

Tension crawled into Sammy's shoulders, but he kept his expression neutral. "I do not, in fact, 'know what.'"

"Olivia."

The tension intensified, as it always did when he saw, heard, or so much as thought about Olivia Tang. Her name created knots that would take the city's best massage therapist hours to undo.

"What about her?"

Jessica's eyes narrowed. She was a beautiful woman, and Sammy could see several men in the vicinity throwing covetous glances in her direction. Too bad she'd never be interested in them. "Does she still think you and I are dating?"

"I have no idea what she thinks." He refocused on the most important issue at hand. "Udon. I'm definitely ordering the udon."

His dinner date let out an exasperated sigh. "Do you think it's a coincidence she's in town this summer? Maybe it's a sign."

"No, it's not." Sammy snapped his menu shut and set it on the table with no small amount of irritation. "She's in town because she's studying at Stanford. She chose Stanford because it's ranked the number one MBA program in the country alongside Wharton, and sunny Palo Alto—with its proximity to San Francisco's food scene—is more appealing to her than Philadelphia. She probably stayed in California this summer instead of going back to New York because she wants to expand her network for career-building purposes. So, no, I don't think it's a sign at all."

The low chatter of other diners and the clink of knives and forks against porcelain plates were the only sounds punctuating the charged storm brewing around Sammy. He rarely got this riled up, but Olivia was, as always, the exception to all his rules.

Jessica appeared unfazed by his outburst. "For someone who claims he has no idea what she's thinking, you possess a rare insight into Olivia's reasoning."

"When it comes to her career, she's an open book," Sammy said flatly. "Ambition above all else."

He had no issues with ambition. It was one of the many things he'd loved about Olivia—her drive, her intelligence, her determination to succeed in an industry known for being a boys' club. She was strong, smart, and loyal, and she loved the people in her life as fiercely as she did her work.

Or so he'd thought.

Perhaps that was why he'd been so blindsided by her actions

after she realized his vision for his future—*his*, not hers—no longer fit into her neat, color-coded, perfectly planned-out life.

Love blinded even those with perfect vision. It was a lesson Sammy had never forgotten.

Their server took their orders, and Jessica waited until he'd left before she resumed her interrogation. "You must've known she was in town. Farrah must've told you," she pressed. She'd only met Farrah twice, but she had a steel-trap memory. It was one of the reasons why she was one of the most sought-after lawyers in the Bay Area.

Sammy's jaw flexed.

Farrah hadn't told him, but he bet it would come up in their next conversation. She'd never given up on the hope that Sammy and Olivia would get back together, and her matchmaking attempts had intensified after she and Blake tied the knot. Blake and Farrah had had a nasty breakup in Shanghai, but they finally got back together after years apart. It took a lot of pain and heartache, but they got there. They were now so blissfully happy, Sammy expected music to soar and spontaneous rainbows to arc over their heads whenever they were together.

He was happy for them, truly, but just because they sorted out their issues didn't mean happily-ever-after was in the cards for Sammy and Olivia too.

Blake and Farrah broke up because of a fucked-up lie from a third party; Sammy and Olivia had no one to blame for their relationship's demise except themselves.

Besides, they'd ended things eight years ago. It was time for Farrah to let that shit go.

How about you try taking that advice yourself? a smug, unwanted voice in Sammy's head whispered.

He batted it away and refocused on the blond sitting across from him.

"It doesn't matter," he said. "So what if she's in SF? It's a big city, and we're not friends."

Not anymore.

Once upon a time, Sammy and Olivia had been best friends. Lovers. Dreamers. They'd shared and held each other's hopes and wishes in their hands and woven a glittering tapestry of what the future would look like. But when those hopes and wishes changed, the threads frayed, and the discordance stretched the tapestry thin until the fabric tore, ripping itself and its owners apart.

"Let's talk about something else," Sammy said before Jessica could push him further on the subject. "Like your well-deserved promotion, which is why we're here."

Deflection: the world's greatest weapon.

A grin spread across Jessica's face. "One step closer to partner."

"You deserve it."

Sammy flashed a genuine smile. Jessica was a killer lawyer, famous among Silicon Valley's movers and shakers for her sharp instincts and talent for reading people. She worked harder than most people Sammy knew, and she'd been promoted after helping her firm's most important client—a major tech company—win a massive legal fight against the European Union. If she kept going at this rate, she'd make partner before she turned thirty-five.

They clinked glasses, and Sammy downed his sake in one smooth gulp.

He'd missed Jessica's official celebratory dinner because of a last-minute emergency at the bakery. She'd insisted it was fine, but he'd been adamant about treating her to a make-up dinner.

He just hadn't expected to run into his ex-girlfriend at the same restaurant.

What were the odds?

Then again, Sammy shouldn't be surprised. Food was Olivia's

weakness, and she was always on the hunt for great new restaurants. He still remembered her spreadsheets crammed with information about various establishments—the type of cuisine, price point, number of Yelp stars, signature dishes, and additional notes (awards, dress code, cash only, etc.). It was both impressive and terrifying.

Ishikawa was the city's latest culinary hotspot, so of course Olivia would be here. With a date.

The server returned with their food, and Sammy dug into his noodles with a frown. Her date had left soon after she did, and he'd seemed too intoxicated to realize the woman he'd arrived with had ditched him while he'd been in the restroom.

When did Olivia start going out with overgrown frat boys who couldn't keep their drinks down and their shirts on? Why did Sammy care?

I don't. Sammy stabbed a piece of beef with his fork while Jessica talked about the new case she was working on. Luckily, she didn't mention Olivia again for the rest of dinner, and their conversation topics stayed in neutral territory.

The first time Sammy introduced Jessica as his girlfriend had been at his Fourth of July barbecue three years ago, and it'd taken a helluva lot of convincing before she agreed to the ruse. Neither she nor his best friend, Nardo Crescas—who'd grown up with Jessica and had connected her with Sammy after she moved to California—had approved of him faking a girlfriend to get under Olivia's skin.

To be fair, such games *were* childish, but Sammy had been so rattled by being around Olivia again after years of avoiding her that he hadn't been thinking straight. His bakery had had a pop-up in New York that summer, and he'd temporarily moved to NYC to serve as the face of the new venture. It'd been easy to sidestep Farrah's efforts to throw him and Olivia together when they lived on opposite sides of the country; it was nearly impossible when they were in the same city. Jessica happened to be in town that weekend for work—yes, work during Fourth of July—and had reluctantly agreed to play the part of his girlfriend.

Not that it mattered. Olivia hadn't blinked an eye—not then and not the second time around, when Sammy brought Jessica as his plus-one to Farrah and Blake's wedding. That time, it'd been to ensure he didn't do anything stupid, as people were wont to do when they were drunk at a wedding and in proximity with the ex-love of their life.

By the time dinner ended, Sammy had sunk into a brooding silence. If Jessica noticed, she didn't say anything.

"Thanks for dinner." Jessica wound her scarf around her neck. Unless there was a heat wave, San Francisco evenings were substantially chillier than its afternoons—a fact that always surprised tourists who came to the Bay Area expecting the same hot, sunny weather as in Southern California. "You really didn't have to."

"I wanted to." Sammy's phone buzzed with an incoming call. When he saw the name on the screen, his blood iced over.

Olivia.

She hadn't called him in nearly a decade. It was like he'd conjured her call simply by thinking of her throughout dinner.

Or had she been thinking about him after they ran into each other?

"Who is it?" Jessica asked.

"No one." The call ended, replaced with a missed call notification. "You want a ride home?"

"Nah, I'm meeting Mara for drinks. You can join us if you'd like."

"Thanks, but I'm gonna call it a night." He hugged her. "Congrats again. Don't forget us little people once you make it big."

Jessica's laugh pealed through the night. "Says the Insta-famous baker. What was it *Zagat* called you? A 'pastry virtuoso'?"

"Good night," he said pointedly, earning himself another laugh.

Sammy grinned and waited until Jessica had ducked into a cab before he walked to his car. There, his smile faded, and he stared at his phone, torn.

"Dammit." He pulled up his recent calls list and dialed Olivia back.

One ring. Two. Three.

He was about to give up when she finally answered, sounding out of breath. "Hey."

"Hey." He put her on speaker and connected his phone to the car so he could navigate out of his parking spot, freeing it up for the Prius waiting to take his place. "You called?"

There was a brief pause. "It was nothing." A faint tinge of embarrassment colored her tone. "I butt-dialed you."

"You're a bad liar, Olivia, and you wouldn't have called me unless it was an emergency."

Frankly, Sammy was shocked she called even if it *were* an emergency. He'd expected her to have purged him from her contacts list years ago. The fact she hadn't made his heart squeeze in a worrying way.

"I'm an excellent liar," Olivia huffed. His mouth quirked up at her indignation. "Look, it's been a long day, and I wasn't think-ing clearly. You're the only person I know in the city besides my coworkers, which is why I called you, but I've got it under control."

Sammy stopped at a red light. Concern twisted through him. "Got what under control?"

She told him, and when he asked for her address, she hesi-tated before giving it to him.

He cursed under his breath. The glowing numbers on his

radio console told him it was half past ten, and her apartment was in the opposite direction of his house. He should hang up and let it be. She said she had it under control, and he believed her. Olivia always had things under control.

The light turned green, and Sammy's hands flexed on the steering wheel.

"Don't go anywhere. I'll be there in half an hour," he said grimly.

Sammy hung up, merged into the next lane so he could make a U-turn at the next intersection, and cursed again.

He would regret this later. He was sure of it.

———

Twenty-eight minutes later, Sammy pulled up in front of Olivia's apartment building. He input the code she'd texted him and stepped inside, taking in the marble floors and freshly painted walls. The building was on the older side but well-maintained, and apartments here must cost a pretty penny even if they didn't boast luxury amenities. Hell, San Francisco was so expensive a shoebox could go for $1,500 a month and be considered a steal.

Why am I doing this?

The question pounded through Sammy's head for the hundredth time as he climbed the stairs to Olivia's apartment.

"Because my mom raised me to have manners. Or because I'm a masochist," Sammy mumbled, his voice echoing in the empty stairwell.

It didn't take long to find Olivia's apartment once he reached the second floor—the door was ajar, and he heard the faint sounds of water splashing through the crack.

He rapped his knuckles on the wood and waited for her "Come in" before he nudged the door open and took in the chaos with wide eyes.

"Holy shit."

The place looked like Poseidon had pitched a mini fit and drowned it out of rage. Bedsheets and towels covered half the floor, so soaked they were nearly transparent. Olivia was mopping the areas not covered with cloth, but it didn't help much—there was so much water, she'd need a sump pump to suck it all out. Every inch of table surface and counter space groaned beneath the weight of clothes, household products, and various knickknacks, while a pile of wet, crumbling cardboard boxes sat in the corner, flattened and forlorn.

She hadn't been kidding when she'd said the place was a mess.

"My reaction exactly." Olivia blew a stray strand of hair out of her eye. She wore the same outfit she'd worn to dinner, except she'd changed her shoes—good call, considering she'd had on heels—and thrown her hair up in a messy bun. Her skin gleamed with perspiration, and Sammy tried not to stare at the bead of sweat snaking its way past the hollow of her throat and into the V-dip of her dress.

"What happened?" He stepped cautiously through the apartment, avoiding puddles where he could.

"Flood."

He slanted her a sardonic look. "No shit, Sherlock."

Olivia stopped mopping and leaned her weight against the mop handle. "Washing machine flood," she clarified. "The washer wasn't on, but I called my landlord and he said floods can happen even if it isn't running. Something about a burst water supply line."

"Is he on his way?"

"He said it's too late and he'll come in the morning."

Annoyance blasted through Sammy's system. "What the hell? What are you supposed to do until then? Where are you going to sleep?"

Olivia lifted one shoulder. "I'll clean up as much of the mess as possible and rent a hotel room for the night." Her lower lip disappeared between her teeth, and pale pink stained her cheeks. "Like I said earlier, I called you because I panicked and wasn't thinking clearly, but I got it under control, so you can enjoy the rest of your night. Sorry for making you come all the way out here."

"It's almost eleven p.m. Not a lot of 'night' left to enjoy," Sammy said dryly.

The pale pink darkened into a dusky rose. "I said I was sorry." Olivia patted her hair, keeping her gaze averted from his. "Thank you for coming. I'll reimburse your gas or cab fare, but you don't need to stay. I'm fine."

"No, you're not."

"Yes, I am."

"Half your stuff is ruined, you look like you're about to collapse from exhaustion, and do you even know where the closest hotel is? Or whether they have any rooms available?"

"That's what Google is for."

Irritation curled through Sammy's stomach. Seriously? He'd gone out of his way to help her—after *she* called *him*—just to get snipped at and told his help wasn't needed?

Screw that.

He should've never come. Hell, he should've blocked her number and erased her from his life a long time ago, mutual friends be damned.

"Fine. Don't bother with the gas money—I'll consider that my charity donation for the month." Sammy's jaw clenched. "Good luck with this mess, not that you'll need it. After all, you always figure your shit out. You're perfect."

He turned and stalked toward the door, silently cursing himself for his stupidity. He already had one foot in the hallway when he heard a soft sniffle.

Sammy froze and clenched his jaw harder.

Don't do it, man. Just don't.

He did.

He looked over his shoulder and saw Olivia had resumed mopping. She wasn't crying, but her eyes shone suspiciously bright.

She really did look exhausted. Her movements were sluggish, and her eyes drooped as she pushed the mop across the same spot for what must have been the dozenth time. It was close to midnight; knowing her, she'd been up and going nonstop since five or six in the morning.

Sammy also knew with dead certainty that Olivia would've never called him or anyone else if she didn't need help. She was the one people ran to when they had problems, not the other way around. It must've stung her pride that she'd had to reach out to someone else for support—and that her only option had been Sammy; hence why she'd pushed him away when he'd showed up. She didn't like appearing weak.

Their relationship had died a long time ago, but he still knew her like the back of his hand.

God. Damn. It.

His anger fizzled as fast as it came. Sammy exhaled a sharp breath and raked a hand through his hair, already hating himself for what he was about to do.

"Leave it," he said roughly. "The place is as dry as it's gonna get, and there's not much else you can do till the morning."

"It could use another go-over with the mop." Olivia wiped her nose with the back of her hand. "*Go.* I got it."

"Liv, I swear to God." Sammy flinched the instant the words left his mouth. He hadn't used her nickname in years, but it fell out as easily as if they were still together. It tasted bittersweet, like memories of a bygone era.

Olivia's shoulders visibly tensed as Sammy stomped through the apartment and wrested the mop from her hands. "I'll mop; you pack what you need for the night," he said, tone curt. "If you keep going at this rate, you'll pass out on the floor and drown."

She rolled her eyes. "It was never *that* flooded."

He simply stared at her.

"Fine, Sir Bossy McBosspants." Olivia walked toward a pile of folded clothes on the coffee table. "I'll pack."

Half an hour later, Sammy had dried the floors as best he could, and Olivia had packed an overnight bag and changed into a T-shirt and leggings.

"Let's go." Sammy wiped his hands with a paper towel. "I'll drive."

"But I haven't picked a hotel yet," she protested.

"It's past midnight. We don't have time to go through your spreadsheets and figure out which hotel has a Michelin-starred restaurant or offers designer amenities."

"A Michelin-starred restaurant isn't a requirement," Olivia muttered. She followed him into the hall, turning off the lights and locking the door behind her as she did so.

It wasn't until they were ensconced in his car that she spoke again. "Where exactly are we going if not a hotel?"

"My house."

Sammy would have smiled at the sputtering that filled the car if he weren't so damn annoyed and uneasy. He shouldn't be taking Olivia to his house. He shouldn't be taking her anywhere. Yet here he was, playing knight in not-so-shining armor to the woman who'd smashed his heart into smithereens a lifetime ago.

Masochists had nothing on him.

"We are not going to your house," Olivia said after she got her indignant sputters under control.

"According to the driver a.k.a. me—we are."

"*Why?*"

"Because I'm tired, you're tired, and I don't want you murdered while searching for a shady hotel room in the middle of the night," Sammy growled. "I don't have any Michelin stars or a spa, but I have a clean bed and a bathroom. You're using them. Tomorrow morning, we'll figure out the mess with your apartment. And don't tell me you don't need help—you called me for a reason. So stop arguing and let's have some peace, quiet, and rest for a few hours, okay?"

Olivia's jaw unhinged. She blinked slowly, her long dark lashes sweeping across her cheeks in a shocked flutter.

Sammy turned the ignition and ignored the voice chanting in his head: *Bad idea. Bad idea. Bad idea.*

His whole night had been plagued with bad ideas. What was one more?

"Okay." Olivia sounded subdued when she finally answered.

They didn't speak again until they arrived at Sammy's house. The two-bedroom, one-bathroom abode wasn't fancy like Blake and Farrah's condo in New York or Kris and Nate's mansion in Beverly Hills, but it was home. Sammy had saved for years before he could afford the down payment, and it was finally all his. That made it the best damn place on the planet, in his opinion.

"This is your room." He flipped on the light in the guest room, revealing a full-size bed with a royal blue comforter, a matching blue rug, and a sleek white desk and chair. He always had friends or family staying over when they were in town, so he kept the place well maintained. "My room's next door, bathroom is across the hall. Guest towels are the green ones—if you need extra, they're in the closet next to the bathroom. Feel free to grab anything in the kitchen if you get hungry. And, uh, I guess that's it."

Sammy rubbed the back of his neck, aware of how absurd

this whole situation was. He and Olivia hadn't spoken more than a dozen words to each other in eight years, and now she was staying in his house. In the room next to his.

It's only for the night, he assured himself.

As much bad blood as there was between them, he couldn't bring himself to turn away from a—well, not friend exactly, but someone he knew who was in need.

Sammy couldn't read her expression, but he thought he caught a glint of emotion in Olivia's eyes before she shifted her gaze and focused on the bookcase next to the desk. He'd stuffed it with books from high school and college that he never read anymore but couldn't bear to throw out. The collection contained everything from classic fiction like *The Great Gatsby* to his favorite statistics textbook.

Was it weird that he had a favorite textbook? Probably. But in a world where people hoarded stranger's toenails and plastered their houses with creepy dolls, it could be worse.

"Thank you." Olivia tightened her grip on the strap of her duffel bag. "I appreciate it. Really."

"Sure. Whatever," Sammy said, embarrassed. "G'night."

"Good night."

Spoiler: it wasn't a good night *or* morning. Because as Sammy lay in bed, unable to sleep after hours of tossing and turning, all he could think about was the woman in the room next door.

Fuck.

CHAPTER 3

OLIVIA WOKE TO THE SOUND OF HER PHONE ALARM blaring and the smell of eggs and bacon.

Her stomach rumbled in anticipation even as her eyes remained closed, desperate for a few extra minutes of shut-eye.

She hadn't fallen asleep until two in the morning, and she'd set her alarm for seven thirty—her landlord had said he'd come by her apartment at nine—which meant she was way behind on her usual eight hours of sleep.

You'll stay in bed for five more seconds. That's it.

One...two...three...four...five.

When she hit the mental count of *five,* she threw off the covers, swung her legs over the side of the bed, and turned off her alarm before she could be lulled back into La La Land.

Olivia had learned the mental count strategy from a podcast she'd listened to a few years ago and had been using it since for things she didn't want to do. The trick was to set a defined period of time (e.g., the count of five) and take action the second you hit the last count so your body didn't have time to protest. Olivia had done it so many times, she'd conditioned herself to react without thinking much about it.

She blinked the sleep from her eyes and took in her surroundings. She'd been so tired, she hadn't taken a good look at Sammy's guest room last night, but in the light of day, she could fully appreciate the soothing decor. The blues and whites were a balm to her soul, and everything was neat but not *too* neat. Plus, the bed felt like a giant cloud—or maybe that was her exhaustion talking.

After Olivia freshened up in the bathroom and changed into street clothes, she padded into the gourmet kitchen. Other than the bedrooms and bathroom, Sammy's house was open plan, with nothing but a marble counter and three cushioned barstools separating the kitchen from the dining nook and living room. Instead of the dark colors you typically found in a bachelor pad, Sammy's house boasted cheerful yellows, whites, and blues. Light streamed through the giant windows in the living room and bathed the furniture in sunshine, while framed prints of food puns decorated an entire wall of the kitchen.

Olivia smirked when she spotted a picture of a smiling lemon and orange duo with the words *Squeeze the day!* printed beneath them. It was so corny and cute at the same time.

The sizzle of oil in a pan drew her gaze away from a dancing radish that proclaimed, *You're radishing!* and toward the man standing in front of the stove. Shirtless. Barefoot. Cooking.

Her throat went bone-dry.

Hot. Damn.

She hadn't seen Sammy sans shirt in a *loooong* time, and damn if he hadn't filled out since their college years. Not that his body had been anything to sneeze at back in the day, but—once again for the people in the back—*hot. Damn.*

Bronzed skin stretched over broad shoulders and a lean, muscular back that rippled with strength. His arms were corded with thick muscles that flexed every time he flipped a piece of bacon or reached across the counter, and his gray sweatpants hung low on his hips, revealing a sliver more skin than was decent.

Olivia wheezed.

Sammy glanced up, his handsome face calm and unreadable, his hair tousled from sleep. "Good morning."

"Morning." She slid onto one of the counter stools and tried to keep her eyes above his neck. The last thing she needed was to get caught ogling her ex-boyfriend. She was embarrassed enough, calling him for help yesterday.

"How did you sleep?"

"Pretty good."

An awkward silence filled the air, punctuated by the continued sizzle in the pan until Sammy shut off the stove.

Olivia remembered the days when they couldn't *stop* talking to each other—about their hopes and dreams, and funny YouTube videos and articles they'd read online, and the merits of pie versus cake. Anything and everything they could think of. She also remembered the days when they didn't speak at all—endless hours of silence laden with unspoken accusations and broken promises until those, too, exploded in anger. Then there were the years when they'd been as far apart physically as they were emotionally, separated by time and distance and heartbreak.

Now here they were, eight years later. So different from who they used to be and yet still the same. A little older, hopefully a little wiser, but still holding on to regrets from the past.

"You want breakfast? I made enough for two." Sammy slid a plate heaped with scrambled eggs, bacon, and toast across the counter before Olivia could answer.

Her mouth watered at the sight and smell. He'd made the bacon chewy and tender, the way she liked it. A lot of people preferred it crispy, but she thought crispy bacon tasted like charred smoke.

"I'm always down for abs—eggs!" Olivia corrected herself, her cheeks flaming as she forced herself not to stare at the chiseled six-pack in front of her. "I'm always down for *eggs.*"

A tiny smile with a hint of smugness hovered on the corners of Sammy's lips like he was well aware of her slipup but was too much of a gentleman to call her out on it—which he was.

Damn him.

Olivia spooned some eggs in her mouth and evaded Sammy's gaze by examining the kitchen. Sammy was a baker by trade, but he loved cooking as much as baking, and he'd clearly spared no expense in outfitting his favorite room of the house. Sleek pale wood cabinets lined the walls above gleaming counters that boasted glass containers of flour and sugar, a stand mixer, a state-of-the-art espresso machine, and a three-tier ceramic cake stand. An eight-burner stove and Sub-Zero fridge stood sentry to the right of the sink; a glass-fronted cabinet filled with plates and glasses shone on the left. Copper pots and pans hung from hooks on the ceiling above the wood-topped center island, and a vase of beautiful sunflowers added a touch of homey cheer to what would've otherwise been a too-magazine-perfect scene.

"Farrah helped design it," Sammy said when he noticed her scrutiny. He leaned against the counter and sipped his coffee. Somehow, the simple action made him look even hotter. "Virtual consultations."

"Right." Olivia remembered Farrah mentioning it to her a while back, but she'd been so busy with business school, she'd glossed over the information. "It looks great." She swallowed another mouthful of eggs. "The food is great too." She felt the need to compliment him because there were only so many times a girl could say, "Thank you," before it got annoying. She wasn't lying either—breakfast *was* good. Sammy could turn the most mundane dishes into a gourmet meal.

"Thanks." He finished his coffee, and she snuck a peek at the way his throat flexed when he swallowed before averting her gaze.

What was *wrong* with her?

This was Sammy. Her ex-boyfriend. Her first love. The only man who'd ever made her cry, and the one who walked away when he'd promised her forever.

Yet he was the one she'd called when she'd needed help, and he'd shown up. He hadn't needed to, and she hadn't expected him to, but he'd shown up. Not only that, but he went above and beyond by opening his house to her for the night—and now she was so fucking confused. Were they friends or not? Did she like him or not? She was attracted to him, but she couldn't control her hormones, and they had nothing to do with her feelings.

Olivia wished she were back in her mess of an apartment. Nothing cleared her thoughts like a good deep-cleaning session. Like she always said: clean house, clean mind.

"When are you supposed to meet your landlord?" Sammy asked.

"Nine. I should head over soon if I want to make it on time." Olivia finished the last piece of bacon and stood.

"'Kay. Give me five minutes."

"Excuse me?"

"I need to change, then I'll take you to your apartment."

"But..." She floundered, searching for an excuse. Spending more one-on-one time with Sammy was a bad idea on so many levels. "It's Saturday. Don't you have...stuff to do?"

Won't Jessica be mad you're spending the morning with your ex? And that you let me stay the night?

Olivia kept that question to herself. Judging by Jessica's enthusiastic reception last night, the answer was probably no, and she had no desire to discuss the blond with Sammy.

"Not until later in the day." Sammy shrugged. "Five minutes. Be right back."

He disappeared down the hall, leaving a flummoxed Olivia in the kitchen.

Don't read too much into it.

Sammy wasn't being nice because he still carried a torch for her—not that Olivia wanted him to carry a torch for her. He was nice to everyone; he couldn't help himself. It was in his DNA.

Except, of course, for the day they broke up, but that was neither here nor there.

"That was a long time ago," she muttered. "*Stop* thinking about it."

Olivia glared at herself in the microwave door. Her midnight-dark hair hung sleek and straight past her shoulders, and thanks to the magic of concealer and mascara, she looked bright-eyed and alert despite her restless night of sleep. Her shirt was crisp, her pants fitted but comfortable.

She was a mess inside, but at least she looked perfect on the outside.

She tore her gaze away from her reflection and bounced her eyes around the room, strangely on edge. In the cold, harsh light of day, she couldn't believe she'd broken down like that last night.

She'd called Sammy. She'd nearly cried. Thank God she hadn't, but the impulse had been there. Over what? A little flood? Yeah, a lot of her belongings were trashed, but they could be replaced, and she was alive and unharmed. Why had she freaked out?

Olivia was the one who always stayed calm during emergencies, like when she and her friends almost burned down their hotel villa during Kris's bachelorette weekend (don't ask). She'd never met a crisis she couldn't handle on her own.

"You got this," she said. "You'll go to your apartment, sort out this mess with the landlord, and book an Airbnb or hotel room until you can move back in."

She loved writing her to-do lists, but saying them out loud helped too. It was her version of positive affirmations.

"That's gonna be expensive."

Olivia jerked her head toward the hall, a wisp of disappointment curling through her when she saw Sammy had put a shirt on. *Duh, he can't run around San Francisco shirtless.* The black T-shirt and jeans he'd donned did incredible things for his tall, muscled frame, though, so it wasn't a total loss.

"What?"

"Based on what I saw yesterday, it'll take weeks before your apartment is habitable again." Sammy slid his wallet into his back pocket. "It's gonna be expensive as hell to rent an Airbnb or hotel room for that long, especially during peak tourist season."

Her brows knit into a frown. "I doubt it'll take weeks."

His knowing smirk made her want to punch him in the face, last night's hospitality and excellent abs—eggs! Excellent *eggs!*—notwithstanding.

"Maybe it won't," Sammy agreed, but the smirk remained.

Olivia's frown deepened.

Her studio had a little water damage. How long could repairs *possibly* take?

———————

"*Seven weeks!* It's going to take *seven weeks* before I can move back into my apartment," Olivia sputtered, disbelief and anger swirling in her veins as she pictured her landlord's apathetic expression when he broke the bad news. "That's half my summer!"

"It's unfortunate." Sammy didn't say it, but she heard faint echoes of *I told you so* beneath his words.

She pressed two fingers to her temple and tried to calm her nerves. She was *this* close to regurgitating her breakfast.

Olivia had a plan for the summer, as she did for all areas of her life: kick ass at her job, eat her way through the city's best restaurants, and date around for a bit before meeting her future husband. She'd had high hopes for love in business school, but after a year in Stanford's MBA program, she'd given up on the idea that her one and only lurked in the suited, uptight ranks of the Graduate School of Business. A majority of her classmates were male, but they were either taken, insufferable, or—more often than not—both, so she'd pinned her hopes on a whirlwind summer of romance instead.

It'd worked for Kris and Nate, who met the summer after study abroad and were getting married in a few short months. Why couldn't it work for her?

While Olivia didn't *need* a man, a simple calculation told her she had to meet someone this year to stay on track for her five-year plan: finish her MBA, become a vice president at Pine Hill Capital by thirty-two, get married by thirty-three, and have two children by thirty-five. The children would have to be twins, of course—preferably one girl, one boy, to maximize the efficiency of the process. Why deal with morning sickness and mood swings for eighteen months when you could get it done in nine?

Since Olivia was twenty-nine going on thirty, she had three years to get hitched. She figured she and her future husband had to date for at least a year before getting engaged, plus she needed time to plan the wedding.

The timing was tight, but it'd work—as long as she found her happily-ever-after partner this year.

But now, her apartment mishap had thrown a wrench in her plans. She was already exhausted from work most days, and she'd have to spend weeks running around San Francisco, looking for a new apartment. There was no way she could wait seven weeks before moving back into her studio. As much as she hated to admit it, Sammy was right—it would be wildly expensive to rent a hotel room for that long, and Olivia didn't deal well with instability. A week or two, she could handle. Seven? Forget it.

Stress did not a happy Olivia make.

"This is a nightmare." She tilted her head back and counted silently to ten. She *knew* she should've brought her calming lavender face mist with her. "I should sue him for gross negligence."

The burst pipes had been the landlord's fault. She'd only lived in the apartment for a few days—she hadn't even touched the washing machine yet. He'd explained the restoration process would take almost two months because the studio was old and the water had caused extensive damage.

The landlord had offered the option to break her lease without penalty and $500 to replace her damaged items.

Five hundred dollars. Her mattress alone cost more than that.

"But I won't sue him," Olivia continued, talking to herself. "More time and money wasted. Searching for a new place to stay would be a better investment."

A low chuckle filled the car.

She cast a half-confused, half-annoyed glance in Sammy's direction. "What's so funny?"

"You." He made a right turn. "You are so...you."

He said it in a way that she couldn't tell whether he meant it as a compliment or an insult.

"I am, and I'm fabulous," Olivia said, choosing the I'll-pretend-that's-a-compliment route. She was so not in the mood to argue.

Sammy's face broke out into a full-fledged grin, and a swarm of butterflies took flight in her stomach. "What are you going to do while you search for an apartment?"

"I'll stay at a hotel. Not ideal, but hopefully the search won't take too long." She tapped her fingers on her thigh, her mind racing with a million to-do items. She needed a spreadsheet ASAP, with neighborhoods, rent prices, a list of amenities, proximity to her office, and the nearest public transport option—

"Since we're not near a computer and you can't create a spreadsheet at the moment, how about a cupcake? It'll make you feel better." Sammy cut the engine, and Olivia realized they were at his bakery instead of his house.

"How did you know I was thinking about spreadsheets?"

"You're always thinking about spreadsheets."

Valid point.

"C'mon." Sammy got out of the car. "Cupcake's on me."

Olivia's stomach twisted. She didn't want to go in there, but she had no good excuse for staying in the car and turning down her favorite dessert, so she reluctantly followed him into the bright, airy shop.

The smell of freshly baked pastries and sweets slammed into her nostrils the minute she stepped inside. Crumble & Bake was one of San Francisco's most-visited food spots and a tourist destination unto itself. A chalkboard menu of the different items on offer took up the whole wall behind the registers, and the store comprised three sections: one for classic Chinese bakery items like Hong Kong–style egg tarts and pineapple buns, one for Western baked goods like croissants and muffins, and one for desserts. Crumble & Bake's famous cupcakes lined an entire counter, with each flavor displayed in its own glass jar.

Customers packed the shop this Saturday afternoon, and more than a few customers stared and whispered when they saw Sammy. He wasn't movie-star famous, but he'd been featured in the media enough times and had a large enough social media following that he inevitably got recognized in public—especially in his own shop.

A few curious glances fell on Olivia as well, which she ignored.

She trailed Sammy behind the counter and into the kitchen, where she garnered more curious glances while he conversed with a large blond man in a white double-breasted chef's jacket. He introduced himself as Liam, Sammy's pastry sous chef.

Olivia smiled politely and tried to melt into the walls so she wasn't in anyone's way.

After ten or so minutes, Sammy seemed to remember he hadn't arrived alone. "Sorry, this is going to take a while. There are a few things I need to handle before we leave," he told Olivia with a hint of apology. "Feel free to explore, taste test, et cetera. My office—the one with the green door—is quiet, or there's a window seat by the cupcake counter if you want to see the action."

"Sure, no problem. I'll figure it out." There were worse things than being "trapped" in a bakery.

"Try the lemon-and-raspberry cupcake!" Liam yelled before the kitchen doors swung shut behind her. "It's our signature!"

Olivia took his advice and paid for the cupcake—she could've had it on the house, but she already owed Sammy too much—before parking herself in the window seat behind the cupcake counter. One bite told her all she needed to know: it was the best freakin' cupcake in the world. *Wow.* No wonder it was Crumble & Bake's signature item. Her taste buds were in heaven.

She munched on the lemon-and-raspberry confection while Googling hotels near her office—ideally within walking distance. If she had to spend a king's ransom on accommodations for the next few weeks, she wanted to cut down on transportation costs.

But no matter how hard she tried, Olivia couldn't focus. She kept looking around, unable to take her eyes off the bustling bakery. A framed copy of Sammy's first magazine cover—taken two years after his business opened its doors—hung on a nearby wall. His smile seemed to mock her, saying, *You thought I couldn't do it. Well, here I am, doing it.*

Her stomach churned with guilt. She wished she'd been more supportive when he first came to her with his plans. She wished she hadn't let her mother's words and insecurities get to her. But the truth was, no matter how strong she stood in all other areas of her life, she'd never been strong enough to face off against Eleanor Tang—and win.

Speaking of the devil...

Her phone lit up with an incoming call. She was tempted to ignore it, but that would only delay the inevitable.

Olivia picked up the call and turned her head away from the crowd, like that would somehow diminish the background noise. "Hello, Mother."

"Olivia, where are you?" Eleanor's cool, crisp voice flowed over the line like ice water. "It's loud."

"I'm shopping," Olivia lied. "For more work clothes."

"Why? Did you gain weight?"

She rolled her eyes and prayed for patience. "No. I simply needed a wardrobe refresher."

"Fine," Eleanor said. "Make sure not to buy anything pastel. It washes out your complexion."

Olivia couldn't resist countering with "Alina's bridesmaid dresses are pastel."

She could practically see her mother waving a dismissive hand in the air. "Yes, well, peach flatters most of the bridesmaids' complexions. It's a shame it does nothing for yours, but majority rules. Speaking of your sister, you'll be here for the rehearsal dinner?"

It wasn't really a question, nor was it a request—never mind the fact that Alina had chosen their cousin Kayla as her maid of honor instead of her only sister. Not that Olivia *wanted* maid-of-honor privileges. Normally, she loved wedding planning, but

Alina made Bridezilla look like a cute, innocent puppy, and that was *before* you factored an overbearing Eleanor into the equation. Still, it hurt like hell to be passed over for the role by someone who should've been her ride-or-die. Then again, she and Alina hadn't had that type of sisterly relationship in a long time.

"Yes, Mother, I'll be there." *Like I said I would, the past five times you asked.*

"Good."

While Eleanor rattled on about Alina's wedding, Olivia tuned her out. Her mother hadn't stopped talking about Alina's engagement to Richard Barrons III since Richard popped the question with a four-carat Cartier last year. He was Eleanor's dream son-in-law—a wealthy, generically handsome, Harvard-educated hedge fund manager from a good family whom she could brag about in her weekly ladies-who-lunch meetings.

Personally, Olivia thought Richard was a douche nozzle and total sleaze, but she wasn't the one marrying the guy. At least her mother, sister, and future brother-in-law lived in Chicago, and she could keep her physical contact with them to a minimum.

"I have to go," Olivia said when she saw Sammy step out of the kitchen. "I'll see you at the rehearsal dinner. Bye!"

She hung up before Eleanor could rope her into another conversation she didn't want to take part in. Talking with her mother always made her blood pressure spike.

"Sorry about that," Sammy said as they exited the bakery. Afternoon sunshine spilled over them, warming Olivia's chilled skin. "Things took longer than I expected."

"Don't be sorry. It's your job, and you've already been driving me around all morning." Olivia climbed into the passenger seat. "Besides, I had your cupcakes to keep me company."

A smile flitted over his face. "You okay with going back to the house right now? I can make lunch."

"Yes, but I just need to grab my bag. I'm not hungry yet." Olivia had left her overnight duffel at Sammy's house. The rest of her belongings were stuffed in his trunk and back seat—they'd spent hours packing and getting rid of her furniture after her landlord left that morning. "I can call an Uber XL that'll fit all my stuff and have them drive me to a hotel. I don't want to inconvenience you any more than I already have."

"It's not an inconvenience." Sammy stared straight ahead, his jaw flexing like he was holding a silent debate with himself. "Did you already book the hotel?"

"No. I'll do it now." Olivia pulled up the relevant tab on her phone. She'd already decided on a hotel and had been ready to check in before her mother called.

"Wait."

She raised a questioning eyebrow, and Sammy delivered his next words so casually, so innocuously that she didn't realize their import until much later.

"Instead of a hotel, why don't you move into my place?"

CHAPTER 4

SAMMY HAD A REPUTATION FOR BEING A NICE GUY. HE had an even temper, helped those in need, and rarely raised his voice.

But here was the truth: he wasn't actually that nice. He did nice things, but he also got angry and petty and jealous and vindictive. Maybe he did so with less frequency than the general population, but Sammy was human and possessed all the flaws of one.

Case in point: Olivia's apartment disaster.

A small part of him sympathized with her. A much larger part of him delighted in schadenfreude.

In all the time Sammy had known her, he'd never once seen Olivia be anything other than perfect. Perfect grades, perfect looks, perfect clothes, perfect job. Her life was a Pinterest board and *Forbes* 30 Under 30 list wrapped in an Excel spreadsheet and topped with a gold star sticker.

Call him an asshole, but seeing her freak out was so fucking satisfying. She hadn't even freaked out when they broke up. She'd just stared at him for a long minute, turned, and walked out the door like the year they'd spent together had meant nothing.

Even now, the memory stung.

"That's the last of the croissants." Liam rinsed his hands in the sink. "Just in time. Store opens in…" He checked the clock. "Ten minutes, and according to Cordy, there's already a line."

"There's always a line." Cordelia breezed into the kitchen in time to catch the last half of Liam's statement. "I swear half the city is addicted to carbs."

"Not that we're complaining. The carb addicts pay your salary," Sammy reminded her with a grin. "How's it looking out there?"

"Five waiting to pounce the minute we flip the OPEN sign. More to come once we hit the eight a.m. rush, I'm sure." She sighed. "Bryce chose the worst day to call in sick."

"Is there ever a *good* day to call in sick?" Liam mused. "It's always busy."

"Yeah, but Mondays are a whole other beast. Dontcha know? Croissants and muffins are the highlight of the corporate grinders' start of the week. That and coffee, but we don't serve coffee." Cordelia popped her gum. "We should serve coffee."

She'd been on Sammy's case about adding drinks to the menu since she started working as a bakery assistant six months ago. A theater enthusiast with hair that changed colors along with the seasons—it was currently dyed pale blond with pink tips for summer—she was bold, brash, and one of Sammy's best employees. She handled even the fussiest customers with aplomb, and she worked the register with ungodly speed.

Sammy knew it was only a matter of time before Cordelia made it big onstage and quit. Her passion was the stage, not bakeries, but until then, she'd hold down the fort—and continue bugging Sammy about the menu.

"Maybe next year," Sammy said, like he always did. "I don't have time to think about expanding the menu right now."

Business was booming, and while he was thrilled with Crumble & Bake's success, it meant more work on the corporate side of things and less time for the culinary side. Sammy had hired an operations manager last year to oversee all three of the brand's existing branches—San Francisco, LA, and San Diego—but they were also expanding to the East Coast. Soon, there'd be a permanent Crumble & Bake in New York and one on Thayer University's campus in Maryland, right on the DC border.

Sammy also had to keep up with his social media presence. A digital operations associate maintained and updated the accounts, but Sammy had to star in the videos and photos. His personal brand fed into Crumble & Bake's success as much as the corporate brand fed into his success. It was mutually beneficial, even if Sammy was tempted to shut down all his social media some days. Being a public figure online was more draining than a long day in the kitchen.

"It's just coffee," Cordelia argued. "Buy a couple o' espresso machines and boom! You're done."

"Don't think it's that simple." Liam came to Sammy's aid. "We've been here since three a.m. Cut the man some slack."

"I'm cutting, I'm cutting." Cordelia made scissor motions with her fingers. "You're the boss," she told Sammy. "Just wanted to throw my two cents in, is all. Plus, the closest coffee shop to us is Three Lions and their lattes are nasty." She glanced at the clock and heaved a sigh. "One minute. Here we go."

She swanned out of the kitchen. Soon after, Sammy heard the bells above the entrance jangle and the low persistent hum of excited chatter fill the air through the swinging doors.

While Cordelia worked the counter, Sammy and the rest of the kitchen staff busied themselves with the behind-the-scenes work. He had a tight-knit family at the bakery—Liam, his right-hand man; three production bakers; a cake decorator; a kitchen helper to assist with nonbaking tasks like dishwashing and refilling ingredient bins; and Cordelia and Bryce, who manned the front of the house. Sammy's operations manager and digital associate worked remotely, and he had Zoom meetings with them twice a month.

"Who was the woman you brought in the other day?" Liam asked casually after they finished making and packing the lunchtime goodies.

"Hmm?" Sammy wiped a counter down.

He didn't come into the bakery every day like he used to, but when he did, he followed a standard baker's schedule: arrive at 3 a.m. to sanitize the kitchen and prepare the day's baked goods for a 7 a.m. opening, begin making the lunchtime items while the morning crowd got their fix, clean the kitchen just before noon for the lunch rush, prep the next day's ingredients and products, clean the kitchen (yes, again—hygiene was critical), and close at four. It was an unconventional schedule for anyone except bakers, but Sammy had gotten used to it over the years.

"The woman from Saturday," Liam repeated. "Dark hair, yay tall, Asian?"

Sammy paused for a second before he continued wiping. "Oh. Olivia."

"Yep. First time you brought a woman here."

"Don't read too much into it." Sammy swept a few crumbs off the counter into his hand and disposed of them in the trash. "I helped her with something that morning and the bakery was on the way to our next stop."

He didn't mention Olivia would be staying with him for the foreseeable future. That was no one's business except theirs.

"She's beautiful."

Sammy shrugged in response.

His sous chef persisted. "You two dating?"

"I didn't realize we were playing Twenty Questions." Sammy's tone was curt. "Toss me that flour, will ya?"

Liam obliged. "That's not an answer."

This was what Sammy got for cultivating close relationships with his employees. Derek, his operations manager, kept telling him to treat them as employees instead of friends, but Sammy liked the camaraderie at the bakery—except in situations like this, when said employees insisted on getting on his nerves.

"We're not dating." Sammy stored the flour in its allotted spot. "We know each other from study abroad."

"As in college?" Liam let out a low whistle. "Long history."

He looked like he was about to ask another question, but Cordelia saved Sammy by poking her head through the door and yelling, "Boss, someone's here to see you!"

Sammy frowned. Cordelia knew better than to ask him to do a meet-and-greet with a fan, but who else could be here to see him?

He checked his phone for a clue—a call or a text, maybe. Nothing.

Whatever. He'd meet the person regardless—anything to avoid Liam's inquisitive stare.

When Sammy saw who was waiting for him at the counter, however, he wished he was back in the kitchen enduring Liam's endless questions.

"Hey, cuz." Edison's eminently punchable face carried its usual semismirk. "How's it going?"

"What are you doing here?"

Sammy kept his tone civil, but irritation darted through his system and formed a solid block of resentment in his stomach. Out of all his cousins, Edison had always been his least favorite, but it hadn't been until that summer in New York that he'd vaulted to the top of Sammy's short but mighty Most Hated list.

"To support my cousin, of course," Edison said in an oily voice. He swung a white paper bag stamped with the Crumble & Bake logo in the air. "Nice little place you've got here. It ain't NASA, but it's cute."

Sammy's jaw tensed at the backhanded compliment. Edison, a corporate lawyer, looked down on anyone who didn't have a high-paying career in the medical, legal, or engineering fields. His office was only a few blocks from the bakery, but as far as Sammy knew, he'd never dropped by before.

Sammy still remembered the other man's sneer when he found out Sammy had turned down a job offer from NASA to open a bakery, of all things. Edison had always resented Sammy for "stealing his thunder," as he put it when their grandparents wouldn't stop raving about Sammy's SAT scores (he'd beaten Edison's score by forty points). Sammy's career U-turn had finally given Edison the justification he needed to look down on his "rival."

"I appreciate the business. Now, if you'll excuse me, I have business to attend to."

"Sure." Edison remained where he was. "By the way, Mom asked if you were coming to dim sum this Sunday. We haven't seen you in a month."

Sammy's extended family ate dim sum together every Sunday. It was a Yu tradition, and he tried to attend whenever he wasn't busy with work. Unfortunately, he was always busy with work these days, and he'd had to help Olivia settle in yesterday.

"Maybe. We'll see."

"Well, I suggest attending this week's gathering." Edison adjusted his tie. "I have a big announcement."

Sammy flashed a tight smile. "Like I said, we'll see."

"Sure, sure." His cousin chuckled. "Have a good day, cuz. See you this weekend...maybe."

He winked at Cordelia and strode out the door, smug and pompous in his thousand-dollar Armani suit.

"That's your cousin? What an ass," she said the second the door shut behind him. "Are you sure you're related?"

Sammy's mouth flattened into a grim line. "Yeah."

"Never seen you be so curt with someone." Cordelia straightened a cupcake in its case. "Not that I blame you. He must have been hell to grow up with."

Edison *had* been hell to grow up with, but Sammy hadn't hated him until eight years ago, when he'd caught Edison and Olivia kissing less than an *hour* after Olivia and Sammy broke up.

That's right. Edison and Olivia. Kissing.

Renewed anger simmered in Sammy's stomach as he remembered stumbling on the scene. Remembered the disbelief, the devastation, the heartbreak. He wouldn't put anything past Edison, but Olivia *knew* he despised the man. Their breakup had been messy, but he'd thought she respected him enough not to pull such a low move—even if neither she nor Edison knew he knew. Sammy had stumbled away before they saw him and never confronted them about it. Technically, Edison and Olivia had both been single, so they hadn't cheated on anyone, but it was the fucking principle of the matter.

Now, part of Sammy regretted offering Olivia a place to stay. He wasn't sure what made him do it. The words just fell out of his mouth yesterday when she mentioned booking a hotel. Not only that, but she'd declined and he'd *insisted*, like an idiot. He'd said her stuff was already in his car and reminded her it would be cheaper than paying hotel rates for God knew how long. She'd relented on the condition they sign a lease and she pay rent like any normal tenant.

By nighttime, Sammy had whipped up a week-to-week lease, they'd signed on the dotted line, and Olivia's belongings had been transported into her new room.

Out of all the bad ideas Sammy had had since he ran into her Friday night, taking Olivia in as his roommate was possibly the worst idea of them all.

Or was it?

The nice part of him said he should help her find a new place as soon as possible. The not-so-nice part insisted he kick her out next week. The downright devious part encouraged him to make the most of the situation—by making her regret the day she walked out on him.

Olivia living in his house and at his mercy meant plenty of opportunity for mind games.

Sammy wasn't a mind-games person. They were cruel and a waste of time and energy. But nothing about his feelings toward Olivia had ever been "normal," and like he said, he wasn't as nice as people thought he was.

The devious part won.

CHAPTER 5

OLIVIA DEBATED THE PROS AND CONS OF STABBING someone in the eye with a pen versus bludgeoning them over the head with a stapler. She wasn't a violent person by nature, but she could learn and adapt. A few Google searches and YouTube tutorials, maybe a couple of grisly movies. She'd be on her way to Violentville in no time.

Her coworkers deserved it.

They spilled into the office on a loud, chattering, postlunch high, sleeves rolled up and faces gleaming with sweat from tromping through downtown San Francisco in the middle of a summer afternoon in suits. It was warmer than usual today, and the scent of their musk invaded Olivia's nostrils.

She wrinkled her nose.

"Olivia!" Logan slapped a heavy hand on her shoulder, causing her fingers to slip on the keyboard. She gritted her teeth and deleted the resulting nonsensical string of letters and symbols on-screen. "Working hard, I see."

"Someone has to," she said with a mix of tart and sweetness that made it difficult for the receiver to discern whether she was joking. She wasn't.

Next to her, Cassidy continued typing like she was the only person in the room.

Besides the office assistant, Olivia and Cassidy were the only women in Pine Hill's San Francisco office. Cassidy was a senior analyst like Olivia, but she carried a chip the size of Alaska on her shoulder. Olivia had tried getting lunch with her the other day and received a bland, silent glare in response.

So yeah, zero help or female bonding there.

Logan laughed. "You're funny. Pretty girls usually aren't funny."

Pen stabbing. Definitely.

If only because the pen was closer and it would take less time to dispatch the blond tool hovering over her shoulder.

While the rest of the office settled into their seats—a few of them casting amused glances in Olivia and Logan's direction as they did so—Logan perched on Olivia's desk and obscured her view of the monitor.

She exhaled a long breath. "Can I help you with something?"

Olivia had played the Wall Street game for close to a decade. She couldn't blow up—especially not here, where she had no allies. Her new manager in the New York office had been a sexist pig, but at least she'd had colleagues who had her back. Here, she was the new girl. She was only in California for the summer, and none of her coworkers seemed keen on getting to know her beyond some of the men's thinly veiled come-ons.

She'd worked too hard and too long to throw her future away over some idiot finance bro who had nothing better to do with his time than annoy her.

"The question is whether or not I can help *you.*" Logan flashed what he must've imagined was a dazzling smile. Objectively, he wasn't bad-looking, but his personality canceled out any charm his golden hair and lean build might have had. "You're new to the city, and I can show you around. I know some great nighttime activities we could do after work."

His voice dropped, making his insinuation clear.

Disgust crawled into the pit of Olivia's stomach. She flicked her gaze toward the gold wedding band on Logan's finger. "Your wife might not like that very much."

Translation: *I would rather bathe in acid than spend time with you outside the confines of this godforsaken office, you cheating ass.*

He didn't blink at the mention of his spouse. "Don't worry about her."

"Okay. I won't." Olivia scooted her chair to the left so she could see her monitor again without Logan blocking the way. She purposely didn't respond to his offer to show her some "great nighttime activities."

Logan opened his mouth again, but before he could speak, their boss poked his head out of his office.

"Olivia, I need to speak with you."

Olivia pushed back from her desk and sauntered past a disappointed-looking Logan. Hopefully, he would be back at his desk—on the other side of the room from Olivia—by the time she finished her meeting.

She entered the managing director's office and sank into the chair opposite Michael, curious what this was about. She hadn't interacted with him much beyond a perfunctory greeting on her first day, but Michael Berman sat high on Pine Hill's hierarchy, and it couldn't hurt to butter him up.

They made small talk for a minute or two—how Olivia liked Stanford, her impressions of San Francisco, and so on—before Michael got down to business.

"Have you heard of Ty Winstock?"

The name sounded vaguely familiar. Olivia flipped through

her mental files until she zeroed in on where she'd heard it before. "He's the cofounder of Mosaic," she said, naming a popular workspace and productivity app that had exploded on the scene a few years ago. Since then, Mosaic had been praised by everyone from *Forbes* to Oprah. The company went public last year with a huge IPO (initial public offering) that made its founders two of Silicon Valley's newest tech billionaires.

However, Ty Winstock was notoriously press-shy; his partner was the one who made the media rounds. Olivia didn't even know what he looked like.

"That's right." Michael nodded, looking pleased with Olivia's quick answer. "We're hoping to acquire him as a new client, but he's quite...eccentric. I'd like you to put together a dossier on him. Anything you can find that'll give us a better understanding of his likes, dislikes, et cetera. We have our first meeting with him in two weeks. You'll join me."

Surprise and pleasure zinged through Olivia's veins. She hadn't had a lot of client-facing opportunities so far—most of her work involved tracking investments and conducting special projects, such as analyzing the firm's private equity holdings and industry trends, all of which she could do at her desk—but she thrilled at the challenge.

"I'll have the dossier ready by next week," she said, trying to hide her excitement.

"Excellent." Michael tapped his pen on his desk. "I've heard great things about you from HQ. I know you're only in the city for the summer, but who knows?" He smiled. "Maybe you'll want to stay after you graduate."

Olivia made a noncommittal noise and smiled back. She loved New York, and she hated the majority of her coworkers here. The chances of her staying in San Francisco were slim to none.

When she returned to her desk, she found a Post-it Note stuck to her mouse pad.

For nighttime shenanigans, call 415-768-2898 ;)

No signature, but it wasn't necessary.

Olivia's good mood dimmed, and she glared across the office at Logan, who winked and puckered his lips when he saw her watching him.

Ugh.

This was going to be a long summer.

———————

Olivia got home—correction, got to Sammy's house—at half past eight. She'd stayed late to work on the dossier and had gone down the internet rabbit hole researching Ty Winstock. He was an interesting character, to say the least. Thirty-three years old, never married, no children, a high school dropout who'd taught himself coding and created his first app at fourteen. He was unique among billionaires in that he didn't own a house or any personal real estate holdings—he traveled a ton and moved from five-star hotel to five-star hotel, but since he was based in the Bay Area, he spent a majority of his time at the Z Hotel San Francisco. She still had to do more digging on the guy's current investments, but the ache in her eyes alerted her it was time to shut off the computer and resume her investigation tomorrow.

"You're home late." Sammy sat at the kitchen counter, eating a bowl of noodles and watching as she off slipped her shoes and placed them neatly on the shoe rack by the entrance. The kitchen was the one room that offered a view of all other parts of the house—the entryway to the right, the hall of bedrooms straight across, the dining and living area to the left.

"Not that late for finance people." Olivia hesitated, wondering if she should make small talk before beelining to her room for a change of clothes and a shower.

She'd spent all of yesterday moving in, and the task had taken her mind off how weird it would be for her to live with her ex. Now that she had no boxes to unpack or clothes to organize, she was at a loss as to what to do.

How would their relationship work? Would they be roommates who made small talk in passing? Would they eat meals and binge-watch *The Bachelor* together, cackling over how cheesy but addictive the show was?

She couldn't imagine the latter happening, but it seemed wrong to treat Sammy as just a roommate given their history and the fact that he'd gone out of his way to help her. Regardless of how much he'd hurt her back then, she owed him, and that threw a whole new wrench in their dynamics.

Not that she could complain. She'd chosen to accept his offer, so it was up to her to figure it out.

"Have you eaten yet?" Sammy asked, interrupting Olivia's silent debate. "I made extra noodles, if you want them."

"No, thanks. I already ate." Olivia had a list of the best restaurants that delivered to her office and planned on rotating between them in the upcoming months. Honestly, she wouldn't have minded a second meal—Sammy's noodles were amazing, and her sushi dinner hadn't filled her stomach as much as she would've liked.

But she didn't want to eat dinner with Sammy. Didn't want to sit in proximity to him while those dark eyes of his caressed her skin and the rumble of his voice stirred things inside her that she hadn't known still existed.

They stood across the room from each other, their tones casual and their conversation mundane, but a strange charge danced in the air between them, twisting the molecules into a rope of tension that sizzled and tugged at Olivia's stomach.

"If you change your mind, the leftovers will be in the fridge." Sammy shifted, and his muscles bunched under his shirt.

Gulp.

"Sounds good." Olivia ran a nervous hand through her hair. "It's been a long day, so I'm just going to shower and call it a night."

She might've imagined it, but she thought his eyes flared with heat at her words, and the charge in the air danced faster.

An inane part of her wondered if he was picturing her in the shower. The possibility shouldn't have thrilled her as much as it did.

Don't be ridiculous. There's no sexual attraction between us. It's...static. Like the kind you find on sweaters during winter.

Olivia admired him the way she'd admire any good-looking man, but that didn't mean she wanted to sleep with him. Or kiss him. Or do anything else of that nature.

As for the way Sammy was looking at her...well, that was her overactive imagination playing tricks. She read too much erotica.

"Good night," Olivia blurted before he could say anything else.

She practically ran out of the kitchen, holding her breath until she was within the safe confines of her room.

She leaned against the door and closed her eyes, her heart pounding for no discernible reason. Sammy hadn't said or done anything untoward since she ran into him at Ishikawa, and she had no reason to be this nervous. But even though he'd been nothing but pleasant—almost suspiciously so—Olivia couldn't shake the sense that she was prey trapped in a house with her hunter.

CHAPTER 6

OLIVIA AND SAMMY HAD THEIR FIRST ROOMMATE ARGU-
ment less than a week after she moved in.

"I can't believe you did this." Sammy's head pounded with
anger as he stared at his kitchen. "What were you thinking?"

Olivia planted her hands on her hips. "I was *thinking* I would
do something nice and help you organize your things. This place
is—was—a mess."

The pounding intensified. "It was *my* mess. I knew where
everything was. I had a system. I use the kitchen all the time. You
don't even cook!"

"I could."

The snort slipped out before he could stop it. "No, you can't."

Wrong thing to say.

Olivia's cheeks flushed red, and defiance sparked in her eyes.
"It's been eight years. I've improved."

"Hate to break it to you, but there was nowhere to go but up."

Harsh? Perhaps. True? Absolutely.

Sammy had eaten Olivia's cooking once, and his stomach still
rebelled at the thought.

"It wasn't *that* bad." Olivia's chin jutted out even as pink tinted her cheeks.

He stared at her in disbelief. "We got food poisoning!"

"Once! We got food poisoning *once!*"

"Once is enough!"

"Stop yelling!" Olivia took a deep breath and pressed two fingers to her temple. "We're off topic. The issue is not that one *tiny* mishap years ago—"

"We threw up for three days. My throat was so raw I could barely speak afterward. I had to call in sick to my internship."

She continued like he hadn't spoken. "—it's that you're throwing a fit over a rearranged spice rack. You had no system. The spices weren't arranged alphabetically, by height, or by category of flavor. It was chaos, and I brought order. They're now in alphabetical order because that's the easiest organizational method. The containers' different heights are irritating, but that's nothing a quick trip to the Container Store won't fix. We can buy a pack of labels and matching spice shakers—"

"We're not going to the Container Store," Sammy gritted out. "We're not buying labels or new spice shakers. You know why? Because there's nothing wrong with the old ones or the way the spices were organized."

"They were *not* organized."

"They were to me. And I'm putting them back." He didn't take his eyes off Olivia as he picked up the chili powder—currently nestled between the ground cardamom and cinnamon—and shoved it on the bottom rack, next to the turmeric powder.

Take that, alphabetical order.

Olivia gasped. "You did not just do that."

"Oh, I'm just getting started." Sammy opened the fridge—because contrary to what she said, Olivia hadn't reorganized just the spice rack but the whole damn kitchen—and stuck the milk on a shelf instead of the door storage.

Her eye twitched.

When he retrieved a half-empty box of green tea packets from his new "tea and coffee cabinet" and placed it on the counter next to the hot water dispenser, angling the box so it didn't line up perfectly with the wall, she stormed over and shoved the tea back in the cabinet.

He took it out.

She put it back in.

There was a dirty joke lurking there somewhere, but Sammy was too riled up to concentrate on anything except not strangling the woman in front of him.

"This is *my* kitchen."

"It's *our* kitchen," Olivia corrected. "I signed a lease. I'm paying rent. The kitchen is a communal space, which means it's mine and yours."

"You don't even use the damn kitchen! You eat dinner at your office half the time, and the other half you order takeout."

"I have to look at it," she fired back. "You know I dislike clutter."

Sammy's molars ground together until his jaw hurt. "Right. I forgot. Everything has to be perfect for the mighty Olivia Tang. Your house, your career, your fucking relationships. How's that working out for you? Living in your ex's house, still single because no man on earth can live up to your unrealistic expectations. Careful, Olivia, or you'll end up like your mom always feared you would."

The second the words left his mouth, he wished he could take them back.

Olivia reeled like she'd been slapped, her eyes wide.

This time, Sammy was the one who rubbed his temples. Shame and regret lodged in his throat. "I didn't mean—"

She turned and walked away. A minute later, he heard the firm thud of her bedroom door slamming shut.

Sammy let loose curses that would have his mom washing his mouth out with soap.

He'd been cruel, and he never wanted to be cruel. But that was what happened when you fought with someone you knew so well—you understood which buttons to push and which words would cut the deepest.

"What are you looking at?" Sammy growled at the green tea in the cabinet. He slammed the door shut and, with another curse, shoved the chili powder back between the cardamom and cinnamon and placed the milk in the fridge's door storage before he stalked to Olivia's room and knocked.

No answer.

He knocked again.

"Go away." Her voice was calm, and he heard the distinct sound of a zipper unwinding.

"Olivia, open the door."

Nothing.

Sammy released a pent-up sigh. "I'm sorry, okay? I shouldn't have said what I said. It was shitty of me. Can we please talk about it face-to-face like adults?"

The door flew open, and Olivia glared at him. He could see an open suitcase behind her, half-filled with clothes. "There's not much to talk about. I shouldn't have moved in. I appreciate you helping me when my apartment flooded, but I won't let you hold it over my head."

The shame thickened. "I'm not holding it over your head."

"Yes, you are. We had an argument, and you said—and I quote—'living in your ex's house, still single because no man on earth can live up to your unrealistic expectations.' That was a low blow." Olivia turned her back on him and wedged a neatly folded

T-shirt into her suitcase. "We should've known this wouldn't work. We have too much history for us to be normal roommates. I'll stay in a hotel until I find a new place, and I'll pay you—"

"Don't leave."

She paused for a second before she resumed packing. "—prorated rent for the time I've—"

"Olivia." Sammy placed a hand on her arm. He hadn't realized he'd stepped into her room until now. "Don't leave."

Olivia stilled, though he detected a slight tremor beneath his hand. The surrounding air thickened and sizzled, the heat sliding over Sammy's skin and setting every nerve ending on fire.

"You can stay as long as you like. I'll treat you like I would any other roommate. I'm sorry for what I said, and I won't say anything like that again. It's not fair, especially when I was the one who asked you to move in."

Wariness crept into Olivia's eyes. "Why are you being so nice? You don't even like me."

"That's not true."

Olivia shot him a skeptical look.

"We've had our differences," Sammy acknowledged. "But what happened between us happened a long time ago. How about we call a truce?" He held out his hand. "No arguing over the past or using it as a weapon. From now on, the only arguments we'll have—if we have any—are normal roommate arguments. Who left the toilet seat up, who left dishes in the sink overnight..."

"I never leave the toilet seat up or leave dishes in the sink overnight, so the answer will always be you." A small smile graced Olivia's lips when Sammy glared at her. "Fine, we can be adults about this. Truce."

She grasped his hand, and a bolt of electricity almost knocked him on his ass. Judging by the shock that flared in her eyes, he wasn't the only one affected.

Olivia's smile faded, and Sammy's heart crashed against his chest. They'd seen each other multiple times over the years, but this was their first skin-to-skin contact since she walked out of their apartment that fateful summer in New York. The chemistry was as devastating now as when they'd first started dating.

Fuck. This threw a wrench in Sammy's plans. He'd thought he had better control over his hormones, but suddenly, all he could think about was how soft Olivia's lips looked and how good she smelled—like freshly washed linens with a hint of jasmine.

Other than the sound of their breathing, it was silent. So silent he could hear his pulse thrumming in his ears.

Olivia stared up at him, the wariness in her eyes replaced by a heat that stirred him to life. If he leaned forward a few inches—

The loud, harsh ring of the doorbell shattered the spell that had kept them suspended in a state of tense anticipation.

They yanked their hands—still entwined in an unmoving handshake—apart and leapt back at the same time.

"I'll get that—"

"I'll unpack again—"

Their words overlapped and jumbled together.

Sammy ducked his head and got out of there like the hounds of hell were on his heels. Adrenaline pumped in his veins.

If someone hadn't rung the bell...

He shook his head. He wouldn't think about that now. He had bigger things to worry about—like the person on his front step.

There was only one person he knew who'd pop in unannounced on a Saturday afternoon.

Sure enough, his mother beamed when he opened the door. "Sammy!" She looked him over and clucked. "Have you been eating enough? You look thinner. I hope you haven't been working too hard," she said in rapid-fire Mandarin. "That's what you hired employees for. You need rest."

She said the same thing every time she saw him. If Sammy really had lost as much weight as she said he had, he'd be invisible.

"Hi, Mom." He stepped aside so she could come in. "Let me take that for you."

Amy Yu's arms were laden with shopping bags from Wing Fa, a popular Asian supermarket near his parents' house.

"No, no. I got it."

She slipped off her shoes before winding her way to the kitchen. In her pale pink polo shirt, white cropped pants, white sneakers, and pink-and-white tennis visor, his mother looked as young and spry as someone in her thirties, even though she was pushing fifty-six.

"I was already at Wing Fa and thought I'd buy you some groceries." Amy unloaded boxes of silken tofu, bunches of bok choy, and bags of frozen dumplings onto the marble counter. "When was the last time you had soup? You look tired. I'll make you lotus root and pork soup," she decided. "Good for energy."

Sammy leaned against the kitchen island and folded his arms over his chest. "Okay, who is it?"

His mother blinked, innocent as a doe. "Who is who?"

"The girl. Who's the girl you want to set me up with this time?"

Sammy was twenty-nine, hardly old or decrepit, but his mom had been on his case about getting married for years. She wanted grandchildren, and she wanted them *now*.

Once she realized Sammy was nowhere as pressed about his marital status as she was, his mom took it upon herself to set him up with every eligible woman she knew. He'd indulged her in the beginning, but after more than a dozen blind dates—some okay, some downright horrible, none earth-shattering—his patience was wearing thin.

His mother knew it too, which was why she always showed

up with food whenever she wanted him to go on another match-making date. Food was his weakness.

"I have no idea what you're talking about." Amy opened the freezer door and started stuffing the dumplings and shrink-wrapped foam trays of oxtail, pork, and beef inside. She'd bought enough groceries to feed a small army for a month. "By the way, are you going to dim sum tomorrow?" Her tone was casual. Too casual. "We haven't seen you in weeks, and your grandparents miss you."

Yep, she was definitely going to spring Mystery Woman on him at dim sum.

"I call them every week."

"Calling isn't the same as seeing, is it?" Amy arched an eye-brow, and he suddenly felt like he was ten again, tracking mud through the house after she'd mopped the floors. "They're old, and your grandfather's health isn't so good. Who knows how much longer they'll have?"

No one could guilt-trip like an Asian mom.

Sammy sighed. "I'll be there." He'd learned to pick his battles a long time ago.

"Great! Your grandparents will be thrilled. I heard Edison has big news too." Amy snorted. "He probably bought a new car or something equally tacky. Your auntie Ling's always brag-ging about him like he's something special because he went to Harvard and is a big-time lawyer, but I know better." She patted Sammy on the cheek. "You *turned down* Harvard. Who needs a degree from that big overhyped university anyway? Harvey Mudd is smaller, more prestigious, and you work for yourself instead of some corporate boss. Plus, you're taller and more handsome." His mother looked smug. "Edison's only one and a half meters tall, and he's not the one all the waitresses at Wah Sing go crazy over."

Even though she'd lived in the U.S. for over three decades, Amy still used the metric measuring system, instead of the American Imperial system. Old habits die hard.

Sammy's cheeks colored. "Mom!"

"What? It's the truth." She leaned in and whispered, "I heard from your auntie Felicia that Edison got implants for that receding chin of his, which does look stronger nowadays."

The one thing his relatives loved more than guilt-tripping their children was gossiping.

"I'm not touching that topic with a ten-foot pole." Sammy helped his mom unpack the rest of his groceries. "How's Dad?"

"Fine, fine." His mom shoved a bottle of hoisin sauce into a cabinet. "He went hiking with your uncles. Imagine! A bunch of old men trying to act like they're still young. I told him if he made it to the top, I'd eat my shoe." Her words were harsh, but her tone was loving.

"Not your new Coach sneakers, I hope." Sammy laughed when she punched him playfully in the arm.

"Don't sass me—"

A door opened and closed in the back of the house, followed by the faint but unmistakable sound of a shower running.

Sammy's shoulders stiffened. *Oh no.*

His mother's head twisted slowly toward the hallway that housed the bedrooms and bathroom. The shower sounded unbearably loud in the otherwise silent house. Then she twisted her head around until she faced Sammy again.

The glee in her expression made him take a step back.

"Who's in the shower?" she asked, her eyes wide. "Is it a girl? Do you have a girl over?"

She couldn't have been more excited if she found out she won free round-trip tickets to Hawaii.

The jackhammers in Sammy's head pounded anew. Between

this and his earlier argument with Olivia, they'd had a busy day. "No. I mean, yes, but no."

Amy frowned. "You're not making any sense. Is it a girl or not?"

"It is, but—"

She flew toward the bathroom, leaving him alone in the kitchen.

"—it's not what you think," Sammy finished. He followed his mother into the hallway, where she stood outside the bathroom door with anticipation gleaming in her eyes. His stomach pulsed with dread. "Mom, she's in the shower. You can't wait for her outside the bathroom like this. It's creepy."

"I need to use the toilet," she said. "What's creepy about that? People wait outside public bathrooms all the time."

This isn't a public bathroom, he wanted to say, but he knew it wouldn't get him anywhere. There was no arguing with his mom once she set her mind on something.

Sammy could only watch in slow-motion horror when the bathroom door opened a few minutes later and steam poured out, partially obscuring an unsuspecting Olivia as she stepped into the hall. For once, he wished she were one of those women who took forever in the shower—no way would his mom wait here for an hour—but she was quick and efficient, as always.

Olivia's tanned skin glistened with crystal droplets of water, and her damp dark hair was slicked back, highlighting her cheekbones. She held onto the top of the towel wrapped around her slender frame with one hand and reached for her bedroom door with the other. Judging by the far-off look in her eyes, she was deep in thought and didn't notice she had company in the hall.

In any other situation, Sammy would've been turned on as hell—*hot girl in a towel!*—but it was hard to feel lustful when you were watching an imminent car crash.

"Hello," Amy said in English.

Olivia jumped and screamed, which caused his mom to scream in response.

"Aaaaaaah!"

"Aaaaaaah!"

Olivia's grip on the towel loosened, and the pale green terry-cloth slid onto the floor, revealing her in all her naked glory.

"*Ai-yah!*" his mother exclaimed while Sammy gulped, torn between averting his gaze and soaking in the visual feast.

The gentleman in him won out—barely. He raised his eyes to the ceiling, jaw tight, but the image of Olivia's smooth bare skin and luscious curves had been ingrained in his mind. He'd seen her naked before, but damn, the years had been good to her. Those breasts, those hips...

Fuckity fuck fuck.

His tranquil Saturday had turned into an epic shit show.

"Olivia." His mother recognized the woman Sammy had once introduced as The One. He'd been young, stupid, and in love, and when he'd broken the news about his and Olivia's split, Amy had looked at him with sad eyes and fed him what she'd claimed was a "Love Cure" soup. It hadn't worked. "This is a surprise."

Olivia snatched her towel off the floor and covered herself once more. Her face matched the reds in the sunset painting hanging next to the bathroom door. "Mrs. Yu. Hi," she squeaked.

"Sammy didn't tell me you were here. In his house. Naked." Amy's laser-beam stare drilled into Sammy, whose grimace deepened.

He chose not to point out that Olivia had been in the shower and therefore had to be naked—it wasn't like she was strolling around the living room in her birthday suit. That wouldn't go over well, and he'd like to live to see thirty, thank you.

Olivia didn't respond. For once, she appeared speechless.

"Well," his mother said wryly, switching back to Mandarin. She knew Olivia was fluent in the language. "At least now I know why Sammy was so besotted with you back in the day. You have beautiful breasts."

Aaaand they blew right past Awkward territory into the town of Highly Inappropriate.

Olivia's face went from fire-engine red to purple, and Sammy squeezed his eyes shut, wishing with all his might that the floor would open up and swallow him whole.

It didn't.

Bastard.

CHAPTER 7

WAH SING WAS ONE OF SAN FRANCISCO'S OLDEST AND most popular Chinese restaurants. Spread out over two floors in bustling Chinatown and open 365 days a year, it was a Sunday dim sum staple for local Chinese residents and the place where they went to celebrate all special occasions—Thanksgiving, Christmas, birthdays, graduations, promotions.

Sammy's family had frequented Wah Sing for years, and they had a standing weekly reservation for the two largest tables on the second floor, right in front of the wood carving of a flying dragon and phoenix that took up half the wall.

When he arrived at the restaurant a little past noon on Sunday, less than twenty-four hours after the cringeworthy incident between his mom and Olivia, Sammy found a majority of his relatives already seated and gossiping loudly over cups of *pu-erh* tea.

The weekly gatherings were less about familial bonding and more about swapping intel on members of San Francisco's Chinese community, showing off one's newest handbag, and bragging about a child's latest accomplishment.

"Sammy!" His mother spotted him first and waved him over. Gone were the polo shirt and tennis visor; in their place was the silk blouse he'd bought her for Mother's Day and her best gold jewelry. She sat at a table with his father, brother, grandparents, and various aunts, uncles, and cousins. Thankfully, Edison wasn't one of them—Sammy's least favorite cousin held court at the other table.

Edison smirked and raised his cup when he saw Sammy.

Sammy ignored him and slid into the seat next to his mother.

"Sammy, it's good to see you." His grandmother reached across the table and patted his hand with a smile. "I'm so happy you're here."

His face softened. "It's good to see you too, Po Po," he said, slipping easily into Mandarin as he used the Chinese address for maternal grandmothers.

His grandparents on his father's side, who lived in Houston, were wealthier but more standoffish than his mother's side of the family. He called them on holidays, and they sent him red packets of money for his birthday, Lunar New Year, and Christmas, but other than that, he had limited interactions with them. They'd never quite gotten over the fact that his father had turned his back on the bride they'd chosen for him and married Sammy's mother instead.

His *gung gung* (maternal grandfather) and *po po,* though, he loved with all his heart. They'd babysat him and his siblings while his parents had been busy working and attending night school for English lessons. His grandfather had taught the Yu children how to write Han characters, while his grandmother snuck them sweets and introduced them to the world of Chinese television dramas—much to his parents' consternation.

"Ah, it all makes sense now." His brother, Kevin, smirked and sipped his tea.

Older than Sammy by two years, Kevin worked as a civil engineer and had married his college sweetheart last spring.

His marriage was the reason their mother had redoubled her efforts to set Sammy up. Now that Kevin's wedding was in the rearview mirror, she'd set her sights on her second child's love life.

"Are you going to clarify, or are you going to be cryptic?" Sammy picked up a shrimp-stuffed eggplant with his chopsticks and deposited it on his plate.

Kevin grinned. "You'll see. This is going to be good."

"Shush," Amy scolded, treating Kevin like he was thirteen instead of thirty-two. "Don't scare your brother."

While Auntie Felicia distracted Amy with a juicy tidbit about one of their friends' husbands running off with his massage therapist, Kevin leaned across their fifteen-year-old cousin, Gina—who was too engrossed in her phone to notice—and whispered, "Hope you sharpened up on your flirting skills before you got here."

"I know I'm being set up," Sammy said. "Mom came by with food yesterday."

"Yeah, but do you know *who* she's setting you up with?"

"No." Sammy lifted his shoulder in a shrug. "I never do."

Kevin's grin widened. "This is going to be good," he repeated.

"How the hell do you know who it is and I don't?"

"I overheard Mom on the phone when I swung by to fix their water heater," Kevin said matter-of-factly. "She should be here soon. Can't wait." He rubbed his hands.

Sammy snorted. "You're a grown-ass man. Act like it."

"*Excuse* me," Gina huffed, looking up from her phone. "I'm *trying* to watch a TikTok video, and you are *distract*ing me."

She overenunciated her words until each syllable hit like a bullet to the chest.

Kevin ruffled her hair and earned himself a threatening teenage scowl. "That's what earbuds are for, kid."

"I am *not* a kid, and my mom won't let me use earbuds at the table. She said it's rude, and she'll take away my allowance if she sees me doing it, so I would *appreciate* it if you lowered your voices."

"Someone's big mad," Kevin teased.

Gina shot him a flat look. "Don't use teenage slang. You're old, and it's so cringe." She returned her attention to her phone.

Sammy couldn't hide a grin at his brother's offended expression. "You were worse as a teenager," he reminded him.

"Yeah, yeah." Kevin turned to his wife, Lydia, who'd watched the entire interaction with amusement. "We're never having kids."

She patted him on the hand, her eyes dancing with laughter. "Let's revisit this later when the hurt's worn off."

Ten minutes later, Sammy understood why Kevin was so gleeful and why his mother had brought him so much food yesterday.

He watched, stunned, as a familiar brunette walked to their table and greeted everyone with a pleasant smile.

He whipped his head toward his father, who sipped his tea and avoided his son's gaze. "Dad. You let her do this?"

"Don't look at me." Richard Yu set his cup down and raised his hands. "I don't involve myself in your mother's shenanigans."

"They're not 'shenanigans,'" Amy interrupted. "I'm trying to secure our son's future. Don't you want him to be happy? Don't you want grandchildren?"

"Kevin will give you grandchildren," Sammy said, ignoring his brother's squawk of protest. *Too bad.* That was what older brothers were for—serving as the first line of defense against meddling mothers. "You don't need me."

Horror washed over Amy's face. "Don't be ridiculous. I want grandchildren from *all* my babies. I gave your brother leeway on getting married because he and Lydia dated for years before he proposed—finally—but you don't even have a prospect. No girl-friend, no dates—"

"I go on dates! I just don't tell you about every one."

"—other than the ones I set up for you. Now, don't be rude and say hi to Lucy." Amy's smile widened. "Lucy! Come here. You look so beautiful—doesn't she look beautiful, Sammy?—and that top is so pretty. Blue is Sammy's favorite color, you know. What a coinci-dence. Here, sit in my seat so you youngsters can talk. No, no, it's no trouble at all. I'm sure you don't want to listen to old people gossip."

Before Sammy could protest, his mother had vacated her seat, plunked a fresh plate and teacup on the table, and moved to the other side of his father, who shook his head and poured himself another drink.

I'm going to kill her.

Matricide was frowned upon, but surely people would understand.

Sammy's ex-girlfriend slipped into the seat next to his and flashed an apologetic smile. Funny how all his exes were showing up in his life lately. "Sorry if this is awkward," Lucy said, getting straight to the point. "Your mom ran into mine the other day at the supermarket and invited us to dim sum. My mom got sick yes-terday, but I didn't want to be rude and bail at the last minute, so here I am." She looked self-conscious. "I had no idea it was a..."

"Setup?" Sammy finished.

He'd dated Lucy in high school. They'd lost their virginities to each other, and he'd fancied himself in love, though it would be another four years before he truly fell in love and realized what he'd felt for Lucy had not been the big *L*. Real love consumed you and demanded sacrifices you'd never thought you'd give. What he and Lucy had had was lust coupled with companionability and friendship. It'd had all the ingredients of love, but it'd been miss-ing that spark that bound one heart to another.

Still, Sammy had been devastated when Lucy's family moved to Colorado in the middle of their junior year. They'd agreed they should break up—long-distance was hard enough for adults; it was all but impossible for hormone-riddled teenagers. After she left, Sammy had holed up in his room for a week with the bottle of rum he'd found stashed under Kevin's bed. His brother must've left it behind during his last visit home from college. Drunk and depressed for the first time in his life, Sammy had penned a letter so sappy, so cringe-inducing that he still squirmed with mortification whenever he thought about it.

Lucy had never replied to his letter, and he'd never settled on whether that was another punch in the gut or a small mercy. He hadn't heard from or about her since her move, except for the occasional update from his mom, who'd been good friends with Lucy's mom and had already cast Lucy in the role of her daughter-in-law. She'd been even sadder about the breakup than Sammy had been.

"I didn't realize you were back in the city." Sammy hoped to God Lucy didn't remember his letter. He'd sent it a decade ago. There was no way she could remember...right?

He ignored Kevin's shit-eating grin. He'd committed the grievous mistake of telling his brother about the letter when Kevin had been in the dumps himself over a breakup. In true sibling fashion, Kevin had never let him live it down.

That was what Sammy got for trying to empathize.

"My parents are still in Colorado, but I moved back for work. Software engineering," Lucy explained.

Edison interrupted their catchup by clearing his throat—loudly—and tapping on his teacup with a chopstick.

Sammy and Kevin exchanged *can you believe this guy?* expressions. Kevin held the same low opinion of their cousin that Sammy did.

"Sorry to interrupt everyone's meal," Edison oozed, as sincere as a commission-starved car salesman. "But I have a big announcement." He prattled on for a few minutes about nothing in particular before he cleared his throat again. Sammy resisted the urge to offer him a cough drop. "Mom, Dad, Po Po, Gung Gung, beloved aunties and uncles and cousins—"

Gina rolled her eyes so hard Sammy was surprised she didn't enter another dimension. "Get to the fucking point, bighead," she muttered, tapping furiously on her phone.

Sammy's mouth twitched. *Atta girl.* He didn't reprimand her for cursing. She clearly had good judgment if she could see through Edison's bullshit.

"I'm proud to announce that..." A dramatic pause long enough for Sammy to replicate Gina's eye roll. "You are looking at the newest junior partner of Sterling, Wilson and Cartwright!"

There were exactly two seconds of silence before everyone reacted. Sammy's grandparents beamed. Gina yawned. Kevin shoved a shumai in his mouth, no doubt to prevent himself from saying something snarky. Auntie Ling jumped from her seat and squealed, hugging her smirking son and talking loudly about how *of course* Edison made partner because he'd always been the smartest person in the room.

Gee, thanks, Auntie.

Sammy's mom snorted. "Whatever. People make partner all the time," she sniffed. "But *you*, Sammy, you're on magazine covers! You were named one of *Forbes* 30 Under 30!" She glared at Auntie Ling. "I'll bring copies next week. Edison, the smartest person in the room my ass."

Her husband coughed.

She whirled on him. "You agree? You think Edison is smarter than our son?"

Sammy made a sympathetic face at his father, who resembled a deer caught in headlights.

"Of course not." Richard poured himself another cup of tea and stirred in a sugar cube. "My drink merely went down the wrong pipe."

Before Amy could say anything else, Edison raised his voice over the chatter. "Wait, that's not all! To celebrate my promotion..." He puffed out his chest. "I'm treating everyone to a weekend trip to Lake Tahoe! I've rented a big chalet—"

Loud, excited chatter drowned out the rest of his words. His promotion was big news, but nothing got the Yus atwitter like a free vacation. Even Gina looked up with interest.

"Wow," Lucy said. "That's really generous."

"That's Eddie," Sammy said dryly. "Generous to a fault."

While the rest of Sammy's family discussed what they would pack and do at Lake Tahoe—even his mom got into it; clearly, an all-expenses-paid trip was enough to overcome her lifelong rivalry with Auntie Ling—Sammy and Lucy finished catching each other up on their lives. She was pleasant, smart, and kind, as always, but there was zero chemistry. Whatever romantic attraction they'd had in high school had fizzled, and while Sammy enjoyed talking with her, he knew they'd never date again. He could tell she felt the same way.

"I don't get it," his mother complained after they'd finished dim sum and Lucy excused herself to run errands. "You and Lucy are perfect for each other! You looked so cute together in high school. Remember when you two went to homecoming? You in your little bow tie and she in that pink dress. I still have the pictures. She'd give me beautiful grandchildren." She glared at him. "Don't you want me to have grandchildren, Sammy?"

"Don't start." Sammy crossed his arms over his chest. "I have a bone to pick with you about trying to set me up with *Lucy Wang*, of all people."

He couldn't really blame his mom, since he'd never told her about the letter, but he was mortified enough from having to face Lucy again that reason had jumped out the window.

"What's wrong with Lucy?" She sounded indignant. "She's pretty and she works for Google. *Google!* As a software engineer!" Amy waved her hands in the air. "Do you know how much money software engineers make?"

"I don't need her money, Mom. I make enough on my own."

"Well, of course you don't. But if she has her own money, it means she won't leech off yours. You have to be careful. Don't want to attract gold diggers." Amy heaved a sigh laden with the thousand burdens that came from having a son who wouldn't see reason. "I figured since you didn't click with any of the new women I set you up with, you might have better luck with an ex. Who knows? If she hadn't moved to Colorado, you two might be married right now!"

"I doubt it." Sammy glared at Kevin, who was loitering to the side, eavesdropping and chuckling to himself.

His mother narrowed her eyes. "Is this because of Olivia?"

What? Why the hell was she bringing up Olivia?

"No."

"Are you sure?"

"Yes."

"Are you lying?"

"No."

Her eyes narrowed farther, and he could practically see the gears turning in her head.

Unease prickled the back of Sammy's neck. Nothing good ever came of the look his mother was giving him now.

Abruptly, her frown disappeared, and she smiled.

Oh, fuck. His unease intensified.

"All right." Amy patted his arm. "I understand about Lucy."

"You do?" Kevin asked from the sidelines. Lydia hushed him,

and Sammy and Amy ignored him. Richard had wisely ducked into the Chinese market next to Wah Sing for that day's newspaper while his wife and son argued over said son's love life.

"Sorry I invited her without asking you first," Amy continued. "Have a wonderful rest of your day. I'll see you soon." She waved goodbye and swanned into the market, yelling, "Richard!"

"You're in deep shit," Kevin said.

Sammy had to agree. Red flags had popped up left and right the second his mother apologized. She would *never* apologize for matchmaking unless she had something more nefarious up her sleeve.

Too bad he had no clue what that something was.

CHAPTER 8

IN HINDSIGHT, OLIVIA ACKNOWLEDGED THAT SHE *might* have been in the wrong when she'd rearranged Sammy's beloved kitchen without asking for his input first. She really had thought she'd been doing him a favor—what kind of monster left dozens of spices unorganized like that?—but she supposed any baker or chef would chafe at having their culinary sanctuary upended.

Since she couldn't put everything back the way it was—she didn't remember all the original placements—she settled for an apology dinner. Sammy had said some hurtful things during their argument, but he'd sucked it up and apologized. It was time for her to do the same.

Plus, she needed to stop hiding from him. She'd locked herself in her room since she accidentally flashed him and his mother yesterday, so mortified it took a good half hour before the crimson faded from her face. She'd even waited until she heard Sammy leave the house that morning before she chanced sneaking into the bathroom to brush her teeth and wash her face—and he hadn't left until eleven.

Olivia couldn't hide from him forever, though, so she might as well get their first post-accidental-nudity encounter out of the way.

"It's not that big a deal," she said out loud, touching one of the takeout boxes to ensure it was still warm. "He's seen you naked before."

The reminder didn't help as much as she thought it would.

She glanced at the clock and drummed her fingers on the table. It was almost seven. From what she'd observed over the past week, this was when Sammy usually ate dinner, but if he didn't come home soon, the food was going to get cold. Olivia would've worried he was dining out, but she'd heard him on the phone that morning saying he would be home all night working on bakery stuff.

Ten more minutes, and then I'm digging in. She could save the leftovers for lunch tomorrow.

Disappointment niggled at her, which was ridiculous. It wasn't like she'd been looking *forward* to dinner with Sammy. This was an apology meal. It was an obligation, not desire.

To keep herself preoccupied, Olivia opened the Community app on her phone and scrolled through the local listings, looking for anything that sounded interesting. She was feeling lonely, and she could use some new female friends in her life. Farrah was only a phone call or FaceTime away, but she lived in New York and was married now. Plus, her interior design business was booming, and she was always busy. Ditto for Kris, who lived in LA and was juggling her job at MentHer—a nonprofit for girls who'd lost their mothers—with her charity work, wedding planning, and flying back and forth to various exotic locations to visit her movie star fiancé on set. Courtney was single and ready to mingle, but she also lived out of town, in Seattle.

None of Olivia's grad school friends had stayed in the city either, choosing instead to take their summer internships in New

York or London. The classmates who *were* in San Francisco, she didn't care for.

She sighed and scrolled aimlessly through Community, where people could form groups and post meetup opportunities for others with similar interests in their city. Knitting, bird-watching, photography, dodgeball...

Olivia stopped on a black-and-white profile photo of a shirtless man lying on a bed with his head thrown back in ecstasy. *EROTICA BOOK CLUB* the bold black letters next to the photo proclaimed.

Interesting...

Olivia had read her fair share of high-brow literature and popular fiction—Proust, Austen, Dostoyevsky, Toni Morrison, Dan Brown, Stephen King. She was familiar with all of them. But she had a particular weakness for erotic fiction. It was the perfect escape from the sometimes mundane nature of reality, and who didn't like hot sexy times? Besides, the books contained excellent ideas for spicing things up in the bedroom.

Given the social stigma against the erotica genre, Olivia didn't flaunt her reading preferences, but she didn't hide them either. Her friends understood but didn't share her tastes, and it would be nice to find some like-minded readers she could connect with.

Olivia scrolled down and read the description.

Not your average book club! This is a group for people who enjoy reading and discussing sexy, smutty books. Each month we will choose an erotic romance or erotic thriller book to read and discuss. Join us for book discussions, drink specials, and raunchy jokes (because all work and no play makes Jill a very dull girl). We meet on the first Tuesday of every month at the Catalina Restaurant & Bar, 7 p.m. Hope to see you there!

It sounded promising. Too bad it only met once a month—Olivia could only attend two meetings before classes started again, but what the hell. She'd take fun where she could find it.

She'd just finished adding the next book club meeting to her Google calendar when the sound of a car door slamming caused her to look up. A minute later, Sammy strolled in, looking devastating in a black T-shirt and jeans. Surprise flickered over his face when he saw Olivia and the spread on the dining table.

Her nerves jumped into overdrive. "Hi."

"Hi." He flashed a quizzical smile. "You must be hungry." A faint tinge of amusement colored his voice.

Okay, she may have gone a *little* overboard with the Thai takeout. The still-closed containers took up almost the entire table.

"It's not for me," Olivia said. "It's for you. Well, for us. It's an apology dinner."

Sammy's smile faded. "Dinner."

"Yes."

"With you."

An inexplicable stab of hurt pierced her chest. "I was trying to be nice. You were right—I shouldn't have rearranged everything without asking you first yesterday—but if you don't want to eat with me or you already ate, that's fine." She busied herself with opening a container of chicken pad thai.

"I didn't mean it like that."

She felt rather than saw Sammy walk up to the table. The faint scent of sandalwood mingled with the delicious aromas wafting from the open takeout boxes.

"I'm surprised, that's all. You've never wanted to eat dinner with me." Sammy reached into one of the large brown paper bags and took out plastic utensils and napkins. "If I didn't know better, I'd think you were scared of me."

"Ha!" Olivia snorted, overcoming her earlier nerves. "As if."
Despite her bravado, he wasn't entirely wrong. She *was* scared of being around him—he brought out too many emotions she thought she'd quashed. But they were roommates now, so she needed to get over it.

They worked in silence, setting the table and unpacking the food until Olivia's mouth watered from the smells. Her greedy gaze skimmed over the spread as she tried to decide what to dig into first. The classic pad thai or the creamy green curry? The eggplant thai basil or the duck with honey plum and ginger sauce?

She settled for the pad thai. Whenever she tried a new Thai place, she always ordered the pad thai first. If they couldn't get such a classic dish right, then chances were their other items weren't great either.

Olivia and Sammy sat on opposite sides of the dining table, eyeing each other warily. The clock ticked on the wall, loud and insistent, as if impatient for the humans in the room to *say* something so it wouldn't be the only one filling the silence.

"You look nice," Sammy said. "I almost didn't recognize you with your clothes on."

Scarlet washed over Olivia's face while his mouth broke out into a huge grin.

"I can't *believe* you brought that up!" She should've spiked some dishes with laxatives. She'd avoid those herself, of course, and Sammy would've had to spend hours on his porcelain throne. It would've been glorious. "You have no manners. A gentleman would've forgotten all about it."

"Trust me, no man—gentle or not—would've forgotten it." Sammy's eyes dipped to her chest, and the heat on her cheeks tripled.

"My eyes are up here."

"I'm aware." He raised his gaze to meet hers again—lazily,

sensually, stopping for detours at places he had no place detouring to.

Who *was* this man? Not the sweet, lighthearted Sammy she once knew.

This Sammy was unapologetic, carnal, and—as much as she hated to admit it—sexy as hell.

Olivia stuffed a forkful of noodles in her mouth so she had something else to focus on. As she'd suspected, the pad thai was excellent.

"You get all the embarrassment out of your system yet?" Sammy smirked when she shot him a look that would've put anyone else six feet in the ground. "You would've never brought it up, and it would've been the elephant in the room for weeks. This way, we get over it and move on with our lives. Don't think I didn't know you were hiding from me this morning. You never wake up so late."

"I was not *hiding*. I have a new morning ritual that takes longer than usual."

"Lie. You'd never allow a 'morning ritual' to take up so much of your time."

Damn him for knowing me so well.

Olivia was not, in fact, one of those people that meditated and journaled and did yoga for an hour in the morning. She subscribed to the Six-Minute Miracle Morning method: one minute each for silence, affirmations, visualizing, scribing, reading, and exercise. Efficient and effective, just the way she liked it.

"Whatever," she said coolly. "Now that the elephant has been discussed and removed, let's move on to other topics."

"Sure." Sammy leaned back and laced his fingers behind his head. "Let's hear it."

"What?"

"Your apology." He raised his eyebrows. "You said this was an apology dinner."

Olivia's lips pressed together into a thin line, but she wasn't one to go back on her word. "I'm sorry."

"I didn't quite catch that."

"I'm sorry," she gritted out in a louder voice.

"My hearing must be off tonight. Repeat that again?"

"I'm sorry!" she exploded. "I'm sorry for rearranging your stupid kitchen without asking first. I'm sorry for calling you last week and making you feel like you have to deal with all this. I'm sorry about New York. I'm sorry about my mom. I'm sorry, I'm sorry, I'm sorry! There! Are you happy?"

By the time she finished, her chest pumped with heavy pants, and her words hung frozen in the air—she was too shocked to move.

Sammy stared at her, equally frozen.

Olivia covered her face with her hands, mortified for the umpteenth time in a week. What was *with* her lately? The stress from work, her fruitless-thus-far apartment search, and sharing a house with her ex-boyfriend must be getting to her; she'd balanced on the knife's edge of losing it for days now. Well, turned out tonight was the night she tipped over the edge.

The clock's ticking filled the room once more, this time in admonishment. *That's not what I meant when I said* talk, the accusing march of its minute and second hands said.

Great, now she was hearing voices from inanimate objects. She really was going crazy.

"Olivia." Sammy's tone was far gentler than she'd expected, and it was worse than if he'd yelled and refused to accept her apologies. "You didn't *make* me do anything. I was the one who chose to drive to your apartment that night, and I was the one who invited you to move in—though I did second-guess myself when I saw what you did with my spice rack." His mouth tipped up, and Olivia snorted, grateful for the touch of levity. "Apology for rearranging the kitchen accepted, though the point might be moot. You were right—we're both living here now, and it'll be easier if there's a system in place. I went to the Container Store today and bought some labels and new spice jars, so you can arrange them to your heart's content."

Olivia's face lit up before it fell again. "You went to the Container Store without me? What type of spice jars did you buy? What do the labels look like?"

Sammy shot her an *are you kidding me?* look.

"I was just asking," she said defensively.

She was also well aware that he hadn't touched what she'd said about New York. Judging by the way he returned to his meal, he wasn't planning to.

Olivia felt curiously deflated. She didn't want to discuss their breakup per se—talk about reopening an old wound—but a part of her had been relieved for the opportunity to discuss the *real* elephant in the room. The one that had sat between them, immovable and unforgettable, for eight long years.

Guess it would have to sit there longer because she sure as hell wasn't bringing New York up again.

"If you went shopping today, why don't you have a shopping bag?" she asked.

Sammy dug into the green curry. "I left it in the car. I'll grab it later."

"Oh." Olivia poked at her duck. "The next time you see your mom, can you tell her I apologize for, um..."

"Flashing your breasts?"

Among other things. Her breasts weren't the only thing she'd flashed, though hearing the word *breasts* come out of Sammy's mouth sent a spear of heat ricocheting through her insides.

"No need," Sammy continued. "She knows you didn't mean to do it. She told me so today."

So *that's* where he'd been all day! With his mom.

A strange relief fizzled through Olivia's veins.

"It's sweet you spent your Sunday with your mom." She was half-teasing, half-serious. She wished she had that type of relationship with her mother, but if wishes were horses, yadda yadda.

Pink tinged Sammy's cheekbones. "Yu family Sunday dim sum. It's a tradition, though I missed the last few," he said. "She made me promise to show up today."

"Why?"

"Why else? To set me up with what she hoped would be her future daughter-in-law, who also happened to be my ex-girlfriend." His mouth twisted into a grimace.

Olivia frowned. *She* was Sammy's ex-girlfriend, and she sure as hell hadn't been invited to dim sum. She could've used some egg tarts that morning too.

Then it hit her that, duh, of course Sammy had had other girlfriends other than her. In fact, he was dating Jessica—

"Wait a minute!" She slammed her palms on the table. The takeout boxes trembled with shock. "Why's your mom setting you up when you already have a girlfriend? Doesn't she know about Jessica?"

Was it possible Sammy had kept Jessica a secret from his family? Maybe they didn't want him dating anyone outside their culture, but three years was a helluva long time to keep such a secret.

The pink spread across Sammy's face. "Jess and I are no longer dating," he said cagily.

Olivia's heart revved. "But I saw you together at Ishikawa."

Sammy had been in high spirits all week—except for when he saw what she did to his spice rack—which meant they couldn't have broken up since then. You don't end a three-year relationship and walk around looking all hot and happy afterward.

"We were there as friends." He'd composed himself and returned to wolfing down his curry. He continued between bites, "She and I broke up, uh, a while ago."

What's "a while"? Weeks? Months? Years?

He'd brought Jessica to Farrah's wedding, so their breakup couldn't have been *that* long ago.

"Why didn't you tell me?" Olivia demanded.

He looked at her like she was crazy. "Why would I tell you?"

She opened her mouth, then closed it. Why *would* he tell her? His love life had nothing to do with her. Until a week ago, they'd barely acknowledged each other when they were in the same room, much less updated each other on their relationship statuses.

Olivia switched subjects. "So? Is your mom one step closer to gaining a daughter-in-law?"

Sammy's dark eyes glittered. "Fishing, Olivia?"

"You wish. Merely worried for the poor woman who might have to put up with your appalling organizational skills."

"I have other talents that would make that a nonissue, as you well know," he said silkily.

A host of unwanted erotic images invaded Olivia's mind. *Strong hands gripping her hips as he thrust into her from behind. Her legs wrapped around his waist as they fucked against a wall. Waves of bliss punctuated by throaty screams of pleasure.*

Olivia's body reacted instantly. Her nipples puckered, her thighs clenched, and moisture pooled between her legs, warm and honeyed.

She was so stunned by the unexpected onslaught of arousal that she couldn't come up with a response.

"To answer your question, no, Lucy and I are not rekindling our relationship," Sammy said. "We're exes for a reason."

His words cooled her ardor faster than a bucket of ice water dumped over her head.

Olivia forced a smile, her skin feeling too tight for her body. "True. It's a bad idea to get involved with exes again."

"Exactly." Sammy played with his chopsticks while keeping his gaze locked on Olivia. "How are things with you and Stripper Boy? Have another fun date on the town planned?"

Stripper—oh. Wesley.

She hadn't heard from him since she'd ditched him at Ishikawa, thank God.

"He's not my type." Olivia shrugged. "But I have other dates planned."

The only upcoming date she had was with her trusty vibrator, but he didn't need to know that. Pride prevented her from telling the truth: that her string of mediocre dates over the past few years was more unsatisfying than not dating at all. Dating in New York had sucked—gorgeous, successful people abounded, but they were all too busy, too flakey, and/or too self-absorbed to commit to a real relationship—and while single men outnumbered single women in San Francisco, quality counted more than quantity.

Something dark flickered in Sammy's eyes. "I'm sure you do. Let me guess—all Ivy League–educated, upwardly mobile finance types you can bring home to Mom?"

Olivia suppressed a flinch. "You know my type," she said with forced lightness.

His smile was devoid of humor. "That I do."

They ate the rest of their meal in silence.

Olivia poked at her food, trying to relish what was objectively a great dinner, but it was too late. She'd lost her appetite.

CHAPTER 9

OLIVIA REDOUBLED HER DATING EFFORTS OVER THE next few days. Her conversation with Sammy reminded her of her self-imposed timeline for finding a boyfriend, and she could use the distraction. It didn't help that Sammy hadn't eaten dinner at home since her apology meal. It was stupid, but she couldn't help but wonder whether *he* was on a date during the nights he was out. Maybe he'd caved and was going out with the ex his mom had set him up with. Or maybe he was going out with someone else. Hell, he could be dating a different girl every day for all she knew.

Or maybe he was just hooking up, not dating. Sammy was a successful, good-looking bachelor; a hyperactive sex life wasn't out of the realm of possibility.

The thought made her stomach cramp.

"I just think he overreacted," Olivia said, sweeping blush over her cheeks. "I did nothing wrong. I bought him dinner, for chrissakes." She enhanced the blush with a dusting of highlighter. "I mean, fine, I did it as an apology, but still."

Farrah's laugh pealed out of the phone. Olivia had her on

speakerphone while she got ready for her date, so it was *almost* like the old days when they pumped each other up before a night out.

Olivia frowned. "What's so funny?"

"Do know you've been talking about Sammy for the past forty-five minutes?"

"I have not." Olivia finished her makeup and sat on the bed so she could put on her shoes.

"Yes, you have." Farrah's amusement came through loud and clear. "Do you think *maybe* you still have feelings for him?"

"I have feelings all right," Olivia muttered. "Homicidal ones."

The more she thought about it, the more pissed she was about how Sammy had acted in the last half of dinner the other night. What right did he have to give her the silent treatment? She'd tried her best to be civil!

Farrah snickered. "Fine. Maybe he was upset because he's jealous you're dating other guys."

"Please. He's not jealous. He's probably out with a girl right now, acting all charming and gentlemanly like he isn't a...a..." Olivia couldn't think of the right word, so she settled for a frustrated, "Ugh!"

"Liv." Farrah sounded like she was suppressing wild laughter. "Are *you* jealous?"

"No!" Olivia stared at her phone, horrified. "Why would you *think* that?"

"Because you sound jealous."

"Clearly, the distance has warped your brain and you don't know me as well as you used to," Olivia declared. "I have to go. I'm meeting Malcolm in half an hour, and who knows what the traffic will be like?"

"Wait. Your date's name is *Malcolm*? Like *Malcolm in the Middle*?"

Olivia scowled, ruing her decision to call her so-called best friend for a predate pep talk. "Goodbye."

Farrah was laughing too hard to respond, so Olivia hung up and swept out of her room in a huff. Her steps faltered when she saw Sammy in the living room, watching an old Bruce Willis movie on low volume. She'd been so distracted by her date prep and call with Farrah that she hadn't heard him come home.

He glanced up, then froze. His eyes swept from the top of her head to her toes, taking in the sleek blue dress that hugged her curves and the silver heels that added three inches to her height. It was her favorite first-date outfit; it never failed to make her feel like a million bucks.

Olivia's skin heated beneath his perusal.

"Hot date?" Sammy drawled. His tone was light, but his gaze was dark.

She clutched her purse, willing herself not to tremble. Her breasts ached and her stomach swooped, but that must have been first-date jitters. It had nothing to do with the man sitting less than ten feet away. "As a matter of fact, yes."

"Not with Stripper Boy, I hope."

"His name isn't—" Olivia shook her head. "Never mind. It's not him. It's with someone else. He's in tech. He's nice. His name is Malcolm."

Why was she telling him all of this?

Sammy's mouth curled up. "Malcolm?"

Oh, for Christ's sake.

"Don't start," she snapped. "Farrah already gave me grief for it. I'll have you know, Malcolm is a perfectly respectable name."

"Of course it is—for middle-aged professors who smoke pipes and wear jackets with tweed patches on the elbows."

"I don't have time to argue with you. I have a date to go

on." She turned on her heels and stalked toward her front door, Sammy's laugh ringing in her ears.

"Have fun with Malcolm the Tech Guy!" he called after her.

Argh! She was going to strangle him in his sleep one day. She really was.

Malcolm the Tech Guy turned out to be as respectable as his name—and as boring. Olivia had screened him thoroughly after the Wesley debacle, but what came off as humble and intellectual online turned out to be mind-numbingly dull in person. To make matters worse, he'd chosen a horrible restaurant for dinner. She took one bite of her chicken, decided there was a seventy-five percent chance it'd give her salmonella, and spent the rest of the meal drinking while Malcolm rambled on about some app he was developing.

Needless to say, she declined his invitation for postdinner drinks.

Two hours later, Olivia trudged up the stone path toward Sammy's house, exhausted and annoyed. How hard was it to find a decent, dateable guy in a big city? She wasn't asking for a harem. She just needed *one*.

"I would've had a better time with my Kindle and vibrator," she muttered as she unlocked the front door.

Thankfully, the house was dark, and she didn't have to do a reverse walk of shame in front of Sammy. The last thing she needed was for him to see her come home after yet *another* failed date. The Wesley incident had been bad enough.

Olivia showered, changed, and climbed into bed, but she couldn't fall asleep. Her stomach kept growling, pissed that she hadn't fed it all night. It was too late to order takeout, so after an eternity of tossing and turning, she tiptoed into the kitchen to search for any goodies that might be in the fridge.

She was rummaging through the shelves, looking for

something that *wasn't* raw or liquid, when a voice behind her caused her to jump and slam the fridge door on her finger. "What are you doing?"

"Fuck!" The curse exploded out of her mouth as pain lanced up her arm.

Sammy was by her side in an instant. "Let me see that."

"It hurts," Olivia whimpered.

He examined the injury, his touch gentle as he cradled her hand in his. "No bleeding and it doesn't look broken. There's just some swelling and bruising."

"Just?" Fine, she was being a big baby, but her finger felt like it might fall off, so excuse her for being dramatic.

Sammy flashed a crooked smile that hit her like a ray of sunshine through her fog of pain. "Rest and regular icing should take care of it until it heals—unless you smash it again. Word of advice: don't."

"Thanks, Dr. Obvious."

His smile broadened, and Olivia's heart fluttered in response.

Traitor. It had no business fluttering. It was an organ, not a freakin' butterfly.

He made her rinse the injured area beneath cold water while he prepared an ice pack.

"What are you doing up so late, anyway?" He pressed the ice to her finger, and she sighed at the cool relief.

"I was hungry." Olivia tried not to stare at his bare muscled chest. Now that the pain had subsided, she realized Sammy was wearing her favorite outfit—gray sweatpants and a white T-shirt. If she looked hard enough, she could see the outline of his—

Nope. Nooooot going there.

"Thought you went to dinner. Date with Malcolm the Tech Guy didn't go well?" Sammy asked casually.

"It was fine. I..." Huh. She didn't actually need to look that hard. She could totally see his *No! Stop it!* Olivia tried to push her dirty thoughts out of her mind and prayed to God she wasn't blushing. "What?"

Sammy gave her a strange look. "Date. Hungry?" he prompted.

"Right." She cleared her throat. "We went to a bad restaurant, and I didn't eat. The end."

"You want ramen?"

"What?" She sounded like a broken record.

"Instant ramen," Sammy clarified. "I can make some. It's nothing mind-blowing, but it'll tide you over until the morning. Unless you want eggs and toast."

A warm, gooey sensation oozed through her chest. "Ramen is fine. Thank you." She watched him prep the food, swallowing the lump in her throat. Even though there were moments she wanted to kill him, Sammy was a good guy. No, not good. *Great.* And she'd been stupid enough to drive him away. "What about you? Why are you up so late?"

"Couldn't sleep." Sammy dumped the noodles in a pot on the stove. "Thought I'd watch a show or something till I could."

"What show did you have in mind?"

"Probably *Friends* or something I've already watched. Otherwise, I'll stay up all night to find out what happens next, and that won't solve the problem."

"Good point." Olivia chewed on her bottom lip. "I'm down if you are."

Sammy's eyebrows rose.

"To watch the show," she said. "I can't sleep either, and we're both already up..." She trailed off.

Sammy shut off the stove and ladled the noodles into a bowl. He stayed silent for so long, Olivia was sure he'd say no until he surprised her with a quick nod.

"Let's do it."

They stuck with his original *Friends* suggestion. In between laughing their butts off and arguing over which character was the best friend—Olivia said Phoebe; Sammy was Team Chandler— they talked about everything that came to mind, just like they used to. There was something magical about the late-night to early-morning hours that compelled people to drop their guards, and for once, things between Olivia and Sammy felt like old times: easy, comfortable, and poignant all at once. The awkwardness that had lingered between them since her apology dinner faded more and more until it was nothing but a faint memory by the time Olivia drifted off.

She stayed on the couch next to Sammy, too cozy and sleepy to move, and as her eyes fluttered shut, she found herself thinking that she could get used to nights like this.

CHAPTER 10

OVER THE NEXT TWO WEEKS, SAMMY AND OLIVIA SET-
tled into a comfortable routine. Their unexpected late-night
bonding over *Friends* reruns had erased some of the tension, and
the longer Sammy lived with her, the easier it was to pretend they
were just roommates with a history but no hard feelings. He even
invited Olivia to his friends' annual Fourth of July party. The
fact that she accepted after only a brief hesitation spoke volumes
about how far they'd come in such a short time.

They weren't back to the way things used to be before their
breakup—Sammy didn't think that was possible. But they were
friendly, and that was a helluva lot less exhausting than hostile.

Of course, that didn't mean he couldn't have his fun. He saw
the way Olivia looked at him when she thought he wasn't paying
attention. She was attracted to him, and he took advantage of her
attraction by walking around the house shirtless more often than
he would've otherwise.

A little regret and longing never hurt anyone, and it was fun
seeing her squirm.

Sammy smiled a diabolical smile as he pulled up in front of
Aaron's house.

"What's that look on your face?" Olivia eyed him with suspicion.

He smoothed his features into a mask of innocence. "I'm excited for the food. Aaron is a grill master."

"That wasn't a look of excitement. That was a look of pure deviousness."

"Deviousness? Me?" Sammy doubled up on the innocence. "I would never."

"Hmph." Olivia didn't look like she believed him, but a golden blur distracted them before she could continue her interrogation.

"Hey, buddy!" Sammy laughed as Milo, Aaron's huge golden retriever, nearly knocked him off his feet in its excitement. He scratched the dog behind the ears, and Milo's tail wagged with enough speed to whip up a Category One hurricane. "Excited today, huh?"

"Sorry about that. He's been jumping on people all day." Aaron strolled out of the house and shook his head good-naturedly. "Big fan of parties, aren't ya, bud?"

Milo responded with an enthusiastic bark.

"I'm Aaron." He addressed Olivia and stuck out his hand. "Sammy didn't mention his date was so beautiful."

Sammy snorted. Aaron had been the class player in high school, and though he was happily married now, he could no less turn off his flirtatious nature than a leopard could lose its spots. Aaron would never cheat on his wife, though, and Melissa was confident and good-humored enough to put up with his indiscriminately charming ass.

"Olivia. Nice to meet you." She shook his hand. "I'm Sammy's plus one, but we're just friends."

Friends, huh? Sammy supposed that sounded better than *We're just roommates.*

Aaron threw his head back and laughed. "Friend-zoned. Ouch." He nudged Sammy in the ribs.

Sammy nudged him back. Hard.

"He's a tough guy. He can take it." Olivia bent to pet Milo. "Your dog is adorable."

"He knows it too. Uses those puppy-dog eyes on us every time he can—usually when we're at the dinner table. He can teach you a few things about picking up girls," Aaron added, grinning at Sammy.

"Hilarious." Sammy sighed in exasperation but smiled. "If you're done ragging on me, let's join the party. I'm starving."

The guests had gathered in the backyard, taking advantage of the state-of-the-art grill and pool. They were mostly Sammy's friends from high school, but since it was an open-invitation party, there was a good number of significant others, coworkers, and friends of friends in the mix.

Sammy introduced Olivia to everyone he knew and left to catch up with Aaron and Trey after a group of women drew Olivia into a discussion about Stanford and the best brunch spots in the city.

"What's the deal with Olivia?" Aaron flipped a hamburger patty with a deft motion. "Don't give me any of that 'friends' bullshit either. I can cut the sexual tension between you two with a butter knife."

Sammy cracked open his beer. "I don't think so. Like she said, we're...friends."

"You hesitated." Trey pointed an accusing finger at him. "Didn't he hesitate?" He directed his question at Aaron.

"He did," the host confirmed.

"*Nothing* is going on between us. We're friends," Sammy repeated.

His friends pinned him with matching *that's-bullshit* expressions.

"And roommates," he added grudgingly.

"Really?" Trey's eyes lit up as his gaze swung toward Olivia and raked over her body. She wore a white sundress that bared her long legs and smooth shoulders, and her face glowed with animation as she laughed at something one of the other women said. She looked so beautiful, it almost hurt. "Lucky you. Please tell me she walks around in one of those tiny little pajama sets women love. Or just a T-shirt and panties. Can't decide which is hotter."

Sammy took a swig of his beer and resisted the urge to poke one of his oldest friends' eyes out with a metal skewer. "Stop being a perv."

"I'm not being a perv. Any red-blooded man would wonder the same thing. So, which is it? Pj's or T-shirt and panties?"

"Neither." Sammy's tight smile came off more like a snarl, but he didn't give a shit. "Yo, Aaron, are the burgers done yet? I'm dying here."

"Nuh-uh. You're not getting off that easily." Aaron waved his spatula in the air. "You're friends, roommates, *and*...? Are you banging her?"

Sammy's forced smile morphed into a grimace. "No, and pay attention to the grill. I don't want charred burgers."

"The burgers are fine. Stop deflecting."

"Jesus, you're nosier than a middle school girl."

"Still deflecting," Aaron sang.

This was what Sammy got for staying in touch with his high school friends. They'd known each other too long and could sniff out each other's bullshit like bloodhounds.

"We used to date," Sammy finally said in a clipped tone. Might as well throw them a bone so they'd get off his back.

Aaron's brows furrowed. "When did you...?" Realization dawned. "Wait. Olivia. *Shanghai Olivia?*" He jabbed his finger in her direction.

"*Stop.*" Sammy yanked Aaron's arm down. "Do you have to be so freakin' obvious?"

"But that's *her!*" Aaron whisper-yelled. "You're *living* with her? What the hell? Tell me everything. I want all the details."

Yep, he was exactly like a middle school girl.

"What's going on?" Confusion lined Trey's face. "What am I missing?"

"Remember that girl Sammy was all broken up about after he came back from New York?" Aaron slid the cooked patties onto a waiting tray. "That's her."

It took a few seconds for Trey to connect the dots. Once he did, his eyes bugged out of his skull. "Holy shit, that's *her?*" He cast a second, even more appreciative glance in Olivia's direction. Sammy's jaw tightened. "I totally get it now. She's hot."

"It was a long time ago." Sammy should've gone for something stronger than beer, like tequila. Or bleach. Might as well just end it here and now. He'd rather cut his losses and join the afterlife early than suffer through another second of this conversation. "Not worth discussing."

He'd made the mistake of telling his friends about Olivia when he'd returned from New York lost, heartbroken, and pissed beyond belief. Younger Sammy hadn't been the type to keep his problems to himself. He'd needed to be around people in times of grief, to talk through his troubles and heal under their sympathy.

Now his earlier openness was coming back to bite him in the ass.

"Yeah, but she's your roommate now." Aaron's good-natured teasing melted, replaced with concern. "Look, I know it's been a while since you guys broke up, but I remember how heartbroken you were. It was pretty pathetic, not gonna lie, which was sad in college but would be even *more* pathetic now that you're a grown-ass man. So don't do anything stupid, 'kay?"

"Thanks for the sage advice," Sammy said sarcastically. "But I'm over it." He grabbed a paper plate and arranged one of the freshly grilled patties on a hamburger bun with lettuce, tomato, onions, a few strips of bacon, and a slice of cheese. "Our living arrangement is temporary. She was in a tough spot and I helped her out." He briefly explained Olivia's apartment problem. "She'll move after she finds a new place."

"What if she doesn't find one?" Aaron asked.

"Then it's only for the summer. She goes back to school in the fall." Sammy bit into his burger. *Incredible.* Aaron could be an annoying little shit, but his grilling prowess was out of this world. "It's not a big deal."

"Can I come over to watch a game one day?" Trey asked hopefully. "If not pj's or a T-shirt, she walks around in her underwear, right?"

"No, and no."

Trey's face fell. "So much for being a good friend," he grumbled.

"You'd have better luck with Cherie." Aaron tilted his head toward the pretty blond. "She's been making eyes at you all day."

Trey perked up faster than a dog spotting a bone. "Really? Sweet." The former football player left without another word and bulldozed his way across the backyard toward his target.

"Don't look at me like that," Aaron said when Sammy shot him a look. "She *has* been staring at him, but I'm not sure if it's because she's attracted to him or because he's wearing the world's loudest T-shirt."

Sammy took in Trey's bright red, white, and blue shirt— designed to look like a fireworks explosion—and snickered.

Now that the burgers were done, Aaron moved on to the hot dogs. The meat sizzled as it hit the grill, and mouthwatering aromas thickened the air once more. "Seriously, though. Be careful with Olivia. Last I checked, she's got some strange voodoo magic over you."

Sammy finished his beer. "I can handle her. Don't worry."

The rest of the afternoon passed in a blur of food, laughter, and pool games, including a traumatizing round of Marco Polo during which a mortified Sammy accidentally groped Aaron's aunt's breasts while he was "it."

He'd apologized profusely, but the woman had merely winked and made it clear she was not at all opposed to his groping—or anything else he might want to do to her.

Sammy hadn't been able to look her in the eye since.

Thankfully, Aaron had been busy arguing with another guest about the 49ers' prospects in the upcoming football season and had missed the entire episode. Otherwise, the incident would've been even more awkward, if that were possible.

As the sun sank beneath the horizon and the free-flowing alcohol worked its way through the guests' systems, music soared, inhibitions dropped, and the singles paired up faster than animals lining up for Noah's Ark.

When an impromptu dance party broke out, Sammy found himself squished between Cherie and—*dear God*—Aaron's aunt, both of whom were drunk out of their minds.

"Are you single?" Cherie threw her arms around his neck and ground her hips against his. "You are so cute."

"Good musculature. Nice, strong shoulders," Aaron's aunt—what was her name? Gail? Gwen? Something with a *G* and three letters—added, sounding like she was describing a horse up for auction. She rubbed his shoulders for emphasis.

With the way Cherie was grinding against him, Sammy was forced back against Gail/Gwen's bikini-clad body, which was just so wrong. The older woman wasn't unattractive, but he wasn't interested—in *either* female.

"Ladies." His chuckle belied his nervousness. "I'm flattered, but I'm sure there are other men here who'd appreciate your charms. Trey, for example."

Trey would fuck anyone willing and interested, and Sammy had seen him making out with Cherie in the pool earlier.

Cherie sniffed. "Forget him. He told me I'd look better as a brunette." Judging by her tone, that amounted to a crime against humanity. "Plus, he's busy." She angled her head to her right.

Sammy followed her gaze, and his muscles snapped into a rigid line that sent a jolt of tension reverberating through his body.

Trey was busy, all right. Busy putting his hands all over Olivia. Smiling at her, twirling her around, bringing her in close like they were slow dancing under a star-strewn island sky, instead of bumping it out to Drake at a barbecue in the San Francisco suburbs.

The worst part was, Olivia wasn't pulling away. She was smiling back at him like she *enjoyed* being that close to him.

If she only knew, Sammy thought savagely. If she only knew what a player Trey was, she wouldn't loop her arms around him like that. If she only knew Trey was a mechanic and not a fancy yuppie, she'd walk away without a second thought.

There was nothing wrong with being a mechanic, but Sammy doubted it would pass muster with the status-conscious Tang family.

"Excuse me." Sammy extricated himself from Cherie's arms and stepped out of Aaron's aunt's grip. "I'll be right back."

Cherie pouted, but Gail/Gwen's eyes twinkled with a message that might've been *Go get your girl*—which would be ridiculous, because Olivia wasn't his girl.

She was, however, his roommate, and her room was right next to his, which meant Sammy owed it to his personal sanity and quality of life to ensure he wouldn't have to hear her and Trey having sex. Or see her crying when things with his man-whore friend eventually went south—and they *always* went south. Trey was a great friend, but when it came to women, he had the attention span of a goldfish.

A muscle twitched beneath Sammy's eye as he closed in on the laughing, dancing twosome. They were so wrapped up in each other, they hadn't noticed him yet, even though he was only a few feet away.

"Did you know you could kayak under the Golden Gate Bridge?" he heard Trey say. "It's very romantic." His voice dripped with insinuation.

Olivia's laugh danced in the air, and when she replied, her words carried a teasing lilt Sammy remembered all too well. "I'm sure it is."

Sammy's molars ground against each other so hard, his entire face hurt. *Kayaking under the Golden Gate Bridge? Give me a break.*

Olivia wasn't a kayaking type of person. She was a wine-tasting, weird-but-delicious-as-fuck-conceptual-dinner kind of person.

"Hey, man." Sammy clamped a hand on Trey's shoulder and bared his teeth in a semblance of a smile. "Aaron's looking for you."

"Really?" Trey glanced around. "He looks busy to me."

Dammit. Aaron was indeed busy whispering sweet nothings in Melissa's ear by the pool.

"He got bored waiting for you," Sammy lied. "I'd check in with him now. It seemed pretty urgent."

Trey's gaze flitted between Sammy and Olivia. A slow smirk took over his face. "Sure, dude." He kissed Olivia on the cheek and whispered something that caused her to laugh again before he sauntered off, whistling a jaunty tune.

"What's so funny?" Sammy demanded, inexplicably irritated.

"Nothing." Olivia squashed her smile. "You better have a good reason for chasing away my dance partner. We both know Aaron wasn't looking for him."

"I know no such thing, and is that what you call what you two were doing? Dancing? Looked more like groping to me."

She lifted a perfect dark brow. "Jealous?"

"Not even in your dreams."

"I hate to break it to you, but you have no place in my dreams."

"You sure about that?" Sammy stepped closer, challenge glinting in his eyes.

Olivia's chin lifted. "One hundred percent."

"You're lying." Sammy encircled her waist with one arm and brought her close until their bodies pressed flush against each other. He hadn't drunk much today, but he'd had enough. His thoughts were muddled, and instead of taking a rational course of action—like staying the fuck away from the one woman with the power to undo him—here he was, holding her close and breathing in her fresh, intoxicating scent.

The music and chatter faded away until all he could hear was the *thud-thud-thud* of his heart beating a rhythm as wild and unpredictable as the charged molecules in the air.

Olivia's face bore a pale pink flush from her drinks, and her eyes shone beneath the darkening skies as she stared back at him, her lips slightly parted.

In that instant, they weren't Sammy and Olivia, ex-lovers locked in a silent standoff on a summer California night; they were Sammy and Olivia, slick with sweat and heady with alcohol, dancing the hours away in a Shanghai nightclub.

He blinked, and they morphed into Sammy and Olivia, entangled in passion on lust-drenched sheets.

Blink.

Sammy and Olivia, sneaking kisses in dark, intimate corners of dark, intimate restaurants in New York.

Blink.

Sammy and Olivia, lying on the grass, staring up at the stars and weaving dreams of what their futures would look like. They hadn't discussed how those futures would intertwine or for how long; it'd seemed like a silly question, as irrelevant as asking whether the sun would rise the next day or whether the ocean would kiss the shores. There was an infinitesimal chance it wouldn't happen, but it was for all intents and purposes a foregone conclusion.

What fools they'd been.

"What are you doing?" Olivia didn't wrap her arms around Sammy as any woman in her current position would, but she didn't pull away either.

"Dancing."

"We're not moving."

"It's not that kind of dance."

Olivia's breath quickened. He could hear it, feel it, practically taste it.

Sammy's eyes dropped to her mouth and traced a hungry path over the sensual curves of her lips. The delicate Cupid's bow punctuating her top lip, the lush fullness of her bottom lip. The soft pinkness that he knew from experience would blossom into a passionate red under the right ministrations. A nip here, a graze of the teeth there, and she'd look properly loved.

"Sammy." His name came out as a breathless sigh, its purpose trapped somewhere between a plea and a warning.

He hardened immediately, to the point where his erection

threatened to punch a hole through his jeans. Lust roared in his veins and drowned out everything else—the doubts, the insecurities, the voices warning him what a bad fucking idea this was.

He'd been full of bad ideas lately, and he couldn't bring himself to care.

Sammy fisted her hair with his free hand and tugged her head back. "Say my name again."

He half expected her to fight him, but Olivia obeyed without hesitation. "Sammy." This time, it came out as a whimper.

He couldn't have stopped what happened next if Zeus himself came down from the heavens and ordered him to cease and desist.

Sammy groaned and dipped his head. Olivia arched into him, her eyes fluttering closed.

Just one taste, he thought. *Then I'll get her out of my system once and for all.*

Reason and willpower had fled, leaving only denial in its wake.

Sammy's and Olivia's mouths were centimeters apart. His breath whispered across her lips before he claimed—

Fuck!

Something massive hurtled itself into Sammy and knocked him flat on his ass. Since he was still holding on to Olivia, she crashed down with him—or rather, she crashed down *on* him. Face-to-face, knees straddling his hips, her breasts right in front of his eyes.

His cock twitched with excitement.

Sammy was half tempted to roll them over, pin her to the hard ground, and finish what he'd started, but the fall had hammered some sense into his head.

The lust-drenched fog enveloping him gradually faded, and he exhaled a sharp breath.

He and Olivia weren't alone in their own little world, where the past couldn't touch them and the future remained a hazy mirage. They were lying on the ground, limbs entangled, in front of dozens of bemused partygoers. He'd been *this close* to kissing Olivia, and they would've had to go home afterward and either pretend it hadn't happened or act awkward as hell around each other for the rest of her stay. The other "options" weren't options at all.

Fuck buddies? Fuck no. Not with an ex. That was like pouring gasoline on bone-dry wood—an explosion waiting to happen. And not in a pleasurable, orgasmic way.

Rekindled relationship? Impossible. They'd broken up for a reason, and that reason still existed.

Olivia stared down at him. Her eyes had cleared too, though Sammy detected vestiges of her earlier desire.

The spell had broken, but neither wanted to acknowledge the death of a dream.

Their furry interloper took care of that problem for them.

Milo's sharp bark shattered what remained of the bubble around Sammy and Olivia.

Sammy turned his head and leveled the adorable seventy-pound menace with an aggrieved glare. "Dude, seriously?"

Milo barked again, his tongue hanging out, his tail wagging with sheer joy. Apparently, he now had three favorite hobbies: playing fetch, chasing squirrels, and cockblocking his human dad's friends.

Speaking of which...

Aaron's feet entered Sammy's field of vision, and when Sammy cranked his head up, he confirmed the blond wore the exact smirk he'd imagined he would wear.

Olivia scrambled off him, and Sammy mourned the loss of her warmth before he pushed himself off the ground.

"Didn't mean to interrupt." Aaron's gaze moved from Sammy

to Olivia and back again. Amusement warred with trepidation in his eyes.

"You didn't. Your dog did." Sammy reached down and ruffled the golden retriever's fur, earning himself another tail wag. Milo was too damn cute to stay mad at. Depending on how one looked at it, he may have even saved Sammy from committing a massive mistake.

"He does that a lot," Aaron said in a wry tone that made Sammy wonder how many times Milo had interrupted his parents doing the deed.

He didn't want to know.

"Anyway, figured you guys wouldn't want to miss the fireworks." Aaron's smirk widened. "The ones in the sky, I mean."

Sammy glared at his so-called friend while red washed over Olivia's cheeks. He'd been so caught up in their moment, he hadn't noticed the pyrotechnics lighting up the sky. They were too far out in the suburbs to catch the city's fireworks show, but Aaron had his own supplies. The other guests had set up camp on the other side of the backyard, where no trees blocked the view, and they'd dragged over enough lounge chairs and pillows to make the corner look like an outdoor slumber party.

Sammy couldn't believe he'd missed the migration. That was what Olivia did to him—made him oblivious to everything that wasn't her. Proving once again how dangerous she was.

To his relief and disappointment, she excused herself and slipped inside the house—ostensibly to use the restroom, but he wouldn't be surprised if he didn't see her again until it was time to leave.

"Don't," he warned when Aaron opened his mouth.

"I wasn't going to say anything."

"Uh-huh."

"I mean it. I already warned you earlier, and you're a grown man." Aaron fell silent for a moment before adding, "You know what you're doing."

Sammy tilted his head up and watched the lights paint the night sky in a kaleidoscope of colors, his cock still semihard, his skin still tingling with electricity.

I sure hope so.

CHAPTER 11

THE TOWN CAR SMELLED LIKE LEATHER AND EXPENSIVE cologne courtesy of Michael, who remained quiet as he skimmed through the Ty Winstock dossier Olivia had delivered last week. Other than the rustle of paper as he turned a new page, the company car taking them from the office to Avenue Steakhouse was silent.

Olivia stared out the window, counting to ten in her head to keep her mind off the nerves buffeting her stomach.

Tonight was her chance to make a big impression on her boss. Even though she planned to move back to New York after she got her MBA, Michael was a managing director and a trusted voice. His recommendation would move her that much closer to the vice presidency she craved.

"What do you think of the San Francisco office?" Michael's deep voice rumbled through the quiet and startled Olivia out of her fantasies of the future—striding into the boardroom suited up in badass Armani, kicking Wall Street ass during the day and coming home at night to a beautiful home and gorgeous husband with whom she'd have all the explosive, kinky sex she liked. Somewhere down the line, there'd be children. Even further down the line, she'd be a CEO, gracing the covers of *Forbes* and *Fortune* and carving a legacy for herself as one of the few women who rose to the top of the finance food chain through sheer grit, intellect, and perseverance.

She had it all planned out.

But first, she had to survive this dinner.

"It's different from New York," Olivia said carefully. "That's to be expected. There are inherent cultural differences between the East and West Coast, but I'm grateful for the opportunity to work here this summer. It's a great way to connect with other branches of the firm and meet new colleagues."

Whether she *liked* said colleagues was another matter.

The key to evasion: provide a parallel answer that sounded like what the questioner wanted to know without actually answering anything.

"True," Michael agreed. "What about the people? How are you getting along with the team?"

The men are pigs, and the only other woman seems to be allergic to conversation. They suck and I hate them.

"They're brilliant," Olivia said smoothly. "I learn something new every day."

When it came to their jobs, every employee at PHC was smart as hell, and she *did* learn something new every day. For example, a few weeks ago, she learned Logan was a cheating bastard. The other day, she learned Cassidy could stare right through you like you weren't even there. It was pretty impressive.

"That's good. I've heard great things about you from Kevin." Michael continued paging through the dossier. "Perform well this summer and you have a bright future ahead of you in the company."

Olivia's heart kicked against her chest. Kevin was a partner, her boss's boss's boss. She hadn't interacted much with him in New York, and she hadn't been sure he knew who she was beyond the basic fact she worked at the firm. She certainly hadn't expected him to say great things about her. He wasn't involved in her day-to-day work, and she'd never presented before him. What could he possibly have said? She was dying to know.

But since she couldn't ask Michael, she settled for a demure "Thank you. I won't let you down," while secretly doing cartwheels in her head.

Vice presidency, here I come!

The town car pulled up to the Avenue Steakhouse, a grand building whose sleek lines and understated colors reflected its customers: wealthy, powerful, discreet. Avenue had played host to many a power meeting since its inception twenty-five years ago.

Olivia glimpsed herself in the dark glass windows as they entered the hushed venue. She wore her favorite gray tweed Theory sheath cinched at the waist with a narrow black belt, a tailored black blazer, black Wolford stockings, and black Prada pumps. Her hair fell in a sleek, smooth waterfall past her shoulders, and tiny pearl studs graced her ears. She looked every inch the professional.

Olivia had internalized the fashion rules for women in finance—some official, others unspoken—and used it to her advantage.

Dos: sheath dresses, nice silk blouses, classic heels or flats, stockings, bags large enough to hold pitch books.

Don'ts: cardigans (unless it was casual Friday, which was an increasingly common perk), classic button-down shirts (the buttons almost always gape), open-toed shoes and sandals, anything flashy with logos.

Outside of work, Olivia dressed however she wanted, but

she'd drawn a line between her personal and professional lives, and ne'er the twain shall they meet.

The host showed them to their table, and Ty Winstock arrived soon after.

She gave him a quick discreet once-over, eager to soak in anything she could about the elusive Mosaic cofounder. There were almost no public photos of him from recent years and even fewer interviews. The man was an enigma.

Winstock—it seemed wrong to think of him by his first name—resembled a modern hippie more than a billionaire. Tall and lean, he'd gathered his brown hair into a short ponytail, and a neatly trimmed beard covered his razor-sharp jawline. Bright, inquisitive blue eyes peered out from beneath thick dark brows. Beneath the scruff, he was handsome in that quiet, intellectual way you didn't notice unless you really looked. Instead of a suit or a dress shirt and pants, he wore a white V-neck T-shirt under a black hoodie with Mosaic's logo emblazoned on the back, black jeans, and designer sneakers. Standard tech-mogul wear.

The outfit was a blatant violation of Avenue's dress code, but none of the staff seemed keen on kicking Silicon Valley's latest golden boy out.

"Ty! Good to see you." Michael grasped the other man's hand in a firm handshake. "How was Nevada?"

"Hot." Winstock's bland tone revealed not an ounce of emotion. His eyes flicked to Olivia, and he stepped around Michael to hold out his now-free hand. "Ty."

"Olivia." Her heart thundered against her chest as she shook his hand. She tried not to think about the fact that she was in the presence of a man worth $1.2 billion (give or take a few hundred million, depending on how the markets were faring). Winstock was the highest-level client she'd ever met in person, and it was all she could do not to freak out.

Calm down. You got this.

Olivia had been around famous people before. Heck, Kris was engaged to one of the biggest movie stars on the planet. Then again, the future of Olivia's career didn't hinge on what action hero Nate Reynolds thought of her.

Once they placed their orders and made the requisite small talk, Michael launched into his spiel about why Winstock should invest with Pine Hill Capital. Most pitches involved a presentation of some sort, but according to Olivia's research, Winstock hated traditional pitch decks. He was a talk-it-over-during-a-meal kinda guy.

Olivia, who was usually outspoken in company meetings and client calls, let Michael take the lead. He was her boss, and she didn't want to say something off base and fuck things up.

Winstock was quiet, interrupting only to clarify a point or ask an incisive question. By the end of dinner, it was unclear whether he was sold on PHC or thought everything Michael said was bullshit.

He turned to Olivia as the server arranged their desserts—flourless chocolate tortes with orange essence—on the table. "Tell me why I should invest with PHC instead of a bigger firm. You have two minutes," he said, like Michael hadn't spent the past hour doing exactly that. "In your words, not anyone else's."

Olivia's fork froze halfway to her torte before she regained her composure. She set the utensil down and unlocked her phone, conscious of Winstock's unwavering blue eyes and Michael's burning stare.

This was it. Her test. Make it or break it.

After she set the timer, she smiled coolly and said, "Michael did an excellent job of outlining our metrics and previous success, so I won't go over those points again. I'll be honest—we're not the biggest fish in the sea, but bigger isn't always better. Pine Hill is a family—both employees *and* clients. We manage our clients' portfolios like they're our own, and because of that, we're incredibly selective about which individuals we bring into the fold." She outlined the personalized perks that PHC offered its high-networth investors and tapped her phone screen after she finished. "Twenty-five seconds left. Twenty, if you deduct the time it took for me to set the timer." Another smile. "As you can see, we're also efficient and sensitive to the demands on our clients' time. I assure you, Pine Hill Capital would be happy to keep our briefings to two minutes or less should you sign with us."

The subtle dig, couched in outward respect, was bold, but Olivia sensed Ty Winstock was not a man who held a high opinion of ass-kissers or yes-men/yes-women. He was also, as her painstaking research indicated, big on community and company culture. His employees reported the man went to great lengths to treat them like family. Birthday celebrations for everyone from the janitors to the C-suite executives, holiday parties with extravagant gifts paid out of Winstock's own pocket, monthly town halls—the works.

While Michael choked on his drink, Winstock pushed back from the table. Olivia's heart resumed its thundering. Shit, had she read him wrong? Was he so offended that he was walking out before he ate dessert? No one passed on dessert unless they had to.

Mental images of her career going up in flames plagued her as she fought not to hyperventilate. She could already hear her mother's voice in her head: *Your sister would've never done something so foolish at a business dinner, Olivia.*

"Good pitch. I'll think about it." A fleeting smile touched Winstock's lips—his first of the night. "I'll be in London for the next three weeks—I'll let you know my decision once I return. Enjoy dessert."

"You're skipping dessert?" Olivia blurted.

Another smile, this one containing more amusement than the first. "I don't have a sweet tooth."

With that, the tech billionaire strode out of the restaurant and disappeared into the night.

"Well." Michael brought his coughing fit under control and cleared his throat. "That didn't end the way I expected."

"I'm sorry." Olivia flushed. "I shouldn't have gone rogue like that."

It was unlike her, but Winstock was in the big leagues, and you didn't land someone like that as a client by being boring and conservative. You had to stand out.

Michael waved her apology away. "It's fine. It *was* a good pitch, and your closer seemed to have intrigued him—which is the *only* reason it's okay," he clarified, his expression growing sterner. "Let's keep the sass to a minimum next time."

"Of course." Relief fizzled through her veins. *Next time.* Meaning she wasn't fired.

Her career reconstructed itself after its earlier imaginary death in her mind.

"Do you have any plans right now?" Michael asked after paying for the meal with his company card.

Olivia froze for the second time that night. She couldn't read Michael's expression or tone. Where was he going with this?

"I was planning on calling it a night," she said carefully. "Lots to do at the office tomorrow. I want to make sure I'm well-rested."

"Of course. I was going to ask if you wanted a drink after this nerve-wracking dinner," Michael chuckled. "But that's probably not a great idea for a Monday night."

She smiled, relieved. "Probably not."

Thank God he wasn't pushing her to get drinks with him—or do anything else.

That was the downside of being a woman in a male-dominated industry—you had to be extra careful whenever you were alone with someone of the opposite sex. Olivia refused to let those fears dominate her, but she wasn't an idiot. Her guard was always up, especially when she was with a male colleague outside the office—or even *in* the office. That went double if said male ranked above her in the firm's strict hierarchy.

The tension dissipated from Olivia's shoulders as she waved goodbye to Michael and hailed a cab back to Sammy's house. It was dark when she arrived except for the light in the entryway; he must've realized she wasn't home and kept it on for her.

Such a Sammy thing to do.

They hadn't discussed their near-kiss over the weekend. While Aaron distracted Sammy at the barbecue, Olivia had fled into the house and locked herself in the bathroom, where she'd spent half an hour debating how to handle her momentary lapse of judgment. The truth was, she hadn't been that drunk. Tipsy, perhaps, but not enough that it would've impaired her logic. It had been something else that'd compelled her to drop her guard—something she didn't care to examine. Apparently, neither did Sammy, because he'd acted like nothing had happened when she'd rejoined the party.

Which is for the best. No need to upset the delicate balance of their relationship or whatever the hell they had.

Olivia was halfway to her room when her phone rang.

"Olivia." Her sister's cool voice—so similar to their mother's—flowed over the line. "I hope I'm not disturbing you."

"No, I just got home. What's up?" Olivia was not in the mood to talk to Alina, but she might as well get it over with.

"I'd like to confirm whether you're attending my rehearsal dinner."

Jesus Christ. If one more person mentioned the dinner, Olivia was going to scream. "Yes. I already told Mom I'm going."

"She didn't mention that when I saw her this morning."

"Take that up with her, not me."

"Olivia." This time, Alina's tone carried a gentle rebuke. "Mom is busy planning the wedding. Sometimes, things slip her mind. You should've sent a physical RSVP."

"I did." Olivia rubbed her temple. She could feel the beginnings of a headache coming on. "It probably hasn't reached you yet. But I'm your sister. Of *course* I'll be there."

She and Alina might not be close, but they were family. When Olivia was younger, she'd hero-worshipped her sister. Three years her senior, Alina had excelled at everything she touched, and Olivia had wanted to be just like her—beautiful, perfect, doted on by their proud mother. They'd been best friends before it became clear that Eleanor's love was limited and doled out based on which daughter she could brag about the most. Olivia and Alina's relationship had gradually transformed into a competition with no winner, at least not on paper. Both had graduated summa cum laude from Ivy League schools—Alina from Harvard, Olivia from Yale. Both had been class valedictorian and student body president in high school. Both excelled in their chosen fields—anesthesiology for Alina, finance for Olivia.

But Olivia knew, deep down, that Alina was winning because Alina always won. Perhaps it was because she was older and therefore always a few steps ahead, or perhaps it was because Eleanor had always favored her elder daughter.

At the ripe old age of twenty-nine, Olivia was single and on her way to becoming an old maid in their mother's eyes. Alina had been engaged to Richard at twenty-nine, but they'd waited for her to complete her residency before going through with the actual wedding. Alina had completed medical school and Olivia was only halfway through business school. But the kicker was, their mother fawned over Alina in a way she'd never done with

Olivia, no matter how many A-pluses or promotions Olivia received.

It was what it was. Olivia had made her peace with it a long time ago.

"...coming to San Francisco," Alina said.

Olivia blinked. She'd been so wrapped up in her thoughts, she'd missed the first half of what her sister said. "What?"

Alina responded with the tiniest sigh. It was amazing how much weariness one could pack into a gust of breath. "Mom, Richard, and I are coming to San Francisco," she repeated.

"*Why? When?*" The questions burst out with more horror than Olivia had intended, but if Alina was offended, she didn't let on.

"Richard and I are thinking of moving there after we get married. I've been recruited by a private clinic that's based in San Francisco, one that would pay me double what I'm earning now, and we'd like a better feel for the city before I make my decision."

Olivia couldn't have been more stunned if Alina had told her she'd joined a cult and was traveling to California for a sacrificial ceremony beneath the full moon. Alina *loved* Chicago. She'd left only for school and had promptly moved back after she received her MD from Harvard. Olivia had been the one itching to break free from the confines of their hometown and escape their mother's crushing expectations.

"Why didn't you tell me this before? And why is Mom coming with you?"

Eleanor would never move out of Chicago. That was the seat of her power, where she'd established a name for herself as a grande dame of society and cultivated a circle of admirers and competitors who kept her days filled with drama, party planning, and expensive lunches at the Waldorf Astoria.

"I just got the offer last week," Alina said. "If we move, Mom will visit often, so she wants to look at houses with us."

"I thought you were just 'getting a feel' for the city, not looking at houses already."

"Houses are part of the city, Olivia."

Olivia hated when Alina punctuated her sentences with her name. It was so freakin' condescending.

She was also cognizant of the fact that Eleanor had visited her only once when she'd lived in New York, but of course their mother would visit *Alina* often.

"We'll be there in August," Alina continued. "We're staying at the Z Hotel, but we should have a family brunch. I haven't seen you in a while, and you're one of my bridesmaids. Not to mention my sister."

Maybe I'd see you more if I were your maid of honor.

Olivia bit back her caustic reply. "Sure," she replied instead. "Looking forward to it." *As much as I look forward to a root canal without anesthesia.*

"Excellent. Good night."

"Good night."

Olivia hung up and heaved a deep sigh as she looked around her room, which suddenly felt *too* quiet. She was still apartment hunting in her free time, but nothing that met her budget and requirements had surfaced yet. At this rate, she might as well stay at Sammy's house through the summer.

The idea didn't freak her out as much as it should have.

She'd seen Sammy's car in the driveway, which meant he was home. He was probably sleeping—he had early nights when he planned to go into the bakery the next day.

Olivia was horrified to realize part of her was tempted to wake him up just so she had someone to talk to. Sammy was one of the best listeners she knew, and when they weren't sniping at each other, she loved talking to him. If they were dating, she wouldn't think twice of barging in his room and laying her troubles at his feet—not to mention rewarding him afterward with a blow job. She'd done that in Shanghai more often than she cared to admit.

Since they *weren't* dating, she settled for a few chapters of her latest erotica read instead. Reading was the closest thing she had to therapy without actually going to therapy. Plus, her first book club meeting was tomorrow, and she couldn't wait.

Olivia needed new friends in the city, stat. Otherwise, she'd go crazy—or *do* something crazy, like sneak into Sammy's room and finish where they'd left off on the Fourth of July.

CHAPTER 12

"I'M TELLING YOU, ANAL IS SO GOOD IF YOU DO IT right!" Natalie waved her arms and nearly whacked Kat in the face in her enthusiasm.

"No way." Donna shook her head. "I tried it once, and it felt like I was dying."

"Did you use lube?"

"Of course I used lube!"

"Did you use *enough* lube?"

Donna pursed her lips. "Look, it doesn't matter. I'm down for BJs, sex in public places, rimming, whatever. But anal is a no-go."

Natalie huffed and turned to Olivia. "What about you? Team Anal: yes or no?"

Now that was a question Olivia never thought she'd have to answer.

She cast an apologetic glance in Donna's direction. "Yes, if it's with the right guy." Donna was right—it hurt like hell the first few times, but once she got used to it and understood the proper preparations, it'd become far more pleasurable.

Olivia needed to trust the guy a *lot* to let him in the back door, though. To this day, the only person she'd had anal sex with was Sammy.

Donna groaned at her answer, while Natalie and Tamara high-fived her. Kat merely smiled.

"Yes! I knew we could count on you!" Natalie's eyes glittered with excitement. "I'm *so* happy you joined the club. We finally have a tiebreaker."

Natalie and Tamara were on Team Anal; Donna and Kat were not. Olivia was indeed the tiebreaker.

"Plus, we like you," Kat added.

"Yes." Natalie nodded. "That too."

Olivia grinned, happily buzzed from her first jumbo-size margarita. "I like you guys too."

Two hours into her first erotica book club meeting and she was having a *blast*. The club was small—she was only the fifth member—but the other women had a playful camaraderie that instantly put her at ease. They'd welcomed her with open arms, and for the first time in months, she felt like she *belonged*. It was weird because she'd only known them for a few hours, but she could already tell they were her people.

Donna was a thirty-six-year-old dental hygienist who'd founded the club last year because the other book clubs she'd been in were too "boring." She was married and had the most infectious laugh Olivia had ever heard. Her bubbliness would give Olivia's preternaturally chirpy friend Courtney a run for her money.

Kat, on the other hand, was quiet and observant. She was a PhD student studying comparative literature at UC Berkeley, and she possessed a dry sense of humor that Olivia took a shine to immediately. Kat was one of those women who was beautiful but so unassuming you didn't notice until you looked closely and saw the shiny honey-brown curls, warm brown eyes, and delicate, lightly freckled features.

Natalie was Olivia's age, the daughter of a major tech executive, and an aspiring romance author in addition to being an avid romance reader. She proudly declared she could blaze through one or two books a *day*. With her razor-cut platinum bob, sharp cheekbones, and designer clothes, she resembled a Russian supermodel/heiress, but her cold looks were at complete odds with her outgoing personality.

Tamara, a freelance graphic designer, was the person Olivia never would've imagined read erotica or romance. She had spiky, black hair, eyes so blue they looked violet, skin pale enough to qualify her as Edward Cullen's long-lost sister, and piercings in her left eyebrow, nose, and—judging by what Olivia could see through Tammy's thin cotton tank—nipples. She looked like she'd be way more into gothic horror or kick-ass action novels, but the minute the thought crossed Olivia's mind, she admonished herself for stereotyping. If someone saw Olivia on the street, they wouldn't think she read erotica either.

On the surface, the book club members couldn't be more different, but they were all friendly, open, and nonjudgmental. They'd spent the first hour of the club discussing that month's pick—a dark erotic romance about a woman entering a BDSM relationship with her ex's father—before they segued into a general conversation about relationships and sex. The book had featured a hot-as-sin anal scene, hence why they'd started debating the pros and cons of the act.

Kat's phone buzzed. She glanced down and flinched, her cheeks paling.

"Who is it? That asshole again?" Natalie demanded. "*Don't* answer, Katty Kat. He doesn't deserve it."

Kat's bottom lip disappeared between her teeth. "Yeah, but—"

"No buts. He's your ex for a reason, and if he had a hot

father, I'd tell you to do what Jaimie did in the book and fuck him. The father, I mean."

Kat snorted out a laugh. "It'll only take a few minutes, okay? I'll tell him I'm busy and that'll be that. I'll be right back."

Natalie's face scrunched with frustration as the brunette disappeared outside so she could take the call away from the noise and general mayhem of the Catalina restaurant.

Olivia was dying to know what was going on, but she didn't want to be too nosy at her first meeting. Luckily, Donna filled in the blanks for her.

"That was Ben, her ex-fiancé." The blond made a face. "They were together for six years and all set to be married until Kat found him banging her best friend two weeks before the wedding."

Olivia gasped. "No."

"Yes." Tamara nodded, her piercings glinting with anger beneath the lights. "To make matters worse, he blamed *her*. Said she was always busy with school, never made time for him, so of course he got lonely, blah blah blah."

"Worst part is, Kat believed him," Natalie jumped in. "I mean, she dumped his ass, but she also feels guilty because his fucking gaslighting got into her head and she thinks it was partly her fault. She still carries a little torch for him, and the jerk keeps stringing her along by always calling her about stupid shit—whether she has one of his shirts, what the name of the restaurant they went to that one time was. Probably so he can have a backup once he's done screwing his way through the city. Smug bastard thinks he can get her back with a snap of his fingers, and at this rate, he might be right."

Olivia felt sick. "That's horrible." Kat was so sweet, and even though she barely knew the woman, she knew she didn't deserve to be treated that way.

"We keep telling her to cut him off, but she won't." Donna looked glum. "She's too damn nice. We—"

She fell silent as Kat returned to the table.

"Sorry about that," the brunette said, cheeks flushed. "I'm back."

"I hope you told him to shove his cock through a woodcutter." Natalie shrugged at Kat's frown. "What? A girl can hope."

After a short, uneasy silence, the women resumed their conversation about their favorite and least favorite sexual acts, making a conscious effort *not* to mention Kat's love life. Eventually, the tension disappeared, and they were laughing their asses off once more at Natalie's increasingly outrageous statements.

By the time Olivia left the restaurant, she was several margaritas deep and grinning like a madwoman. The club met officially once a month, but she'd received a standing invitation to their weekly happy hours, where they met up just to chat and hang out—book discussions not required. Whoever made it, made it; there was no pressure to attend.

Olivia fully intended on joining, though she might scale back on the number of drinks.

Was drinking this much on a work night out of character and a bad idea? Yes.

Did she deserve a fun night out? Also yes.

Fuck it, she worked *hard*, and tonight was the first time in a year she'd vibed with other women who lived in the same city. She was still going to show up and kick ass in the office tomorrow. She'd just need a little more help than usual from aspirin.

With that reassurance in mind, Olivia tiptoed into the house, not wanting to wake Sammy up. He worked crazy hours, and she was never sure if he had a regular day the next day or if had to go into the bakery at unholy hours in the morning.

Quiet...quiet...quiet...

THUD!

She flinched as she knocked over the coat rack in the front

hall. The heavy brass tree toppled to the floor and landed on her toes.

"Dammit!" Olivia let loose a string of colorful expletives as pain burst through her foot. She heaved the rack off and hopped on one leg while she raised her other foot and tried to massage away the throbbing ache. "Freakin' tree. I will murder you. I don't care if it's bad for the environment," she said, her drunk mind not processing the fact that it was a coat tree and not, in fact, an actual tree. "I will melt you down and use your brass for jewelry, which I'll sell on Etsy for extra income, and I'll get rich and buy all your sister and brother and cousin trees and melt them down too—"

"Olivia?"

The kitchen light flicked on, and she winced, blinking rapidly while her eyes adjusted to the new brightness level.

Sammy stood next to the counter with one eyebrow raised. His hair was tousled from sleep, and he was wearing those damn gray sweatpants again—the ones that hung so low on his hips they were in danger of falling off. No shirt.

His penchant for distracting shirtlessness was worse than Matthew McConaughey's.

His eyes moved from Olivia's frozen form—she was still clutching one foot in her hand—to the toppled coat rack and back again.

"I see there's been an altercation in the entryway." His mouth twitched with amusement.

"It's your stupid tree." She was technically the one at fault, but he didn't need to know that. "It got in my way."

"Ah." Sammy walked over and righted the brass abomination. "I see the tree has gone rogue and attacked you while you were coming in. That's unacceptable. I'll give it a stern talking-to in the morning."

"Good." Olivia nodded, then narrowed her eyes. "Wait. Are you making fun of me?"

Sammy's mouth twitched again. "I would never make fun of you."

"Lies!" She released her foot and jabbed his chest with her finger. It was like poking a brick wall—a sexy brick wall. His skin was smooth and warm beneath her touch, and awareness sizzled in her lower belly.

Olivia shook her head to clear the unwanted thoughts and immediately regretted it.

The room spun, causing her to lose her balance. In her panic, she grabbed on to the nearest source of stability...aka Sammy.

Her hands clutched his rock-hard biceps, and her body pressed against his naked, chiseled torso. The sudden urge to wrap herself around him like a vine curling around a tree trunk overwhelmed her.

Olivia tilted her head up, and her stomach swooped and dipped faster than a roller coaster ride. Because the look in Sammy's eyes? Hot enough to set the iceberg from *Titanic* on fire.

A heavy ache blossomed between her legs, and her nipples tightened. She wondered if he could feel them through her thin bra and top. She wondered a lot of things, actually—like whether Sammy was as good a kisser as he used to be or if he'd gotten even better over the years (*a pox on any woman he'd kissed who wasn't her!*), and if his tastes in bed had changed or if he was still as adventurous as ever (*dear God, please*).

Olivia's thighs clenched when she remembered some of their reenactments of the scenes from her books. There was one scene in particular from tonight's book club pick that Sammy would knock out of the ballpark—he would look hot as hell in a CEO getup. Suit and tie, black-rimmed glasses, a nice watch on his wrist. *Yum.*

Olivia found guys who wore watches hot as hell, especially if they paired it with a button-down shirt with the sleeves rolled up. Maybe it was because she valued punctuality? Whatever it was, it got her going faster than one of the cars in those Vin Diesel movies guys liked so much.

The molten heat in Sammy's eyes turned to lava. "Olivia." Her name came out as a hoarse rasp. "Stop looking at me like that."

She sniffed him discreetly. *God, he smells good.* Clean and fresh, with a hint of sandalwood. "Like what?"

"Let's get you to bed. You're drunk," he said, ignoring her question.

"No, I'm not," she slurred. Okay, maybe a little. But she only had, what? Three margaritas? Three was *nothing*, even if said margaritas had been jumbo size. On a scale of one to drunk, she was not. Or something like that.

Olivia squealed when the world tilted upside down and she found herself staring at the ceiling. The blood rushed to her head, precipitating what she suspected would be a massive headache in a few hours. "What are you doing? Let me down!"

"No. You might knock down the poor coat tree again." Sammy marched them down the hall toward her room.

"This is kidnapping!"

"Yes, I'm kidnapping you inside your house and taking you to your room. The horror," he said, tone dry.

"This isn't my house." Olivia blinked. The hallway looked so different upside down. *Is that a smudge on the ceiling? How did that get there?* She made a mental note to look for a stepladder so she could clean it tomorrow. "This is your house. I'm only living here. Temporarily."

Her apartment search hadn't been going well, in the sense that Olivia had stopped searching. It was unlike her—usually, she'd already have dozens of viewing appointments lined up—but work had been crazy. She'd get around to it. Eventually.

Sammy nudged her door open with his foot. "How much did you drink tonight? I haven't seen you this hammered since K-town karaoke."

Olivia giggled, remembering her and Sammy's epic night in New York's Koreatown years ago. Their innocent dinner had segued into an hours-long party at a nearby KTV (karaoke) spot with a bunch of Russian tourists who'd ordered enough alcohol to down a large elephant. Sometime between knocking back vodka shots—*blech*—and belting out the lyrics to the Backstreet Boys' "I Want It That Way," she and Sammy had snuck into one of the bar's bathrooms for sex.

The bathrooms had been surprisingly clean, though Olivia had been too inebriated to dwell on the hygiene ramifications of their actions anyway. She didn't regret it—it had been the hottest sex of her life.

"That was a good night," she mumbled as Sammy set her down on her bed. "We had a lot of good nights, didn't we?"

A small pause. "Yeah," Sammy said softly. "We did."

Olivia closed her eyes, breathing a sigh of relief when she felt Sammy unbuckle and tug off her shoes. She hadn't realized how constricting they were until they were off.

"Sammy?"

"Hmm?"

"I'm sorry."

He froze, his hand lingering close enough to her calf for the warmth to soak into her skin. Funny how a small almost-touch could send her heart into palpitations.

"For what?" There was a new, strange note in his voice.

"For New York." Olivia kept her eyes closed and sank into the comfort of her bed and the wells of her memory. She felt like she was in a dream, and that made it easier to get the words out. "I think I've said this before? I don't remember. But anyway, I'm sorry for not believing in you. For lying and hurting you. You're the best man I know. You always have been—even in the moments when I hated you for hurting me back. Though I guess that's hypocritical of me." She frowned at the thought.

There was a pronounced silence. "I appreciate that, and I'm sorry too," he said, still in that strange voice. "For the things I said."

"I forgive you. Can we be friends again? Beyond the truce, I mean." Olivia's lower lip wobbled. "I miss you a lot." She'd missed him for years. It wasn't something she would ever admit during the day, but under the cover of darkness, she couldn't have held back the truth if she tried.

Sammy had been her rock, her best friend, her cheerleader, and her partner in crime. He'd been the love of her life, and his absence had left a huge, gaping hole in her chest. Even in the moments when she despised him, she'd missed him with an intensity that frightened her.

His breathing sounded unsteady, or maybe that was her heart beating a drumbeat she hadn't heard in a long, long time.

"I'm right here." Sammy moved her leg so he could drape the blanket over her.

Olivia may be drunk, but it didn't escape her notice that he'd avoided answering her question about being friends again. *Real* friends, not friendly acquaintances the way they were now.

She opened her eyes, her gaze tracing the strong lines of Sammy's profile. The lights were off and she couldn't see his face clearly, but she'd memorized every feature—the deep chocolate eyes, the broad cheekbones, the firm, full lips and square jaw.

"That's not what I meant."

Sammy muttered something that sounded like "God help

me." He exhaled a long breath and adjusted the blanket so it was tucked securely around her. "Let's discuss this in the morning when you're sober."

"I'm sober." Olivia hiccupped. "Well, I'm the *teensiest* bit tipsy. Margaritas will do that to ya, ya know?" She flung her arms open dramatically. "Sammy."

"Olivia." A faint note of teasing entered his voice.

She pouted. "I don't like it when you call me that."

"That's your name." More amusement.

She shook her head. "You should call me Liv. That's what all my friends call me."

The intensity of his stare warmed her already flushed skin. It was scorching in here, and all she wanted was to rip off her clothes and burrow herself into Sammy's delicious warmth. Which made no sense because she'd be trading heat for more heat, but Sammy's kind of heat sounded way better than suffocating beneath her comforter.

"Is that what you really want? For us to be friends?" His hand lingered near her shoulder, and Olivia instinctively reached up and clasped it to her chest. He made a strangled noise but didn't move away.

"Yes," she said dreamily. If she said it, it'd come true. *#Manifestation*

Was it normal to want to have hot sweaty sex with your friends? Well, one friend in particular whose name rhymed with Tammy, who—hey! Tammy was a new friend. Friends were great. Olivia loved friends, especially her new book club ones. Now that she thought about it, perhaps the book club discussion was what had gotten her all hot and bothered. Sammy's current shirtless state only amplified her hot-and-bothered-ness.

She shifted in her bed, wishing she were naked. *Why was it so freakin' hot?*

Olivia lifted Sammy's hand so she could throw off her covers. "Turn up the AC. I mean, turn down the AC." Her brow knit in puzzlement. "Make it colder," she clarified. "I'm burning up."

Concern sharpened in his eyes. "It's sixty-eight degrees."

"Then why aren't you cold?"

"Because I was under my covers—until someone knocked down a coat rack and woke me up."

She didn't dignify that with a response. "It's not. I'm hot." She giggled. "That rhymes."

Sammy rested his free hand on her forehead, and she sighed with contentment at his cool touch. "Jesus, you *are* burning up. How much did you drink?"

"Like...*threeeee* drinks?" Olivia squinted one eye as she tried to remember. "Four? Five? Ten?"

"You could be sick. This feels like more than an alcohol flush. How do you feel? Nauseous? Fatigued? Any abdominal pain?" He fired off the questions like he was a doctor.

She thought about it. "Horny."

He went still, so still she couldn't hear him breathe. "What?" There went that strangled noise again.

Golden warmth—the good kind, not the kind burning her skin—melted and trickled throughout her body, sensitizing each nerve ending as it flowed past.

"I went to my first erotica book club meeting tonight." Her eyelids drooped. It'd been a long day, but she didn't want to stop talking yet. She wanted Sammy to stay for a while longer. "It was a good book. They had this scene where the couple has sex in his office. He blindfolds her with his tie and fucks her up against the glass—one-way, so people outside couldn't see them, but she didn't know that. She hated it but loved it, and she screamed so loud he had to cover her mouth with his hand so the rest of the office couldn't hear her."

The warmth in her lower belly pulsed as Olivia pictured the scene in her mind.

She'd been wrong—she *could* hear Sammy breathing. Loud and ragged, like he couldn't draw enough oxygen into his lungs.

"Fuck." He yanked his hand out of hers so fast Olivia would've stumbled had she been standing. "Go to sleep, Olivia." Every inch of his muscular frame radiated tension. It filled the room, pressing into her eyes and causing her lids to droop farther.

Her body was primed and hungry for touch, but her mind was ready to knock the hell out.

"I don't want to go to sleep yet. I want—" A huge yawn interrupted her train of thought. "I want—" Another yawn.

What *did* she want? A lot of things. But at that moment, there was one thing she desired most.

"I want you…" Olivia's voice faded as she lost her battle with exhaustion and sleep overtook her.

CHAPTER 13

OLIVIA WOKE UP IN HELL.

An army of jackhammer-wielding assholes slammed against her skull in a torturous rhythm so loud she could *feel* her brain rattle. Her throat burned, and her stomach sloshed in a way that brought yesterday's dinner dangerously close to the surface. She needed to run to the bathroom before she upchucked all over the beautiful sheets in Sammy's guest room, but lead weights pinned her limbs to the bed.

She wanted to close her eyes and drift back into slumber, where her aches and worries would disappear, but in the dim recesses of her mind, she realized it was Wednesday. She had to go to work.

The thought of getting up—much less dressing, commuting to the office, and spending the entire day at her desk, staring at her computer and fending off inappropriate come-ons from Logan—made her want to die.

You can do this, Olivia tried to say, but the words didn't come out, so she settled for a silent pep talk instead.

On the count of five. One...two...three...four...five.

She rolled onto her side. She'd moved, which was good. But she was still in bed, which was bad.

Her stomach gurgled, and Olivia would've thrown up had it not been for sheer force of will.

Hell. No.

No way was she puking all over *her* room. The smell of vomit lingered, even after you cleaned it, and the room was her sanctuary. She refused to taint it.

Olivia stared at the drawn shades—if she closed her eyes, she might not open them again for the next, oh, twenty hours—summoned every ounce of willpower she had, and lurched off the bed.

Success!

Now all she had to do was make it to the bathroom.

"Fuck," she rasped, her voice sounding sick and scratchy to her own ears.

After an eternity, Olivia managed to half stumble, half lurch her way across the hall into the bathroom, where she promptly hurled her guts in the toilet. Just when she thought it was over, another wave of nausea overtook her, and she resumed the disgusting exercise.

Sweat slicked her skin, hair stuck to her face, and her throat felt like it was scraped raw by razor blades.

She wasn't sure how long she knelt there, puking out the contents in her stomach, but in the middle of her misery, she felt someone—obviously Sammy, because they were the only people in the house—gather her hair back from her face. It reminded her of her party days, when she, Farrah, Courtney, and Kris would take turns holding each other's hair while they threw up after drinking too much.

Maybe that was the problem. Olivia remembered only bits and pieces from last night, but she knew she'd imbibed more margaritas than she should've. It'd been a dumb move, drinking that much on a work night. She rarely fucked up like that, but Olivia had been so happy to have female friends again that she'd slipped.

But whatever monster was raging through her body felt more serious than a hangover. Besides, weren't you supposed to throw up the night you drank too much, not the morning after? Maybe—

Aaaannd there went her dinner again. Or maybe it was yesterday's lunch or breakfast. She couldn't possibly have any of the burger and fries from Catalina left in her stomach.

After an eternity, the vomiting finally, blissfully ceased, and Olivia slumped on the floor.

Sammy knelt until they were at eye level, worry etched all over his handsome face.

"G'way," Olivia moaned. She didn't want him to see her like this. She felt and no doubt looked like shit, there were bits of vomit in her hair—*gross*—and her complexion probably resembled that of a wax figure.

Embarrassment snaked through her, which was so messed up. She might be *dying*, and she was worried about what she looked like in front of Sammy?

Talk about screwed-up priorities.

Sammy's mouth tilted up for a moment before it flattened again. "You're not dying, and you look...well, not fine, but not worse than what anyone else in your situation would look like."

Shit. She'd voiced her thoughts out loud?

Her day kept getting worse and worse.

"What time is it?" Hopefully, she had time to shower. Even if she didn't, she *had* to shower. She couldn't walk out of the house like this.

"A little past eight."

Olivia squawked in dismay. "I'm late!" By the time she

showered, got dressed, and hoofed it to the office, it'd be well into the workday.

She grabbed Sammy's hand. "Phone. Call," she wheezed.

He knew what she was asking before she spelled it out. "No," he said. "You're sick. You can't even stand, much less go to work."

"Can too." Olivia pushed herself off the ground. Two seconds later, her ass hit the cool white tile again—and stayed there. "Cannot," she amended.

"Anyway, I already called your office and told them you couldn't come in because you have a stomach virus."

What? When? Olivia hadn't heard him on the phone. Then again, she'd been too busy acquainting herself with the toilet to pay attention to much else.

The adrenaline from missing work dissipated and left her more drained than before. She couldn't remember the last time she'd been this sick. She hadn't even caught a common cold in three or four years—her immune system was titanium.

Sammy left and returned a minute later with a little plastic stool that he plunked in the shower stall. Olivia didn't protest when he hauled her into the shower, sat her down on the stool, and helped rinse out her hair. She knew how to pick her battles.

Sammy worked briskly, shampooing and conditioning the sticky strands until they were nice and clean again. She closed her eyes and savored the sensation of his strong, sure hands massaging her scalp. The jackhammers in her head eased, lulled by the massage, the soothing sound of the water, and the comforting male presence beside her.

After he finished, he dried her hair and carried her into her bedroom, bridal-style. Somehow, he'd avoided spraying water on her torso in the shower, so Olivia didn't need to change before he tucked her back into bed.

Her stomach growled its displeasure at the new horizontal position. "Sam—"

A trash can appeared before she finished saying his name. She leaned over and dry heaved while he held her hair again and rubbed soothing circles on her back, but nothing came out.

After a while, she flopped onto her back and waved the proverbial white flag. "I'm sick."

"I know." Sammy smoothed a gentle hand over her hair.

The next few hours—days? weeks?—passed in a blur. Olivia was out of it half the time, caught up in feverish hallucinations or fitful dreams. It must've been days, because if it were weeks, she'd be in a hospital. Every time she woke up, Sammy was there, feeding her ice chips to help with the dehydration. He seemed to know what she needed, when she needed it, without her saying anything, including when she needed to use the restroom or throw up again.

Yeah, the symptoms from whatever she had were not pleasant. Things came out on both ends.

It would've been deeply humiliating, except Olivia was too miserable to feel embarrassed. She was only grateful that she wasn't living alone, dealing with this nightmare by herself.

Perhaps her apartment flood had been a blessing in disguise.

During her bedridden stint, Olivia started talking to Sammy about nothing and everything: Her mother. Her sister. Her sister's douche canoe fiancé, whom she was pretty sure she caught staring down her shirt the last time she'd gone home. Her brilliant five-, ten-, and twenty-year life plans. Why Charmander was the best Pokémon. Why Sammy needed to stop walking around shirtless.

He listened to her ramble and took part in the conversations, even though half were absurd and the other half ended abruptly when Olivia fell asleep or lost her train of thought.

However, he took a special interest in her verbal dissertation on why Sammy's shirts needed to stay on.

"It's distracting." Olivia sucked on an ice chip until it melted and the cool liquid trickled down her throat, soothing her fever. Bless whoever invented ice chips. They deserved a statue in every city and an annual bash with cupcakes shaped like their face. "I can't think when your six-pack is staring at me."

"Just my six-pack or any six-pack?"

She pondered the question. She hadn't thrown up in hours, which was a good sign. Fatigue clawed at her and sweat dampened her brow, but she'd choose that over bodily ejections any day of the week. "Just yours. And Chris Hemsworth."

"Chris Hemsworth, huh?" Sammy looked thoughtful. "I suppose I could have worse company than Thor."

"Uh-huh." Olivia's lids fluttered, her breath shallow. "'Specially not fair when you wear those gray sweatpants."

"What's wrong with my sweatpants? They're my favorite pair."

"I can see your dick through them."

He choked. "Excuse me?"

"The outline," she clarified. "Those sweats are like a push-up bra for your dick. Shoves it in everyone's face without revealing anything. It's a cocktease—literally. And when you wear them while cooking—" She licked her lips, both at the mental image and because her lips were bone-dry. "I kinda wanna jump you."

Not kinda. Definitely. But she didn't want to scare him away. Sammy was the only thing keeping her sane during these long, feverish eternities where night bled into day and the specter of death hung in the air.

Olivia was the *teensiest* bit dramatic when she was sick.

Sammy fell silent, and Olivia cracked her eyes open to assure herself he was still there. He was—hair mussed, mouth soft, eyes speculative. Her guardian angel. She wanted him by her side always.

"That's good to know," he finally murmured.

He asked no more questions after that, and Olivia drifted off into sleep again. This time, instead of nightmares about a mountain of paperwork chasing her through the halls of PHC or dreams of Charmander lighting candles with its fire breath in her future home, her brain dug up a memory she'd buried deep in the recesses of her mind.

"Sammy, it's not what you think!" Olivia followed him into the living room of their New York apartment rental, her panicked heart crashing against her rib cage repeatedly in an attempt to escape—or punish her. Like it, too, was too disgusted to stay around her any longer. "You don't know the whole story."

He gripped the edges of the back of the couch, his shoulders taut, his lean frame vibrating with pent-up anger. "What's the whole story, Olivia?" His voice was colder than she'd ever heard it.

Dread coiled in her stomach.

Sammy wasn't cold. He was warm and gregarious and the kindest person she knew—and he deserved so much better than her.

A giant lump formed in her throat. "I only said that to get my mom off my back. I didn't mean it."

He turned, and Olivia flinched at the hurt in his eyes.

"No? So you're going to introduce me to your mom when she visits? How will you explain that one? 'Oh, just kidding, Mom, I didn't actually break up with him because I think he's a loser who's throwing away his future by choosing to be a baker instead of a fucking NASA scientist."

Tears stung her eyes. "I was obviously lying! You don't know my mom. She's... I'm not ready for you to meet her, okay? She's critical and judgmental, and she drives everyone I care about away. You have no idea how harsh she can be. I don't want her to hurt you."

Olivia had fucked up by telling Eleanor about Sammy.

Technically, she'd told Alina in an ill-advised attempt at sisterly bonding, but she should've known her sister would tell their mom. After Eleanor learned Olivia was shacking up with a boy in New York, she'd called immediately and grilled her about said boy's qualifications. That was the exact word she'd used: qualifications, like they were talking about a job candidate instead of a boyfriend.

Olivia should've lied about Sammy turning down his NASA job offer and choosing to open his own bakery instead, but she'd been so shocked by Eleanor's announcement that she was flying to NYC to meet him that she'd panicked. She'd told her mother that she'd already broken up with him because of course she wouldn't date a wannabe baker; she only wanted a successful boyfriend, thank you very much. The words had tasted like poison on her tongue, and she'd felt sick saying them, but they did the trick—Eleanor had been mollified.

Olivia just hadn't expected Sammy to come home early and overhear everything she'd said.

Frost iced over the look of betrayal in his eyes. "You don't have to worry about her hurting me. You're doing that well enough on your own."

Olivia whimpered and turned in her sleep. Her heart was pounding again—from her stomach bug or her nightmare memory, she didn't know.

Pain lanced her chest, mixed with a glint of anger. Yes, she'd said hurtful things, and that was on her. But she meant it when she said she hadn't, well, meant it. She and Sammy had been dating for almost a year. Did he really think she was such a vile person? Was he not going to listen to her or give her the benefit of the doubt?

"I didn't handle things with my mom well, and I should've never lied or said what I said. But you know me. I'm not that type of girl. I would never hurt you like that."

"Do I?" Sammy spoke with lethal softness. "Do I really know you're not that type of girl?"

He might as well have punched her in the stomach. She felt like she got all the wind knocked out of her, and her heart beat a jagged rhythm in her chest. "What?"

A muscle ticked beneath his eye. "You've made it clear that you don't approve of me trying to start a bakery. When I first told you, you stared at me like I had two heads. It's been weeks, and you've never said—not once—that you supported my decision. Every time I talk about it, you change the subject. The other day, when I went to your company picnic and your boss asked me what my plans were after college? I told him, and you fucking flinched. Like you were embarrassed by me. You never hesitated to tell everyone about my NASA internship, but you're real freakin' quiet now. So tell me, Olivia, how do I know you're not that type of girl?"

The room spun. Olivia opened her mouth, then closed it, because Sammy wasn't wrong. She didn't think the bakery was a good idea. He was an incredible baker, but he was also an incredible mathematician. Success for the latter was all but guaranteed; hell, NASA was practically begging him to accept their job offer. But opening a bakery? It was fifty-fifty at best. The hours, the stress, the uncertainty of starting something from the ground up right out of college—it didn't make sense. If things went south, Sammy could end up buried in debt. Olivia loved him too much to let that happen or to encourage him to throw his future away without trying to convince him otherwise.

As for being embarrassed by him...a tiny, horrible part of her was. And she hated herself for it. Perhaps if Olivia hadn't grown up in an environment where so much emphasis was placed on the "right" degrees and "right" job titles, she'd have felt differently. But all her life, the people around her had drilled into *her the importance of career success—her family, her professors, her classmates and colleagues.* Baker *did not fall under the list of acceptable professions for boyfriends,* aspiring baker *even less so. It was hard to overcome lifelong conditioning, even for someone she loved.*

Her silence caused a bitter, mocking smile to spread across Sammy's face. "That's what I thought."

"I just want what's best for you," *she said weakly.* "Sammy, this is your future. If a bakery is something you really want to do, at least wait until you have a financial cushion or some kind of backup plan. Get a few years' experience in another field so you can fall back on it in case the bakery doesn't pan out. Don't jump into it right out of college."

Sadness eclipsed his face. "Some things make sense in the head; others make sense in the heart. If there's one thing this summer taught me, it's that I would be miserable spending the next few years in a job I don't love. I would wake up every day hating my life. Knowing that, would you still ask me to wait?"

"Maybe it's just *this* job you don't like," *she argued.* "It doesn't mean you'll hate *every* math and engineering job out there."

Sammy shook his head and let out a disbelieving laugh. "You sure you want what's best for *me*? Or do you want what's best for *you*? Maybe you want a status symbol more than a boyfriend. Something nice and pretty to put up there with your Yale diploma and résumé. Maybe, if everything in your life were perfect— including your boyfriend—your mom would finally love you."

The blood rushed in Olivia's ears. Pain prickled at her skin even as the embers from her earlier anger grew brighter. "I can't believe you said that," *she choked out.*

It was the most hurtful thing anyone had ever said to her, even taking into account her mother's insults, because Sammy knew *what a sore subject Eleanor was. She'd confided in him things she'd never told anyone—her doubts, her insecurities, her secret fear that her mother didn't love her at all. Not as a daughter, not even as a person. Eleanor probably liked her hairstylist more than she liked Olivia.*

Regret flitted through Sammy's eyes before his face hardened. "Face it, Liv. You say you hate your mother, but she's screwed *you up so much you can't even see how much you're like her. You only care about whether something makes you look good or fits neatly into one of your fucking spreadsheets. Everything you've ever done has been to gain your mother's approval, and since I can no longer help you with that, I guess I'm yesterday's news."* His mouth twisted. "Hey, look on the bright side. You'll be working in finance. You can date some uptight Wall Street guy like your sister. But that wouldn't work, would it? You'd still be following in her footsteps. Still second best—"

SLAP! *Sammy's head twisted to the side as Olivia's palm connected with his cheek.*

The air pulsed, deafening in its silence.

Olivia's chest heaved with suppressed emotion. She curled her hands into fists and tucked them beneath her armpits—whether to prevent herself from slapping him again or to hold herself upright, she didn't know.

Sammy touched his cheek. She'd slapped him so hard, a bright-red handprint marred his golden skin. A muscle jumped in his jaw.

He didn't say a word. He didn't even look at her as he turned and walked out the door.

It wasn't until Olivia heard the click of the lock that she allowed herself to sink onto the ground and dissolve into sobs.

Something warm and wet trickled down Olivia's cheek, jolting her awake before her mind could take her further down the dark halls of her memory—the actual breakup, the run-in with Sammy's skeezy cousin Edison (who'd been visiting New York at the time), the anger she'd held on to like a lifeboat for years because it was easier than dealing with the hole in her heart.

"Why are you crying?" Sammy's alarmed voice forced her to open her eyes. "Does something hurt? Do we need to go to the hospital?"

His concern was so at odds with the Sammy from her dream, it made her cry harder.

His face paled. "That's it. We're taking you to the hospital. I thought you were getting better—"

"No. I *am* getting better. I'm not crying because I'm hurt." Well, she was, but not in the way he thought. "I'm just emotional. It's almost that time of month," she fibbed.

"Oh." Sammy grimaced. "Define *almost*. Like in the next few hours or next few days? You don't need me to"—he lowered his voice—"help you put in a"—even lower voice—"*tampon*, do you?"

Olivia laughed and cringed at the same time. "No!"

"Thank God." Relief drenched his expression. "I'm fine with puke and poop, but periods are not my forte."

Men. They were all the same.

"Don't say the P-words. They make me want to, you know, puke."

"But not poop?"

"Stop!" She moaned, her cheeks blazing while he laughed. "Guys are *so* gross." Like she needed the reminder that he'd seen her perform just about every bodily function over the past few days. Any sexual attraction he might've harbored toward her must've died by now.

That was the moment Olivia realized something had her staring at Sammy in such a way that he arched an eyebrow in confusion.

She didn't *want* his sexual attraction toward her to die.

She didn't want him to leave her side.

She didn't want him to be set up on dates by his mother and go out with other women.

Because...*she* wanted *him*. His heart, his humor, his loyalty and intelligence—she wanted all of it. Olivia still had feelings for him, and judging by her body's reaction every time he was near—virus-induced abnormalities aside—they were strong ones.

She gulped.

Oh poop.

CHAPTER 14

"I'M SO SICK OF THE BRAT DIET." OLIVIA MUNCHED ON a banana, her expression morose. "Why must it be so boring?"

"Because you just recovered from a horrible stomach virus and you don't want it to flare up again." Sammy sank onto the couch next to her with a fresh bowl of buttery popcorn, which she eyed with unconcealed envy. "Unless you like worshipping the Porcelain God."

"The Porcelain God can kiss my ass."

"Already has."

He laughed when she grabbed a handful of popcorn and tossed it at him.

It was Sunday, five days since Sammy woke up and found Olivia hurling her guts out in the bathroom. The first day had been brutal—he'd had no idea someone could throw up *that* much. Although he had a shit ton of work at the bakery, he'd stayed home to take care of her. There was no way he could leave her here, as sick as she'd been, and he didn't know anyone else who could take over nurse duty.

Luckily, Olivia's fever broke the third night. Today was the first day she'd spent outside her bedroom or bathroom since she contracted the VFH—Virus from Hell. Since she wasn't operating at one hundred percent yet, Sammy had whipped up some snacks and fired up Netflix for a chill day in. Too bad she couldn't eat anything other than the so-called BRAT diet—bananas, rice (white), applesauce, and toast (non–whole wheat)—while her stomach recovered.

For a foodie like Olivia, it was hell.

"I texted the other book club girls. None of them got a virus." Olivia's mouth turned down at the corners. "I don't know what happened. My immune system is top-of-the-line. I felt a little weird at dinner but thought that was the alcohol talking."

"You probably came into contact with someone who had it," Sammy said. "Stomach viruses can be contagious."

"Maybe." Horror dawned on her face. "Wait. Does that mean you'll get it? You've been in the same room as me for days!"

"Nah, I don't have any symptoms. They usually surface one or two days after exposure. Plus, I disinfected everything and washed my hands so much they looked like an old lady's."

"That's what I smelled." Olivia sighed. "The wonderful scent of disinfectant."

She wasn't joking. Olivia was one of the few people Sammy knew who *liked* the scent of Lysol.

"If you do get sick, I'll take care of you," she said. "It's only fair."

"Throw in a sexy nurse uniform and we'll be even."

She rolled her eyes. "Seriously?"

"You get gray sweatpants; I get a nurse uniform," Sammy half joked. He wasn't sure how much Olivia remembered from their weird but enjoyable conversations while she'd been sick. He also wondered whether everything she'd said had been true or if they'd been the ramblings of someone suffering from a 102-degree fever.

Olivia's face flushed bright crimson, and Sammy hid a smile. Oh yeah. She remembered the gray sweatpants conversation—and judging by her mortified expression, she'd been telling the truth.

Even now, his body warmed at the memory of her words. C'mon, a beautiful woman telling him his dick was distracting and she wanted to jump him? He'd have to be dead not to have a reaction. That wasn't even taking into account her ramblings about her erotic book club read after she came home drunk—he'd had some interesting dreams about blindfolds and office sex that night.

"Sweatpants? I don't know what you're talking about," she bluffed, but the rapid spread of scarlet across her cheeks and down her neck gave her away. "Sweatpants are sweatpants. Nothing special about them."

"Really?" Sammy leaned back against the couch cushions and tucked an arm behind his head, the picture of lazy confidence. "Not even when paired with a bare chest while I'm cooking?"

Olivia's lips parted, and her eyes hazed over like she was picturing the image in her head.

Sammy's cock jumped to attention. *Fuck*. He'd been teasing her; he hadn't expected her to react like *that*. Like she really was going to jump him and have her dirty way with him.

He had no issues with that whatsoever.

He set his bowl of popcorn aside. "How are you feeling?" he asked gruffly. "Got nausea or anything like that?"

She shook her head.

"Good." Sammy cupped her chin with his thumb and forefinger.

Olivia's eyes widened. "What are you doing?"

He leaned closer until their mouths were centimeters apart. "I'm going to kiss you," he said calmly. "Do you want me to kiss you, Olivia?"

Sammy couldn't believe he was doing this—it was like all reason had fled his body, leaving behind pure instinct and desire, but he couldn't bring himself to care. Reason was an overrated bastard anyway.

The soft sounds of the movie on screen faded, and the world narrowed until he only saw the woman sitting in front of him. Even if they were out in the city, surrounded by thousands of people, she'd still be the only woman he had eyes for.

It'd been that way for nine years.

Olivia gulped and slowly, ever so slowly, nodded.

Victory slammed into him as his mouth crashed over hers and eight years of pent-up longing exploded. He fisted her hair with one hand and tilted her head back for greater access. *Fuck*, she was even sweeter than he remembered. You'd never know she'd been sick. She tasted like she'd been dining on nectar and ambrosia all day.

A breathless gasp slipped out of her mouth as she pressed her chest against his and curled her hands around his biceps. He was rock hard, and he knew she could feel it because her skin had heated beneath his touch and she was grinding against him in little circles that drove him crazy.

Nothing mattered in that moment except this. Her. *Them.*

Sammy didn't break the kiss as he eased her back until she was lying on the sofa and he was straddling her. His cock was ready to burst from the confines of his pants, but even in his lust-addled state, he realized they were moving pretty fuckin' fast for two people who'd resented each other for the better part of a decade.

Whether he cared was another issue.

Olivia moaned and arched her hips up.

Lust scorched through his veins, and he couldn't decide what he wanted more: to continue kissing her senseless, pull her pants down and feast on her sweet pussy, or flip her around and fuck her until she couldn't walk tomorrow.

Hell, it was Sunday morning, and they were both young and healthy. Why choose?

Sammy reached to tug down her yoga pants just as the sound of the doorbell blared through the house.

You've gotta be shitting me.

He groaned in frustration and pushed himself up on his arms, suppressing a litany of curses.

"I didn't know you were expecting someone." Olivia's eyes were bright, her lips swollen from their kiss, and her chest rose and fell with rapid breaths.

It took all of Sammy's willpower not to drag her into his arms again, but if his hunch was correct, their unwelcome visitor wouldn't leave until they got what they came here for.

"I'm not. But I have a feeling I know who it is."

He sat up and took a deep breath, forcing himself to cool down before he walked to the front door, discreetly adjusting himself along the way.

Sure enough, when he opened the door, he found his mother standing on the front stoop, her arms laden with shopping bags from Wah Sing.

"No," Sammy said flatly.

Amy peered up at him, her brows beetling over her nose. "Is that any way to greet your mother?" she demanded with a wounded expression.

He wasn't fooled. "No," he repeated. "You're not setting me up again."

"Did I say anything about setting you up? Did I say one word before my son—the one I birthed after *hours* of labor and *months* of carrying him, the one whom I raised into the big strong man he is today—flung baseless accusations in my face? No." She heaved an enormous sigh and made a plea to the gods in Chinese. "*Lau tian ye*, what did I do to deserve this? Such an ungrateful son. I go all the way to Wah Sing to pick up his favorite foods because he couldn't make it to dim sum, and he won't even let me in his house." Her shoulders drooped. "I'm an old woman. These bags are heavy and—"

"Okay, okay." Sammy pinched the bridge of his nose. Lau tian ye, *what did I do to deserve this?* He loved his mom, he really did, but she was more dramatic than a *Real Housewives* reunion. "I get it. You can come in. I wasn't really going to leave you outside."

Her wounded expression disappeared. "I knew I raised you right."

Amy marched into the kitchen, where a flustered-looking Olivia stood.

"I can help with that," Olivia said when she spotted Amy's grocery bags.

"You don't have to. You're still—"

Sammy's mom interrupted him. "That would be great! Thank you." Her shrewd gaze moved from Olivia's swollen lips to Sammy's tousled hair to the flickering images on the TV. "Have you been hanging out here all day?"

Sammy's shoulders tensed. Before he could run interference, Olivia answered.

"I was sick for a few days and I'm still recovering. Sammy was nice enough to stay with me so I don't get too bored."

"Hmm. Very nice of him, indeed." Amy cut a glance in her son's direction.

Sammy shifted his weight and tried not to look too guilty. He'd told his mom he couldn't make it to dim sum because he had paperwork to catch up on. He hadn't wanted her to get any ideas about him and Olivia.

Too late. He could practically see the mischief fairies dancing with jubilation in her eyes.

After they finished unpacking the groceries, Amy insisted on making Olivia plain congee seasoned with salt and ginger. It was her go-to food when any of her children were sick.

While they waited for the congee to thicken, Sammy's mother dropped her bombshell.

"So," she said, wiping the counter with a damp washcloth. "Did you see Edison's email?"

Edison had sent the world's most obnoxious email to every member of their family who had an email account, detailing the dates, logistics, and schedule for his grand Lake Tahoe celebration weekend. Sammy wasn't sure why he'd bothered—trying to keep all the generations of Yus on schedule while they were on vacation was more futile than trying to sweep water off the shores of a beach.

"Yes."

"Did you see the part where he said a few of us can bring plus-ones? First come, first serve."

Sammy's stomach lurched when he realized where his mother was going with this. "No, I didn't." He shot her a warning look, which she ignored.

"Well, you can! Isn't that great? Since Edison is being so generous—although, if you ask me, it's just a chance for him to show off to more people because he has nothing else going on in his life—you should take him up on it. Free vacation for you and a guest, Sammy! Don't be a fool and give that up. As a matter of fact..." Amy turned to Olivia with a deceptively innocent expression. "Olivia, have *you* ever been to Lake Tahoe?"

Sammy couldn't believe it. His mother had been there to console him after his breakup with Olivia, and now she was inviting Olivia to go on a fucking family trip?

Shit, she really was serious about going through his exes since he hadn't liked any of the new women she'd set him up with. First Lucy, now Olivia.

It was a god-awful idea, but Amy wanted grandchildren enough that Sammy wouldn't put anything past her.

Olivia cast a panicked glance in Sammy's direction. He responded with a subtle shake of his head, already resigned to his mother's shenanigans.

"Um, no—"

"Excellent! You'll join us at Lake Tahoe. It'll be so fun. Good thing I had the foresight to put Sammy down for a plus-one already." Amy clapped her hands. "Ah, I think the congee's ready. Let me get that for you." She bustled over to the stove, humming merrily.

Olivia and Sammy stared at each other, dumbfounded.

What just happened? she mouthed.

He sighed and mouthed back, *Looks like we're all going to Lake Tahoe.*

CHAPTER 15

FOR ONCE, OLIVIA WAS COUNTING DOWN THE MIN-
utes to the end of the workday. Usually, she got so caught up in
work, the hours slipped by, and she'd look up and realize that it
was already seven or eight.

Not today. She couldn't wait to ditch her overly air-conditioned
office and beeline for Chinatown, where she was meeting Sammy
for dinner. Even now, she could feel his lips on hers, firm and
insistent. She could smell him, taste him, hear him—low and raw,
his groans sending shivers of delight down her spine.

She'd had forty-eight hours to process her realization that she
still had feelings for him, and twenty-four hours to replay their
kiss over and over again until she could point out every minute
detail. If his mom hadn't shown up…

Olivia drummed her fingers against her thigh and stared at
the digital clock on her computer. 6:58 p.m. *Almost there…*

She and Sammy hadn't had a chance to talk after their kiss.
His mother had stayed late into the night, chatting away, but
Olivia couldn't shake the feeling that Amy had been watching
her the whole time, examining her like she was a bug under a

microscope. What the older woman was looking for, Olivia had no clue. All she knew was, she wanted to figure out what the hell was going on between her and Sammy *before* she spent a weekend with him and his extended family.

Hopefully, he wouldn't say the kiss had been a mistake. She was still sorting through her exact feelings toward him, but she knew she didn't regret their kiss one bit.

The clock ticked to 7:00 p.m., and Olivia shot out of her seat. Cassidy was still tapping away at her computer like a robot, but a few other people in the office stirred like they, too, were ready to call it a night. Private equity had better hours than investment banking, but eleven- and twelve-hour days were common.

"Where are you off to in such a rush?" Logan grasped Olivia's wrist on her way out. "Hot date?"

She stiffened and leveled a death stare at his hand until he removed it. One of these days, she was going to stab him with a pencil. She really was. "None of your business."

He seemed unfazed by her cold reply. "Hey, if it doesn't pan out, my offer stands. Lots of fun things to do at night around here." Logan winked, and Olivia almost threw up in her mouth.

The entire office could hear them, but no one said anything. In fact, a few of Logan's friends smirked, and one of them slid his gaze over her body in a way that sent shivers of revulsion down her spine.

Fucking assholes. Olivia had put up with more than her fair share of inappropriate and sexist comments over the years, but no one had dared be as overt about it as Logan.

"Thank you, but my idea of fun doesn't involve shotgunning beer and buying another Patagonia vest." Even now, she spotted *five* of the same vests in the room.

She left the office to a chorus of *ooh*s and guffaws. Her coworkers were supposed to be adults, but they acted like overgrown frat boys half the time.

"This is why I'd never stay in San Francisco," she muttered under her breath. The only thing keeping her sane this summer was the thought that she only had to endure Logan and the rest of the Dickface Squad for another month and a half.

Of course, that also meant she only had a month and a half left as Sammy's roommate. The thought depressed her more than it should. But Olivia had officially given up her apartment search, so at least she could enjoy her remaining time with Sammy in peace.

She found him waiting for her at what he claimed was the best dim sum restaurant in the city, looking disconcertingly gorgeous with his wind-tousled hair and gray sweater.

"Hey." He grinned, and she couldn't resist grinning back. Sammy had a smile that instantly improved the receiver's mood. "You ready to get your socks knocked off?"

Olivia responded with a playful harrumph. "We'll see. All your hype has given me high expectations, so don't be surprised if I'm disappointed."

"You won't be. Trust me." Sammy led her inside. "My family comes here every week, and they have the pickiest palates in the Bay Area."

He was right. The dim sum at Wah Sing *was* out of this world. Olivia had never eaten dim sum at night, but hell, she'd tromp down here after work every day just for the shrimp dumplings.

"I need the recipe." She hoovered up another dumpling. "Immediately."

A laugh flew out of Sammy's throat. "You don't cook."

"Not for *me*. For *you*. They give me the recipe, I give the recipe to you, and voila! Dim sum at home."

"Seems like we're missing a few steps," Sammy said wryly. "Like the part where I agree to act as your personal chef."

"You'll be *our* personal chef. Since you'll be cooking for yourself too, it doesn't count as extra work, does it?"

He chuckled. "Finish eating. We've got a lot on our schedule tonight."

He could laugh all he wanted, but she *would* get that recipe. Where there was a will, there was a way.

Olivia hid a devious smile as she thought about all the home-cooked dumplings in her future.

When Sammy found out she hadn't explored much of the city yet because of work, he'd offered to take her on a whirlwind tour of San Francisco at night.

Unlike Logan's sleazy proposition, Olivia took Sammy up on his offer immediately.

Their first stop, which they just completed: food.

Their second stop: after-hours at a science museum.

"This is so cool." Olivia cast an impressed glance at the museum's soaring walls and spotlit exhibits. "The last time I attended an after-hours museum event, Farrah and I got drunk and almost knocked over a priceless statue."

"You could get drunk if you want. There's a themed party in the main hall with a dance floor, DJ, and everything."

"No, thanks. Not tonight." She wrinkled her nose. She was still traumatized from last week's virus. She hadn't contracted it from alcohol, but her mind had linked the two together and she didn't plan on imbibing cocktails anytime soon.

Instead of joining what sounded like an admittedly wild party, they wandered through the exhibits, cracking silly jokes and coming up with crazy stories for the animals they passed along the way. Olivia wasn't a big museum person, but between the interactive demonstrations, the novelty of visiting at night, and Sammy's dry, witty commentary, she was having a blast.

"Do you ever miss it?" she asked as they passed under a tunnel in the aquarium. Brightly colored fish swam over and around them, making her feel like Ariel under the ocean.

"Miss what?" He placed a hand on the small of her back and guided her to the side to allow a group of giggling college girls past. Her traitorous heart fluttered at the small, simple touch.

"Math. Science. You know." Olivia waved a hand in the air. "Do you ever think of going back to those fields?"

"No." A simple answer. "I'm happy with where I am in my career."

"That's good." Olivia fiddled with her bracelet, her heart aching when she remembered how little faith she'd had in him but also bursting with joy because Sammy had done it. He'd made his dream come true, and she was so freakin' proud of him. "I'm happy you're happy. You deserve it. What you've done with the bakery is amazing."

Sammy's throat bobbed. A shadow of an unidentified emotion crossed his face before it disappeared. "Thank you. That means a lot."

They stared at each other, and the world fell away. Olivia wanted nothing more than to kiss him again, but she wasn't sure where they stood, and she didn't want to make things awkward, especially since they were leaving for Lake Tahoe tomorrow.

"Are there any other exhibits you want to see?" Sammy broke eye contact first. "Museum's closing soon."

Disappointment snaked through her, which was silly. What had she expected him to do? Grab her, pin her against the wall, and kiss her senseless with all the fish and other museumgoers watching?

Yeah. Kinda.

"No, I'm good." Olivia pasted on a smile. "What's next?"

The answer: a ride in one of San Francisco's iconic cable cars, which was far less crowded this time of day. In fact, there were only three people in Olivia and Sammy's car besides them and the driver.

Olivia's earlier disappointment faded as the city whizzed by in a blur of lights. The clanging of the bells, the groaning of the car every time they went up and down a hill—it fed the innate sense of adventure that she'd been buried beneath work and school for too long. Whenever they passed a famous landmark, Sammy would throw out a fun fact or piece of trivia. She informed him he would make an excellent tour guide, to which he merely laughed.

They ended the night at Twin Peaks, where they soaked in sweeping views of San Francisco laid out in all its glittering glory. Luckily, there was no fog, and Olivia could see all the way down Market Street, downtown, and the lit-up Bay Bridge. An entire city at their feet, sparkling like a thousand fallen stars.

Olivia shivered, her pulse pounding at the sight. At that moment, she could see herself falling in love with the city. New York was her first love, but there was something magical about seeing San Francisco like this, here, with Sammy by her side. It felt...right.

"You cold?" Sammy wrapped an arm around her shoulders, and she shivered harder—not necessarily from the chill penetrating her layers of clothing.

"A little." She sank deeper into his warm embrace. She wasn't *that* cold—she'd had the foresight to bring her warmest coat—but she *was* a shameless opportunist. So what? Like any woman would turn down the chance to snuggle in Sammy's arms.

"I have an extra jacket in the car. I can grab it."

Olivia snorted. "If I put on another layer, I won't be able to move. I already feel like the Marshmallow Man."

Sammy flashed a crooked grin. "A very cute Marshmallow Man."

She couldn't tell if he was flirting or just being nice. Regardless, her heart rate picked up and her cheeks warmed. At least it was dark and he couldn't see how red she was. "Ha-ha." *Oh God.* Her laugh sounded like a horse braying.

Sammy, fortunately, didn't comment on it.

They sat in companionable silence for another half hour before the cold got too much and they went home.

That was how Olivia had come to think of Sammy's house—as home. The best one she'd ever had, to be honest. She loved the years she'd spent in New York as Farrah's roommate, but whereas that had felt like an endless slumber party with her best friend, living with Sammy felt like home.

Olivia paused in the hall outside her bedroom. "Thanks for tonight. I had a great time."

"Hey, I couldn't let you leave San Francisco without a solid tourist experience."

"It wasn't *that* touristy. I enjoyed it. It was the best night I've had in a while," Olivia admitted. "Also, I *will* get that dumpling recipe and you *will* make them for us both."

"Sure, it's for 'us both,'" Sammy teased, smiling. "You know it's less about the recipe and more about technique, right?"

"I'm sure your technique is great." *Crap, that came out wrong.*

Heat flared in Sammy's eyes, and liquid warmth trickled through Olivia's stomach in response. Should she mention their kiss the other day? Because she *really* wanted to know where they stood—so they could do it again, hopefully.

Screw it. It was now or never.

"Listen, about Sunday and our k—"

"We should get some shut-eye," Sammy interrupted. "Early morning tomorrow."

True. They were leaving for Tahoe at seven—God bless summer Fridays; Olivia didn't have to take personal time off for this trip—but her stomach fell at his blatant dismissal.

"Sure. Uh, see you tomorrow."

In her room, Olivia stripped off her clothes and had just

pulled her nightshirt over her head when she heard a knock on her door. She opened it to find Sammy standing there.

"I forgot something," he said.

Her brow furrowed. "What—"

The rest of her sentence died as Sammy's lips claimed hers and pleasure exploded throughout her body.

Every thought flew out of Olivia's mind. All she could focus on was his heat, his taste, and the hard contours of his body pressed against hers.

She moaned, enjoying the small shudder the sound provoked in him as he backed her up onto her bed. His erection pressed against her stomach, and the need to feel him inside her swirled through her and muddled her thoughts.

Just as Olivia reached to tug off his shirt, Sammy broke the kiss, his face flushed and his eyes gleaming. "That's what I forgot. Good night, Olivia."

She blinked, dazed. "G-good night."

Olivia touched her lips and watched, stunned, as he walked out of the room and closed the door, plunging her in darkness once more.

What the hell just happened?

CHAPTER 16

THE CHALET EDISON RENTED SAT RIGHT ON LAKE Tahoe. Sammy hated to admit it, but Edison had done a bang-up job choosing the place. It was huge—two stories, with seven bedrooms, five bathrooms, and a vaulted living area, as well as an attached rear unit with two additional bedrooms. There was more than enough space to house the entire Yu clan and their plus-ones. But the best feature wasn't the massive fireplace or the tricked-out kitchen—it was the extra-large hot tub in the backyard.

Sammy had been itching to check out the tub all day, but now that he was here, he'd rather drown himself in the lake.

Because guess who was in the tub with him? Olivia, dressed in a bikini that made him glad no one could see what was happening south of the border, so to speak; his twin horndog cousins, Kyle and Lyle (yes, the rhyming was on purpose), who couldn't stop drooling over her; Kevin and Lydia, who kept shooting shit-eating grins in Sammy's direction for no discernible reason; and fucking Edison.

Sammy would have more fun at an execution party with Attila the Hun and Vlad the Impaler.

"Are you sure you're twenty-nine? You don't *look* twenty-nine." Kyle stared at Olivia's chest. "Do you like younger men?"

Sammy groaned while Olivia stifled a laugh. Kyle and Lyle were juniors in college but well on their way to becoming the biggest players in the family. It didn't help that they were both athletes at the University of Michigan—football for Kyle, hockey for Lyle—ensuring they had a steady stream of girls throwing themselves at them. They were so cocky, they made Kanye look humble.

"Thanks. I'll take that as a compliment." Olivia didn't touch the "younger men" question.

"Are you and Sammy dating?" Lyle asked. "He's never brought a plus-one to a family outing before."

"No." Olivia snuck a glance at Sammy, who was too busy fighting the urge to strangle his cousins—all three present—to notice the flash of uncertainty in her eyes. "We're old, uh, friends and current roommates."

"Roommates?" Kyle and Lyle chorused, eyes wide.

"How the hell did that happen?" Kyle pointed an accusing finger at Sammy. "You never told us you had a roommate."

"Because it's none of your business."

"Screw that. Tell us," Kyle pleaded, turning to Olivia.

She laughed and gave a quick rundown of what happened to her apartment. Even Kevin and Lydia got into the story, making sympathetic noises when she told them how half her belongings got ruined and how her landlord offered her a measly $500 as compensation.

"How nice of you to let her stay with you, Sammy-poo." Kevin's grin grew as he used the childhood nickname Sammy despised. "You're a stand-up guy."

"Sammy's always been a gentleman," Lydia piped up. "Don't you agree, Olivia?"

"So, since you're roommates, do you bang every night?" Lyle asked before Olivia could respond. "What?" His tone turned defensive beneath his older cousins' glares. "Isn't that the point of having a roommate of the opposite sex?"

"No, dumbass. Stop making Olivia uncomfortable or I'm kicking you out of the tub," Sammy threatened.

Lyle scowled. "You can't kick me out. It's not your tub."

"*Anyway.*" Edison's loud voice interrupted their bickering. He wore an annoyed frown, clearly irritated that their attention wasn't focused on *him*. "We all know Sammy's great, yadda yadda. But you should've come to me, Olivia." He slicked a hand over his hair. "I'm a lawyer. I could've sued the hell out of your landlord and gotten you a huge settlement. I'm *that* good. Did I tell you I made partner?"

"You made partner?" Kyle's eyes widened, his tone dripping with sarcasm. "Why didn't you tell us earlier?"

Edison had, of course, seized any and all opportunities to brag about his new partner status throughout the day. There was a running bet among some of the Yus as to how many times he would utter the P-word that weekend. Sammy had bet ten bucks on thirty to forty. Hell, they were already at thirteen, and it was only the first day.

He covered up his laugh with a cough as Edison glared at the football player. He took it back—the twins weren't that bad.

"That's all right." Discomfort filled Olivia's face. "I didn't want to sue anyone. I just wanted a clean place to live."

Sammy had been nervous as fuck about seeing Edison and Olivia in the same room before the trip. Memories of their kiss still haunted him, and he'd had no clue what to expect. But the two had mostly ignored each other—which Sammy was more than fine with—until now.

If Edison didn't stop leering at her, he was going to rip off his cousin's arms and beat him to death with them.

In any other circumstance, Sammy's violent thoughts would've alarmed him, but this was Edison they were talking about. He would've been alarmed if he *didn't* have violent thoughts toward the jerk.

"Well, you know you can reach out at any time." Edison smirked. "You have my number."

What the fuck?

Sammy's head snapped toward Olivia, who looked like she wanted to sink beneath the water and stay there. Why the *fuck* did she have Edison's number? Had their kiss been more than a kiss? Had they *dated*, and Sammy didn't know about it?

Lydia leaned over with a worried frown. "You okay? There's a vein throbbing in your forehead," she whispered.

"I'm fine." *Or I will be after I murder Eddie in the most gruesome way possible.*

His sister-in-law looked unconvinced.

"Actually, I don't," Olivia said stiffly. "I got a new phone years ago and lost all my contacts."

Lie. She still had Sammy's contact at least.

"Wait. You guys knew each other before this?" Lyle's head swiveled between Olivia and Edison. "How?"

Olivia's mouth opened, but Edison beat her to the punch. "Oh, we met when I visited Sammy in New York. Remember when he was interning for NASA?" He chuckled. "Good ol' days. Everyone thought he would be a big-time engineer or something along those lines, but he turned out to be a...baker. Which is *fine.* But it ain't NASA. Right, Sammy boy?"

A heavy, awkward silence suffused the air.

"Uh, we're gonna grab some snacks," Kyle said. "Man, we're hungry."

"Yeah, we're growing boys." Lyle chuckled nervously. "Be right back."

The twins hauled ass out of the hot tub and disappeared into the house. Lydia, who hated confrontation, murmured something about checking on Amy and slipped out as well, leaving Kevin, Edison, and Olivia behind.

"Dude, not cool." Kevin glared at Edison.

"What? It's the truth. Besides, Sammy knows I didn't mean anything by it." Edison smirked at Sammy. "Right?"

"Right. But hey, you didn't go to New York to visit *me*, remember?" Sammy lifted his shoulder in a casual shrug. "You went to meet with the dean of Columbia Law."

Edison's face clouded.

"Shame you never convinced him to let you in," Sammy continued. "Not many people would've gone to the extra effort to show up in person to dispute an admissions decision."

"Fuck you," Edison snarled. "I got into *Harvard*. I fucking made *partner* before I'm forty. Who cares about Columbia?"

Updated *partner* word tally: fourteen. Sammy was definitely winning the bet.

"Weren't you on the waitlist for Harvard?" Kevin draped his arms along the edge of the tub. "And didn't you get in after banging the dean's daughter? Funny how that works."

"Shut up, Kevin. You didn't even attend an Ivy League."

Olivia spoke up. "Where you go to school isn't the be-all and end-all." She glared daggers at Edison, and damn if the sight didn't send satisfaction curling through Sammy's stomach. "I know plenty of Ivy League graduates who are jerks or miserable in their job, and plenty of non–Ivy League graduates who are happy and thriving. And I think being your own boss and building a business empire from scratch—the way Sammy did—is way more impressive than being a run-of-the-mill lawyer."

Warmth glowed in Sammy's chest.

"Really?" Edison's eyes glittered with danger. "That's not

what you said when you called and asked me to come over after you and Sammy broke up in New York." He flicked a triumphant glance in Sammy's direction. "Oops. You didn't know that, did ya? But you two were already *kaput*, so there was no reason for you to know."

Just like that, the warmth died, and Sammy's skin iced over. Olivia had *called* Edison? He'd assumed this cousin had come looking for him and they ran into each other. What the fuck was Edison insinuating? Had they done more than kiss? Had they *slept* together?

Sammy wanted to throw up.

Out of the corner of his eye, he saw Kevin's jaw drop and Olivia's face turn bone-white.

"You're a real fucking asshole, you know that?" Kevin shot a death glare at Edison.

"Aw, so sweet that big bro is coming to little bro's defense. Maybe if Sammy wasn't such a pussy—" The rest of Edison's words came out as a strangle when Sammy closed the distance between them and slammed the asshole against the side of the tub. He closed his hand around his cousin's throat—not enough to kill the guy but enough to make him *think* he might kill him.

The smugness melted from Edison's face, replaced with fear.

"Don't mistake my tolerance for weakness," Sammy said quietly. "I put up with you because we're family, but if you say another nasty word toward me or anyone else I care about—if you so much as *look* at us the wrong way—I will rearrange your face until you're unrecognizable to your own mother. And guess what? Other than your parents, no one will care."

Everyone liked Sammy better, and they both knew it.

"Are we clear?"

Edison didn't answer, his features a mask of angry defiance.

Sammy's grip tightened. "I said, 'we clear?'"

"Yes," Edison finally choked out.

Sammy released him, and the other man sagged, clutching his throat.

"You're a crazy son of a bitch," Edison gasped. "I'll fucking sue you for assault."

No, he wouldn't. Edison was too vain and image-conscious to let other people know that Sammy—whom he'd always considered his "weaker" cousin because Sammy had a conscience—got one up on him.

Sammy didn't bother responding. He splashed out of the tub and walked into the house, ignoring Olivia's and Kevin's calls.

Thank God he had his own room in the annex so he could stew by himself. There was an uneven number of guests, and they'd drawn straws to see who would get the single. Sammy had lucked out.

He stopped for a quick shower in the annex's shared bathroom and wrapped a towel around his waist before heading to his room. He felt numb, and the events of the past hour floated through his head like scenes from a movie instead of his messed-up life.

What Edison and Olivia did or didn't do that summer shouldn't bother him, but dammit, it did. Because Edison was his cousin and Olivia had been the love of his life. Because their hookup stabbed at all of Sammy's hidden insecurities about not being good enough or measuring up. Because it was a fucking betrayal, even if Sammy and Olivia had already broken up.

Sammy's shoulders stiffened when he saw Olivia waiting for him outside his room. She must've come straight here after he'd left.

"I'm not in the mood to talk," he said curtly.

She stepped aside so he could open the door, but she followed him inside before he could close it in her face.

"We *have* to talk." Her skin was blotchy and her eyes pleaded for forgiveness, which told him all he needed to know, didn't it?

"No, we don't."

"Nothing happened between Edison and me."

Now she was *lying* to him? Sammy had seen them kissing with his own eyes! She didn't know that, though, and he wondered if she was really going to take the denial route.

"Nothing, huh?" He crossed his arms over his chest. "So you didn't call him after we broke up? You guys didn't hook up, didn't kiss?"

Last night had been the best night he'd had in years, and their kiss had knocked his fucking socks off, but it might as well have happened a lifetime ago. There were zero similarities between last night's easy companionship and tonight's hostile tension.

"We did kiss. Once," Olivia said, her voice so low Sammy almost couldn't hear her. "He made the first move, and I should've pushed him away, but it happened so fast that I—" She exhaled a shaky breath. "It was a mistake, okay? But we didn't do anything more than that, and I called him because of *you*, not because I wanted *him*. I knew you guys weren't close, but I'd hoped he could help me—" She stopped.

"Finish that sentence," Sammy said, his voice hard. "Help you what, Olivia?"

"Help me make you see reason." Her cheeks flushed with guilt. "About the bakery. Or help me make things right with you. I don't know." She shook her head. "I don't know what I was thinking."

"Olivia Tang, doing something without a clear plan?" Sammy mocked. "Excuse me if I don't believe you."

She threw her hands up. "How many times do I have to apologize? I fucked up. I admit it. Can we please move on? I thought we had a truce."

They did—but all truces eventually ended.

"No, we can't. Not yet. You know why?" Anger heated Sammy's stomach, slow and insidious. He stalked toward her, causing her to inch back until she hit the wall and had nowhere left to go. He rested his forearm on the wall above her and a hand to the side of her head, caging her in. "Because I *saw* you kissing him." He chuckled at her horrified expression, but the sound was devoid of humor. "Yeah. You didn't know that, did you? I saw you making out with my fucking cousin, the one you knew I despised, less than an hour after we broke up. You know the worst part? I came back to apologize. I thought I'd been too harsh and that maybe we could work things out. Turns out, the joke was on me. It didn't take you long at all to get over me, did it?"

The scabs on his old wounds had been ripped wide-open, and he was bleeding all over the place, his emotions a groundswell that threatened to drown him.

Olivia's eyes shone with unshed tears. "I didn't get over you, Sammy. I never did."

Sammy's chest cracked in two. "Stop. Lying."

He hated this. Hated fighting and arguing and feeling vindictive. Just when he and Olivia were almost on good terms again, something had to come along and fuck it all up. In this case, that "something" was five feet eight inches of pompous ass with whom Sammy had the misfortune of sharing a family tree.

They couldn't catch a break.

"I'm not lying." Frustration echoed in Olivia's words. "I was young and stupid and let my mom make me doubt myself. I did a lot of things I'm not proud of, but our breakup *destroyed* me. All these years, I held on to my anger over the things you said because it was easier than owning up to the fact that I still want you. I always have." Her lower lip trembled. "I'm not lying," she repeated.

Sammy closed his eyes, the pain and hurt from the past mingling with a seed of hope. He didn't know what to think. Part of him wanted to let bygones be bygones, but this was one of those cases where the mind and the heart did not line up. He hadn't realized how messed up he was from Olivia's rejection all those years ago until now.

He'd proved his naysayers wrong and grown Crumble & Bake into something bigger than he could've imagined, but the knowledge that the person he'd loved more than anything hadn't believed in him? Had been ashamed of his choices, even? That cut deep.

When Sammy opened his eyes again, they glittered with challenge.

"Prove it."

CHAPTER 17

OLIVIA GULPED AS SHE STARED UP AT SAMMY'S HARD, handsome face. Tension poured off him like heat from a stove, and his eyes locked onto hers, making it hard to breathe. The world had narrowed until it was just the two of them and the wild, erratic beats of her aching heart.

Prove it. How?

If she could split her chest open and reveal all the broken pieces of herself, she would, but since she couldn't, she settled for the only option left.

Olivia grabbed Sammy's face and kissed him.

It wasn't the same passionate, lust-fueled embrace as their last two kisses. Yes, the desire was there, but so was everything else she'd ever felt for him—love, longing, regret, joy, anger, sadness, shame, and a million other shades of emotion.

It was funny. She tried so hard to be perfect, but her relationship with Sammy—the messiest, most imperfect thing in her life—was the one thing that made her feel most alive.

Olivia wrapped her arms around his neck and swept her tongue across his bottom lip, seeking entry.

He remained stiff and unyielding until she tugged his hair and gently bit his lip in reprimand for making her wait. A shudder rolled through his body, and he finally yielded, his mouth branding hers with a possessive urgency that left her reeling.

Just like that, the dynamics shifted. Olivia was no longer the one in control; Sammy was. Claiming her, marking her, making her burn with every glide of his tongue and sweep of his palms up her body.

A blast of cold air hit her when he yanked her towel off and tossed it on the ground. It lasted for all of two seconds before he covered her body with his, his heat searing her from the inside out. His towel was gone too, and she could feel every hard, throbbing inch of him between her thighs.

Olivia whimpered with need.

"Is this what you want?" Sammy's voice was low and guttural as he pinched her nipple through her bikini top. Her core clenched at the brief but scorching sensation, and she almost sobbed when he did the same to her other breast. He'd barely touched her, and she was already soaking.

"Yes." She hardly recognized the breathless moan that left her mouth, but she was beyond caring about how wanton she sounded.

"Say it," he ordered, and fuck if that didn't turn her on more. Olivia loved control outside the bedroom, but she had a real weakness for dominant males *inside* the bedroom. It was the one place where she could let someone else take the driver's seat. "Tell me what you want."

"I want you." She whimpered when he pulled back, mourning the loss of his touch.

"You can do better than that." Sammy tsked, looking disappointed. "Be more specific."

"I want you to—" She flushed, her chest hot with embarrassment. "I want you to fuck me."

"Where?"

"Anywhere." The answer slipped out of its own accord.

A wicked gleam entered Sammy's eyes. "You shouldn't have said that."

Olivia didn't have time to react before Sammy picked her up and put her on all fours on the bed. A second later, her bikini was gone, and she was bared to him—body, heart, and soul.

He dragged a finger through her slippery folds, hissing when he felt how wet she was. "Fuck, you're dripping."

Olivia whimpered again and wiggled her hips, urging him to hurry up already. She needed his mouth, his fingers, his cock—*anything*. She was dying here, so turned on the only thing she could focus on was the orgasm teasing her from a distance.

Sammy chuckled. "Oh, no. It's not going to be that easy. I'm still mad at you for kissing Edison, and we'll have to address that before we give you what you want, won't we?"

Her pulse thrummed in her ears. She knew what was coming, and equal parts excitement and fear coiled in her stomach.

"Do you trust me?" He dipped a finger inside her, causing her to moan.

"Yes." Olivia tried to thrust back and finger fuck herself to relieve some of the ache in her core, but Sammy removed his hand before she could get a rhythm going.

A disappointed whine escaped her throat.

"Don't move."

Silky heat pooled between her thighs at his commanding tone, and Olivia obediently stayed still while Sammy grabbed something from the closet behind her. A minute later, he covered her eyes with a soft cotton bandanna and secured it with a tight knot. The room plunged into darkness, heightening her other senses— the smell of wood from the walls and floors mixed with her arousal and Sammy's faint sandalwood scent, the rustle of air as he moved into position, the smoothness of the sheets beneath her hands and knees.

"Grab onto the headboard and put your head down."

Olivia's forehead hit the bed at the same time her fingers curled around the iron bars of the headboard. In this position, with her ass raised and her legs spread, she was even more vulnerable than she'd been on all fours, but she trusted Sammy. No matter her sexual tastes or how much she'd wanted this over the years, he was the only person she'd allow to see her this way— submissive and at his mercy.

She heard his breathing quicken as he glided a palm over the curve of her ass.

"You're going to count for me, baby. Can you do that?"

"Ye—" Olivia didn't get the whole word out before his palm landed on her skin with a sharp crack. She jerked, pain and pleasure radiating from the strike, but she had the mind to count like he'd ordered. "One."

Another slap, this time on her other ass cheek. "Two."

Her body jerked again at the sharp sting. "Three," she bit out.

By the time they reached ten, she was a mess of pain and arousal. Her ass throbbed in rhythm with her core, and her clit was so swollen and tender, she was sure she would come if Sammy so much as touched it.

"Did you learn your lesson?" He was breathing hard, and Olivia wished she wasn't blindfolded so she could see him. Seeing him turned on turned *her* on.

"Yes." Another moan fell out when his tongue touched her skin, and he licked and massaged the burn away. Shivers rolled down her spine, sensitizing every nerve ending and turning her nipples into diamond-hard points.

By the time Sammy finished, she was on the knife's edge of arousal again.

Olivia heard the telltale rip of foil before the bed dipped and the tip of his cock teased her entrance.

"Hold on tight," was the only warning she got before he slammed home.

Olivia cried out in pleasure as she felt his full steel length moving in and out in a fast, hard rhythm that sent her body sliding across the bed and the headboard crashing against the wall. His fingers dug into her hips, and his groans mingled with hers. The air was heavy around them, drenched with arousal and stifling the sounds of skin slapping against skin.

One of his thrusts hit the spot that made her unravel, and she came apart, her screams rising in volume while fireworks of sensation exploded inside her. Her orgasm spread through her like liquid fire, melting her down into a pool of honeyed pleasure.

Olivia was so caught up in the intensity of her orgasm, she didn't notice Sammy had pulled out until she felt him slathering something cool and slick on her ass.

"Remember when you said you wanted me to fuck you anywhere?" He bent forward, his words a whispered breeze across her ear. "This is your one chance to take it back."

She bit her lip, her heart hammering. For the briefest moment, her mind flew to the book club discussion. She'd said she was Team Anal, but in truth, she hadn't done it in years. Not since she and Sammy broke up. She might as well be an anal virgin all over again.

But she had liked it when she did it. She just needed to warm up first.

"I don't want to take it back. Just...go slow, okay? It's been a while."

There was a pause. Her blindfold disappeared, and Olivia had to blink several times before her eyes adjusted to the light again.

Sammy cupped her chin and turned her head so she was looking back at him. His eyes were molten with lust, but there was a sharp, incisive glint in them as he examined her face. "Define *a while.*"

"Eight years."

Surprise blossomed on his face, quickly replaced with pure male satisfaction. "Am I the only man you let fuck you in the ass, Liv?"

Pink stained her cheeks. She was tempted to bluff and tell him that was only because no one else had been interested, but he'd know it was bullshit. No man would turn the act down. Besides, she was so tired of lying and pretending. It hadn't exactly done her much good in the past.

"Yes."

Her word of the night. But fuck, it felt good to give in. To stop resisting. She wanted him, and she wanted him to know it.

Sammy's gaze and touch gentled. No doubt he knew her admission wasn't about the act itself—it was about the trust that came with it.

He resumed his ministrations, and once he'd applied the adequate amount of lube, he slowly inserted a finger into her ass. Olivia tensed at the invasion. She was mentally prepared, but her body remained skittish.

"Relax," he murmured. "That's it. Good girl."

More slow thrusts.

Olivia closed her eyes, trying to get used to the sensation. *Breathe. Just breathe.*

Eventually, the alien, uncomfortable feeling faded, and she squirmed with need again—especially when Sammy started lapping up her juices with his tongue while he worked her from behind.

"Oh, God!" Olivia's back bowed as he scraped his teeth

over her clit and finger fucked her pussy with his free hand. *"Ohgodohgodohgod."* The knot of pleasure at the base of her spine tightened. "I'm going to come. I'm going—"

He inserted a second finger into her ass, and she exploded for the second time that night. Olivia went crazy, her hips bucking and thrashing as a wave of orgasmic bliss swept over her and left her gasping for breath.

Sammy kept his mouth on her until she came down. Only after she collapsed on the bed in a boneless heap did he clean them both off with tissues, crawl up, and brush his lips over the back of her neck.

"How do you feel?"

"Fucking amazing," Olivia said, eliciting a soft laugh. She turned to look at him. "But you didn't..."

"Next time. You're too tight. We'll work up to it."

It was stupid, but the promise of "next time" got her all hot and bothered again.

Her eyes dipped to Sammy's still-rock-hard cock. "Okay," she murmured throatily. "But in the meantime, how about I take care of that for you?"

Sammy didn't get a chance to respond before she shifted positions and engulfed him in her mouth, earning herself the world's sexiest groan. She pulled back and took him in again, and again, and again, each time taking more of him until he hit the back of her throat. She worked him over with her lips and tongue, licking and swirling and sucking until she felt him stiffen.

"Coming," he gritted out, his hands tightening in her hair.

Olivia doubled down and increased her pace until he flooded her mouth, his hoarse cry echoing in the room, and she didn't pull away until she'd swallowed every drop.

She glanced up, her lids heavy.

Sammy's face was flushed, his eyes bright with arousal. She'd never seen anything hotter in her life.

"Did that convince you?" She swiped a tongue over her bottom lip, and he groaned again.

After he regained a semblance of control, he hauled her to her feet, his gaze roaming her face. "I'm convinced you want me in bed," he said. "But that's never been our problem, has it?"

Definitely not. Their sexual chemistry was liable to set the room on fire if they weren't careful.

"No. The problem was…" Olivia faltered. She'd never been big into the whole self-martyr thing because there were better uses of her time, but she was also willing to admit when she'd been wrong. She was the one who'd set their relationship on its downward spiral, starting with her refusal to support him when he announced he wanted to open a bakery and ending with her ill-advised kiss with Edison. Granted, the kiss had happened after she and Sammy broke up, but now that she knew Sammy saw them, she understood why he'd been angry at her for so long. "Me." She swallowed hard. "The problem was me."

Sammy's face softened. "No, it wasn't. You were never a problem, so don't say that shit again."

"Sam—"

"Hold that thought." He walked over to the dresser and pulled out a T-shirt, which he handed to her. "I don't want you to freeze while we're having this conversation."

Olivia realized then that, duh, they were both still naked.

She slipped his shirt over her head. It was so large, it fell to her thighs, and she detected faint notes of Sammy's scent clinging to the material.

It wasn't until Sammy also got dressed and they were sitting on the bed that she continued speaking.

"It was me," she said. "I didn't support you, and I *was*

ashamed that you chose baking over NASA. Plus, the Edison thing…" She picked at the hem of the shirt. "I shouldn't have called him."

Sammy blew out a breath. "It wasn't just you. I said some pretty hurtful things too. I knew what a sensitive topic your mother and sister were, and I threw it in your face." He shook his head. "We were both at fault, but the problem wasn't you or me. The problem was *us*."

Olivia's skin chilled. "What does that mean?"

"It means we were young and naive. We loved each other, but it wasn't enough. Our lives were going down different paths and neither of us was mature enough to handle it. If we hadn't broken up, we would've had to deal with different obstacles— you in New York, me in Cali. Even if I stayed in New York, you'd have worked crazy hours in banking while I worked crazy hours building a bakery from scratch. We never would've seen each other, and I'm not convinced that wouldn't have been the death of us eventually." His eyes grew sad. "I think we knew that deep down, and I think the thought freaked us out to the point where we lashed out. We weren't ready for what the real world had to throw at us. Sometimes," he said softly, "it's not about love. It's about timing."

Everything he said made sense, and it had already happened, so Olivia wasn't sure why her heart ached so much. Maybe it was because deep down, beneath the layers of logic and practicality, she was a romantic at heart, and the idea that love wasn't enough to conquer all depressed the hell out of her.

"What about now?" she asked. "How's our timing now?"

Emotion flared in his eyes before it dimmed. "You're only in SF for the summer. Stanford for another year. After that, you're back in New York. I wouldn't say the timing is great now either."

Olivia was quiet for a long moment while her brain whirred,

spitting out pros and cons and hypotheticals so fast she almost couldn't keep up. "I don't *have* to go back to New York," she said, watching his face carefully. "I've worked in the SF branch all summer, and I've done a good job. I'm sure I could convince management to let me transfer here if I wanted."

Sammy's eyes widened. "Are you saying—" He cleared his throat. "You would move to SF for me?"

"Who says I'm doing it for you? I could be doing it for me," she teased, because hey, she couldn't give him *all* the power. "*But* if that's the only thing standing between us, then I...wouldn't be opposed to asking for a transfer."

"Us?" This time, Sammy's tone was teasing.

"If you want there to be an 'us' again." Olivia hated being this vulnerable. She wanted to sink into the floor out of embarrassment, but it had to be done. Trying to act all tough because of her pride had netted her nothing but trouble in the past. "Because I do. Out of all the guys I've dated—"

Sammy scowled.

"—you're the one I've never been able to let go of." *I'm falling in love with you all over again.* She bit back the confession—it was too soon for that—but it was true. All it took was a few months near Sammy and she'd gotten sucked in all over again. His charm, his humor, and his intelligence—not to mention those abs—paired with their chemistry and the way her heart flipped every time she saw him? She hadn't stood a chance. "I agree we were young and naive the first time, but we're not *that* young and naive anymore." She let out a shaky laugh. "We could make it work. I *want* to make it work."

Sammy yanked her toward him, squeezing her so tight it was hard to breathe. "Liv." Gravel filled his voice. "Fuck."

Was that a good fuck *or a bad* fuck?

Olivia buried her face in his chest, trying to enjoy this moment while it lasted in case the answer was the latter. Perhaps having this conversation while they were stuck on vacation together may not have been the best idea. If he broke her heart again tonight, Olivia wasn't sure she could put up a happy face for the rest of his family tomorrow.

Sammy pulled back and stared at her. "When we broke up, I thought you ruined my life," he said. "I couldn't eat. I couldn't sleep. I was a pathetic mess—just ask my friends. And no matter how many years passed or how many dates I went on—"

This time, Olivia was the one who scowled. The thought of Sammy so much as smiling at another woman made her want to scratch said woman's eyes out.

"—I never recaptured that spark we had. With you, I felt my emotions to the fullest. Joy, anger, sadness...both the good and the bad. But with everyone else, I was a shadow of the person I could be." He swallowed hard. "Then I realized, you didn't ruin my life. You ruined me for other women."

Olivia's head snapped up in shock.

Sammy flashed a crooked smile. "So yeah, to answer your question, I want to make it work too. Otherwise, I'm fucked."

Her tears blended with her laughter, which seemed appropriate because she was a hot mess. "How romantic."

"Thanks. I thought so."

Olivia smiled before growing serious again. "So are we really doing this? You and me?"

Between Edison and their sex session and this conversation, the night had been a roller coaster of emotions. Everything seemed so sudden, but when she thought about it, they'd been building toward this moment for a while. From the minute she called Sammy the night her apartment flooded, this—them—was a foregone conclusion. Because she'd known, deep down, that Sammy would show up. He was just that type of guy. She hadn't anticipated becoming roommates with him, but she had known she was opening the door for him to enter her life again beyond a few secret glances at mutual friends' get-togethers.

Their attraction had never died. Maybe their love hadn't either. It'd just been buried and covered with the disguise of hate.

Now that their past had been laid out and stripped bare, and there were no more secrets between them, maybe they could finally move on.

Whether they'd do so together remained to be seen.

"You and me, part two." Sammy sealed the promise with a soft kiss. "Let's do it."

CHAPTER 18

THE REST OF THE WEEKEND PASSED WITHOUT INCI-
dent (unless one counted all the times Sammy and Olivia snuck
off to make out and have sex). Sammy must've scared Edison off
for good because his cousin didn't so much as glance in his or
Olivia's direction after the hot tub incident.

Good. Sammy hadn't been kidding—he really would've
punched Edison's lights out had he said or done anything
untoward.

Did he feel bad about his threat considering Edison was the
one bankrolling the weekend? A little, but not enough to take
back his words. Edison had the money, and Sammy had put up
with him for almost thirty years. Hell, he deserved the whole
freakin' chalet for not snapping earlier.

With the specter of Edison's snide remarks gone and his relationship with Olivia renewed, Sammy had a blast at Lake Tahoe.
He went hiking, fishing, mountain biking, paddle boarding—all
the things he couldn't do in the city. Sometimes Olivia joined him;
other times she parked herself lakeside with her latest read and
baked herself into a golden bronze color. He didn't mind—those

books always got her going, and they were a source of...interesting scenarios she liked to reenact in the bedroom.

He also won the family bet. Final count for how many times Edison uttered the word *partner* over the weekend? Thirty-six.

It wasn't all fun and games, though. They had more hard conversations about the future, including what they were going to do when Olivia left for Stanford or if her company turned down her request for a transfer. Although Palo Alto wasn't far, business school was a killer, so she wouldn't have much free time once classes resumed.

Unlike in college, these conversations focused on reality, not fantasy. That meant they might not always have the answers, but at least they wouldn't be blindsided when real life crept up on them as it had a habit of doing.

By the time Sammy and Olivia left Lake Tahoe, it was an open secret they were hooking up again, though they hadn't told anyone they were officially dating yet. Sammy swore he saw his mother's eyes mist over with happy tears when she waved goodbye.

"Tip: never give her your number," Sammy said as they entered his house. It felt good to stretch his legs after four hours of sitting in a car—it would've been three, but traffic was hellish on Sunday evenings. "She'll blow up your phone with 'subtle' hints about how she's getting old and how much she wants to hold her grandchildren before she dies."

"Ah, Asian-mom guilt. I know it well." Olivia's eyes sparkled with laughter. "Don't give her my number. Got it. Except I already did."

Sammy stared at her in horror.

"She ambushed me," Olivia said defensively. "She told me she needed an emergency contact in case she couldn't reach you. She looked so worried... Asian-mom guilt, remember?"

"Oh, Liv." He patted her on the shoulder. "You have no idea what you got yourself into."

She responded with a puppy-dog look. "I don't. Make me feel better?"

He did. Gladly, and multiple times.

The next two weeks passed in a blur. Sammy and Olivia spent their days texting each other during work breaks, their weekends exploring the city, and their nights doing things that would make a porn star blush.

Sammy had forgotten how *good* dating Olivia felt. How much he laughed, how excited he got when her name popped up on his phone or when he finally saw her after work—which, by the way, was a pain in the ass. Not the baking part but the management part. The paperwork and minutiae that came with the expansions in DC and New York made Sammy want to bang his head against the wall, and he would rather eat glass than have to sit through another Zoom call about licenses and tax filings.

"Have you thought about hiring a CEO?" Olivia asked one night after a particularly steamy session between the sheets where Sammy finally divested her of her second anal virginity. Was that a thing? Maybe not, but even after weeks of easing her into it, she'd still been so tight, Sammy had resorted to picturing his grandparents' dentures and mentally reciting the 49ers' entire roster in order to not blow his load early. "Someone who can run the management side of things while you do what you do best?"

"What's that?" Sammy asked lazily. He cupped her breast with one hand and swept his thumb over her nipple until it peaked beneath his touch. He lowered his head and flicked his tongue over the hard nub, enjoying the way Olivia's breath hitched in response.

"Baking," she breathed. A low moan escaped her throat when he turned his attention to her other breast.

"You sure that's what I do best?" He tugged gently on her nipple with his teeth and sucked hard before releasing it with a pop.

"At work, at least." Olivia rolled her hips up to meet his.

"Hmm. I'll think about it." Hiring a CEO was a good idea, but Sammy was too distracted to think through the details right now. His hand inched between her legs, where he found her wet and ready for him.

"I can help you look—*ohmygod*."

They didn't speak again for a good half hour, unless you considered screaming and groaning *speaking*.

After the postcoital bliss faded, Sammy draped an arm over Olivia's shoulder and pulled her close. As much as he loved the sex, this was his favorite part of the night. Just lying next to her, talking to her, knowing she was all his and he was all hers.

"I wish Kris's wedding were this weekend." Olivia switched topics from their earlier discussion and snuggled closer to Sammy, draping one leg over his and one arm over his stomach. "Would give me an excuse to avoid the terror of Tangs."

"The terror of Tangs?"

"You know how a group of lions is called a pride and a group of wolves is called a pack? Well, a group of Tangs is called a terror. Specifically, if said group includes my mother, sister, and future brother-in-law."

Sammy coughed to hide his laugh. "Technically, your brother-in-law isn't a Tang. Neither is your sister after she marries him."

"You know what I mean," Olivia grumbled. "Whose side are you on anyway?"

"Yours, of course." He ran an absent-minded hand through her hair. "How long are they here for?"

"Just the weekend, but that's long enough. They want to have brunch." She sounded about as excited as a kid who'd just been told Christmas was canceled.

"Brunch is bad?"

"The last time we had brunch together, my mother made the waiter cry and my sister made us listen to her keynote speech for an upcoming conference. Three times."

Sammy winced. "Ouch. Do you want—" He hesitated. "If you need moral support, I'm here." *If you need me to go with you, I can,* he clarified in his mind. But he didn't want to be presumptuous and invite himself to a family affair. Besides, the last time Olivia's mother entered the picture, Olivia hadn't been too keen on introducing him.

This was a different situation, though. He wasn't some wannabe baker who'd turned down a once-in-a-lifetime job at NASA. He was a *successful* baker, businessman, and all that jazz. But what if that wasn't enough?

Sammy forced himself to step back from his self-pity party. The problem with the past was that it was a bitch to shake off, no matter how much you wanted to leave it in the rearview mirror. But he was trying.

"...handle it," Olivia was saying. "I may need one of your cupcakes to console me afterward."

"Done." He kissed the top of her head. "Speaking of Kris's wedding," he said, bringing them back to the original subject. "Did you buy your tickets for Italy already?"

"Not yet. Kris offered to fly all the bridesmaids out, but we agreed it was too much, considering she's already paid for so many things she didn't need to, like accommodations at the freakin' *castle* where she's holding the wedding." Olivia traced a circle on his abs. "I set a low-fare alert for SF to Tuscany, but it hasn't gone off yet. I might buy my ticket tomorrow, though. The date's getting close, and Tuesdays are the cheapest day to book flights."

Sammy grinned. *What an Olivia response.*

"I was planning to buy mine tomorrow too." He'd wanted to book his flight earlier, but he'd been so busy, it'd slipped his mind. He only remembered when Nardo texted him asking if Kris had *really* put a $600 cheese tray on her wedding registry, considering she didn't even like cheese.

The short answer: yes. It wasn't even the most expensive item on the registry. The whole thing was a little rich for Sammy's blood, but a majority of Kris's wedding guests were big Hollywood types, so they could afford it. Sammy himself had stuck with a (slightly) more reasonably priced Le Creuset pot for a wedding gift.

"How about we buy ours together? Would be nice to have some company on a long flight, and as Tahoe proved, we travel well together."

Olivia's eyes gleamed with amusement. "We traveled together before that," she said, referring to their study-abroad adventures. Even back then, Kris had been extravagant in her spending and had paid for their group of friends to spend a weekend in Macau for Courtney's birthday.

"That was different. That was part of a group. This will be just the two of us. So?" Sammy tried to sound casual. "What do you think?"

For some reason, this felt like a turning point. He wasn't asking her to vacation together as a couple per se—because Kris's wedding technically wasn't a vacation—but flying and showing up in Italy together seemed oddly intimate.

If she said yes, that was.

Olivia propped herself up on one elbow and planted a soft kiss on his lips. "I think it sounds great. Hey, maybe we can join the Mile-High Club."

Sammy laughed, if only because the chances of Olivia having sex in a dirty, cramped airplane bathroom were slim to none.

This was the same woman who would rather dehydrate herself on purpose than risk having to use a plane restroom.

"Only if we get upgraded to first class, though," she added. "And only after the restrooms pass my hygiene check. I'll bring some extra Lysol wipes just in case...what? Why are you looking at me like that?"

"Never change, Liv." He chuckled. "Never change."

The next morning, Sammy had a YouTube baking tutorial shoot, an interview with a local culinary magazine, and a meeting with his operations manager, so he didn't show up at Crumble & Bake until well past noon.

He was accosted the moment he stepped inside the shop.

"You!" A short stocky man with a 49ers cap and a startling resemblance to a bulldog jabbed his finger in Sammy's direction. "You're the asshole who's sexting my girlfriend!"

What the fuck?

Sammy cast a glance at Bryce, who gave a helpless shake of his head. He'd always been the nicer, less confrontational of Sammy's two front house managers. Cordelia was off today—otherwise, she would've shut this nonsense down already.

Luckily, the bakery was empty, though it wouldn't be long before the lunch rush started.

"Sir, I think you have the wrong person." Sammy was tired, hungry, and in no mood for any bullshit, but as the business owner, he had to keep his cool.

"Nah. It's you." Bulldog glared at him. "Sammy Yu."

Well, fuck.

"I assure you, I'm not sexting anyone, least of all your girl-friend." Sammy had been paranoid about cybersecurity ever since his Instagram got hacked a few years ago, and he knew better than to send anything too personal out in cyberspace. He didn't even sext Olivia.

"Yeah? That's not what the naked picture my girlfriend sent you says." Bulldog's eyes glinted with anger.

Double fuck.

Sammy sometimes received raunchy photos and messages on his social media accounts, but he never responded. He sure as hell never sexted any of his female fans.

"Did you see me message her back?"

Bulldog flushed. "You didn't get a chance before I made her block your ass."

Sammy almost laughed out loud. "With all due respect, this seems like an issue between you and your girlfriend." *Especially if you distrust her enough to go through her social accounts.* Then again, if she was sending naked pics to other men, perhaps some distrust was warranted. Either way, it wasn't his problem. "That being said, I'm going to have to ask you to leave the store, sir. This isn't the time or place to air personal grievances."

Lady Luck shone down on Sammy at that moment because the door jangled open and Officer Mike, a regular who stopped by several times a week for donuts (fulfilling every pop culture stereotype about his profession), walked in dressed in full uniform.

"Hey, Sammy." He glanced between Sammy and Bulldog with a curious expression.

"Good afternoon, Officer." Sammy stared at Bulldog, who scowled but backed down.

"This isn't over." Bulldog stormed out, and Sammy released a long-held breath.

Jesus. The last thing he needed was boyfriends jacked up on testosterone causing trouble in his shop. Nothing like that had ever happened before, but there was a first time for everything—unfortunately.

"Everything all right?" Mike asked.

"Nothing I can't handle." Sammy shook it off. Hopefully, Bulldog wouldn't swing by again, but if he did, Sammy was calling the cops. "The usual?"

Mike always ordered the salted caramel chocolate donut.

The officer grinned. "You know it."

The rest of the day passed uneventfully, thank God, but the Bulldog situation had already soured Sammy's mood. He really hated social media sometimes. He'd liked it fine when he was a private user, but as a semipublic figure, the shit he had to deal with was draining. He knew he shouldn't complain, considering his success on social media had played a huge role in getting him where he was now, but he'd never wanted to be famous. He just wanted to bake. Now, because he had a certain number of followers and had been on the cover of a few magazines, everyone felt entitled to him, like he was a piece of public property.

Sammy retreated into his office and rubbed his eyes, staring at the mountain of papers waiting for his signature. He swore, they multiplied every time he left the room. He didn't remember there being so many documents yesterday.

He got to work, dutifully reading and signing paper after paper until his vision blurred. How was he more exhausted sitting at his desk than running around the kitchen during peak hours?

"Liv was right," he muttered, pressing his pen so hard to the page he broke its nib. *Shit.*

He really needed to hire a CEO.

CHAPTER 19

"YOU SHOULDN'T WEAR SHORTS, OLIVIA. YOU DON'T have the thighs for them." Eleanor Tang surveyed her younger daughter with a critical eye. "Have you tried working out?"

Olivia pressed her lips together. "Yes, Mother. I work out every day." Sex counted, right? At Stanford, she usually went for a morning jog, but the streets near Sammy's house were too hilly. That type of cardio was above her pay grade.

"Interesting." Eleanor reached for her water glass, her tastefully sized emerald ring flashing in the light. "Perhaps you should step it up. You don't want to get fat."

Eleanor Tang, the Queen of Political Correctness. *Not.*

"I think her thighs look great." Richard winked and stared at Olivia like he could see right through her clothes. "Men like a little meat on their women's bones."

Ugh. Their food hadn't even come yet, and Olivia already wanted to hurl.

I should've taken Sammy up on his offer. While she didn't want to subject him to her family's company, she could have used a friendly face. As it stood, she had to deal with the terror of Tangs on her own.

"What are you trying to say?" Alina asked playfully. She, of course, was a perfect size zero and had been her entire postpubescent life.

Olivia was slim by any standard except Eleanor's, but she wasn't a size zero and had no desire to be one. She liked her hips and thighs, thank you very much.

"You know you're beautiful." Richard kissed Alina's cheek.

Alina giggled, Eleanor beamed, and Olivia rolled her eyes.

"How's the house hunt going?" Olivia changed the subject.

"It's not a hunt per se, because Richard and I don't know if we're moving here for sure yet, but I have to say, I'm loving San Francisco." Alina leaned back to allow their server to set their food on the table. "We saw some great houses yesterday. Didn't we, Mom?"

"They were acceptable," Eleanor acknowledged. "But not perfect. Keep looking."

The meal dragged on. Olivia was convinced she'd been sitting there—downing mimosa after mimosa to soothe her nerves—for days, but in reality, brunch lasted less than two hours. Their conversation topics were the same as always: Alina's wedding, Alina's job, Richard's job, Eleanor's social obligations, etc.

Olivia's dad had left them when she was less than a year old, but Eleanor had gone through three more marriages since then—all to wealthy, successful men who were the polar opposite of Olivia's deadbeat father and who left Eleanor a good chunk of their money in their divorce settlements. Say what you wanted about Olivia's mother, but she was a master at manipulating men into forgoing a prenup. Her last husband had parted with several million dollars and his summer house on Lake Michigan.

"Olivia, where are you living right now?" Alina asked, finally realizing that none of them had asked about Olivia or her life since the discussion about her thighs. Not that she minded—the less her family knew, the better. They were more critical than Simon Cowell in his worst *American Idol* days. "Maybe we should look into that neighborhood too."

Olivia gulped down another mouthful of orange juice and champagne. No way was she telling them she was living with Sammy. Her mother had a steel-trap memory, and she'd definitely remember Sammy as the guy who threw away a NASA career to be a baker. Sammy may be successful, but Eleanor's tolerance for creative types hovered near the same level as her tolerance for public transportation and white after Labor Day, aka close to zero.

"You don't want to live there," Olivia said. "The place isn't, uh, in the best neighborhood."

Sammy lived in an excellent neighborhood, but her family didn't need to know that. The thought of any of them coming within a mile radius of him made her stomach churn. She wanted to protect him from the Tangs at all costs.

Alina's eyes widened. "It's not in..." She lowered her voice to a whisper. "*The ghetto*, is it?"

"*No*, and don't use that word. It's offensive."

"Why?"

"I don't think it's offensive," Richard added.

Olivia sighed. There was no use in explaining. She'd tried multiple times in the past, but it always went unacknowledged and led to heated arguments.

"By the way, I meant to tell you earlier, but it slipped my mind with everything else I had going on." Alina sipped her drink. "I received an invitation to speak at a conference the weekend of my bachelorette, so I moved the celebration up. My bachelorette is now the weekend of September nineteenth."

Olivia's french toast turned to ash in her mouth. "*What?*"

"Is that a problem? I thought that was a suitable alternative."

"That's the weekend of Kris's wedding." Olivia strove to maintain control. "I've talked about it for months, and I already bought my tickets for Italy."

"You have?" Alina blinked.

"Yes." Irritation pumped through Olivia's veins. "Is there another alternative? Maybe you can decline the conference invite. You've had the bachelorette date set for a year."

Alina's face collapsed into a frown. "I can't decline the invite. It's the most prestigious conference in my field. One of their original speakers pulled out, and they're counting on me. Plus, September nineteenth is the only weekend that works for all the bridesmaids."

"Except me." The metal from Olivia's fork dug into her hand. "I didn't realize you'd already checked with everyone else before you told me."

"I was going to tell you earlier." A defensive note crept into Alina's voice. "Like I said, I forgot."

"Olivia, this is your sister's bachelorette," Eleanor cut in. "Your *only* sister. You have other friends besides Kris. Family comes first."

Olivia's head was *this close* to pulling a Mount Etna and exploding. "I'm a bridesmaid in Kris's wedding."

"You're a bridesmaid in Alina's wedding too."

"Well, maybe if I'd been the maid of honor—since I'm her only sister and all—we wouldn't have this problem," Olivia snapped. "I would've sorted out the logistics better."

Alina paled, but Eleanor looked bored. "Don't tell me you're still upset about that. Holding a grudge is not classy."

"You know why I asked Kayla!" Alina burst out, causing their mother to shoot her favorite daughter a rare frown. Eleanor despised scenes. "She lives in Chicago, she enjoys planning, and you're always so busy. I thought I was doing you a favor so you could focus on school instead of worrying about my wedding. You didn't want to be my maid of honor anyway."

Olivia was so done with this conversation, this brunch, this whole *day.*

"Fine, whatever. You're right. But I'm sorry to say that I won't make it to your bachelorette because I'll be in Italy. Now, if you'll excuse me, I need to use the ladies' room." She pushed her chair back, stood, and speed-walked to the restroom, blinking back tears.

It was dumb for her to feel so hurt over her sister's bachelorette party, considering she'd been dreading the event, but it was further proof that Eleanor and Alina barely listened to her or considered her a part of the family.

Olivia had come to terms with her father's absence in her life. She'd never known the guy, and she had no interest in seeking him out. Any man who walked away from his family didn't deserve her energy. Her mother and sister were different. She'd grown up with them, and she had no clue why they disliked her so much. The one time she tried to bring it up with them, her sister had interrupted because her Pottery Barn order had arrived and needed her attention, and her mother had dismissed her as being "paranoid."

Olivia splashed cold water on her face and fought to regain control of her emotions. *Fuck it.* Kris had been more of a sister to her than Alina had ever been, and she wouldn't feel guilty about choosing Kris's wedding over Alina's bachelorette.

The restroom door opened. She didn't pay attention to the newcomer until she heard a familiar male voice.

"How're you doing?"

Olivia yelped and glared at Richard, who leaned against the wall with a smirk, looking every inch the preppy douche in a pale blue button-down shirt and pink pants.

"This is the women's restroom," she snapped. "Just because you're wearing pink, doesn't mean you belong here."

"I wanted to check on you. You seemed upset." Richard walked over, faux concern shining on his face. "I totally get it. It's a bummer, missing your sister's bachelorette."

"Sure. Now get the fuck out."

"I can make you feel better." He ran the back of his finger down her cheek, and she shuddered with revulsion. "I've always thought you were hot. Different from Alina, but hot." He leered at her legs. "I know you're attracted to me too. We don't live in the same city, which is a shame, but Alina and Eleanor are going to a wine tasting tonight that I'm skipping. Our hotel room will be free for hours..."

Olivia gaped at him, certain she was hearing wrong. Was her sister's fiancé seriously *propositioning* her in a public bathroom in the middle of brunch with said sister? And was he seriously asking her to come over to *the hotel room he shared with Alina?*

He either had a serious abundance of balls or a serious lack of brains. She'd bet on the latter.

"Are you fucking kidding me? I am in no way, shape, or form attracted to you." Olivia stepped back, her stomach roiling with disgust. "I also don't think my *sister*—who's sitting *right outside*—would appreciate your invitation."

Richard didn't look fazed. "Hey, it was worth a shot. Good way to get back at her, you know what I mean?" He winked. "If you change your mind, you know where to find me."

He sauntered out, looking for all the world like he hadn't offered to cheat on his soon-to-be wife.

What. The. Fuck.

Olivia pressed the heel of her palm to her eye, struggling to sort through what just happened. She'd always known Richard was an asshole, but she hadn't thought he was idiotic enough to act on his sleazy impulses. Judging by how casually he'd walked out of here, he wasn't at all concerned that Olivia would tell Alina—or, if she did, that Alina would believe her.

Which begged the question: Was he right?

Olivia's conscience demanded she tell Alina, but there was a real possibility her sister would think she was lying. Richard had Alina wrapped around his pampered finger. But Olivia had to try, right? Or would it just drive a deeper wedge between her and her family? Eleanor for sure wouldn't take her side. Her mother and sister would probably think she was jealous and trying to break up Alina's engagement because she was a bitter shrew or something.

Olivia groaned and covered her face with her hands.

Her day had gone from bad to worse to hall-of-fame hellish.

CHAPTER 20

WHEN IT RAINED, IT POURED.

The Monday following Olivia's disastrous family brunch, fog drenched most of the city in an eerie mist and put a damper on her mood before she'd even arrived at the office.

Once she did, she beelined straight to the kitchen for her caffeine fix. She was waiting for the espresso to brew when Logan breezed in, wearing a pink button-down the exact shade of Richard's pants at brunch.

Was that color in the Douche Nozzle Handbook or something?

"Morning, Olivia." He raked his eyes over her body. "You should wear that skirt more often. It makes your ass look *good.*"

Maybe it was because she was still chafing from her encounter with Richard or maybe it was because she hadn't had her coffee yet and it was too early for this shit, but Olivia was *over* Logan's creepy-ass comments.

She'd held her tongue in the past, afraid of rocking the boat when she was so close to what she wanted career-wise, but honestly? Fuck him. Logan was a harassing asshole and not even *that* good at his job. Olivia was better, and everyone knew it. She'd only been at the San Francisco office for two months, but Michael had already assigned her to some of the most high-profile projects. Case in point: Ty Winstock.

Sure, Winstock was still stringing them along, but he hadn't signed with any other firm, and he'd asked for Olivia by name during his last check-in with Michael.

She wasn't naive enough to think she was indispensable, but she was a huge asset to the company and PHC was all about the profit-loss margin.

With that in mind, Olivia slammed her mug on the counter and whirled around, not bothering to hide her ire. "Please do not comment on my attire or my body. It's inappropriate and makes me uncomfortable."

A startled look slid into Logan's eyes before he waved her response off with a smirk. "C'mon, I was just complimenting you. No need to get your panties in a twist."

Olivia was glad her coffee wasn't ready; otherwise, she would've poured the scalding hot liquid over his head and earned herself an assault charge.

"It may not have been your intention, but I *am* uncomfortable." She had to walk a fine line here—make Logan realize his comments weren't okay without outright accusing him of sexual harassment. Office politics were a tricky beast, and despite her contributions to PHC, Olivia wasn't confident enough in her standing to take on someone who'd been with the company longer than she had. Plus, Wall Street culture wasn't known for being female-friendly. "I would appreciate it if you kept your comments to work-related matters. I'm sure HR would agree."

She couldn't resist throwing in the last part. Otherwise, she was sure Logan would ignore her request.

His face darkened at the veiled threat. "Fine," he said in a clipped tone. "I was trying to be nice, seeing as how you're new to this office and all, but I'll stick to 'work-related' matters like you want. Quick tip from someone who's been here for a while, though? It never hurts not to be a bitch." He stormed off.

Olivia's hands shook as she poured her coffee. She'd done what she had to do, but dammit, it wasn't even nine thirty on a Monday morning and she was already drained.

She wished she could deal with the Richard issue in the same manner, but family was even more complicated than office politics. She hadn't decided whether she'd tell Alina what happened, but she needed to, fast—Alina and Richard's wedding was in three months.

"Don't worry about Logan."

Olivia jumped in surprise. Luckily, she caught herself before her coffee spilled all over the front of her white shirt. That would've been the poison cherry on top of a shit sundae.

"Sorry. I didn't mean to startle you." An uncomfortable-looking Cassidy stood in the doorway. She shifted from foot to foot. "I didn't mean to eavesdrop either."

"It's fine." Olivia placed a hand over her racing heart. "How long have you been standing there?"

"Long enough." Cassidy's nose scrunched. "I came to grab some coffee, but I heard you and Logan talking, and I didn't think it was a good time for me to step in." She looked around and lowered her voice. "He's had issues with sexual harassment in the past, you know? Not anything physical as far as I know, but he always makes inappropriate comments, and several employees have filed HR complaints against him. That's why he got transferred to this office a few years back; he was originally based in DC. Anyway, he's on thin ice. One more complaint and he's out."

Olivia blinked, shocked both by the revelations and the fact that Cassidy was, well, talking to her. The other woman hadn't said more than two words to her before now, despite Olivia's attempts to strike up a friendship.

"Why does PHC keep him on if he's such an issue?" It didn't make sense. Based on what Cassidy said, Logan was a lawsuit waiting to happen.

The blond shrugged. "His father is best friends with the chairman of the board."

Oh. *Now* it made sense.

"Right. Thanks." Olivia cleared her throat, feeling awkward. "Uh, *why* are you telling me this, though? Not that I don't appreciate the insight, but we haven't..." She trailed off, trying to think of a way to say *we haven't gotten along* without sounding rude.

Pink blossomed across Cassidy's cheeks. "I thought you should know. Women need to stick together and all that. I'm sorry I haven't been friendlier this summer, but I've had a lot going on, and I get so wrapped up in work. Plus, I don't have a lot of female friends, so I'm not the best at...that sort of thing."

Sympathy flooded Olivia. Now that she thought about it, she could see how what she'd perceived as coldness on Cassidy's part had instead been social anxiety. Cassidy had never been outright rude to her; she'd just turned down her past invitations.

"You know what they say, practice makes perfect." Olivia smiled. "Any chance you're free for lunch today? It's okay if you're not, but if you are, there's a great new sandwich shop nearby that you might like."

For a second, Olivia thought Cassidy would say no again, but then the other woman returned her smile. "That sounds great."

When Olivia got home that night, she found Sammy baking cupcakes—shirtless.

That sneaky bastard. He *knew* what seeing him like that did to her.

"Seriously?" She hung her jacket on the coat rack, her mouth watering at the delicious aroma swirling in the air. "That's unfair."

"What? I'm working," he said innocently. "Here, try this. New cupcake recipe. Tell me what you think."

Olivia took the proffered dessert and bit into it. The flavor of pumpkin spice exploded on her tongue. "Oh my God, this is amazing, and I don't even *like* pumpkin spice."

"Yeah?" Sammy looked pleased. "I've been working on the recipe all day. Thought I'd finally sell my soul and do a limited-run of pumpkin spice cupcakes for the fall. Tap into the trend and all."

"It's a great idea." She wolfed down the rest of the cupcake. "People will love it."

"I hope so. By the way, I thought about what you said the other day and decided I'll hire a CEO."

He delivered the news so casually, it took a few seconds for Olivia's brain to catch up. "Really?"

Crumble & Bake was expanding so fast, bringing on a CEO would be a smart business decision, especially since Sammy hated the management side of things, but Olivia hadn't expected him to agree or make a move *this* fast.

"Yep. I'm drawing up a job description tomorrow. I'll still have a say in big decisions, and I'll be the Chief Baking Officer overseeing all store operations and production, but the CEO will take care of the pesky paperwork and all that." Sammy's cheeks pinked. "I, uh, overheard the podcast you were listening to the other day, and they were talking about sticking to your zones of genius. Capitalize on what only you can do and do well, delegate the rest. It made sense."

Olivia grinned. "Told you podcasts are good."

"Eh, maybe that one episode. Give me good music instead any day of the week."

"Yeah, yeah." She hopped onto a kitchen stool and watched Sammy ice the remaining cupcakes. "I have a hypothetical for you."

"Shoot."

"What would you do if, say, the girlfriend of a close friend propositioned you?"

Sammy's head snapped up. He set his piping bag down and crossed his arms over his chest. "Who propositioned you?"

"No one. It's a hypothetical."

"Hypotheticals are things that have happened but the people asking them don't want others to know have happened."

Olivia made a face. "You have some tongs I can use to toss that word salad with?"

"Funny." Sammy didn't budge from his crossed-arms position. "Now tell me whose ass I need to kick."

Was it bad that her stomach fluttered at his commanding tone? "No one important."

"Liv."

"*Fine.*" She blew out a breath. "It was Richard."

She received a blank stare in response. "Who's that?"

"My, uh, sister's fiancé."

"*What?*"

"Yeah." Olivia gave a quick rundown of what happened at brunch. It actually felt really good to get it off her chest and have someone to talk it over with.

When she finished, Sammy looked like he was ready to fly to Chicago and introduce Richard to his fist. "What a fucking a-hole. Has he done something like this before?"

"He gave me creepy looks, but this was the first time he's said anything. The question is, should I tell my sister?" Olivia listed the pros and cons that had been running through her head since brunch. "I don't know. I wish it were black and white. If I were closer to her, it might be, but we don't have that level of trust between us. There's every chance she won't believe me."

A thoughtful expression crossed Sammy's face. "I don't know your sister, so admittedly I'm not sure how she'll react. But if the roles were reversed, what would you want her to do? He's marrying into the family, so you'll have to see him at every holiday and family gathering. What if he keeps making moves after they're married? You'll either have to keep quiet about it until he stops being an ass—if that ever happens—or you'll have to tell your sister what her husband is doing. Trust me, fiancé is bad, but husband is worse, especially if she finds out you knew before the wedding and didn't say anything."

He was right, of course. Olivia had been leaning toward telling Alina, but she needed someone else to say it for it to sink in.

"That conversation is going to suck." She propped her chin in her hand, already dreading it.

"Here. Have another pumpkin spice cupcake."

She cracked a smile but accepted the offering. "You know how to cheer a girl up."

"Sure do. Now, about Richard's address. What is it?"

"Stop. You can't get arrested for killing him. Who will bake for me then?"

"I'll only get arrested if I get caught."

Olivia set her cupcake down and rounded the counter, where she looped her arms around Sammy's neck. "I like the way you think."

He waggled his eyebrows. "My brain is one of my most attractive qualities."

"Absolutely." No lie. Looks and all that were nice, and Olivia had a major soft spot for his abs, but deep down, she was a sapiosexual. Intelligence was a huge turn-on. "Thank you for talking it through with me." She planted a kiss on his lips. "So... are you done recipe tasting, or can you spare a half hour?"

A slow smile spread across Sammy's face at her suggestive tone. "Half an hour? You underestimate me."

Olivia shrugged. "I just wanted to watch another episode of *Friends*, but if you want to binge—" She squealed when he swept her up and carried her into his bedroom.

"You think you're funny, huh?" he growled, tossing her on the bed.

"As a matter of fact, I do. I'm a great—"

Sammy's ringtone interrupted her. He declined the call, only for his cell to ring again less than a minute later.

"Sorry, let me take this first. It's my digital associate. She never calls, so it must be an emergency."

"I'll be here." Olivia leaned back and rested her elbows on the bed, watching with mild concern as Sammy answered the phone.

"Hey, Penny... No, I haven't checked social today." Sammy's face paled, and Olivia's concern ratcheted up another notch. "You're kidding. Yes, okay. Let me just...get a handle on the situation first. Thanks for calling. Yeah. Good night."

He hung up and looked something up on his phone. His face paled further.

"What's wrong?" Olivia asked, her concern morphing into full-blown anxiety.

Sammy handed her his phone without a word. She glanced at the tweet he'd pulled up, and her stomach plummeted.

Shit.

CHAPTER 21

THERE WERE CRISES, AND THERE WERE *CRISES*. THE roach claim fell into the latter category, hands down.

Sammy's digital associate, Penny, had alerted him to a viral tweet showing a photo of a cockroach baked into one of Crumble & Bake's cupcakes. The user was anonymous, known only by the screen name @raiderssucks23, but the post had garnered over fifty thousand likes and spread to other social media platforms—Instagram, TikTok, Facebook, and even YouTube, where drama-thirsty channels declared Crumble & Bake "canceled."

In the days following the tweet, Sammy barely slept. There were meetings upon meetings on how to respond and whether it was a real claim or sabotage (from a rival bakery, perhaps). There were calls to and from the city's Department of Public Health. The media went crazy over the story, and both Sammy's and Crumble & Bake's social accounts were inundated with messages. Some were from supporters, others were trolls or people screaming for answers on how, exactly, a cockroach had made its way into one of the company's signature products. It wasn't just social media either—it was email, phone lines, reporters showing up outside the bakery unannounced. Sammy was ready to delete all his personal accounts, but Penny convinced him it would make him look guilty and that it would be a horrible PR mistake. Business dwindled, and expansion plans for DC and New York halted as the staff got all hands on deck to manage the fallout from one fucking tweet.

It was a nightmare—especially because Sammy didn't know for sure if the claim was real.

What if someone really *had* found a roach baked into their cupcake? He trusted his staff, and he prided himself on running a tight ship, but things slipped through the cracks.

"Fuck!" He tugged his hair in frustration. The thought of such a huge screwup made him sick.

He'd poured years, most of his money, and all of his blood, sweat, and tears into his business. Not to mention, there were dozens of people counting on him for their jobs and livelihood. Crumble & Bake was booming—or it had been until a few days ago—but it was still a small business. It wasn't a giant corporation with decades of name recognition and that, yeah, might suffer during a PR crisis but likely wouldn't go under because of some bad press. If Sammy didn't figure this shit out and stem the tide of negative public opinion, he'd fail not just himself but everyone around him.

"Fuck, fuck, *fuck!*"

Not helpful, but he needed to vent. He hadn't slept or eaten in seventy-two hours, and he was dangerously close to losing his sanity.

The door opened on his last *fuck*. Liam poked his head in, his face pale and withdrawn. He loved the bakery as much as Sammy did, and as Sammy's second-in-command, he'd been equally tortured over the idea that such a huge hygiene violation might have occurred during his watch. "They're here."

Sammy rubbed a hand over his face and wrested his frustration under control. "Bring them in."

The crisis communications consultants he'd hired piled into his office in a whirlwind of suits and leather. Sammy spent the next few hours with them hammering out a strategy. It didn't escape his notice that he should have already had a plan in place—another sign that management wasn't his forte. But he'd never had a PR issue before, and the need for a crisis comms plan had fallen by the wayside as he dealt with the million other things on his plate.

Both he and the consultants agreed they needed to get to the bottom of what happened. How did the roach get into the cupcake? Who was responsible? Sammy also needed to issue an official statement on behalf of Crumble & Bake, retrain staff on food safety protocols, and make sure all external messaging about the incident remained consistent. The consultants warned Sammy not to get defensive or sucked into negative message spirals and to never respond to media requests with "No comment." Instead, he should explain what happened, how it happened, and the concrete steps he was taking to fix the issue and prevent a reoccurrence.

By the time the consultants left, a migraine pounded behind Sammy's temple and he was tempted to break out the whiskey, even though it was only two in the afternoon.

There was another knock on the door.

"Come in," Sammy grunted.

He'd expected to see Liam or maybe Cordelia, who kept popping in with food to make him feel better, but to his surprise, Olivia entered.

Sammy's heart lifted at the sight of her. She was the one person who could make him feel somewhat better these days. "What are you doing here? Don't you have work?"

"I have one summer Friday left, and I took it." Her face creased with sympathy. "How are you holding up?"

"I'm holding." Sammy sighed. "This is the longest week ever."

"It'll blow over." Olivia came up behind him and wrapped her arms around him. "C and B went years without any food safety issues. Surely people wouldn't hold one mistake against you."

People were petty enough to do just that, but Sammy tried to see the glass as half-full. The last thing he needed was more pessimism.

"We'll see. C'mere." He pulled Olivia onto his lap. "I can't believe you came all the way down here."

"I had to take care of some things at the office even though it's a summer Friday, or I would've come sooner." Olivia brushed her lips against his. "I'm not keeping you from anything, am I? Because I can hop right back out. I just wanted to make sure you're okay. We haven't had the chance to talk much this week."

"Nah, I could use a break."

"Good. Any chance you can take the rest of the afternoon off? You can go back into crisis-management mode later, but it's a beautiful day." She gestured out the window, where the sun blazed against a cloudless blue sky. "Fresh air always helps clear my mind."

Sammy thought about it for two seconds. "That's the best idea I've ever heard." His brain was fried, and he'd been staring at the walls of his office for days on end. Fresh air *would* do him good.

"Perfect. Before we leave though…"

He raised a questioning brow.

"There's something I've always wanted to do in an office. Might help you relax too."

His cock jumped in interest when she pulled a silky red tie out of her bag.

"I borrowed this from your closet. I hope you don't mind."

Olivia twirled the material around her finger, her voice warm and seductive. "There's a scene in one of my books where the guy blindfolds the woman…"

Oh, yeah. He remembered that scene. Or rather, he remembered her telling him about that scene the night she'd come home drunk from her book club. He'd been so turned on, he'd had to jack off in the shower before falling asleep.

But as Sammy bent a blindfolded Olivia over his desk, hiked her skirt up, and pounded into her, releasing days of pent-up frustration and energy, he was reminded that reality was sweeter than fantasy—at least as far as sexual scenarios went.

The only thing missing was the one-way glass from the scene, but she didn't seem to mind. Olivia screamed so loud he had to clap a hand over her mouth so his staff didn't think he was committing bloody murder in here.

Sammy's orgasm ripped through him seconds after hers. His cock pulsed hard, and his thrusts grew erratic until he'd spent himself.

"Fuck, that was so hot," he panted, kissing the side of her neck before he withdrew and disposed of his condom. He made a mental note to take out the trash himself later. "I approve of your office conduct. One hundred percent."

A husky laugh emerged from Olivia's throat as she straightened her clothes and fixed her hair. He'd untied the blindfold after they both came, and her eyes shone with postcoital satisfaction.

"Next time, let's do it in a conference room," she purred. "Glass walls. Big table. The whole shebang."

"You're a freak. I love it." Sammy drew her in for another kiss. She could always make a shitty day better, and it wasn't the sex. It was her. Just seeing her face and hearing her voice made him feel like ten pounds had been lifted from his shoulders.

Yeah, the roach crisis still hung over his head and he had

a ton of stuff on his plate, but for a few hours, he would enjoy himself, dammit.

Surprisingly, he did. They went to the Ferry Building, where they ate their way through the food stalls. They walked along Fisherman's Wharf and soaked in the warm sunshine. They grabbed ice cream cones from Bi-Rite and hung out at Dolores Park, where they kissed, cuddled, and even joined a group of stoned hippie types playing hacky sack.

Sammy laughed for the first time since he'd seen the tweet, and the fresh air untangled some of the mess in his head. Olivia had been right—he'd needed this.

"I'm a hacky sack *goddess*! Admit it." Olivia hip-checked him when they left the park a little after sunset. "Did you see me back there? I was unstoppable!"

"Easy there, Hacky Sack Goddess. I was taking it easy on you."

"Says the guy who dropped the sack, what, five times?" Olivia squealed when Sammy picked her up and spun her around.

"I was rusty, you little devil," he growled. "I'll do better next time."

"That's what they all say," she taunted. She looped her arms around his neck, her face glowing. "I hope you had fun today."

"I did." Sammy kept her feet off the ground as he pecked her on the lips. "Thank you."

"Anytime. Besides Hacky Sack Goddess and Spreadsheet Extraordinaire, I'm also the Mistress of Fun."

"That sounds kinky. I like it."

Olivia laughed and slapped him on the shoulder. "Is sex all you think about?"

"Nah. I think about other stuff two percent of the time." He set her down so he could give her a longer, proper kiss. "Seriously, though. I needed this afternoon. I appreciate you spending it with me."

"You don't need to thank me. I *want* to spend time with you." Sadness flitted over her face. "I wish the summer could last longer."

Sammy swallowed hard. They had precious little time left as roommates before Olivia returned to Stanford. It wasn't a *huge* deal—Palo Alto was less than an hour's drive from the city, and they'd agreed to visit each other on the weekends. But he was going to miss seeing her every day. Miss coming home to her, falling asleep and waking up next to her...

Sammy realized with horror that the emotions buffeting him at that moment weren't new. He'd felt them once before, a near-decade ago, when he'd been head over heels for a girl who'd taken his breath away the first time he saw her. Now here he was, experiencing those *same feelings* for the same girl, all grown up, except the intensity eclipsed the first time a hundredfold. He supposed he should've expected it, considering they were dating again, but he hadn't expected it to come on this fast or this strong.

Sammy was in love with Olivia again—more than he'd ever been. And he had no clue if she felt the same toward him.

Aw, fuck.

CHAPTER 22

"CHEERS! YOU DID IT, BITCH!" NATALIE'S EYES SPARkled as she clinked her drink against Olivia's. "They'll *have* to make you VP now."

"It's not a sure thing yet," Olivia said humbly, but she was doing cartwheels on the inside. That morning, Michael had called her into his office and informed her that Ty Winstock had officially signed on as a PHC client and that he'd credited part of his decision to her pitch. Michael hadn't seemed annoyed that Winstock liked Olivia's short, off-the-cuff pitch more than he'd liked Michael's presentation; he was just thrilled they'd landed a big fish like Winstock.

"Nuh-uh. None of that false modesty. *Own* it, babe," Tamara ordered. "Vice President Olivia Tang. Sounds good, doesn't it?"

A grin spread across Olivia's face. "Yeah. It does."

Her book club friends erupted in cheers that turned the head of every other patron in the bar. They'd gathered for their weekly happy hour meetup, which had turned into a mini advance celebration of Olivia's promotion. Olivia wouldn't formally be promoted until after she received her MBA, but with the Ty Winstock win under her belt, she was ninety-nine percent sure she had the vice presidency in the bag.

Kat's phone rang.

"Don't think about it," Olivia said before the brunette could answer. "Put your hands up and back away slowly."

She could see the caller ID clearly from where she was sitting: *Ben*. The asshole ex.

She'd bonded hard with her fellow book club members this summer, and she was comfortable enough with them now to tell them what she really thought—and she *really* thought Ben could go suck a dick.

"But it might be important," Kat protested.

"The only important thing that man has to say is when he's getting a vasectomy. God knows we don't need any mini-Bens running around," Natalie said, direct as always.

Kat frowned. "That's a horrible thing to say."

"Horrible words for a horrible person." Natalie grabbed the phone off the table over Kat's objections. "Nope. New rule: none of us can check our phones while we're together. Let's throw it back to the dinosaur era."

"I agree." Donna sipped her drink. "Things were so much simpler before we were glued to our devices."

"That includes you, Tam." Natalie nudged the pierced designer, who tapped on her cell like her life depended on it.

"Sorry." Tamara glanced up with a distracted expression. "I'm texting my girlfriend. I hope you guys don't mind, but I invited her to join us and she's bringing a friend. I know happy hour is sacred, but she's so busy, I haven't seen her in a week, and she's only a couple of blocks away."

Olivia shrugged. "I'm fine with it." The more, the merrier. Hell, she was so happy, she wouldn't object if Tamara invited an entire marching band to join them.

The others chorused their agreement.

Tamara had mentioned her girlfriend a few times before, and Olivia was curious to see what she was like. All she knew was the girlfriend worked some high-powered job that required her to travel often and take meetings at ungodly hours of the day.

Ten minutes later, she got her answer.

A beautiful blond sauntered into the bar, looking like a model in her red pea coat and heels. "Hi, babe." She dropped a kiss on Tamara's lips.

Olivia spewed her drink on the table, earning her several strange looks.

"Sorry," she choked out.

The blond glanced up. Shock filled her perfect features. "Olivia?"

"Jessica."

The two of them stared at each other, too stunned to say anything else.

Holy hell, Tamara's girlfriend was *Sammy's ex*? That was a development Olivia couldn't have dreamed of in her wildest dreams. Did that mean Jessica was bi? Or was she a newly-come-out lesbian? Did Sammy know?

Tamara's gaze ping-ponged between them, bright with curiosity. "You know each other?"

Jessica recovered first. "We have a mutual friend."

That's one way to put it.

"Speaking of friends, this is Ty. Ty, this is everyone." Jessica gestured to the man who came up behind her.

Aaaannnd Olivia spewed her drink for the second time that night, because Ty was none other than Ty freakin' Winstock.

She couldn't believe it. She was at happy hour with her boyfriend's ex, her company's biggest client, and her erotica book club.

This had to be a nightmare.

Winstock's mouth twitched. "Hello, Olivia."

Now Jessica was the surprised one. "You've met?"

"I signed on with her firm as a client." Winstock—Olivia still couldn't bring herself to think of him as "Ty"—sat next to Kat, who turned bright red and scooted a few inches away from him. His eyes shone with amusement. "Olivia made quite the pitch."

Donna leaned over and whispered in Olivia's ear. "Damn, girl. For someone new to the city, you know *everyone*."

"Not really. It just so happens everyone I know came to the same bar tonight." Olivia half expected Sammy to come strolling in the door, but he was having a guys' night with Aaron and Trey.

The initial furor over the cockroach-in-a-cupcake claim had died down somewhat—now everyone was focused on the news that a huge fast-food chain's CEO had been in a relationship with one of his employees for a year, against company rules—but the problem hadn't gone away. Sammy and his team still didn't know how the cockroach had gotten into the cupcake or if the anonymous Twitter user was lying. Still, the lessened media scrutiny gave them some breathing room to relax and focus on getting to the bottom of what had happened.

As the night wore on, the initial awkwardness from seeing Jessica and Winstock faded, but Olivia burned with questions. She finally got her chance to ask them when Donna and Natalie excused themselves to go to the restroom, Kat and Winstock went to grab fresh drinks, and Tamara—whom Jessica apparently called "Mara"—broke the no-phones rule and stepped outside for an emergency client call, leaving Olivia and Jessica alone.

"Yes, I'm a lesbian. I've been out since I was fifteen, and I've been dating Mara for over a year." Jessica's lips curved at Olivia's mortified expression. "Sorry that came out so direct, but I can tell you've been dying to ask me all night, so I figured I'd save you the trouble."

"Since you were fifteen? But..." Olivia faltered. "You dated Sammy."

"Would you believe me if I said he's such a great guy, I made an exception for him?" Jessica burst into laughter. "*Kidding.* You should've seen your face. He is a great guy, but he and I never, uh, officially dated."

"What?" Olivia's brows furrowed. "He introduced you as his girlfriend in New York. He took you to Farrah's wedding!"

Now Jessica was the one who looked embarrassed. "Yes, well, those were special circumstances."

"What the hell does that mean?"

The blond shifted in her seat. "It means, those were the *only* times we dated."

"I don't—" Olivia froze when the pieces clicked into place. "Wait. He *lied?* He used you to—"

Tamara returned, interrupting her train of thought. "What's going on?" Her eyes moved from Jessica's sheepish expression to Olivia's outraged one.

"Nothing. Except I might commit murder tonight," Olivia muttered.

"What?"

"Babe, can you order me a drink?" Jessica placed a hand on Tamara's arm. "Another apple martini would be great."

Tamara made a face. "I can take a hint. Be right back—hopefully, I won't interrupt Kat and Ty's little lovefest."

Hmm. Kat and Winstock *did* look cozy at the bar. They both carried fresh drinks but didn't seem in any hurry to return to the group. They'd been semiflirting all night—or rather, Winstock had been flirting with Kat while she blushed like crazy, until she'd found out he was also a history buff. After that, they couldn't stop talking about the Ottomans and Byzantines or whatever.

Winstock was surprisingly down-to-earth for someone with a ten-figure net worth, and if he hadn't been a client, Olivia could see herself being friends with him.

Once Tamara left, Olivia resumed her and Jessica's conversation. "Sammy used you to, what, make me jealous?"

Jessica fiddled with her earring. "You should talk to him about it. I shouldn't have mentioned it." She frowned. "Martinis always get me in trouble."

"I'll talk to him about it, all right." Olivia took a deep, steady breath. "Okay. Second question before I go home and commit a felony—how do you know Win—er, Ty?"

"I was a lawyer for Mosaic back in their start-up days. We clicked and stayed friends even after our business relationship ended." Jessica shrugged. "I don't see him that often since we both travel so much. Tonight was our first time meeting up in months, which is why I brought him. I should've asked first—I know it's ladies' night."

"It's fine. It's a *little* awkward since he's my company's client, which is why I'm not drinking anymore—" Olivia gestured to her martini glass, which had been empty for the past hour. The last thing she needed was to embarrass herself in front of Ty freaking Winstock. "But Kat doesn't seem to mind."

Jessica grinned. "Neither does he. I've never seen him so animated with a woman before. Actually, I've never even seen him date."

"Really?" Olivia's eyebrows shot up. "He's a billionaire. He must have women throwing themselves at him." Winstock wasn't bad-looking either, but he could look like Gollum and he'd still be a babe magnet given how many zeros were in his bank account.

"Oh, he does. He just hasn't been interested in any of them.

He brings them to events where he's expected to have a date, but otherwise, he spends most of his time working, traveling, and hanging out with his dog. German shepherd named Bear. It's adorable."

"Huh." Olivia examined Winstock with new eyes. "Maybe that's about to change."

Jessica's baby blues twinkled. "Maybe."

Olivia hoped so. Maybe then, Kat would forget about Ben.

The group stayed at the bar for another hour before they split, and everyone pretended not to notice when Winstock and Kat exchanged numbers.

"Tell Sam I'll see him for drinks next week." Jessica buttoned her gorgeous coat.

"Will do." Olivia liked the woman a helluva lot better now that she knew she'd never dated Sammy.

"Olivia." Winstock made his way over while she waited for her Uber. The rest of the group had already left, and Olivia was passing time answering work emails—including a passive-aggressive one from Logan about her latest report that made her want to punch him in the face. He'd really turned his asshole-ness up after she called him out on his inappropriate comments.

"Yes?" She looked up from her phone and instinctively adopted her professional voice. She felt like she was at a client meeting now that they were one-on-one.

A shadow of a smile crossed Winstock's lips. "Don't worry. I'll pretend tonight never happened."

"I'm not sure what you mean."

"You're uncomfortable hanging out with a client outside of work."

Well, yeah. Schmoozing clients was de rigueur on Wall Street, but randomly seeing one pop up at happy hour with your friends was a whole other matter. Thank God no one discussed anal or their latest erotic read tonight. Olivia would have died of mortification.

"Tonight was unexpected," she acknowledged.

"For both of us." Winstock stuffed his hands in his jeans. He wore a hoodie and sneakers again, and he could've passed for a college student if you didn't know who he was. "But you're a great analyst, so it won't change anything about our business relationship—not that you did anything tonight that would've changed it. Like I told Michael, your pitch clinched my decision to invest with PHC."

"Thank you." She wondered whether she should ask the question that'd been hovering in her mind since their dinner at Avenue, but what the hell? She'd gotten this far. "May I ask why you asked for my pitch during our first meeting? Michael is more senior than me, and he gave an excellent presentation."

"It was all right." Winstock shrugged. "I was more impressed by the details you got right. The meeting venue, the decision not to include a slide deck—I hate those things—the details in the pitch that were personalized for me. I don't do a lot of press, so it's difficult to dig up information about me, but you did it. And I know you're the one who did the research because that's way too in the weeds for a managing director like Michael." He smiled at Olivia's blush. "I run a big company, but I don't like impersonal relationships even in business. Every other pitch I've heard from PE and investment firms felt impersonal. Yours didn't."

He nodded at the black car that'd just rolled up in front of them. The driver peered at his phone and then peered at Olivia. "I think that's you. Good night."

Winstock walked away, and she climbed into the back seat of her Uber, unable to hide her blossoming smile. Besides Sammy—whom, after some deliberation, she was no longer mad at for deceiving her about Jessica because she didn't want to waste their remaining time together as roommates being upset over stupid stuff—nothing made her happier than excelling at work.

After a string of bad luck, things were finally looking up.

CHAPTER 23

"…RECEIVED THE HIGHEST MARK POSSIBLE FOR ALL areas evaluated, which shouldn't come as a surprise." Michael adjusted his tie. "You've been an extraordinary employee, but I'm sure you know that."

"Thank you." Normally, Olivia would've glowed beneath all the compliments and her top-notch performance review, but all she could focus on was what Michael *hadn't* touched on yet: her official request to transfer to the San Francisco office after she graduated next May.

Even though she disliked a majority of her SF coworkers, she'd do whatever it took to make her and Sammy's relationship work this time around.

Sammy had offered to look into moving to New York as well, but Olivia wouldn't let him. He was too close to his family to move across the country from them, and while there'd soon be a Crumble & Bake in New York, San Francisco was his company's headquarters and flagship store. It held special sentimental value. Plus, he already owned a house here. He had far more roots tying him to San Francisco than Olivia did to New York. She loved the Big

Apple and all it had to offer—the food, the shopping, the energy and endless sources of entertainment—but besides her job, Farrah was the only thing keeping her there. She'd miss having her best friend in the same city, but Farrah was married now, and she and Olivia were no longer roommates, so even that tie had loosened.

The fact Sammy had offered, though, reinforced Olivia's belief she was doing the right thing. He was willing to make sacrifices for her; she'd do the same for him.

Except her company had to, you know, approve her request first. She'd applied for the transfer after returning from Lake Tahoe, and the status was still pending.

Michael leaned back in his chair and steepled his fingers beneath his chin. "However, there is one thing we need to discuss that isn't part of our official performance metrics but that is still an important requirement for employees of Pine Hill Capital."

Olivia's brow creased. *Huh.* Whatever the "thing" was, it had never come up in her past performance reviews. "Of course."

Her boss clicked something on his computer and spun the monitor around. "Have you seen this?"

Surprise washed through her. Was that…an *Instagram post*? Why the hell was her boss—who had no personal social media except for LinkedIn—showing her an Instagram post?

When she looked closer, though, Olivia realized why, and her blood iced over.

The post was a carousel by @influencerstea, a massive account that specialized in gossiping about (i.e., dragging) social media–famous personalities. Michael clicked through, and the temperature continued to plummet when images of Olivia and Sammy kissing and playing hacky sack in Dolores Park flashed past. The photos themselves weren't scandalous—it wasn't like they were having sex or anything. It was the caption that twisted things all out of proportion:

Baking influencer and Crumble & Bake founder Sammy Yu spotted canoodling with a mystery woman in Dolores Park. Yes, that Crumble & Bake—the one that still hasn't gotten to the bottom of the roach-in-a-cupcake incident that blew up earlier this month. Guess a food-safety crisis isn't enough to keep an influencer down. Now the real question is: Did those stoners he's playing hacky sack with offer him a roach? ;)

The roach pun was so bad, whoever came up with it should be arrested, but the post still had over sixty thousand likes and hundreds of comments.

Tornadoes of fury, disgust, and disbelief tunneled through Olivia's system. There was so much wrong with the post, she didn't know where to start. Was it a fucking crime for a man to enjoy *one* afternoon out without getting lambasted for it? Yes, his business was in crisis, but that didn't mean he had to flog himself until the public deemed it an appropriate time for him to live his life again. He worked so hard, especially after the tweet broke, but none of the people behind the account or the keyboard warriors trolling in the comments would know, would they?

She was also sketched out by the fact that someone had been snapping photos of them without their permission. She'd figured some people might recognize Sammy, but he wasn't Harry Styles or anything. Stolen wannabe-paparazzi shots had not factored into the equation.

Finally, Sammy barely fell into the influencer category. He had a large social following, but he didn't build his name purely based on social media. He was a businessman, so why the hell was @influencerstea going after him?

Olivia wanted to scream. She hated people sometimes. She really did.

"Another employee brought it to my attention this morning," Michael said. "Someone identified you in the comments, and they were concerned it would reflect poorly on the firm. The post is already gaining traction on Facebook and online news sites— some of which mention you by name."

She took a long, shaky breath and forced herself to count to three before she spoke. "With all due respect, sir, I understand your concern, but I didn't know I was being photographed. I was out with my boyfriend on my personal time when someone invaded our privacy and posted our activities online. I also want to note that I'm not doing anything illegal or scandalous in those photos. I was simply enjoying the day."

"Yes, well." Michael cleared his throat, looking mighty uncomfortable. It was clear he didn't want to have this conversation any more than she did. "That's up to interpretation. Many of Pine Hill's clients are quite conservative, and they wouldn't take kindly to photos such as this one." He stopped at a picture of Olivia and Sammy kissing. She had her arms around his neck, and you could see a sliver of her stomach from where her shirt had ridden up. "You did nothing wrong, but it's often more about perception than the facts. It's imperative clients take our analysts seriously if we want to survive as a firm. I'm afraid, er, *indiscretions* such as this—whether or not they're your fault—would negatively affect your reputation and, by extension, the company's reputation."

Our clients aren't on Instagram or gossip sites! Olivia wanted to yell. The average age of the PHC client was sixty-two, and they were too busy worrying about their net worth to pay attention to online drama. It wasn't like she'd been called out by the *New York Times*, for God's sake.

Besides, what did Michael want her to do? Stop going out in public?

She took another deep breath. "I understand. It won't happen again."

"Good." Michael tapped his fingers together. "Unfortunately, despite your best intentions, there's no way to guarantee it won't happen again unless…"

The hairs on the back of her nape prickled.

"You stop seeing this gentleman—or any public figure whom people might be tempted to sneak paparazzi shots of. I realize that may sound unfair, but it's the only way to ensure more unwanted photos—perhaps even ones of a more scandalous nature—won't pop up in the future."

Olivia stared at her boss, mouth agape. She couldn't believe what she was hearing. They wanted her to stop dating Sammy because they were afraid of—what? More photos of her enjoying her damn life?

A small part of her understood where Michael was coming from, but a larger part was too stunned and pissed for her to apply her usual verbal filters. "Sammy isn't a public figure," she argued. "He's a baker. He's just in the news right now because of…unfortunate circumstances that'll blow over soon."

Perhaps it hadn't been the smartest idea to bring up his PR troubles, but she meant what she said. Sammy wasn't a celebrity; the chances of more shots like the ones on-screen were razorthin.

"I understand, but the fact that one of his followers recognized him in public, took a photo of him, and posted it online—and that said photo got picked up by online news outlets—is proof he's more than your average baker. If someone photographed him once, they can do it again."

Olivia's fists clenched and unclenched in her lap. "With all due respect, sir." She should stop saying that, but it was the only thing she could think of to soften the blow of telling her boss he was dead fucking wrong. "This is my personal life. I give a lot to

Pine Hill Capital. I am, as you mentioned not half an hour ago, an exemplary employee. I come in early and stay late. I helped close the deal with Ty Winstock, our firm's biggest client. I am one hundred percent committed to PHC, but my personal life is my personal life."

Silence invaded Michael's sprawling corner office.

Olivia forced herself not to shake as she met her boss's steely gaze. Other than a furrowed brow, his expression was unreadable.

"Yes," he said slowly. "It is. Under normal circumstances, Pine Hill wouldn't dream of interfering in its employees' personal lives—unless, as stated in your employment contract, your personal life directly affects the firm. Your continued relationship with a public figure—*any* public figure—would fall under that category."

She should've left her blazer at her desk. Olivia was sweating balls in here.

"I'm sorry, but I think that's a bit of a stretch. Sir," she added stiffly. She clutched the edges of her chair with sweaty palms. "May I ask if any clients complained about the photos?"

"No, but that doesn't mean they haven't seen them or they're *not* concerned." Michael smiled a thin smile. "We'd both agree that PHC didn't become what it is by managing problems *after* they arise. We anticipate issues and fix them before they emerge as issues. That's what's happening now. Look." He leaned forward, his tone turning conciliatory. "I understand this is difficult in the short run, but you're not married to this man. You'll find someone else to date. Whereas you're on the cusp of a vice presidency here." His smile grew when Olivia startled. "We both know it's happening once you receive your MBA, so I see no reason to play coy. VP, director...hell, maybe even C-suite down the line. As I mentioned earlier this summer, you have a bright future at PHC. Don't throw it away over some man."

A migraine set in behind Olivia's temples. There was too much happening—her brain was scrambling to keep up.

"Also, don't think I've forgotten your request to transfer to San Francisco after you graduate." Michael tapped his pen against his desk. "I'd be delighted to have you here full-time. I spoke with New York, and they agreed to the transfer as well if it's still what you want next spring. We'll reach out in early March to reconfirm and get the paperwork rolling. But everything I mentioned is, of course, contingent on what we just discussed regarding public image."

"Of course," Olivia said, her voice hollow. How ironic. She wanted to transfer to San Francisco *because* of her relationship with Sammy, and now her company was telling her she could only transfer if she *ended* her relationship with Sammy.

The universe had a sick sense of humor.

"You don't have to give me an answer now. Take some time to think about it," Michael said with the confidence of a man who knew he'd get his way. "In the meantime, let's refrain from any public outings where you could be caught in a compromising position, shall we? You have until your last day to make a final decision about your, er, relationship. And, Olivia?" he called as she made her way out of his office.

She paused with her hand on the doorknob.

"Choose wisely."

"Thank you, sir." It was the only thing she could think of besides *fuck off*, which probably wouldn't go over well. She hesitated, then turned. "One more thing, sir. Out of pure curiosity, may I ask which employee brought the post to your attention? I won't confront them; I just want to know."

Discomfort flitted across Michael's face. "I'm sorry, Olivia, but that's confidential."

She'd figured, but she'd asked anyway on the off chance he'd tell her. She had a pretty good idea who the snitch was anyway.

Olivia walked back to her desk, her palms slick with sweat and her heart slamming against her rib cage with the force of a two-ton truck. She felt like the lead in a rom-com, stuck choosing between her job and love—only there was no comedy and no guaranteed happy ending.

The situation was a total cliché and a total nightmare.

"You okay?" Cassidy whispered. "You look like you just saw a ghost."

Olivia and Cassidy's relationship had warmed since their run-in in the kitchen, and while they weren't workplace BFFs, they were friends.

"Yeah." Olivia turned on her monitor and forced a smile. "I'll be fine."

She glared across the room at Logan, who'd stopped hitting on her since she threatened to report him to HR but who had since taken to undermining and making snide remarks toward her every chance he got. It was subtle enough that she couldn't call him out without looking paranoid and petty, but she trusted her female instincts: Logan was definitely the one who'd told Michael about the photos.

He noticed her glare and smirked, his eyes gleaming with smug superiority.

Ugh. She needed a better solution to the Logan Problem because she couldn't keep working in such a hostile office environment if she transferred to San Francisco.

But first, she needed to figure out a solution to the Sammy Problem, or the point was moot. One misstep and she wouldn't be transferring at all. She might not even have a job.

"You made this." Sammy stared at the plate of shrimp dumplings on the counter.

"Yep."

"You made these dumplings from scratch."

"That's what I said."

He eyed Olivia with suspicion. "You don't cook."

"I learned. I'm an excellent student, as you know."

"Not in the kitchen. Remember the meatloaf disaster?" Sammy picked up a dumpling and held it away from him like he was handling a rabid animal. "Tell me the truth. What are the chances I'll get food poisoning again?"

Olivia scowled. "I can't believe you'd ask me that. I am hurt. I am offended. I am—"

"Answer the question, Liv."

"Fine. More than zero and less than a hundred." She heaved a sigh. "Just *eat* the damn thing. Tell me what you think. If you do get food poisoning, I'll nurse you back to health."

Sammy grimaced. "That doesn't inspire confidence." He made the sign of the cross over his chest before he bit into the dumpling with the look of a man on his way to the gallows.

What a drama king.

His eyes popped open, and Olivia tensed with anticipation.

Sammy pointed an accusing finger at her. "You dirty liar."

"Me?" She widened her eyes with exaggerated innocence. "What did I do?"

"You ordered these from Wah Sing! I'd recognize the taste anywhere."

Olivia choked back a laugh. "Maybe I convinced them to give me their secret recipe and made it from scratch like I said I did."

"Right. And I'm the Queen of England." Sammy ate the rest of the dumpling and shook his head. "How? They don't do takeout."

"I can be very persuasive." Translation: Olivia had shown up in person and offered to pay them double the cost of the dumplings if the restaurant boxed them up for her. "But fine, you caught me. I didn't cook them, so you can eat them without fearing for your health. I just wanted to see how you'd react if I told you I'd cooked. Clearly, you have no faith in me."

"I do, as long as it doesn't involve you being within two feet of a stove or oven." Sammy kissed her on the lips. "Thanks, babe. I needed this."

"No problem."

Olivia's chest squeezed as she watched him eat. Dark circles smudged the skin beneath his eyes, and his wan complexion reflected his stress and lack of sleep. He'd insisted on spending time with her instead of resting, since he "couldn't fall asleep anyway" and they had so little time left before she was due back at Stanford.

"How'd your performance review go?" Sammy asked.

Olivia stuffed a dumpling in her mouth, using it as an excuse to delay answering. She chewed slowly while Sammy watched her with a curious expression.

"Fine," she mumbled after swallowing. "Highest marks across the board."

Pride lit up his face. "I knew it! No way your boss won't approve your transfer. You're the best employee they've got."

"Yeah."

Guilt prickled her throat. Sammy was amazing. Some men couldn't handle successful women, but even in college, he'd been nothing but supportive. He celebrated with her when she was up and cheered her up when she was down. He'd believed in her every step of the way—more than she'd believed in him in the beginning.

She shouldn't be this torn between him and her career—but she was. Because while she loved Sammy, she loved her job too. She'd spent her entire life to get where she was now. She couldn't throw all that away without thinking the situation through.

Sammy's face clouded at her unenthusiastic response. He examined her carefully. "You do still want to transfer, don't you?"

"Of course I do." Olivia squeezed his hand. "Sorry. It's just been a long day."

She didn't want to dump her troubles on him. She hadn't come to a decision yet, and until she did, there was no need to add more stress to his plate.

"It's okay if you change your mind." He sounded pained but sincere. "Don't feel like you *have* to move to San Francisco. Do I want you here permanently? Hell yes. But I know how much you love New York, and if you want to move back after B-school, we'll make it work. They invented phones and Skype and airplanes for a reason."

Olivia's heart hurt so much it was hard to breathe. "That's not it. I *want* to stay here with you." Her chin wobbled.

Sammy's expression grew alarmed. "Then what is it? Why do you look like you're about to cry?"

"Nothing." She shook her head. "Like I said, long day."

"Liv, we promised we'd be honest with each other." His firm tone brooked no opposition. "So be honest. Tell me what's wrong and we'll work it out—together."

"You have enough to worry about. I don't want to stress you out more."

"You not telling me *will* stress me out more. C'mon." Sammy's mouth quirked. "What could be worse than having a customer find a roach in one of your products?"

Olivia cracked a smile. At least he'd reached the point where he could joke about it—sort of.

He was right, though. He'd stress more if he didn't know what was going on than if he did, so she told him about Michael's ultimatum. She barely got the words out without screaming in frustration.

Once she finished, Sammy drew back, looking like he'd been sucker punched. "Your boss really said that to you?"

"Yeah." Olivia reached for another dumpling for comfort, only to discover there were none left. *Great.* "It's so stupid. I have to talk to HR about this. There's no way—I mean, they can't police my personal life like this. There has to be a loophole or something I'm missing. Or I can find another job," she rambled, her mind running a million miles a minute as she searched for a way out of this mess. "I have a great résumé, and there are other private equity firms in San Francisco."

"But will you be able to land a vice presidency right out of B-school at those other firms?"

She faltered. They both knew the answer: no. She'd have to work for another two years at least before she could earn a VP slot at a new company, and the chances of her getting hired straight into the position were slim to none.

"It's just a few extra years." Her stomach churned with nausea. "I'll work my way up like I did before."

Sammy scrubbed a hand over his face. "Liv..."

"It's not a big deal."

"Yes, it is. It's a huge deal. The VP position is all you've talked about."

"This whole thing will blow over." Olivia said this to convince herself as much as Sammy. "Those stupid wannabe-paparazzi shots were a one-time thing. Look, I don't have to decide until the end of summer. I'll come up with a convincing argument before then. I'll convince PHC our relationship isn't a threat to my reputation—which is such bullshit, anyway—once the heat dies down, and they'll agree. The end."

Sammy's jaw tensed. "I don't want you to throw away your career for me. What if they don't agree? What if they fire and blackball you?"

The nausea intensified.

"I'm not throwing away anything." Olivia lifted her chin, trying to project calm confidence. "Let's see how this plays out first, okay?"

"Sure." Sammy's tone was muted, his expression shuttered.

"It'll be fine." She pressed her lips to his and sent a fervent prayer up to the heavens. "*We'll* be fine."

Please, God, let us be fine.

CHAPTER 24

IT WAS D-DAY, A.K.A. DECISION DAY.

Olivia didn't leave for Palo Alto until Sunday evening, but today was her last day working at PHC this summer, which meant she had to tell Michael whether she was ending her relationship with Sammy.

Her heart thudded against her chest as she knocked on his door.

"Come in."

She entered, her eyes roaming over Michael's book-lined shelves and the neatly organized mahogany desk. She'd only worked here for a few months, but it felt like she'd been here for years. It would be strange diving back into her classes at Stanford.

"Please, sit." Michael gestured at the seat opposite his.

She did, folding her hands in her lap. The pounding in her chest intensified.

They made small talk—when she was leaving for Palo Alto, what her second-year schedule looked like, blah blah blah. Olivia responded robotically, too distracted by the elephant in the room to elaborate on any of her answers.

Finally, they got to the point.

"I'm happy you've made a decision." Michael smiled. "I admit, it took longer than I'd expected, but you've always been thorough in your analysis."

Uh-uh. He might sing a different tune once he heard what she had to say. "Thank you for your patience. I did think this through carefully, and—"

"I'm so glad you're sticking with PHC. It's the right move for your career, and I'm happy to say your request to transfer to San Francisco is officially granted." Michael's smile broadened. "As I mentioned during your review, we'll reconfirm in March. Otherwise, we're all set."

Olivia stared at him, baffled. "What?" She shook her head. "I'm sorry. That's great news, but I thought you wanted to hear my decision first."

A puzzled frown eclipsed his smile. "I did. I received your email this morning."

Her heart started pounding again, this time in triple time. She hadn't sent Michael an email that morning. "I see."

Michael shot her a strange look. "Anyway, I wanted to approve the request in person and thank you again for your contributions this summer. Ty Winstock is delighted with your performance. We'll shift his portfolio to Cassidy while you finish out your year at Stanford, and it'll shift back to you after you graduate, per his request."

When Winstock had heard that Olivia would be taking a leave of absence from PHC, he'd asked her thoughts on who should take over his account while she was in school. She'd recommended Cassidy; apparently, he'd taken her recommendation to heart.

"That sounds great," Olivia said woodenly. She was still stuck on *I received your email this morning.*

Her mind flashed back to earlier that day. She usually checked her email before she left the house, so she could delete the spam and flag the important messages requiring her attention. Today hadn't been any different. She'd left her laptop and bedroom door open while she showered, as she always did. Sammy must've snuck in and sent the email.

She wanted to throw up.

She mumbled her thanks and some platitudes about how great it'd been to work with Michael before she hauled ass to her desk and pulled up the Sent Messages folder in her account.

There it was: from Olivia Tang to Michael Berman, 6:45 a.m. PDT.

She scanned through the email, the bile rising in her throat the more she read.

What. The. Fuck.

"Sammy!" Olivia stormed into his house after work, so angry steam practically poured out of her ears. He was home; his car was in the driveway. "Get your ass out here!"

Two seconds of silence, followed by the sound of a door opening and the shuffle of Sammy's footsteps.

He entered the living room. "I had to do it." He didn't ask what she was pissed about; he already knew.

"No, you didn't." Olivia planted her hands on her hips. "It was *my* decision, not yours. How could you do that? How could you sneak behind my back and email my boss? *It wasn't at all what I'd wanted to say.*"

"Exactly!" Sammy threw his hands up in the air. "I knew what you were going to say, Liv. I could tell by your reaction every time I brought it up. You were going to say no to your company and put your job at risk. I couldn't let you do that."

Olivia's cheeks flamed with fury. "It. Was. My. Decision."

"And this is our relationship," he fired back. He rubbed a hand over his face. "Look, I'm sorry I went behind your back. It was shitty of me. But if you'd said no, they would've denied your transfer request. They might've even fired you. That wouldn't have helped us either."

"So what? We keep dating and keep our relationship secret, hoping none of my coworkers see us and no crazy fans sneak more photos of us and post them online?" Olivia shook her head. "How long can we keep that going before it all falls apart?"

San Francisco was a big city, but unless she and Sammy never went out together again, the risk remained.

Sammy stared at her, his expression tortured.

A chill crawled up her spine and dug its icy claws into her organs, freezing her from the inside out. "You want to actually break up."

"Liv..." He reached for her, but she backed away, her chest caving in on itself.

"I can't believe it." Every word scraped against her throat on its way out. "I can't believe you're giving up so easily. All that talk about us being honest and working things out together, that was all *bullshit*. Because if it'd been true, we wouldn't be having this conversation after one fucking obstacle." Moisture gathered behind her eyes, and Olivia didn't bother stemming the tide as tears leaked down her cheeks in salty rivulets. "You didn't even ask me what I wanted. If you had, you'd know I would've chosen you. I can always find another job. I'll never be able to find another us."

If Sammy had given her any sign that he was willing to make this work, Olivia would've gone back to Michael and told him she'd changed her mind—and taken any fallout that came with it. Because she'd come to a conclusion these past few weeks: she'd choose Sammy over anything. Yes, her career meant a lot to her; she'd never throw it away willy-nilly. But she'd be able to find a similar job if PHC let her go. She might have to work her way up again and throw her original five-year plan in the trash, but it would've been worth it.

Yet Sammy hadn't given her that chance. He'd decided for her, and if that weren't bad enough, he seemed perfectly willing and ready to end their relationship with no discussion whatsoever.

Pain raked across his features. "I don't want to do this, Liv," he said, his voice tight with emotion. "You think I *want* to give you up? You mean the fucking world to me, and the thought of not being with you—" He exhaled a shuddering breath. "But I also don't want to hold you back. I don't want you to resent me—us—down the road, and that's what would've happened. You love Pine Hill—maybe not the SF office but the company. You've worked so hard and are so close to your dream. I can't let you throw that away for me. You might be willing to make that sacrifice, but I'm not."

A wild laugh bubbled out of Olivia's throat. "I'm not a child, Sammy. I don't need you to decide what's best for me. But you know what?" Her pulse thundered in her ears, and she swallowed back the urge to vomit. "Maybe you did do the right thing. At least now I know where we stand and how hard you're willing to fight for us."

Which is to say, not at all.

She needed to get out of here. The walls were closing in, and it was getting harder and harder to breathe. If she didn't get fresh air soon, she might faint.

Olivia ducked her head and shouldered her way past Sammy, trying to keep the pieces of heart together until she was far enough away to break down in peace.

He tried reaching for her again, but she shrugged him off.

"Liv, please." Sammy's voice broke. He sounded devastated. *Good.* "Don't—"

She tuned him out and quickened her pace until she was outside, where she ran. She ran and ran until the oxygen in her lungs dwindled and her legs turned to jelly from pumping up and down the hilly streets surrounding Sammy's house. She ran like she could somehow escape reality, but when she collapsed on the bench in a nearby park—mentally, emotionally, and physically drained—there was reality, staring her in the face and smirking like the inescapable bastard it was.

Olivia sniffled and wiped her face with the back of her hand, ignoring the concerned looks from passersby.

Her phone rang. She was tempted to ignore it, but conditioning overrode her instincts. A pathetic part of her hoped it was Sammy; instead, she saw her sister's name flashing on the screen.

Fuck. Olivia still hadn't told Alina about Richard's come-on at brunch. She'd meant to, but she kept making excuses and pushing it off because it was one talk she *really* didn't want to have.

"Hello?" Olivia attempted to steady her voice. She wouldn't tell Alina about Richard now either. She would, eventually, but she didn't have the capacity for another tough conversation today.

There was a short pause. "You sound different."

"I'm getting sick," Olivia lied. She'd never told Alina about her and Sammy's rekindled relationship either. She'd made *that* mistake before.

"Drink some tea and honey; it helps. Anyway, I wanted to make sure you received my email about wedding logistics. I need you to tell me what entrance song you want for the reception and which hairstyle option you prefer..."

While Alina rattled through Olivia's to-do items, Olivia stared straight ahead, numb.

She found it hard to care about Alina's wedding.

She found it hard to care about anything at all.

CHAPTER 25

OLIVIA MOVED OUT SOMETIME BETWEEN THEIR breakup and Sammy waking up the next morning. He hadn't heard her come home. He'd stayed up late, hoping to catch her on her way in. He didn't know what he'd say to her; he just knew he needed to see her, talk to her, before she left.

Only she hadn't come home, not even after the clock ticked past midnight. His body had finally rebelled, and he'd fallen into a troubled sleep. When he woke up a little past nine, he found Olivia's door ajar and her room cleaned out. Nothing in the closet, on the desk, or in the dresser drawers. Nothing in the bathroom. No note, text, or voicemail. She was just...gone.

Sammy sank onto her perfectly made-up bed and covered his face with his hands, pain shredding his heart into a million ribbons. The silence was deafening. Other than the faint trace of her perfume, it was like she'd never been there at all.

"I'm sorry," he whispered. The words echoed back at him, heavy and sorrowful.

He closed his eyes, trying to breathe. It hurt. The air, the silence, everything. It hurt so fucking bad, he may as well have fed his heart through a wood chipper and stomped on the resulting pieces for good measure.

Sammy thought he'd done the right thing. He loved Olivia too much to let her give up on her dream for him. She'd gotten into her predicament *because* of him. If he hadn't fucked up somehow with the roach thing, the post never would've circulated online, and her company wouldn't have had an issue with their relationship. It wouldn't have made her choose.

I would've chosen you.

He released a shuddering breath, wishing not for the first time that life hadn't fucked them over.

Sammy loved Olivia. Olivia loved him. They hadn't said it out loud over the summer, but they hadn't needed to. It'd been there in every kiss, every smile, every moment they'd spent together. And still, it wasn't enough.

His phone pinged with a text. Then another. Then another.

He snatched it up, hoping it was Olivia, but it wasn't. It was Penny with a simple message: We found out who it was! Check your email.

Sammy's stomach lurched.

His team had been working like crazy to figure out who'd been behind the viral tweet. Other than his or her username, @raiderssucks23 was anonymous. They hadn't posted since the cupcake incident, nor had they spoken with reporters.

After a thorough review of the bakery's protocols and interviews with all the staff, Sammy had doubted the veracity of the tweet's claim more and more. Their food safety standards were top-notch, his employees excelled at their jobs and were loyal as hell to Sammy, and Crumble & Bake had received an A grade from the Department of Public Health for as long as it had been in business. Perhaps it was wishful thinking, but Sammy was convinced the roach accusation was sabotage. Unfortunately, without knowing who the accuser was, that was impossible to prove.

Sammy opened his email. The blood drained from his face as he scrolled through the attached screenshots and pictures. By the time he reached the last attachment, the smoldering embers of anger in his stomach had erupted into full-blown fury.

Thanks. I'll take it from here, he texted back.

He stood, got in his car, and drove to Telegraph Hill. He parked in front of the modern two-story house with the Hummer in front and rang the doorbell. The Hummer no doubt got plenty of stink eye in environmentally conscious San Francisco, but the driver likely didn't give a shit.

Sammy rang the doorbell again. After three more rings, he heard footsteps before the front door flew open.

"What the hell?" Edison demanded. He was barefoot and wore a loosely belted bathrobe that was in danger of unbelting. "Are you—"

Sammy's fist slammed into his face before he could finish his sentence.

Edison howled and clutched his bleeding nose. *"What the fu—ugh!"*

Another punch, this time to the other side of his face.

Sammy stepped into the foyer and kicked the door shut behind him while he dodged Edison's pathetic attempts to retaliate.

"I'll sue you for this, you fucking asshole," Edison babbled, his words muffled through the hand over his face. "I will *destroy you*. I will—"

He squeaked in terror when Sammy grabbed him by the collar of his shirt and slammed him against the wall. The fury burned bright inside Sammy, fueling his adrenaline, but he kept his face and voice calm when he spoke. "What will you do, Eddie?" he asked, using Edison's hated childhood nickname. "Will you hire someone to fake finding a cockroach in one of my cupcakes and post the photo online?"

Edison's eyes bugged, and Sammy smiled thinly. "Yeah, I know. Found out today—I hired an investigator to do some sleuthing, and he finally uncovered @raiderssucks23's real identity. Seen him before?" He pulled up the relevant screenshot on his phone and shoved it in front of Edison's face. The photo showed a stocky guy with dark hair and a mean mug. Sammy had seen him only once before, but he recognized him on sight. It was Bulldog, the guy who'd accused him of sexting his girlfriend all those weeks ago.

Real name: Bobby Cooper. Girlfriend: Amanda Lerning. Girlfriend's profession: paralegal at Sterling, Wilson & Cartwright, aka Edison's law firm.

Edison sneered. "No clue who that is, but it sure don't look like me."

"No, but it sure does look like your paralegal's boyfriend."

"So? It's a small world. You can't prove—"

"My investigator had an interesting chat with Bobby, who happens to be quite a whiz in the kitchen. Works as a production baker for a rival bakery, in fact. He also happens to have loose lips once he's threatened with a lawsuit. Said you paid him a thousand bucks to replicate one of my cupcakes, bake a roach into it, and post it online. Now, why would you do that, Eddie?" Sammy's tone remained conversational. "I thought we were family."

"Fuckin' Bobby," Edison snarled. "That man doesn't have two brain cells to rub together. He's always hated you, you know. Amanda is a big fan—but then, she's always been dumb too, and a shitty paralegal to boot—and he couldn't stand it. Always hanging around outside our office waiting for her, complaining, being a useless piece of shit. Thought I'd fuck with him one day and said I overheard Amanda telling her friend she was sexting you." He chuckled. "The stupid oaf bought it. He even showed up at your little shop. Too bad he was too much of a pussy to do anything. Hey, at least it was easy to convince him to mess with you. Business has boomed at the bakery he works at ever since the tweet went viral. Of course, most of that money goes to the owner, not Bobby, but that's not my problem."

Sammy forced himself not to throw his piece-of-shit cousin on the ground and beat him senseless. A few punches were one thing; murder was another, and he refused to go to jail because of Edison.

"Why?" he demanded. "We've never been close, but we're family. Why would you do something so despicable?"

"Why?" Edison's voice rose. "Because I can! Because *I'm* the star of the family, not you! I went to Harvard. I'm a fucking *partner* at my law firm. But all anyone talks about is you. Sammy, Sammy, Sammy. Even when we were kids, you were everyone's favorite." His eyes flashed with venom. "No one except me sees what a loser you really are, so I have to show them. How's business been lately?" His sneer returned. "Heard you had to pause the expansions on the East Coast. What a shame."

Sammy felt sick. He couldn't believe he was related to someone so vindictive. Psychologists would have a field day with Edison—he was the textbook definition of a narcissist.

"Sorry to disappoint, but the expansions are going ahead as planned. Crumble & Bake will survive. So will I. But you?" He tightened his grip on Edison's shirt. "You'll always be a sorry excuse of a cousin and human being. Oh, and thanks for your little speech." He waved his phone in the air. "I got it all on tape."

Then, because he couldn't help himself, Sammy punched Edison one last time for good measure. While the other man screamed and crumpled to the ground, he got back in his car and drove to the bakery.

He had a business to save.

CHAPTER 26

OLIVIA WAS IN A FUNK. SHE DIDN'T GET INTO A FUNK often, so she had no clue what to do. Her usual methods of coping with stress all failed.

Deep-cleaning her off-campus apartment until the place sparkled like a Tiffany diamond? Failed.

Purging and donating half her closet to Goodwill and re-color coordinating the rest? Failed.

Eating her weight in Ben & Jerry's while watching every Meg Ryan rom-com ever made? Failed.

"Get it together." She glared at her reflection. She was wearing her only pair of sweatpants and an old tie-dye shirt she'd forgotten she owned. Eleanor would have a heart attack if she saw her dressed like this. *Too freaking bad.* Olivia was over trying to live up to her mother's unrealistic expectations. She hadn't spoken to Eleanor since that terrible brunch with her, Alina, and Richard, and she didn't want to. She was stressed enough, thank you.

Olivia's phone buzzed with a text—a photo of Kat and Ty (whom Olivia could finally think of using his first name), holding glasses of wine in what looked like Napa. Kat was beaming; Ty was more reserved, but his eyes twinkled with contentment.

Messages in the book club's group chat flew fast and furious.

Natalie: Omg this is so freakin' cute! YOU GUYS.

Tamara: Jess says to tell Ty he owes her a hundred bucks. Lost a bet, something about Zuckerberg?

Tamara: P.S. Pic is cute. I almost gagged, which means it's epically adorable. 👍

Olivia: Agreed.

Olivia: With the cuteness part, not the gagging part.

Olivia: Have you eaten at the French Laundry yet? It has three Michelin stars.

Donna: Can you bring me back a bottle of wine?

Olivia: If you go to TFL, try their salmon cornets. Heard they're good.

Kat: Lol thx, yes, and I will.

Kat: Ty says Jess cheated because she had inside info so it doesn't count.

Tamara: Oh ffs. Now I'll have to hear about this all day!

Tamara: Dude's a billionaire. He can pony up a hundred bucks.

Kat: This is Ty. Please tell Jessica it's not about the money; it's about the principle.

Tamara: 🤦 Gawd, men suck. This is why I'm a lesbian.

Natalie: LMAO

Donna: 😂

Olivia smiled a small but genuine smile for the first time in two weeks. Her instincts had been right—Kat and Ty had hit it off at happy hour, and they'd secretly gone on several dates since then before they announced they were officially dating. It was the definition of a whirlwind relationship, but Olivia was happy her friend had ditched her toxic ex and was now with a great guy—a billionaire, to boot. From what she could tell, Ty treated Kat like a queen, and they could nerd out about Roman emperors and obscure trivia all they wanted together. It was a match made in history-nerd heaven.

Even though she was in school, Olivia made time to attend the book club meetings and weekly happy hours virtually. Since she was joining by computer, the club had pledged to host all their events at the members' homes on a rotating schedule. She felt bad that they had to give up the Catalina's margaritas for her, but they insisted they would rather see her than drink jumbo-size cocktails that gave them massive hangovers anyway.

She was about to ask whether they'd read the latest release by L.M. Slade, her favorite erotica author, when an incoming call from her sister interrupted her.

Alina had the worst timing when it came to phone calls.

Olivia groaned. If she had to confirm one more time that yes, she was attending the damn rehearsal dinner, she was going to lose her shit.

Nevertheless, sisterly obligation compelled her to answer. "Hey, this isn't—"

The stream of hysterical gibberish stunned her into silence. Alina was *never* hysterical, and the last time she'd uttered gibberish had been when they were in diapers.

Something was seriously wrong.

Adrenaline flooded Olivia's system, and she clutched her phone tighter. "Slow down," she commanded, injecting as much calm into her tone as possible. If she freaked out, Alina would freak out more, and the world did not need two Tang women freaking out at the same time. "Breathe. Enunciate. What's wrong?"

"Kayla," Alina choked out. "He's cheating on me with *Kayla!*"

Shit. *Fuck me sideways with a spoon.*

Olivia gulped, her pulse drumming with shock and guilt. She *still* hadn't told her sister about Richard's sleazy proposition during brunch. She'd meant to; Sammy had convinced her when she'd talked about it with him. But life got crazy, and the more time passed, the more she'd leaned toward *not* telling Alina. It wasn't like she would've taken him up on it, and she'd assumed his indiscretion had been a one-time thing. In hindsight, that'd been foolish thinking. *Of course* Richard was a horndog that fucked anything that moved—including his fiancée's maid of honor.

"I was cleaning the apartment and found a burner phone that he's been using to communicate with her. Unlocked—I guess he thought I'd never find it. I thought it was a work phone or something, but then I saw their messages—" Alina's voice broke into a sob. "You know what he said when I confronted him about it? He said I was overreacting. That it meant nothing and that I needed to chill before I stressed myself out more."

A rush of anger surged through Olivia. "Fuck him. He's a lying, cheating asshole, and you're better off without him."

Silence.

Olivia gripped her phone tighter. "Linny." She used the nickname she hadn't used since they were children. "Tell me you left him."

More silence.

"*Alina.*"

"You don't understand." A defensive note crept into Alina's voice. "Richard and I have been together for *years.* I can't throw away a yearslong relationship on a whim."

"It's not on a whim. He *cheated* on you with your cousin and maid of honor, for God's sake!" Olivia paced her apartment. Sure, Richard was rich and good-looking in a generic douche kind of way, but she'd never understood how he'd persuaded her smart, beautiful, successful sister to fall in love with him. She and Alina may not have been close, but she'd be the first to admit that Alina was way out of his league. "Does Mom know?"

"Yes." Alina sniffled. "She told me to turn the other cheek. She said I would be a fool to throw away my engagement over one mistake."

"Of course she did." Eleanor probably freaked out more over potentially losing a status-symbol son-in-law than she did over the fact that her daughter got cheated on by her fiancé.

"She's right." Alina released a long, slow breath, and Olivia could practically see her wiping away her tears and straightening her shoulders. "Richard has been so great to me before this...incident, and he'll be the perfect husband. He's handsome, successful, and sophisticated. Do you know how hard it is to find men that possess all those qualities, are over the age of thirty, *and* who are ready to settle down in Chicago? Plus, the invites for the wedding went out already. We've booked the venue, the band... We spent a fortune on the flowers. It would be so embarrassing to have to cancel."

Olivia couldn't believe it. "You're staying with him because *you spent a lot of money on flowers?*" A few months ago, she might've been more sympathetic to Alina's point of view. She had zero tolerance for cheaters, but from a purely cost-benefit analysis, going through with the wedding rather than calling it off over "one mistake" (if it really was *one* mistake) made sense.

Now, she couldn't help but realize how, well, shallow it all sounded. Even when she'd described why Richard would be the "perfect" husband—*gag*—Alina hadn't mentioned his personality. She hadn't said he was funny or loving or had a great sense of humor. She focused on surface-level things that made *her* look good by association—his looks and his money.

"Don't be so judgmental," Alina snapped, sounding more like her old self. "You don't get it. You're not even dating anyone. You don't understand the pressure I'm under—"

"I don't have to be dating someone to know cheating is unacceptable—"

"This is my *life* and *reputation*, Olivia. I can't throw it all away because of one indiscretion—"

"It's not just one indiscretion!" Olivia shouted.

There was a long, loaded pause. "What are you talking about?" A tint of fear stained Alina's words.

There was no going back now.

Olivia swallowed hard. "Remember when we went to brunch? We got in an argument over your new bachelorette date, and I went to the restroom to cool off. Richard followed me and propositioned me."

No response.

"He asked me to come to your hotel room while you and Mom were at a wine tasting. Me. Your *sister*. While you were sitting just outside. Of course I said no, but if he was brazen enough to do that, he's definitely brazen enough to try it with other women. Kayla is the one you know about, but who knows how many—"

"You're lying," Alina said flatly.

It took Olivia a few seconds to process the words. When she did, she held her phone away from her ear, slack-jawed. "*What? Why would I lie about that?*"

"If it were true, why didn't you tell me earlier? It seems awfully convenient to only bring it up now when you want me to leave Richard."

"Of course I want you to leave him!" Olivia was *this close* to losing her shit. "He's a sleazy, entitled, cheating douchebag! I didn't tell you because I thought it was a one-time thing, and since nothing happened, I didn't want to hurt you. I gave him the benefit of the doubt because of *you* and how much you love him."

And because I was too chickenshit to bring it up with you.

The guilt clamped around her neck like a noose and drained some indignance out of her reply.

"That's a total crock," Alina said. "Admit it. You want me to call off the wedding so I'll be single and lonely like you. You've always resented me, Olivia. You've always wanted what I have—my grades, my clothes, my relationship with Mom. Don't think I haven't noticed. In fact, how do I know *you're* not the one who propositioned *him*? You're almost thirty and you're nowhere near married. You know what they say—misery loves company."

The words slammed into Olivia with the force of a two-ton truck. Hurt washed over her, sucking the oxygen out of her lungs and causing her vision to blur. "Are you kidding me?" she said shakily. "*You're* the one who called *me*. I tried to protect you and make you feel better, and you throw it in my face. I admit I copied you when I was younger—because I looked up to you. You were my older sister. I *worshiped* you, but at some point, you decided this was a competition. Not me, Linny. *You* were the one who stopped cheering me on first, who tried to one-up me at every turn. And you know what? After he propositioned me, Richard didn't look concerned that I would tell you because he *knew* you'd take his side. Even your douchebag fiancé knew you wouldn't believe your own sister. That's why I didn't tell you what he did earlier—because deep down, I knew it too. Perhaps I should've told you sooner anyway, but if this is how you react *after* you already found out he's cheating on you, I don't want to know what you would've said then. So *screw* you, and screw Mom." The burning behind her eyes intensified. "Go ahead with your wedding, but I'll no longer be there. Consider this my official resignation as your bridesmaid. Face it—you never wanted me to be one anyway."

Olivia hung up before Alina could respond. She wasn't interested in anything her sister had to say anymore.

Then she walked to her bed, buried her face in her pillow, and screamed her heart out.

Olivia didn't hear a peep from Alina for days after the Phone Call. She threw herself into school and preparing for Kris's wedding. She both dreaded and longed to see Sammy again; they'd booked tickets for the same flights to and from Italy, and the thought of spending hours sitting next to him in a cramped airborne vessel made her anxiety skyrocket.

She'd been a coward, packing and sneaking out of his house in the middle of the night, but she couldn't bear the thought of saying goodbye. Instead, she'd booked a hotel for her last night in San Francisco before taking the Caltrain to Palo Alto.

She hadn't talked to Sammy since.

Olivia stared at her applied behavioral economics notes. She'd been working nonstop this week to finish all her schoolwork before she left for Italy so she could enjoy the weekend, and her body was punishing her for it. Her vision blurred, her head ached, and she couldn't stop jittering from all the espresso she'd consumed in the past seventy-two hours.

She'd just dragged herself back into the world of habit loops and dual-system theory when someone knocked on the door—once, twice. Short, impatient knocks, like they were annoyed they had to announce their presence.

A frown creased Olivia's brow. She wasn't expecting anyone.

Warily, she got up and peeked through the peephole.

Shock zipped through her, rendering her speechless.

Her mother stared back at her, cold and elegant as always in a green brocade jacket and St. John knit.

"Olivia, open the door. I know you're there. I heard your footsteps," Eleanor said coolly.

Dammit.

Olivia swung the door open, trying to steady her breathing. "Mother, this is a surprise."

"Aren't you going to invite me in?" Eleanor raked her eyes over Olivia's Phi Beta Kappa T-shirt and plaid PJ pants with displeasure. "I see it's laundry day."

"It's not laundry day. I'm wearing these clothes because they're comfortable." Eleanor had been here for ten seconds, and Olivia already wanted to tear her hair out.

She stepped aside, allowing her mother to enter and take in her off-campus apartment with the same expression she'd use if she found dog poop on the bottom of her shoe. The place was small but neat and decorated in shades of soothing lavender, gray, and white. The wooden dining table doubled as Olivia's study nook, and it groaned beneath the weight of her laptop, coffee, textbooks, and thick business case studies. Small succulents lined the window ledge, and a giant poster of Audrey Hepburn from *Breakfast at Tiffany's* hung on the wall.

"Comfort is overrated." Eleanor shifted her eyes away from the stuffed panda that Olivia bought in a Shanghai market during study abroad. It sat on top of a bookshelf, slightly worn after eight years but still cute as hell. "You should hire a decorator. Your apartment decor could use some polishing."

"No." Olivia shut the door behind her. "I don't have the money for that, and I don't own this place. I'm moving out next spring. What are you doing here, Mother?"

"Straight to the point without even an offer of tea. I thought I raised you to have better manners." Eleanor smoothed a hand over her hair, which was still shiny and black thanks to regular visits to her colorist. "Fine. I'm here because I want you to tell your sister you lied."

"Excuse me?"

"Alina broke up with Richard three days ago because *you* told her he hit on you. You didn't know?" Eleanor's smile lacked humor at the shock scrawled across Olivia's face. "The wedding is off. Hundreds of thousands of dollars down the drain. All of Chicago society gossiping behind our backs. Your sister is a wreck. I want you to fix it. Immediately."

Alina broke up with Richard? When? The last time Olivia spoke to her, Alina had seemed intent on staying with the bastard. What had changed?

"I can't fix it. What's done is done, and Richard *did* hit on me." Olivia crossed her arms over her chest, trying not to waver beneath her mother's withering stare.

"It doesn't matter. You *will* tell your sister you lied and save this wedding."

"Why?" Olivia demanded. "So she can marry a cheating asshole? I can't believe you'd want your own daughter to spend her life with someone like that!"

"Stop being so naive," Eleanor snapped. "Everyone makes sacrifices. No one is perfect. Your sister is already over thirty. The chances of her landing an eligible bachelor like Richard again decrease by the day. If you care about her, you'll tell her you lied and convince her to take him back and go through with the wedding before it's too late."

Olivia couldn't help it—she started laughing. Hysterically.

Eleanor frowned. "Stop that. It's unbecoming."

"I can't help it." Olivia hiccupped, wiping tears of mirth from her eyes. "You know what's funny? All my life, I've wanted your approval. School, my career, my relationships—everything I've ever done was colored by what I thought you wanted. But no matter how many As or promotions I got, I've never been quite good enough. Alina was the golden child, and I couldn't understand why you loved her more than me. We're both your daughters. It wasn't until today that I realized you don't love her either. You don't love anyone but yourself."

Eleanor's eyes sparked with fury. "How *dare* you take that tone with me. I'm your mother. I raised you. I fed and sheltered you. I paid for your education, your music and dance lessons—"

"For *you*. Not for us. You molded us into children you could brag about. You never asked us whether we wanted to spend our weekends practicing violin and piano and learning French. You did it because it was what 'good' families did." Olivia shook her head. "Even now, you're more worried about my tone than the fact that I just accused you of not loving your daughters."

"You're an ungrateful brat. You always were—talking back, resisting, giving me headaches Alina never did." Eleanor's tone remained cold. "You've no idea the sacrifices I made to ensure you and your sister had a better childhood than I did. I was born during the Great Leap Forward. I grew up during the Cultural Revolution. There were months when I had nothing to eat except one measly bowl of rice a day, and my chance at an education was ripped away from me. But I made it to the U.S. Even without a formal degree, I was smart. I befriended the right people, dated the right men. Now look at me. Two Ivy League–educated daughters, one of whom was on the cusp of marrying into one of Chicago's most prominent families—until *you* messed it up." A short, bitter laugh. "I should've aborted you like I'd originally wanted. You were an accident; I only wanted one child. But I had a moment of weakness and kept you, and you've been a disappointment ever since. This isn't about *love*, Olivia. It's about survival. Those at the top survive; those on the bottom don't. The fact you've never understood that is exactly why you'll never have my approval."

Pain sliced through Olivia and shredded her insides. *I should've aborted you... You were an accident*

It was one thing to know your own mother hated you; it was another to hear her say it to your face.

Fury and a cold, calm acceptance chased the pain through her system, creating a maelstrom of conflicting emotions. "You know what? I don't want your approval. Not anymore." Her nails dug into the soft flesh of her palms. "You raised me, and for that I'm grateful. But just because I'm grateful doesn't mean I respect you. I finally understand what you value most, and it is nowhere near what I value as a family member, a friend, or a human being. If I ever *do* earn your approval, I'll know I've royally fucked up." Olivia opened the door. "Goodbye, Mother."

You could hear a pin drop in the silence.

Mother and daughter stared at each other, both knowing this was the closing chapter of a long, tumultuous story neither had particularly enjoyed.

Eleanor didn't say a word as she walked out without a backward glance.

Olivia closed the door and pressed her forehead against the solid oak, her pulse pounding in her ears. She might throw up, but she also felt a hundred pounds lighter.

She was finally free—free from her mother's expectations, her judgment, her toxic outlook on the world and messed-up priorities. Olivia could make her own decisions and live her life without worrying about what Eleanor Tang would think.

She didn't know how long she stayed there, head to the door, mind racing with possibilities, but she got to a point where she knew what she had to do next.

One. Two. Three. Four. Five.

On the count of five, Olivia raised her head and made two phone calls.

The first was to New York, where she set her plan in motion. The second was to Chicago—and it was that call that upended her life all over again.

CHAPTER 27

KRIS AND NATE'S WEDDING WAS BEAUTIFUL. THE MUSIC was on point. The food was delicious. And the guest list? So star-studded it made the Met Gala look like a middle school prom.

Sammy couldn't enjoy any of it.

He stared across the dance floor at where Olivia was dancing with Courtney and a couple of guys from the latest hit teen drama. Despite playing high schoolers, the guys were all in their twenties, and one of them was standing way too close to Olivia for comfort.

"What's that I smell?" Luke Peterson sniffed the air. "Déjà vu. New cologne, Sammy?"

"Ha-ha," Sammy said, unamused. "Might want to brush up on your humor alongside your skills on the field."

The burly ex-rugby player—another friend from study abroad—currently assistant coached the men's rugby team at the University of Wisconsin-Madison.

"*Meow.*" Luke stuffed a mini hot dog in his mouth. "Since when did you get so snarky?"

"Leave him alone." Nardo pushed his glasses up his nose. "He's busy wallowing."

"I thought it was Kris's wedding. Didn't realize it was Gang Up on Sammy Day." Yes, Sammy was being a moody boor, but everyone expected him to be happy-go-lucky all the time and that was just not possible. He had good days and bad days, and the latter had outnumbered the former recently, so sue him if he was a little grumpy.

Like a coward, he'd switched flights so he and Olivia wouldn't be on the same plane to Italy. He couldn't do it—sit next to her for thirteen hours nonstop without being able to touch her, kiss her, *be* with her.

Of course, he'd landed in Florence more miserable than when he'd boarded, which was quite a feat, considering he'd been in hell since he and Olivia broke up. *Again.*

"All I'm saying is, we've seen this movie before." Luke gulped down his champagne. Kris would have a heart attack if she saw him chugging Moet, which was not meant to be chugged; fortunately, she was too busy with guests to pay attention to the trio skulking by the appetizer table. "You, Liv, heart eyes emoji, drama, blah blah blah. I dunno what happened, but can't you two take a page from B and F's book, make up, and make out? Cuz all these longing glances and melancholy are bumming me out."

You could always count on Luke not to mince words.

"B and F?" Nardo stepped aside so a pixie-faced actress famous for her gritty indie roles could reach the fruit plate.

"Blake and Farrah," Luke clarified. "Look at 'em. They're disgusting, but at least they're not depressing."

The guys' heads swiveled toward the couple in question, who were dancing and staring adoringly into each other's eyes. The saccharine-sweet display *was* pretty disgusting.

Sammy had never been more jealous.

Deep down, he was a commitment guy. He'd had one-night stands and the occasional fling before, but he craved the stable relationship, the family, the proverbial white picket fence and kids. He'd much rather have a strong, lasting connection with one woman than dozens of flimsy ties with women who didn't care about him and who he'd probably never see again.

The problem was, he'd driven away the only woman he'd had that kind of connection with—because he was a massive idiot. The fact that he'd done it because he'd thought it was the right thing to do did not change the scale of his idiocy.

Sammy's eyes drifted toward Olivia again. The actors were gone—thank God—and she was whispering something to Courtney. She wore the same yellow dress as all the bridesmaids, but she was the one he couldn't take his eyes off of. She glowed with a light that had nothing to do with her outer beauty and everything to do with her inner being, and Sammy was certain he'd always find his way to her, no matter what. He didn't need to see her to know where she was; she was his North Star, his guiding light.

What have I done?

He felt sick.

"Yoo-hoo!" Luke waved his hand in front of Sammy's face. "Earth to Sammy."

"I'll be right back."

"Told ya. Déjà vu," he heard Luke say as he left.

"Shut up, Luke," Nardo said.

Sammy edged around his friends, his long, purposeful strides eating up the dance floor until he reached where Olivia and Courtney were standing.

Courtney saw Sammy first. Her blue eyes widened a fraction of an inch and she nudged Olivia, whose smile fell when she turned and saw who stood behind her.

His heart twisted.

"Hi." She looked wary.

Sammy cleared his throat, feeling hot under the collar. Whoever invented the tuxedo needed to die; he could barely breathe in the damn thing. "Can we talk?" Cardi B came on, and the crowd went wild. He grimaced. "Somewhere a little less loud?"

"Um." Olivia appeared flustered. She glanced at Courtney, who pushed her in Sammy's direction.

"Go. I'm starting a conga line," the brunette announced. "If you think you can't conga to Cardi, you haven't seen me in action." She marched off, leaving the ex-lovers alone.

After an awkward silence and a few false starts, Sammy and Olivia walked through the reception in silence until they reached the line of marble statues and hedges near the castle's main building, where the music became a distant beat instead of a deafening roar.

"So—" They spoke at the same time.

Their nervous laughs mingled in the sweet evening air before they fell silent again.

The last time they'd seen each other, they'd been high on adrenaline and charged emotion. Now, after weeks apart, they were subdued—like they finally understood the import of what had happened, what they'd done.

What *Sammy* had done.

"I heard about what happened with that Twitter guy," Olivia said. "I'm glad you sorted it all out."

In exchange for Sammy not filing charges, Bulldog—Bobby—had gone on record to confess he'd made up the roach claim. He'd been fired for his actions and destroyed online; meanwhile, Crumble & Bake's business spiked back up immediately. They were doing even better now than before the PR crisis.

Edison, whose role Bobby had explained in crystal-clear detail in his public statement, had also gotten fired, not to mention shunned by most of the Yus. Sammy's family had been shocked but not necessarily surprised by Edison's actions, and Sammy hadn't seen or heard from his cousin since the day he confronted him.

Good riddance.

"Thanks." Sammy rubbed the back of his neck. "I didn't see you leave that day. My house, I mean. I thought you weren't moving out till later."

He remembered the blow to his gut when he woke up to find her gone like it was yesterday.

Olivia tucked a strand of hair behind her ear. "I checked into a hotel for the night. It didn't seem right for me to stay after what happened."

"You should've stayed. I wouldn't have kicked you out."

"I know." A tiny shrug paired with an uncomfortable expression. "It was just one night."

One less night I had with you. Though they'd broken up that same day, so it wasn't like they would've binge-watched Netflix or cracked jokes over dinner like they usually did. But even when they weren't speaking to each other, Sammy wanted her nearby.

"I didn't see you on the plane," Olivia added. "I thought—I wasn't sure whether you were still coming."

"I changed my flight. Figured you wouldn't want to be near me for that long. I am sorry, Liv," Sammy said, his voice quiet. "I was an ass. I shouldn't have decided for you." His throat bobbed with a hard swallow. "I miss you. I know that doesn't change anything, but I wanted you to know. I didn't put up a fight because I thought I was doing the right thing—making it easier for you—but I never want you to think it was because I don't care enough. Because I do. The moment I set eyes on you in that crappy orientation room in Shanghai nine years ago, I was a goner. Not a day has passed since that I haven't thought of you, and I wish...I wish I could run away with you and hole up in the mountains somewhere, just the two of us. No internet, no meddling families, no overreaching bosses...just us." He laughed softly. "That sounds stupid, doesn't it?"

"It doesn't sound stupid at all." Olivia's eyes glistened. "I understand why you did what you did—with the email. I'm still upset about it...but I understand. And even though I hate that you decided for me, I don't hate you. I could never hate you."

And then her lips—lips he thought he'd never taste again—were on his, and everything disappeared except this woman, right here, right now.

Sammy tasted her greedily, his tongue delving into her mouth like they'd been apart for centuries instead of weeks. His hands snaked around her waist and snagged her dress in two tight fist-fuls. She felt so good, so *right*, that a pack of wild horses couldn't have dragged him away.

After an eternity that ended far too soon, they broke apart, panting for breath.

He closed his eyes and rested his forehead against hers, waiting for his heart rate to return to normal. He never wanted to leave. He'd give up everything—his business, his family, his life—to stay here with her, in this magical place where the world couldn't touch them, forever.

"I love you."

Three simple words. He'd said them before, a lifetime ago, but they took on new resonance now. Sammy was no longer a young naive college student caught up in the magic of a new city and first love. He was older, more battle-weary from the ups and downs of life. The joys and hardships, the many women his mother had thrown his way—none of whom had inspired an iota of what the woman in front of him did with a blink of her eyes or curve of her lips. That Sammy loved Olivia as deeply, as truly, and as irrevocably as he once had, even after all they'd been through, spoke volumes.

This was endgame.

Olivia's mouth parted, but Sammy barreled on before he lost his nerve. There was more he needed to say, and he wanted to get the words out before Olivia reacted to his confession, since he had no idea *how* she'd react. "It's selfish of me, but when I woke up after you left and realized you weren't there, I was devastated. I thought I could handle being away from you, but I can't. I'll always need you in my life. I know we have the issue with your company to think about, and I know I messed up, but I was hoping, maybe, we could figure it out together. For real." His throat bobbed with a tight swallow. "That is, if you still want to."

"Sammy." A tear slipped down her cheek. He rubbed it away with his thumb, his chest aching. "I love you too. With all of my heart."

A starburst of joy exploded inside him, but the initial sparks hadn't even faded yet before her next words brought it all crashing down.

"But I need some time."

A chill swept through the late-summer air, reminding them that fall was right around the corner and that no season, no matter how beautiful or beloved, lasted forever.

"What does that mean?" Sammy's heart picked up pace, and he regretted all the champagne he'd drunk earlier. "You love me. I love you. That should be enough."

Olivia pressed her fingers to her temple, her face twisted in torment. "Do you remember what you told me in Lake Tahoe?"

He responded with a blank stare.

"It's not about love," she said softly. "It's about timing."

Sammy stepped back. He needed space, air, *something*, because even though they were outside, he felt as though walls were closing in on him. "Is this about your job? Because—"

"No. Yes. No." Olivia squeezed her eyes shut. "It's not just that. It's me. I'm a mess, and I don't—I'm not in the right head-space for us. Not right now."

"Why? What happened?" He scanned her face, searching for something—anything—to pin his hopes to. All he saw was pain and evasion—she wouldn't meet his eyes. "Tell me. We can get through it together."

"I wish I could, but I'm not ready to talk about it right now." Her voice cracked. "I'm sorry. I need some time to sort things out first. Once I do, I'll explain everything. I promise."

Sammy took another step back, his heart tearing itself apart in confusion. "You can do better than that."

Hurt washed over her features. "What?"

"'It's not you; it's me' might be the most played-out excuse of all time." A muscle twitched in his jaw, pulsing in rhythm with his beaten heart. "If you don't want me, just say it. Don't string me along. Don't tell me you love me, then turn around and say you can't be with me. This isn't a game, Liv!" It was his voice's turn to crack. "This is us."

More tears slipped down her cheek. This time, Sammy didn't wipe them away.

Instead, he shoved his hands in his pockets, every inch of him screaming with pain and frustration. Why did it always have to be this hard? What did they do in their past lives that they had to keep going through this cycle? Love, heartbreak, rinse, and repeat. When did it end?

"I know that! I'm not playing a game." Olivia sounded as frustrated as he felt.

"Then what? Are you punishing me for what happened in San Francisco? If so, I'll fucking get on my knees. Beg. Call your boss myself and tell him I'm the one who fucked up—"

"No." She shook her head and pressed her fist to her mouth. "I told you, it's not that. I just need—"

"Time. For a problem you refuse to talk about, but that's apparently turned you into a mess—even though you're never a mess," he said. "Yeah, I heard you the first time. I don't know what would be worse—you lying or you not trusting me enough to let me in on what's happening." Blood roared in his ears, and it was all he could do to remain upright.

"Sammy—"

He paused at the abrupt cutoff in her words and followed her gaze toward the other side of the marble statue they'd been standing behind until a few seconds ago. Kris and Nate, the bride and groom themselves, stared back with bemused expressions.

Shit. Sammy and Olivia had kept their relationship a secret from their study-abroad friends over the summer because they'd wanted time to enjoy each other's company before everyone got into their business and because there'd been so much uncertainty about what would happen once Olivia graduated from business school. The last thing they needed was to announce they were back together only to break up again in front of the people who'd witnessed every moment of their roller-coaster ride.

Sammy had told Nardo after his and Olivia's breakup, but judging by Kris's smirk and Nate's huge eyes, they clearly thought they'd caught Sammy and Olivia—who, in their minds, were supposed to despise each other—making out in the bushes.

Technically, they were correct, except that wasn't the whole story.

"Hello," Kris drawled. "Nice night for a stroll."

Heat scorched Sammy's face; he could see Olivia turn a similar shade of scarlet out of the corner of his eye. Her tears had dried, but he could sense the tension vibrating through her.

"Y-yeah." Olivia inched away from Sammy, clearly unnerved by the audience. "Um, I'm going to rejoin the party. See if... anyone needs help."

She took off, her hair and dress a blur as she practically ran back to the reception, taking with her whatever she'd been about to say before Kris and Nate showed up.

Sammy clenched his jaw so hard his head hurt.

After a short conversation with a now-concerned-looking Kris and Nate, he excused himself and double-timed it back to his suite. There was no way he could stay at the reception for the rest of the night. He was so drained, he barely made it to his room without collapsing.

There, the silence engulfed him, and the scene with Olivia replayed itself in his head on repeat for hours until—*shit.*

Sammy bolted upright from his bed, his heart thundering.

I need some time.

We can get through it together.

I don't know what would be worse—you lying or you not trusting me enough to let me in on what's happening.

He'd accused her of not trusting him—but he was doing the same to her. Not trusting her enough to know that she wasn't lying, that she was going through something she couldn't or didn't want to talk about yet. She'd told him she loved him, but all he'd focused on was her request for time to figure her personal issues out. Not *I don't want you* or *We can't be together*—just time. She'd been willing to sacrifice her job, her dream for him, and he couldn't even grant her one simple request.

No, Sammy wasn't a nice guy. He was an asshole.

He cursed as he shoved his feet into the nearest pair of shoes and ran down the hall toward Olivia's room. He'd gotten her suite number from Farrah earlier, in case he didn't have a chance to talk to her at the reception, and now he prayed she was there as he knocked on the door.

The party should've ended by now—the castle was quiet while

guests slept off the night of revelry, and no music or conversation interrupted the stillness outside the leaded glass windows.

"Yes," Sammy said when Olivia opened the door. She still wore her bridesmaid dress, and it was clear she hadn't gone to sleep yet despite the late hour. She blinked in shock. "Yes, take as much time as you need. I don't care if it takes weeks or months or years. I'm not going anywhere. I'll be here. I'll wait—forever if I need to."

"Sammy," she breathed.

"I don't know what the hell I was thinking earlier, and I don't know what you're going through right now, but I know I'm not entitled to it. If you choose to share it with me, then I will gladly help you shoulder it. If not, I'll give you space." The words tumbled over each other as Sammy tried to get them all out at once. "Whatever you need. I love you."

Olivia wrapped her arms around him and buried her face in his chest. Knee-wobbling relief coursed through him as he squeezed her tight.

"I love you too."

That was enough for both of them.

CHAPTER 28

One Month Later

THE GRAVESTONE GLINTED IN THE PALE MORNING light, one memorial amongst thousands scattered throughout Goldhill Cemetery. It was so early, Olivia and Alina were the only ones there, and an eerie silence hung over the property like even the wind was loath to disturb those resting beneath the ground.

Olivia wrapped her coat tighter around herself, though she wasn't sure whether the chill had more to do with November in Nevada or with the words inscribed on the headstone: BRUCE YEN. REST IN PEACE. 1958–2020.

Bruce Yen, her father, who'd died in a freak car accident on his way back from Vegas three months ago. While Olivia had been cavorting around San Francisco, making love to Sammy, and fretting over her job, her father had been only two hundred miles away, dying.

It was weird. She didn't know the man, didn't even remember what he looked like. Other than shared genetic material, they were strangers. And yet Olivia felt a deep, abiding sorrow—not for the man himself but for what could've been. The father who'd never taught her how to ride a bike and would never walk her down the aisle at her wedding. The parent who could've been a counterweight to Eleanor's viciousness but who'd chosen to run instead, too daunted by the demands of marriage and fatherhood to stick around.

Alina stared at the tombstone, her face pale. "This whole situation feels surreal."

Olivia couldn't agree more.

She'd called her sister the day she cut ties with Eleanor, and they'd had a long, hard conversation that lasted hours. Lots of tears, anger, and angst. Alina admitted that she'd confronted Richard about him hitting on Olivia, and he hadn't denied it. Apparently, he'd thought she wouldn't break off the wedding for all the reasons she'd given Olivia, so he'd barely apologized. That, plus Olivia's words before she'd hung up on their last call, had been the last straw. Alina had called it quits, Richard had flipped out, and Eleanor had flown straight to California to lambast her younger daughter, even though breaking the engagement was Alina's decision.

When Olivia told her sister what happened with their mother, including when she'd asked Eleanor to leave—not just her apartment but her life—Alina had been stunned into silence. But she'd understood. For the first time in forever, she'd understood why Olivia did what she did, and she supported it. Alina's own relationship with Eleanor had been strained since she called off the wedding. They weren't estranged, but they hadn't spoken in weeks.

From what Olivia could tell, Alina was in no hurry to resume communication with Eleanor, who'd withdrawn into icy silence to regroup after the Chicago society papers exploded with news about Richard Barrons III's broken engagement.

"It's ironic." Alina brushed her fingers over the smooth stone. "If it hadn't been for the wedding, I wouldn't have tried to look for our father, but neither endeavor turned out the way I'd expected. No wedding but a funeral." Her mouth twisted. "Ironic," she repeated.

Olivia's breath puffed in the cold air.

During the call, Alina had let her in on a secret: she'd hired a private investigator to track down their father's whereabouts so she could invite him to her wedding. It was sentimental, dramatic, and wholly unlike Alina, but at the end of the day, every girl wanted to dance with her father and have him walk her down the aisle on her big day.

Eleanor hadn't suspected a thing, and the PI had run into brick wall after brick wall until he finally tracked Bruce down to a small town in northwestern Nevada—through police reports about the car crash. A truck ran a red light and slammed into the driver's side of Bruce's car; he'd been dead on impact.

According to the PI, Bruce had moved dozens of times over the years, going from odd job to odd job—most of it paid under the table—to avoid creditors after he'd lost all his money gambling. He'd never remarried or had children after leaving Eleanor, and his car had been registered under a fake name. Ditto for his lease, though the landlord was so sketchy it was a surprise there'd been paperwork at all.

Bruce had lived a sad, lonely life before his demise, and while a tiny shameful part of Olivia thought he deserved it for walking away from his family, a larger part of her mourned the man he'd once been. Eleanor, in a rare slipup, once told her and Alina that their father had aspired to be a poet. He'd wooed her with his beautiful words and romantic visions of the future, and she'd married him despite the voice in her head telling her it was a bad idea. She'd been right—when Bruce's poet dreams hadn't panned out, he'd turned to gambling for solace and left Eleanor to raise two daughters on her own.

Perhaps it had been that fleeting glimpse of humanity that compelled Olivia to cling on to hope for her mother for so long. It'd blinded her to the reality that whatever light had once existed in Eleanor's soul had been snuffed out long ago. For that, Olivia empathized with the woman who'd raised her—mourned her the same way she mourned her dead father, even though Eleanor was alive and well.

But there came a point when enough was enough, and Olivia had reached that point the day she opened the door and watched her mother walk out of her life.

"How are you, Linny?" she asked now, watching the only immediate family member she had left stare at the tombstone with a far-off look in her eyes.

"I've been better." Alina fiddled with the diamond stud in her ear. She was perfectly put together as always, in her sleek black Calvin Klein outfit and black Stuart Weitzman boots, but her complexion had lost its usual glow, and lines of tension bracketed her mouth. "I feel so stupid—about Richard, about Mom, about everything."

"You didn't know."

"I should've believed you when you first told me about Richard. But I wanted so bad for it not to be true..." Alina's gaze dipped. "I'm sorry, Liv. About everything. You didn't have to come—especially when you're so busy with school. I've been a horrible sister—"

"Stop. I *wanted* to come. He was my father too, and you're my sister. Though I wanted to slap you quite a few times over the years," Olivia added with a small smirk.

Alina narrowed her eyes. "I would've kicked your ass."

Shock barreled into Olivia. "Did—did you just say the word *ass?*"

The profanity-spewing Alina doppelgänger shrugged. "Fuck it. My fiancé cheated on me, my broken engagement is splashed all over the papers, my father's dead, and my mother's a bitch. I can say the word *ass* if I want to."

A laugh bubbled out of Olivia's throat, and the pressure that had weighed on her chest for the past few months eased the tiniest bit. "Yes, you can, but no way could you kick my ass." Silence descended again, during which a light bulb went off in her head. "You never got a bachelorette weekend, did you?"

"Thanks for rubbing it in," Alina said, looking miffed. She'd found Richard's burner phone before the event.

"I have an idea." A grin spread across Olivia's face. Ten minutes later, after she explained her plan, Alina answered with a matching grin.

"Let's do it."

They glanced at Bruce's gravestone one last time, bidding farewell to the man they'd never known and never would, and closing another chapter of their lives before they walked to the car Olivia had rented at the airport.

"You sure?" She typed a destination into the GPS and watched Alina for any signs of hesitation. All she saw was resolve.

"Hell yeah." Alina slipped on her sunglasses. "Let's rock this bitch."

Olivia laughed again, still unable to believe those words were coming out of her proper, uptight sister's mouth. She floored the gas, and they were off, speeding past dramatic desert landscapes and narrow slot canyons.

The Tang sisters were going to Vegas.

CHAPTER 29

"JAY-SUS, I AM *EXHAUSTED.*" CORDELIA FLOPPED ONTO the floor in a dramatic heap. "*Why* are so many people buying cupcakes on a random Wednesday?"

"Don't complain." Bryce slouched against the counter and folded his arms over his chest. "I, for one, am happy it's crazy again. We don't want a repeat of late August."

Cordelia shuddered. "True."

Sammy cleared his throat. Loudly. "Guys, I want you to meet someone."

His front house managers jerked their heads around and scrambled to their feet when they saw who stood next to him.

"This is Jude." He gestured to the brown-haired man who surveyed the shop with sharp eyes and a faint glimmer of amusement. "Jude, this is Cordelia and Bryce. They run the front of the house."

"Nice to meet you." Bryce stuck out his hand, then flushed, like he wasn't sure whether that was the right thing to do.

"Nice to meet you too." Jude returned the handshake with an easy smile. "You're right. We definitely don't want a repeat of late August."

"You're the new CEO." Cordelia gave him a once-over. "You're younger than I expected."

Trust Cordelia to speak her mind, even to new management.

Jude laughed. "Thank you, but there's no need to flatter me with words. A cupcake will do just fine."

Surprise flitted across Cordelia's face before she grinned. "I like you, Boss." She paused. "I mean, Boss Two. What should I call you now?" She directed this question at Sammy like he'd have an answer. "'Boss,' 'Boss One,' or 'Baking Boss'?"

"None of the above. Call me Sammy."

"*Boring.*"

He sighed. "Good luck," he muttered under his breath to Jude, who laughed harder.

"The people here are great. I'm glad you brought me on."

"Me too. Trust me, you're a lifesaver." Sammy slapped his new CEO's back before he left him to get to know Cordelia and Bryce better. Jude had asked to introduce himself and speak to all the employees of Crumble & Bake personally, and the front of the house was the last stop since the bakery had just closed for the day.

With the PR crisis behind him and business booming once again, Sammy had thrown himself headfirst into finding a CEO. After weeks of interviews, he'd lucked out with Jude, who was competent, approachable, detail oriented, and experienced—all the things he needed in a chief executive. In his late forties, Jude had worked in the food industry all his life, with his latest role being chief operating officer of a cult plant-burger chain, which he left because of the workplace culture. He'd officially signed the papers last week, and today was his first day on the job. As Sammy had predicted, the staff already loved him.

"Uh, Boss One?" Cordelia angled her head toward the entrance to the shop. "Think someone is looking for you."

Sammy followed her gaze, and the breath whooshed out of his lungs when he saw who stood on the other side of the now-locked front door.

"Hey, isn't that the—" Bryce started before Cordelia jabbed her elbow in his side.

"You guys talk. I'll be right back." Sammy forced himself to relax as he walked to the door and stepped into the warm midday sun. The usually bustling sidewalk was quiet in the lull between lunch and rush hour, and he noticed every sound around him—the quiet pounding of his heart, the jangling of bells as someone exited the shop next to his, the faint honk of a car horn in the distance. "That's quite an outfit."

Olivia blushed. She wore a black tee that bared her stomach and had a sparkly graphic of the famous Vegas sign stamped on the front, tiny denim shorts, and Adidas. Giant palm tree earrings swung from her ears and gleamed gold beneath the sun.

"I lost a bet with my sister." She grimaced. "She told me to wear this to see you. She was drunk at the time, so her judgment may have been off."

His brows knit together. "Alina? I didn't realize you two were drinking and making bets with each other now."

Last he'd heard, the Tang sisters were on barely civil terms.

Then again, he hadn't spoken with Olivia since Italy. It'd killed him not to talk to or see her, but he'd kept his word and given her space to sort out whatever she needed to sort out.

"It's a long story." Olivia blinked up at him, looking so beautiful—even in that ridiculous outfit—that his heart hurt. "Can we talk? I have...a lot to tell you."

He smiled, his heart glowing at being near her again. "I thought you'd never ask."

Two hours and two coffees later, Sammy sat in a nearby café's leather booth, digesting what Olivia had just told him. Her mother, her sister, her father...Jesus, her father.

She'd lived a lifetime in the time they'd been apart.

"I found out about him right before I left for Italy." Olivia swirled a finger over the tabletop, tracing an invisible pattern. "For the first time in my life, I was so overwhelmed, I couldn't think. The situation with us, my job, my family, plus the craziness of school and Kris's wedding—it was too much. I wasn't in the right place mentally or emotionally to jump into a relationship again, and it didn't seem fair to bring you into my mess. I didn't expect to be so affected by what happened with my parents, considering I wasn't close to either of them—I didn't even know my father—but I was. I couldn't talk about it because I didn't know *how* to talk about it. I'm still figuring it out, but the trip to Nevada brought some much-needed closure, and I'm in a better place now. Plus, I wanted to talk to you. To see you." Her voice softened. "To thank you for waiting."

"You don't have to thank me. I said I would wait for as long as you needed, and I meant it." Sammy reached across the table and took one of her hands in his. Her cool palms warmed beneath his touch. "For the record, you wouldn't have been stringing me along. I *want* to be there for you, even when you're a mess—*especially* when you're a mess. That's what a relationship is all about. Being there for each other through the highest of highs and lowest of lows. If you don't want to talk about something, you don't have to talk about it. If you do want to talk about it, I'm here. Like I said, I love you. That'll never change."

That was all there was to it. Love. Such a simple concept that humans liked to twist and complicate with their fears and insecurities, but eventually, everyone had to make a choice—let the doubt consume them or let love carry them through.

Olivia squeezed his hand back, and the glow in his chest burned brighter.

"I have something else to tell you," she said. "I didn't want to say anything until it was official."

He waited, his breath stuck somewhere between his lungs and throat.

"I quit Pine Hill."

"*What?*" The word exploded out of him. "Liv—"

"Let me finish." Her eyes glittered. "I quit, and they hired me back. I agreed—on the condition that I could date whomever I want unless it's a coworker. They have no say in my personal life as long as I don't do anything illegal or anything that conflicts with the business. You and I? Not a conflict, not based on the flimsy reasoning they gave me about 'preventing image issues before they arise.'"

"How?" Sammy managed, still trying to sort through his shock.

"Leverage." Olivia lifted her shoulder in a tiny shrug. "I applied to a bunch of other PE firms and got an offer that matched my current position and salary at PHC. It would've taken a few extra years to become VP, but I didn't care. I made sure they wouldn't care who I dated on my personal time before I put in my two weeks' notice with PHC. I swear I heard their eyes pop out of their head over the phone—I don't think they expected me to push back like that. They asked me to hold off on signing anything until they 'reviewed my case and came to a decision.' But the real kicker was when Ty Winstock found out about my resignation through Kat, and he threatened to follow me to my new firm." A wry smile. "I suspect Kat had something to do with that decision, but Ty told PHC I was the reason he'd signed on in the first place, and he wouldn't stay if I wasn't there. The rest is history."

"So you and I…"

"Are free to do whatever we want." Olivia smiled, but her eyes were worried. "What do you want, Sammy?"

He didn't have to think about it. "I want you."

The worry disappeared, replaced with a sparkle that shone brighter than the stars. "I was hoping you'd say that."

They sealed their promise with a kiss—a declaration to the world that they would be together, no matter what. A kiss that had been a long time coming, that left them both gasping for breath and their waitress's face beet-red when she cleared off their table.

"I realized something," Sammy said as they walked toward his car, parked in front of his now-dark bakery. He hadn't said goodbye to his staff, but he'd see them tomorrow. Maybe. He was tempted to take the rest of the week off and spend it in Olivia's arms instead. "About us."

She raised a questioning brow.

"Our problem wasn't timing. It was self-martyrdom." He leaned against the passenger door. "You lied to your mother in New York to protect me. I pretended to be you and lied to your boss to protect you. You asked me to wait because you didn't want to string me along. And so on and so forth. Self-martyrdom."

Olivia huffed out a laugh. "When you put it like that...we've been idiots."

"Kinda. But we also ended up here, so we're not *total* idiots." Sammy wrapped his arms around her waist and drew her close.

"Here is good?" she teased.

"Here is very good."

He dipped his head and they kissed again, long and slow and leisurely, ignoring the catcalls of passersby as they got lost in a world where nothing existed except the two of them.

CHAPTER 30

Three Years Later

"YOUR TWO O'CLOCK MEETING GOT MOVED TO THREE, your hairstylist confirmed for Sunday, I made reservations for lunch with Ty Winstock at Avenue for Thursday, the mic for your *Women on Wall Street* podcast interview arrived this morning, and"—Lizzy paused for breath—"you have a visitor."

Olivia sent her email update about PHC's progress on the SolarTech deal to the firm's partners and managing directors before glancing up. "Details."

She wasn't expecting any visitors today, but that had never stopped her friends from dropping in when they felt like it— though she suspected their eagerness had more to do with the Chris Hemsworth look-alike analyst who worked on her floor than it did with her.

"Five-foot-six, head-to-toe Calvin Klein, incredibly scary before I got her her caffeine fix."

Olivia grinned. "We're sisters for a reason."

"Don't I know it." Her assistant/secretary/all-around goddess gave an exaggerated shudder. "I have one more message, though."

"Go on." Olivia already knew what it was, but her heart still fluttered like a schoolgirl when Lizzy handed her a cupcake and a note. Sammy sent her one every Monday—to start her week off on a good note, he said (pun intended).

They'd eloped two years ago and tied the knot in Lake Tahoe. Olivia had always pictured her wedding as a grand affair—had relished the thought of all the planning and spreadsheets she'd get to do in the run-up to her big day. But she hadn't been able to stop thinking about the vision Sammy had painted that night in Italy—of running off to the mountains, just the two of them. So that was what they did.

They did host a small reception attended by their closest friends and family when they returned—mostly to prevent themselves from being murdered by said friends and family for not telling them about their nuptials beforehand—but Olivia's most cherished wedding memory would always be their tiny ceremony on a mountaintop.

No fancy decorations, no long list of guests, no crazy wedding dress or elaborate choreography. Just her, Sammy, and the drumbeat of their love rolling through the crisp mountain air.

That was all they'd needed.

"Aren't you going to open it?" Lizzy asked.

"Nope." Olivia knew better. Most of the notes were sweet, but a few were downright filthy. The last time she read one in front of Lizzy, she'd started choking on air and turned so red Lizzy almost called 911. She got her revenge later that night—the handcuffs Tamara bought her as a gag gift one Christmas came in handy—but it was better not to alarm her assistant *too* much.

Lizzy sighed. "Fine. Deprive me of my opportunity to live vicariously through you."

290 | ANA HUANG

"You'll survive." Lizzy was in no way hurting for excitement. She'd once come back from vacation engaged to a duke—only to break off the engagement two weeks later when she found out he had a kid and estranged wife he'd failed to tell her about.

Olivia walked into her sprawling office and draped her coat over the arm of the couch. "How does it feel?" she quipped.

Alina spun one last time in her desk chair before standing up. "Great. That's an excellent chair. Ergonomic, sturdy, comfortable. Adjusted to the perfect height."

"It better be. It cost five hundred dollars." Olivia laughed and hugged her sister. "What are you doing here? Don't tell me the clinic succeeded in wooing you after all."

Alina had been close to signing a contract with the private San Francisco clinic that had wanted to hire her as their anesthesiologist three years ago, but a Chicago clinic had swept in and outbid them at the last minute.

"Not yet." Alina grinned. "I was in LA for a conference and took a quick trip up to see my little sis. How is my niece or nephew doing?"

Olivia flinched. "Shhh!" She closed the door to her office and peered out the window to see if anyone had overheard. The only person nearby was Lizzy, who was busy unboxing her podcast mic. "People will hear."

"Why? What's the big...oh." Alina's eyes grew round. "You haven't told them yet."

"No." Olivia rested a hand on her stomach, her anxiety battling with joy and excitement. Her doctor had confirmed it a month earlier: she was pregnant. Eight weeks along, to be exact. She wasn't showing yet, but it was only a matter of time.

Personally, Olivia was over the moon. Professionally, she was nervous as hell. As far as Wall Street firms went, PHC was pretty progressive, especially since it'd added a woman (finally!) to its board of directors last year and promoted another to partner. But the stigma against pregnant women still existed in the industry, and Olivia had heard too many horror stories about expecting mothers who were treated poorly after they announced their pregnancy and demoted after they returned from maternity leave. Some of them got fired *during* maternity leave.

Olivia knew she couldn't keep her pregnancy a secret forever, but she was dragging out the announcement until she could come up with a solid backup plan in case things went sideways.

"Do you really think they'll freak out?" Alina asked.

"I don't know. Other than Michael, I'm the highest-ranking person in this office, so they won't say anything to my face, but I'm not sure what to expect from HQ." Olivia shook her head. "I'll figure it out."

She'd come a long way since her first summer in California. She was now a director at Pine Hill Capital—one step above the vice president and one rung below Michael's managing director-ship. He'd ceded most of the day-to-day management in the San Francisco office to her, and rumor had it he was planning to retire in the next few years, which would leave an MD spot open.

Olivia already had her eyes set on it. She wasn't obsessed with becoming managing director the way she'd been obsessed with becoming vice president, but she still had goals. Her dreams of conquering Wall Street hadn't vanished just because she'd struck a healthier work-life balance.

"I'm sure you will." Alina's eyes twinkled. "So...you have your first ultrasound today?"

"Yes." Olivia narrowed her eyes. "Is *that* why you came here? So you can tag along to the ultrasound?"

Her sister was the picture of innocence. "I have no idea what you're talking about."

"Bull. Shit. You're as bad as Sammy's family." Olivia planted her hands on her hips. "Do you know who's already coming with me to the sonogram besides Sammy? My mother-, father-, brother-, and sisters-in-law, and my entire book club, plus a group FaceTime call with Farrah, Kris, and Courtney. I swear the sonographer is going to kick me out."

"Great. That means one more person won't make a difference," Alina said, ignoring the last part of Olivia's statement.

It took time, but after she got out from under Eleanor's thumb, Alina had relaxed and blossomed into the warm, loving soul Olivia remembered from her early childhood. Alina and Eleanor still kept in touch—barely—but her sister no longer let their mother run her life, and it'd made all the difference. Alina was thriving at work, dating for fun instead of being laser-focused on finding the "right" husband, and she looked happier than Olivia had ever seen her.

Olivia gave up on trying to dissuade her sister from joining her at the ultrasound appointment. "Fine. Meet me there," she grumbled with affection. "I'll text you the address. Now, I need to get back to work so I can afford the mountain of diapers in my future."

Alina hadn't left for more than a minute before Lizzy knocked and poked her head in. "Michael wants to see you in the conference room."

Olivia's brows furrowed. "Do we have a client meeting?"

They only used the conference room for client and staff meetings, and they didn't have the latter scheduled for today.

"He didn't give any details, but he said it's urgent."

"All right." She sighed. She'd hoped for extra time to review her notes before her three o'clock meeting, but she guessed that wasn't happening. Luckily, she'd already done the bulk of the preparation yesterday.

She followed Lizzy to the conference room. The office had emptied for lunch, and—

"Surprise!"

Olivia's jaw unhinged when she saw her coworkers crowded around the large mahogany table, beaming. Michael, Cassidy (now a VP), Logan (who, unfortunately, still worked at PHC but who'd toned down his snark given Olivia was now his boss)... they were all there. Some wore party hats; others held balloons. A giant white, pink, and blue cake sat in the middle of the table, along with soda, chips, and assorted other snacks.

Her heart picked up pace. *How did they find out?*

She'd been so careful about hiding her pregnancy, but everyone looked happy—except for Logan—and they were throwing her a party, so maybe she'd agonized over the announcement for nothing.

"Who told you?" she blurted.

Her colleagues exchanged glances.

"What?" Cassidy spoke for the rest of the group.

"Who told you I was pregnant?"

You could hear a pin drop.

Michael's eyes widened while Cassidy's mouth fell open. A quick look around the room confirmed they weren't the only ones with that reaction.

Dread slithered into Olivia's stomach at their obvious shock. *Shit.* They *hadn't* known, but then what was—

"No one." Logan snorted, quickly masking his smug satisfaction with a fake smile. "This was your belated surprise birthday party."

"We didn't celebrate a few weeks ago because of the Haldern-Pacific deal," Michael explained.

"Oh." Olivia didn't know what to say. Of all the ways she'd imagined announcing her pregnancy, dropping the bombshell by accident to her entire office hadn't been one of them. She might as well have hit reply-all to an email with a photo of her sonogram. She let out a nervous laugh. "Well, surprise! I'm pregnant."

Fuck it, the secret was already out. Time to embrace it and take the consequences as they came.

More silence.

Cassidy was the first to break it. She ran around the table and hugged Olivia; she'd grown a lot better at showing physical affection over the years. "Congratulations! That's amazing."

The dam broke, and Olivia was soon inundated with more hugs and congratulations. They all looked genuine except for Logan, who sulked in the corner, and Olivia gradually relaxed.

This wasn't so bad.

Michael was the last to approach her. After some small talk, he said, "You may already know this, but we updated our parental-leave policy last year. More paid time off, plus flexible work arrangements after you return to the office. Take advantage of them—you're only a new parent once."

"Thank you," Olivia said with a touch of wariness. She examined her boss's face for any signs he was upset about her pregnancy, but she couldn't find anything amiss.

"I mean it. Don't be afraid to use all those benefits. It won't affect your career trajectory here." Michael cleared his throat. "There's a...stigma against expecting parents in certain parts of our industry, but PHC has always prided itself on being forward-thinking and inclusive."

Olivia guessed the greater female representation on the board and roster of partners helped too.

"I appreciate that," she said. "I'll definitely keep it in mind."

"Please do. My daughter works in finance too," Michael added. "Hedge fund. Refused to take my advice and go into private equity, but what can you do? I know how hard it was for her when she started out. It's still hard, even though she's a senior executive now. But you take it one day at a time."

Olivia murmured her agreement.

In an ideal world, Michael would promote female-friendly work policies even if his daughter *didn't* work in finance, but she'd take her wins where she could find them.

The rest of the day passed in a blur and soon, she was in an Uber on her way to her first ultrasound appointment.

Olivia unfolded the note Lizzy had handed her earlier and frowned. Was that...a recipe?

It took her a minute to realize it wasn't just any recipe—it was the recipe for Wah Sing's shrimp dumplings, the one she'd always wanted but had never been able to get.

Sammy had scrawled a short note at the bottom of the page: *I love you and dim sum.*

A play on the phrase "I love you and then some." The man loved his food puns, as evidenced by the growing collection of food-pun prints in their kitchen.

Olivia burst into laughter, ignoring the strange look her driver shot her in the rearview mirror.

God, she loved her husband.

"Is this everyone, or will more people be joining us?" The sonographer, who'd introduced herself as Mykah, raised her eyebrows at the dozen people crammed inside the room.

"This is it." Amy waved an impatient hand in the air. "So? Do I have a grandson or granddaughter?"

"Do I have a godson or goddaughter?" Farrah asked at the same time, leaning forward like she could somehow see better even though she was watching through a screen instead of in person.

Sammy adjusted the phone so Farrah, Courtney, and Kris could get a clearer view of Olivia.

Mykah laughed. "I'm afraid it's too early for that"—a

collective sigh of disappointment—"but we should have that information at the second routine scan if the mother would like to know the gender ahead of time."

"Trust me, she does," Kris said. She was sitting in what looked like her bedroom. "Liv loves planning for stuff."

Everyone laughed because it was true.

"It never hurts to be prepared," Olivia said primly, eliciting another round of laughter.

Then the technician got to work, and Olivia gripped Sammy's hand, waiting with bated breath while Mykah spread gel over her abdomen and moved the ultrasound device over her stomach until she found what she was looking for.

An image flickered onto the screen, and everyone gasped.

Olivia's and Sammy's grips tightened on each other at the same time. *No way.* She couldn't breathe. Her heart was pounding, pounding so loud she might go deaf from it.

"Is that—"

"Yes." Mykah smiled, her eyes twinkling. "Everything looks fine...and you're having twins."

The room erupted into cheers and laughs.

Sammy's mother was so excited she swooned—her husband and Kevin caught her just in time—and Olivia swore she saw Alina dab tears from her eyes.

"Two for the price of one!" Natalie crowed, earning herself several glares. "What? We all know Liv wanted twins."

"We're having twins." Olivia couldn't believe it. "We're having twins!"

Sammy kissed her, hard and fast. Either his eyes were teary or hers were. Probably both. It didn't matter. *They were having twins!*

"It's in your five-year plan. The universe wouldn't dare mess it up," he joked, but he sounded choked up.

Olivia laughed. "Final test is when we find out the gender. Fingers crossed for a girl and a boy."

Even as she said it, she knew she didn't care. Two girls, two boys, one girl and one boy...she'd love them regardless.

While their friends and family chattered away in excitement, she asked the question she'd been dying to ask since they arrived. "How did you get that recipe?"

Sammy's eyes crinkled at the corners. "A man has to keep some secrets."

"Seriously? I'm pregnant and hormonal. You don't want to mess with me."

His shoulders shook with laughter. "Let's make a deal—I'll tell if you can make those dumplings from scratch *and* they taste similar to Wah Sing's. And if we don't get food poisoning," he added.

Olivia scowled. "You have a death wish, Mr. Yu."

"Good thing you love me so much, Mrs. Yu." He brushed his lips over hers again. "Otherwise, I'd be concerned."

She grumbled and pretended to be upset, but in reality, Olivia had never been happier—even if her husband insisted on making fun of her kitchen skills. Like jeez, the food poisoning thing happened over a decade ago. Let it go. And yeah, she might've almost set the kitchen on fire last month, but that wasn't her fault—some things just happened to be extremely flammable.

Olivia rested her hand over her stomach, her heart already bursting with love for the newest members of their family, and as she looked around at *all* the people she called family—both by blood and by choice—she realized she'd finally found home.

EPILOGUE

Four Years Later

"MY BABIES!" FARRAH BENT LOW AND OPENED HER arms. "Look how big you've gotten! I can't believe it."

Lily and Aiden peeled themselves away from Olivia and toddled toward their godmother with delighted squeals. Farrah smothered them with hugs and kisses while Olivia looked on with an indulgent smile.

"I see how it is," Olivia said with faux anger. "The minute Auntie Farrah arrives, you forget all about your mom, huh?"

Lily peeked back at Olivia shyly. "Wuv you, Mommy."

Olivia's heart melted. "Love you too, sweetie." She blew her daughter a kiss, which Lily returned. Meanwhile, Aiden was too busy searching for presents on Farrah's person to join the lovefest.

"They're only excited to see me because I always come bearing gifts." Farrah fished two gaily wrapped boxes out of her bag. "No, sweetie, not now. We have to wait until tomorrow or your mom will ki—er, get upset."

"Awww!" Aiden and Lily slumped in disappointment at the same time.

"But Everett's out back if you want to—" Farrah didn't get all the words out before Aiden and Lily flew out of the room as fast as their little three-year-old legs would allow. "—play with him," she finished. She set the gifts beneath the Christmas tree.

"Now you know how it feels to get ditched," Olivia teased.

"Yeah, yeah, rub it in."

They stared at each other for a second before they squealed and hugged like two teenage girls reuniting after a summer apart.

"It's so good to see you!" Olivia squeezed her best friend tight. "I thought you didn't get in until five."

"Our flight landed early. We would've arrived sooner, except Blake insisted on stopping for In-N-Out first." Farrah rolled her eyes. "I swear, he practically lives there every time we visit."

"In-N-Out *is* good." Olivia linked her arm through Farrah's and guided her out back, where the rest of the guests gathered around the fire pit. "Sammy will be pissed he spoiled dinner, though."

"Trust me, he didn't. The man eats like a horse."

"You talking about me?" Blake drawled when they stepped through the sliding glass door and into the crisp December air.

Olivia and Sammy had moved into a bigger house after she gave birth to the twins, with a proper backyard for Lily, Aiden, and their friends to run around and play in.

No one had been surprised when a second ultrasound confirmed her twins comprised one boy and one girl—Like I said, the universe wouldn't dare give you anything else, Sammy joked after the reveal—and as Michael had promised, Olivia's maternity leave hadn't affected her standing at PHC, where she was now a managing director. She'd filled Michael's position after he retired two years ago.

Sure, she'd received some side-eyes and passive-aggressive comments while she'd been pregnant—mostly from Logan, who'd finally been fired after another female employee filed a sexual harassment complaint against him—but there would always be assholes.

Plus, she was now their boss, so take that.

"How did you know? I swear you have supersonic hearing," Farrah grumbled.

"I always know when I'm on your mind, babe." Blake dropped a kiss on top of her head before he hugged Olivia. "Always good to see you, Liv."

"Same." She tapped his bicep in warning. "It'll continue being good as long as you treat my girl right. She cries, I'll whoop your ass."

Blake's dimples flashed. "A decade and a kid later, and you still don't trust me?"

"Hell no. Not with those baby blues and that drawl." Olivia narrowed her eyes. "I'm on to you, Blake Ryan."

"Aw, you break my heart, Liv."

"I'm sure." Olivia looked at Farrah while pointing at Blake. "Watch out for this one."

She was joking—for the most part. Blake and Farrah had a rock-solid marriage, not to mention an adorable five-year-old son named Everett. But Olivia would always be protective of her friends, no matter how old they were.

Still, she had to admit, she was in a good place. They all were.

Olivia's chest glowed with warmth as she took in the scene before her. Everett was playing tag with the rest of the kids, including Lily, Aiden, and Ruby, Kris and Nate's daughter. Ruby was the same age as Lily and Aiden—Olivia and Kris had given birth two months apart. Ruby's parents were at the fire pit, talking and laughing with Courtney and her husband, Justin. Justin used to work at the New York branch of Blake's bar Legends before he opened his own tattoo parlor. He and Courtney got together when, by chance, they'd gotten stuck in the same B and B during a freak snowstorm; they'd tied the knot last year.

Nardo, Luke, and Leo Agnelli, another friend from study abroad, were arguing over some movie that'd released last week. Well, Nardo and Leo were arguing—Luke was busy stuffing his face with chips. Olivia was surprised Leo had shown up. She invited him every year, but the famous writer was usually in Europe, where he was based. Other than an abundance of facial hair and a few wrinkles around his eyes, he looked exactly the same.

Olivia remained an active member of the erotica book club, which had gained several members over the years, but tonight, only the originals were here—Kat, Tamara, Natalie, and Donna, plus their significant others, including Jessica (Tamara's now-wife) and Ty. Kat and Ty weren't engaged yet, but Olivia suspected that would be on the horizon soon. At least Kat's ex was way behind her in the rearview mirror. *Ben who?*

And, of course, there was Sammy. He was manning the grill with Aaron and Trey, looking sexy as hell, per usual.

He caught her eye and winked, and her heart melted into a gooey puddle. She blew him a kiss; he grinned and waggled his eyebrows. Translation: *Wait until I get you alone after our guests leave (and our children go to bed).*

Olivia's skin heated at the promise.

"You say Blake and I are gross." Farrah wrinkled her nose. "I think you and Sammy win that award."

"Please. At least you didn't have to watch us defile a Vegas hotel room couch."

Farrah's complexion went from golden to crimson in less than one second. "We thought the door adjoining our suites was locked!" She narrowed her eyes. "How long were you guys watching?"

"Not that long; we're not voyeurs. We were just in shock." Olivia cleared her throat. "*Anyway*, the food is ready."

"Wait. Alina?"

The corners of Olivia's mouth turned down. "She can't make it. There's a big snowstorm and all flights are grounded until tomorrow."

"Huh. Then she must have a twin I don't know about because she's right there."

Olivia whirled around, taking in the green-clad figure stepping through the kitchen's sliding glass door.

"What? I thought you were stuck in Chicago!" she cried, throwing her arms around her sister while Farrah slipped off to grab what looked like a broken plastic toy from Everett before he put it in his mouth.

Olivia swore children bit into everything. She'd initially freaked out—she still did sometimes, depending on what the object was—because *hello*, talk about unhygienic, but Sammy had forced her to do meditation exercises until she calmed down. If she had children and couldn't handle a little dirt and mess...she was in for a rough few years/decades.

Point taken. (But Olivia drew the line at letting Lily and Aiden touch strange objects in strange places. That was how people *died*.)

Alina grinned and hugged her back. "I thought I was, but there was one flight out before they closed down the airport and I managed to grab a seat. I had a transfer in Phoenix, though, which is why I'm late. Did you already start?"

"Not yet. You have perfect timing."

Olivia and Alina squished into the circle ringing the fire pit while Sammy, Trey, and Aaron passed out plates of food. Since it was December, they'd stuck with grilling winter foods: pulled pork, sweet potato and chicken kebabs, butternut squash, pineapple (to remind them of warmer times), and bacon-wrapped corn on the cob.

"This smells delicious." Olivia pecked Sammy on the lips before he took the seat next to her and draped an arm over her shoulder. "Thanks for cooking."

Trey cleared his throat. Loudly.

"You too, Trey," she said wryly. "And Aaron. I appreciate it."

"Anytime." Trey puffed out his chest. "I've become quite a master griller over the years."

Olivia had hosted this annual pre-Christmas party for three years now, and it was the highlight of her year. However, this was the first year that everyone made it; they were usually so busy that it was hard to find a date that worked for the entire group, especially since half of them lived in different cities.

"Sure." Aaron patted Trey on the back. "You've really honed your plating skills."

"Fuck you, dude, I—"

"Language!" Every parent within earshot shouted.

Trey rolled his eyes. He was thirty-five, still a bachelor, and proud of it. "Chill the f—the eff out. The munchkins can't hear me."

"If my daughter starts cursing, I'll kick your, uh, fanny," Nate warned, adjusting the end of his sentence when Ruby ran over with something cupped her in her hands. "Hey, sweetheart, what do you have—oh, shit! I mean, fuck. I mean, *what is that?*"

Olivia pressed her lips together while Sammy buried his face in her neck, his shoulders shaking.

Ruby held up the decapitated doll's head with a toothy smile. "Barbie!"

"Okay, but..." Kris looked like she was trying not to laugh at Nate's freaked-out expression. "Where's the *rest* of Barbie, honey?"

Ruby shrugged. "I'll look!" She dumped the head in Nate's

hand and ran back to the other children, who were rooting in the ground for God knows what.

"Pssst. Kris." Luke lowered his voice to a stage whisper. "I think your daughter's a budding serial killer."

Kris leveled him with a cool glare, looking impeccable as always in a Prada sweater and Rag & Bone skinny jeans tucked into a pair of snakeskin boots that probably cost more than the average American's monthly rent. "Pssst, Luke." She matched his stage whisper. "Why don't you shove your corncob up your ass?"

Pent-up laughter swept through the crowd, both at Luke's offended expression and the way Nate Reynolds—famous for playing some of the big screen's toughest, most macho action heroes—held the doll's head away from him like it would suck his soul out if it got too close.

"Oh, so everyone's cursing now, but *I'm* the only one who gets yelled at for it?" Trey shook his head. "Bull. Shit."

"Technically, doll decapitation is not a proven sign of a serial killer in the making," Nardo said, adjusting his glasses. "More reliable indicators include torturing small animals, arson, voyeurism, antisocial behavior—"

"Can we *not* talk about this at a holiday party with children?" Olivia planted her hands on her hips. "I want tonight to be perfect. Why don't we share—"

She stopped as something flew in front of her and landed in the fire pit.

Leo peered at it. "Is that…?"

"Yes." Olivia pressed two fingers to her temple as a loud wail ripped through the air. "Yes, it is."

Ruby had apparently found the rest of Barbie's body but tripped on her way back to her parents. The doll had gone flying out of her hands and was now dying a slow death in the fire while Nate and Kris consoled their distraught daughter.

Well, Nate consoled—Kris was busy snapping at Luke, who kept muttering, "See? Arson," under his breath.

"That's not arson, you idiot," Kris said. "What do you have against Ruby?"

"Nothing. All I'm saying is, arson, fire, kinda the same thing—"

"No, it's not," Nardo interjected. "Arson is by definition the 'willful or malicious burning of property,' according to *Merriam-Webster*."

"It smells like plastic." Leo glanced at Olivia. "Do you have any Febreze lying around?"

"Ronnie, *no!*" Donna yelled at her son, who was smearing barbecue sauce all over Lily and Aiden's *brand-new white Ralph Lauren shirts*. "What did I tell you about—stop or no YouTube for a week!"

"This is making me question our decision to adopt." Tamara popped a pineapple slice in her mouth. "I mean, we already have a dog. Do we really need a kid?"

"What? We don't have a dog." Jessica's frown melted when Tamara froze. "Wait, did you get us a dog for Christmas? Oh my God!"33

"*Fuck.*" Tamara groaned, but a smile escaped when Jessica peppered her with questions about the breed.

"Language!" Nate roared, waving the doll's head in the air while he kept his other arm around a sobbing Ruby.

"Is it a husky? A golden retriever? A labrador—"

"I swear, Ronnie, if you don't listen to me and stop *right now*, it'll be *two* weeks without YouTube *or* TV—"

"That's not what arson means!"

"*You're* the serial killer!"

"Bite me!"

"*Who ate all the bacon off the cobs and left the corn?*"

"Yo, does anyone know the score for the game tonight?"

"Shut up!"

"You shut up!"

"Screw you!"

"LANGUAGE!"

Olivia collapsed in her seat and buried her face in her hands. "One. I just want *one* holiday party where things don't go off the rails," she said, her voice muffled.

Sammy chuckled and drew her close. "Where would be the fun in that? This is the most entertaining party I've ever been to."

"Agreed." Alina nodded and snuck a piece of bacon into her mouth while casting a guilty look at Blake, who was staring at the pile of naked corncobs near the grill with an outraged expression. "I'm so glad I made it."

"Gee, thanks." Olivia sighed while the noise around her reached a crescendo. "All I'm saying is—"

"Mommy!" Aiden tackled her with a hug—and smeared barbecue sauce all over Olivia's hair, face, and clothing. "Look!" He held up an empty corn on the cob with a toothy grin. "I ate this all by myself."

Sammy snorted out a laugh.

Olivia's eyes narrowed as vengeance brewed in her mind. "That's wonderful, sweetie. Why don't you go show Daddy? In fact, go give him a *big hug*."

Alarm skittered into Sammy's gaze a second before Aiden did as he was told and climbed into his father's lap.

"All right, all right." Sammy laughed and smacked a kiss on Aiden's cheek. "Look at you! You're practically a grown-up now, aren't you?"

"Yep!" Aiden beamed.

Lily, not wanting to be left out, attached herself to Olivia, who resigned herself to another giant laundry day tomorrow.

"Wait, stop. That's so cute!" Farrah pulled out her phone and snapped a photo of Olivia, Sammy, Lily, and Aiden. "I sense a Christmas card in the making."

"You should send it to Mother. She'll have a heart attack," Alina said mischievously.

Olivia snorted. "Right." She hadn't spoken to Eleanor since the twins were born, when Olivia had called her out of courtesy and informed her she was now a grandmother. Eleanor had thanked her for the news and promptly hung up.

If she hadn't grown up with the woman, Olivia would've never believed that someone could be so cold, but she put nothing past Eleanor Tang. She and her mother were basically estranged, and although a part of her would always mourn the maternal bond she'd never had, she'd come to terms with the fact that she and Eleanor would never see eye to eye. Sad though it may be, part of her was glad Eleanor wasn't in Lily's and Aiden's lives—God knew she'd messed Olivia and Alina up enough. She didn't need the opportunity to do it to a new generation too.

According to Alina, Eleanor was dating some guy who owned half the car dealerships in Chicago and was on her way to gaining husband number four.

Olivia didn't care either way. She'd rather focus her energy on the people she loved and who loved her back. Besides, her children already had grandparents who adored them to pieces: Amy and Richard, who babysat whenever Olivia and Sammy needed a date night, snuck the twins candy behind their parents' backs, and played games with Lily and Aiden for hours without tiring (as long as said games didn't require too much physical activity).

The Yus had welcomed Olivia into the fold as one of their own even before she'd married Sammy, and they were the giant, loving family she'd never had. She adored them.

Well, except for Edison, but he'd been excommunicated after he tried to bring down Sammy's business, so he didn't count.

"Next year, maybe we should nix the white clothes." Sammy gently pried Aiden's sticky fingers out of his hair while his son scrambled all over him like he was a jungle gym.

"Good idea." Olivia laughed, but soon, she forgot all about the sauce and dirty clothes as she lost herself in the magic of the warmth and laughter around her.

Later that night, after their guests had left and they'd tucked their children into bed, Sammy and Olivia curled up on the couch in front of the living room fireplace, drowsy but content. They didn't get a lot of alone time these days, so they made every second count when they did.

"You promised," Olivia said. "Spill it, mister."

He shot her a mock scowl. "I'm convinced you cheated."

"I did no such thing." Her mischievous smile lit up her face, and he couldn't get over the fact that this beautiful, smart, amazing woman was his. How did he get so lucky? "I practiced. A lot. But I did it."

"Yeah, after four years."

"You didn't give me a time frame." She nudged his leg. "C'mon. How'd you get the recipe?"

That morning, before Sammy started prepping for tonight's party, Olivia had unveiled her surprise: shrimp dumplings she'd made from scratch. They'd tasted fresh and Wah Sing hadn't been open that early, so it couldn't have been takeout. Plus, they didn't taste *exactly* like Wah Sing's—but they were close.

"Fine, I'll tell you. But you can't get mad."

Olivia's eyes narrowed. "What did you do?"

"I played the my-wife-is-pregnant card. And I, uh, told Wah

Sing's owner we'd name our daughter after her—if we had a daughter. Turns out the owner is quite susceptible to flattery."

"*What?* Lily—"

"Was already on your list of names you liked," Sammy said quickly. "That was a top-secret recipe, okay? And you wouldn't stop talking about it."

"What if her name hadn't been on my list?" Olivia demanded. "What if her name was, I dunno, Helgarda or something?"

"*No one* is named Helgarda."

"I bet a Google search would prove you wrong."

He laughed. "Hey, it all worked out. I wouldn't have made that offer if the owner's name had been hideous. Plus, I doubt she would've held us to it."

"No wonder she always gives Lily an extra egg tart," Olivia muttered. She shoved his chest. "Just for that, you're doing laundry tomorrow."

"Fine." Sammy slid a palm up her thigh, smiling when he heard her breath hitch. "Look on the bright side—you learned how to make your favorite dumplings, our daughter has a beautiful name, and I'll have to work extra hard to make it up to you…"

Which he did, for hours, on an "apology" tour that took them from the living room to the kitchen to the bedroom, where they finally collapsed, exhausted and content, on the bed.

"We have to wake up early tomorrow." Olivia sighed, snuggling closer to him. "We still have to finish cleaning up the backyard. I bet there's stuff we missed tonight—it was so dark by the time everyone left."

"I'll help." Tomorrow was a workday, but Sammy had taken the week off. Jude ran a tight ship as Crumble & Bake's CEO, and Liam had taken on increasingly more responsibilities while Sammy stepped back to spend more time with his family. He still loved the bakery, but it was no longer dependent on him, and that was the way it should be.

Crumble & Bake had only become more successful over the years after it opened its East Coast locations—which were huge hits—and added a full drinks menu to its offerings, much to Cordelia's delight. A rising star on San Francisco's theater scene, she was no longer with the company, but she visited often. They'd even named a latte after her.

"We might have to clean this up tomorrow too." Sammy glanced around his and Olivia's room, wincing at the sight of the clothes strewn everywhere, the bottles they'd knocked over while they'd gone at it against the dressing table, and the dirt they'd tracked onto the floors. "This is a mess."

Olivia had relaxed over the years when it came to cleaning and organization—they had kids, after all—but Sammy still tried his best to keep everything neat when possible.

Olivia rolled them over until she hovered over him. "No," she said, drawing him in for a deep, luscious kiss that had him primed and ready to go for round four. Her eyes were warm and sparkled with love as she stared down at him. "This isn't a mess. This is perfect."

Acknowledgments

This is it. The end of the If Love series. I had never, in my wildest dreams, imagined that I'd publish four books in one year, but anything is possible in 2020!

I had such a blast writing these stories, all of which are dear to me in different ways, and I'm so grateful to the people who've consistently been there to ensure every book got the love it deserved before (and after) it was released into the world:

My beta readers, Aishah, Leslie, and Jen.

My editors, Shelby Perkins and Krista Burdine.

All the bloggers and reviewers who shared this book.

All the readers, new and old, who've taken the time to read one of my stories when there are so many to choose from in the world.

I am honored and forever grateful.

Love you all.

xo, Ana

*Keep in Touch
with Ana Huang*

Reader Group: facebook.com/groups/anastwistedsquad
Website: anahuang.com
BookBub: bookbub.com/profile/ana-huang
Instagram: instagram.com/authoranahuang
TikTok: tiktok.com/@authoranahuang
Goodreads: goodreads.com/authoranahuang

About the Author

Ana Huang is a #1 *New York Times, Sunday Times, Wall Street Journal, USA Today*, and #1 Amazon bestselling author. Best known for her Twisted series, she writes New Adult and contemporary romance with deliciously alpha heroes, strong heroines, and plenty of steam, angst, and swoon.

Her books have been translated in over two dozen languages and featured in outlets such as NPR, *Cosmopolitan, Financial Times*, and *Glamour UK*.

A self-professed travel enthusiast, she loves incorporating beautiful destinations into her stories and will never say no to a good chai latte.

Also by Ana Huang

KINGS OF SIN SERIES
A SERIES OF INTERCONNECTED STANDALONES

King of Wrath

King of Pride

King of Greed

King of Sloth

TWISTED SERIES
A SERIES OF INTERCONNECTED STANDALONES

Twisted Love

Twisted Games

Twisted Hate

Twisted Lies

IF LOVE SERIES

If We Ever Meet Again **(DUET BOOK 1)**

If the Sun Never Sets **(DUET BOOK 2)**

If Love Had a Price **(STANDALONE)**

If We Were Perfect **(STANDALONE)**